W9-AYO-993

7422

RELEASED FROM THE
COLLECTION OF THE
Stratford Public Library
FEB 25 19
MAR 1

DATE DUE

FIC   STRATFORD PUBLIC LIBRARY
Reema   Reeman, Doug
The first to land

3 3028 000 749 4

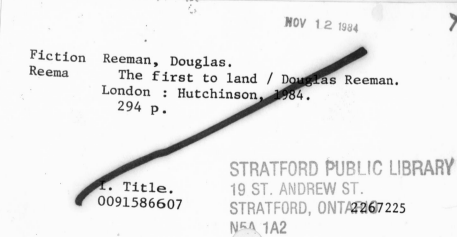

NOV 12 1984   ✗

Fiction   Reeman, Douglas.
Reema   The first to land / Douglas Reeman.
           London : Hutchinson, 1984.
              294 p.

              I. Title.
           0091586607

STRATFORD PUBLIC LIBRARY
19 ST. ANDREW ST.
STRATFORD, ONTA   2267225
N5A 1A2

05/ad

The First to Land

DOUGLAS REEMAN

The First to Land

HUTCHINSON

London Melbourne Sydney Auckland Johannesburg

Hutchinson & Co. (Publishers) Ltd

An imprint of the Hutchinson Publishing Group

17–21 Conway Street, London W1P 6JD

Hutchinson Publishing Group (Australia) Pty Ltd
PO Box 496, 16–22 Church Street, Hawthorne, Melbourne, Victoria 3122
PO Box 151, Broadway, New South Wales 2007

Hutchinson Group (NZ) Ltd
32–34 View Road, PO Box 40-086, Glenfield, Auckland 10

Hutchinson Group (SA) Pty Ltd
PO Box 337, Bergvlei 2012, South Africa

First published 1984
© Highseas Authors Ltd 1984

Set in Linotron 202 Garamond 3 by
Tradespools Ltd, Frome, Somerset
Printed and bound in Great Britain by Anchor Brendon Ltd,
Tiptree, Essex

ISBN 0 09 158660 7

For Caroline Dawnay
With Love.
Tenax propositi.

Contents

Acknowledgement

I wish to thank Major Tony Brown MBE, RM, and his staff at the Royal Marines Museum, Eastney, and all members of the Corps past and present who have willingly given me their help and encouragement in this series.

I

Old and New

The Hampshire countryside gleamed dully after a heavy overnight mist. The big house which dominated the Hawks Hill estate and outlying farm cottages felt damp despite the fires in each room which had been laid and lit long before dawn.

From a window in his study Major General Harry Blackwood gazed out at the grey clouds and frowned. November. At any other time he would have relished this month with its first meeting of the local hunt of which he was Master, but he could not dispel his apprehension, which both worried and irritated him. In a few weeks it was the birth not only of a new year but also of a new century. The thought disturbed him more than he would ever admit to Deirdre, his wife, or anyone else. When 1899 closed he knew his life would somehow lose its purpose. This might even be his last November. He swung away from the window and looked around the room with its dark panelled walls and cheerful log fire. The servants and visitors to Hawks Hill always referred to this as the General's Room. Indeed it contained innumerable relics and mementoes of his life and career in the Royal Marines. A portrait of his father hung on one wall. As he had lived, not as he had died here in this great house. Stern-faced and proud in his scarlet coatee, one hand resting on his sword. Even the sword was mounted in a glass case. Pictures, weapons, fox masks, a bugle with a hole punched through it. It was not difficult to see the expression of horror on the boy's face as he had been cut down by a bullet even as he was sounding the Charge.

Harry Blackwood was sixty-seven years old but in his immaculately cut frock coat he was as straight-backed and trim as the day he had won his majority in the Corps he loved so dearly. But his features told a different story. There were deep crowsfeet around his eyes caused by staring at sun and sky in so many ships, so many campaigns in all parts of the globe. His hair and neatly clipped moustache were white, in marked contrast with his skin, which was like tooled leather.

He crossed to the fire and lifted his coat tails to benefit from the blaze. He had been born here in this house which had been in the Blackwood family for four generations and purchased originally by old Samuel Blackwood: the last of a long line of soldiers. After him all the Blackwoods had been Royal Marines, although Harry had never been able to discover how the change had come about. The main house was a great rambling place which had begun as a fortified Tudor farmhouse. Added to over the years, it spread in several directions with cellars and tiny attics which had once delighted the Blackwood children like a magic castle. It even had a moat, although that was only half filled nowadays; a home for geese and swans.

He heard his wife speaking with one of the maids beyond the door and hoped she would not disturb him. A quiet, faded lady, it was difficult to recall her as the vibrant girl she had once been. She had given him three sons, all of whom were now in the Corps. The youngest, Jonathan, had joined his first ship at Portsmouth just two weeks ago.

Deirdre had been tearful about it but had made no protest when her husband had insisted that his sons should follow the family tradition.

The General had many fixed ideas, one being that women in any kind of authority could not be tolerated. Even the Queen whom he had served for the whole of his life irritated him. Still on the throne after sixty-one years. It did not seem possible. With the British Empire spreading to encompass the whole world you needed strong and decisive leadership, an example for those who had to defend it.

He smiled grimly, the years falling from his features as he did so. It was proclaimed that the sun never set on the Empire. Nor would it while there were still marines.

The door opened slightly but it was Briggs, once his trusted attendant and orderly, now his valet, his shadow.

'Well man?' His voice was sharp. He was not looking forward to the next moments. The thought of them had spoiled the morning, and Deirdre might just be inclined to argue with him.

'Young Mr Blackwood is 'ere, sir.' Briggs eyed him warily. He knew all the General's moods and had been at his side on blood-reddened decks with all hell breaking loose around them. In the desert, and the jungle, wherever the Royal Marines had been called to action.

'Give me a few minutes, Briggs.'

Briggs withdrew. He knew *this* mood. Keep a young officer waiting, even if he was one of the family. Make 'em sweat a while.

Alone again the General walked to the place of honour in his collection. A great painting depicting a battle which had raged in the Crimea, snow, flashing guns, grim-faced marines with fixed bayonets running and dying to the summit of that terrible redoubt. Framed against one fiery explosion was a solitary officer, sword high over his head as he urged his dwindling followers to drive the Russians away from their guns.

Philip Blackwood, Harry's half-brother, was that officer. Now as then he was a hero in the General's eyes. All those years ago when Harry had been a youthful lieutenant like the one he was about to receive in this room, Philip's life had been marked with pain. His wife Davern had died in childbirth, and Philip just ten years later from a fever he contracted in India.

The General had taken it upon himself to care for and raise Philip's only son Ralf. Maybe he and Deirdre had spoiled him because of his background. He had never known his mother, and seen little enough of Philip, who like all serving officers had been more away from the country than in it.

Ralf Blackwood was eighteen, the same age as Jonathan, and was until recently at Woolwich, the Court Division as it was nicknamed. There was no other similarity with the General's youngest son. Ralf had some of his father's good looks, but was resentful of discipline, and inclined to sulk if admonished.

For although the General's military activities were now confined to occasional ceremonials in London or twenty miles away at the Royal Marines' barracks at Portsmouth he retained a close link with the Corps and had plenty of friends who were still serving.

He knew all about Ralf's heavy gambling in the mess. His frequent outbursts of temper when he had been accused of cheating. Being a bad loser usually led to something worse. Had his weakness been women the General would have understood and probably encouraged him. As a boy he had had his first woman, one of the servant girls, right here at Hawks Hill. There had been dozens since of every class and colour.

Deirdre knew the General's record but like most things she never mentioned it.

The door opened and Ralf Blackwood entered. He was in uniform, the scarlet tunic bright in the poor light.

The General said, 'You look well.'

Ralf exclaimed, 'I've come from Portsmouth, Uncle.' He sounded as if he could not believe it himself. 'I was sent to the barracks yesterday. No notice. Nothing. The Colonel must be mad!'

The General snapped, 'Don't be so bloody impertinent! You were sent to Portsmouth to join a new detachment which is going overseas.' He added dryly, 'I can see you know that too. But *I* was the one who arranged the transfer. For your own good and that of the Corps.'

Ralf stood his ground, his face pale and astonished.

'I want to resign, Uncle.'

'Say *sir* when you address me. You are my nephew, but today I am speaking as your superior. You have been gambling heavily. Again.'

'They all do it.' He flinched under the General's cold stare. 'Sir.'

'Three hundred pounds, I believe?' He saw it strike home like a bullet. 'And just *how* did you intend to repay the debt?'

'I – I'll borrow – '

The General ignored him and glanced again at the picture. In the flickering glow from the fire it seemed to be alive. In quieter moments he often relived it. The terrible crack of grenades as he had blown up the magazine on the redoubt, the shock of seeing his hero Philip fall wounded in the bloody snow.

'Your father should have got the Victoria Cross for what he did.' He touched his coat as if to seek the precious decoration. 'Instead I got it. With my eldest son David, that makes two VCs in the family, not a *bad* achievement, wouldn't you say?' It was all he could do to keep the bitterness from his voice as he thought of his mother, elegant and beautiful, but a whore for all that. Society had known of her relationship with the late Lord Cleveland and others like him. It was never mentioned, but like troops in battle society had closed ranks and excluded her. Harry blamed her for the harm she had done him. A major general, and awarded the most coveted decoration the country could bestow, but no knighthood like some of his contemporaries, most of whom had never attained such merit.

A knighthood would have rounded things off and Deirdre would have liked it. He thought of her mild tolerance for some of the things he had done in his life. More than that, she *deserved* it. He thought suddenly of his eldest son David, a captain and somewhere at sea on passage for Hong Kong under orders.

He frowned and did not notice Ralf's sudden apprehension. David had got his Victoria Cross at the capture of Benin. Now he was on his way to the Far East, eventually to China unless the situation there eased. The Chinese mandarins were becoming troublesome again and it was hinted that there might be actual attacks on British trade missions and foreign legations. So why was David being wasted there? With his record, and a captain at twenty-seven, he should have been sent to one of the new iron battleships for further experience and promotion. It seemed almost like a punishment after what he had done in Africa.

He said crisply, 'You will be going to the Far East by troopship. With luck you will be placed under David's command. I say with luck because there are those who would be quick to see your manners as insolence. I will not tolerate any more of this gambling. It will only drive you to something far more serious and bring disgrace on the family. Do I make myself clear?'

'Yes, sir.' He looked at the floor, the corners of his mouth turned down like a pouting child.

The General snorted, 'Resign indeed!' It was strange that Philip, his beloved half-brother, had once intended to resign from the Corps. Philip had imagined he liked action too much. Maybe David's experiences in Africa had hardened him too?

'I shall see Mother before I leave, sir.'

The General relented but only very slightly. There was more at stake than family affections. 'Do that and then return to the barracks. I wish you good luck.'

When he turned his head the room was empty again.

He sat down wearily. The brief interview had drained him. Getting old. Past it.

He would pay off young Ralf's debts. He gave a rueful smile. Could have been worse.

Briggs padded back into the room, a glass of sherry balanced on his small silver tray.

Harry stared. 'Sun's not over the yardarm yet, man!'

Briggs grinned. 'Can't be sure in this weather, sir.' He saw the General's hand shake slightly as he took the glass.

Harry said, 'I'd better see the steward this morning, I suppose.' It was the part of Hawks Hill and all its farm workers and smallholdings he hated. They were always complaining, asking for new roofs, more livestock, it never stopped. He had spent a fortune on the estate. The local hunt, the hounds, and a lavish fashion of entertaining which was the talk of the county.

Trent, the estate steward, was an old woman, he decided. Always hinting at bankruptcy, the need to sell off land to pay for what he had the gall to describe as extravagances.

He thought of Ralf's pale, defiant face and stood up abruptly.

'Maybe the boy'll have lunch before he leaves.'

Briggs looked away. ''E's gone already, sir.'

'*Damn!*' The General left the room and saw his wife watching him from the entrance hall. Reproachful, hurt, it was hard to tell.

'Had to put him right, m'dear.' It sounded defensive and that angered him too. 'Young idiot.'

'Quite so, dear.' She smiled gently. 'But you'll pay off his debts just the same, if I know you.'

The General straightened his back and touched his neat moustache, suddenly pleased with her remark.

He took her arm and led her into the big drawing room where the windows faced a stone-flagged terrace and a line of bare trees beyond. It looked cold and miserable outside these stout walls, he thought.

They sat down and Harry stretched his legs. 'Did I ever tell you how Philip and I chased some slavers halfway across Africa?'

She smiled. 'Remind me, dear.' A hundred times or more. But he obviously needed reassuring, to relive those moments which became more precious with each passing month.

The General leaned back. 'It was this way — '

Briggs walked away. The General sometimes got his facts mixed up when he told his stories. Only his longing to be back with the Corps remained the same.

Captain David Blackwood lay motionless on his vibrating bunk and stared at the slowly revolving fan overhead. He was completely naked, his tanned limbs spreadeagled to catch even the slightest coolness, but there seemed to be no relief.

Around and below him the little paddle-steamer *Cocatrice* squeaked and rattled as her hull deeped over the long undulating swell of the Indian Ocean.

Blackwood was beginning to wonder if he had made the right decision when he had decided to take passage in the small mail and passenger steamship.

When he had received his orders to proceed to Hong Kong he had been serving as acting major aboard the massive battleship *Royal Sovereign* in the Mediterranean. After all the land-fighting he had seen and shared at the capture and burning of Benin in the Niger Protectorate he had felt strangely out of place in a powerful man-of-war, a symbol of Britain's unchallenged might at sea.

Even in the Mediterranean there had been plenty of action when the Royal Navy had taken steps to evacuate Christians who had somehow escaped the terrible Turkish massacre the previous year.

He could have waited for passage in a warship, but the *Cocatrice* was faster if only because of her lack of armament.

He touched his bare skin with his fingers. It was almost dusk and yet he was still damp with sweat. It had been another long, hot day in the Indian Ocean, ninety degrees of blazing sunshine and not a breath of air.

He too had been thinking of Hawks Hill all those hundreds, thousands of miles away. The gardens, the terraces, the agelessness of the rooms with their great pictures and proud portraits.

His youngest brother, Jonathan, would be at sea by now unless there had been some delay. Neil, the middle brother who was twenty-three, was probably still serving as a lieutenant in a frigate in India. Communications might be far superior to those of his father's day, but it still took a long, long while to discover what was happening around the fleet.

He closed his eyes and half listened to the rumble of the great paddles. The passage seemed as if it would never end. They had spent a week at Trincomalee where he had been invited to several dances and receptions aboard ships there. Thank God for the Suez Canal, he thought. It did cut the monotonous journey by weeks.

It would be cold and frosty in Hampshire. Bare trees, sodden hedgerows. He felt his lips smile. Heaven.

Singapore next, then Hong Kong, and then? It was pointless to think further than that. The Chinese situation might have settled itself. He might easily be sent home to England, another ship.

He thought of the day he had joined the *Royal Sovereign* at Gibraltar. The glances in the mess, the way they looked from his Victoria Cross to his face as if to discover something. Even the battleship's captain had received him with something like awe.

'Two VCs in one family.' He had asked dryly, 'Have you finished now?'

And yet the only thing that had made that fight on the Niger River different for Blackwood had been its ferocity and the firm belief that he was going to be killed.

His captain had died within minutes, a sergeant major next, and two experienced marines before Lieutenant David Blackwood had been made to realize that it was upon himself and a small squad of marines that the whole flank depended.

His hand moved up to his shoulder and rested momentarily on a livid scar. The bullet had remained embedded in his body for a whole day before he could find a surgeon. In that climate and under such conditions it was a marvel the surgeon had not lopped of his arm. As it was he still felt pain on occasion. He smiled again, the shadows falling from his face, making him look younger than his twenty-seven years.

There was the girl in Trincomalee. The young wife of an army paymaster who had gone into the interior to visit some isolated infantry unit.

She had made the stay in Ceylon memorable with the fierceness of her passion, her need of him. Her husband was either a lot older than she, or unaware of the luck he should have enjoyed. She had knelt over him in that tall, cool room one night, her loosened hair touching his body until his eagerness for her was roused yet again. She had kissed the scar so that the shame he had felt over it seemed dispersed and forgotten.

He peered at his watch on its stand beside the bunk. It would be laughable but for the discomfort. For even in the little *Cocatrice* you dressed for dinner. Swan, his servant and attendant, would be here soon to arrange a bath and lay out a clean shirt and all the rest of it.

Then in the cramped saloon, with the captain at the head of the table, he would have to endure a hot curry, and some conversation which got more stilted with each league steamed.

There were ten passengers including two Catholic nuns who were intending to join a mission somewhere in China. One was old, the other quite young and pretty. The sailors had been ordered by the captain to mind their language as they worked the ship. He on the other hand, who was a model of good behaviour in the saloon, had a tongue like a lash when he was on his bridge.

Blackwood threw his legs over the side of his bunk and ruffled his dark hair. In the mirror above the small washstand and dressing case he saw his eyes watching himself. Tawny-brown like his mother's. An ordinary face, he told himself, with lines by his mouth as evidence of his suffering after being wounded.

He saw the door open in the mirror, Swan's head coming round it as it always did. The ritual was about to be repeated.

Private Jack Swan of the RMLI had a round, homely face like a polished apple. Hampshire born and bred, he came from a family of marines. That was so common in the Corps it was barely ever mentioned except by exasperated drill-sergeants on the barracks square. 'Don't suppose *yew* 'ad a mother or father, did yer?'

Swan was the same age as Blackwood and the latter had given up trying to make him go for promotion to corporal. Swan was intelligent and quick, both at his duties and in the fury of a battle. He had been with him for three years and whenever Blackwood had mentioned the subject Swan had replied in his round Hampshire dialect, 'Better wait 'n' see, sir. Early days.' It was hopeless.

Swan reached into the canvas wardrobe and took out the mess jacket. Like everything else he supervised it was perfect, but it gave him time to glance at his master. Not the young captain with a VC but the man underneath.

Captain Blackwood had the look of recklessness which made him appeal to women. Swan knew that better than most. He was not one to drive his men when they were doing their best either. But get on the wrong side of him and you would soon know it. They said his father, the old Major General, had been like him once. Blood, guts and women.

Swan gave his secret smile. Promotion indeed. Just being with the young captain was worth all the stripes in the bloody Corps!

Africa, then the Med, next China. In the Corps you took it all for granted. Like their motto. By sea and land. Barracks or frigate, mud huts or stockade, you were still a marine.

The captain's next appointment bothered Swan a bit. He was a hero. Swan had felt quite proud when he had read it in the newspaper. It seemed to rub off on him in some way. He had been with him when those black bastards had tried to cut down the Royals. Swan had lost some good mates on that bloody awful day. He'd not forget that in a hurry.

Unbeknown to either of them, Swan and Captain Blackwood's father thought much the same about the proposed appointment.

The Chinks had learned their lesson back in the fifties in the *Arrow* War as it was called. In 1856 the Chinese had seized a British ship of that name and it had resulted in the bombardment of Canton and a considerable loss of life. In Swan's uncomplicated mind there seemed little likelihood that anything like that would be repeated.

Later at dinner in the *Cocatrice*'s saloon Blackwood had to use something like physical effort to prevent his eyelids from drooping.

The curry had been extra hot, and the captain's wine limp and warm.

The two nuns said nothing, their eyes hidden by their wimples. Only once did the young one glance up as Blackwood replied to the captain's comment about a Boer uprising in South Africa.

Blackwood had been thinking about something else. Of Hawks Hill, and what his brother Neil had written to him about their father's expensive tastes. The farmers did not like the hunt trampling over their fields but could do nothing about it. The labourers on the estate met nothing but rebuffs whenever they tried to have improvements made to their cottages. Trent, the estate steward, had told them to shut up or get out, and jobs were not so easy to find as winter closed in.

Something would have to be done, otherwise Hawks Hill would find itself in serious debt.

He had looked at the captain and had replied, 'If it comes to anything I expect we'll have to go in and finish the fight for the army!' Perhaps it had come out sharper than he had intended. Maybe he was just tired, but he saw the girl's eyes lift to his face. Her empty untroubled expression had made him feel clumsy and childish.

The captain laughed. 'Always spoiling for a battle, you lot are!'

One of the passengers, a rubber planter returning to Singapore with his newly found wife from England, leaned over the table and said loudly, 'I see you have the VC, er, Captain Blackwood. Would you care to tell us how you won it?'

Blackwood looked at him coldly. 'No.'

The planter grinned at his wife. 'Modest too.'

Blackwood stood up abruptly. 'Please excuse me.'

He heard the captain murmur, 'He's had a bad time, poor fellow. Must make allowances.' He also heard the planter's loud guffaw. He suddenly wanted to return to the saloon and tell them in straight, unvarnished words what it was like, *really* like, not just once when someone gave you a medal, but all the other occasions in places which most Britons had never heard of. What right had those nuns to look at him as if he was some sort of animal?

Always spoiling for a battle, the captain had said. He had only been joking, but it was probably true. Aboard *Royal Sovereign* with her endless drills and ceremonial Blackwood had thought of those other times, the fear and elation, the ready comradeship and rough humour which had made his men special. A walk on deck, then some brandy in the cabin. Another day nearer his destination.

There would be some familiar faces at Singapore, rumours to discuss.

He walked to the guardrails and watched the great frothing wash sweeping astern from one of the paddles. Ships such as this one were putting paid to sail. The steam engine and the opening of the Suez Canal through which the square-riggers could not navigate were making sure of it.

Blackwood had been in the Corps for nine years and had

served aboard a sailing frigate when he had first gone to sea. He remembered it clearly. The creaking spars and booming canvas, the sense of mystery which sailing vessels still retained. What was it some old tar had said? Sail is a lady. Steam a bundle of iron. He smiled and returned to the companion way.

Within minutes of his head touching the pillow Captain David Blackwood of the Royal Marines Light Infantry, Victoria Cross and Mentioned in Despatches, was fast asleep.

The Officer Commanding Troops of the big transport *Aurora* leaned back in his chair and pressed his fingertips together. All round the cabin the hull shook to the thump of booted feet, the clatter of tackles and shouted orders as the last of the military came on board.

The *Aurora* was very old and fitted with a single propellor which would probably break down before they reached the Bay of Biscay. He hoped it would not be the case, for the trooper was packed to the deck beams with soldiers, guns, supplies, even some mules and horses, many of which were destined for the latest trouble in South Africa. A whole company of Royal Marines had been the last to arrive on board. The OC Troops did not like the Royal Marines. They were neither one thing nor the other in his view.

Outside the stout hull he heard the muffled sound of a military band on Portsmouth Point as it ran through its repertoire of lively and patriotic tunes. A great crowd had gathered on the harbour wall and pier to watch the old ship put to sea. Mothers and children, wives and lovers. Troopships were only too common as they sailed to the ends of the Empire to restore peace and good order, to attack and destroy the Queen's enemies. But to the watching crowd each ship was different.

The rain was sheeting down. He would be glad to leave. But he had to see a junior second lieutenant of the Royal

Marines. He snapped, 'Enter!'

Ralf Blackwood marched through the door and halted smartly in front of the desk.

The OC Troops said coolly, 'You should see one of your own officers. I have a thousand things to deal with. However – '

He would have liked to have kicked him out of the cabin, but a friend had told him that this young marine came from an important family.

Ralf Blackwood was still not sure what he had been expecting when he had marched with a full company from the barracks to Portsmouth dockyard. Even here in harbour his stomach heaved from a mixture of smells. Horses and men, cabbage water, tar and sweat. Once at sea he would probably be sick.

'My quarters are inadequate, sir.'

'*What?*' He swallowed his anger. 'Four officers to a cabin. When I was your age, your rank, I was lucky to get a berth at all!'

Ralf hung his head. 'I'm not even sharing with a Royal Marine, sir.'

That did it. 'Not good enough, eh?' He flung some papers aside from his desk and stared furiously at a list of names and cabins. 'Three second lieutenants from the Rifles! They're the ones who should be objecting!'

Ralf Blackwood stared at a point above the other officer's left epaulette. Damn him to hell, and his uncle too for landing him in this slum. He thought of London, the bright-eyed girls, the music and the balls he so enjoyed.

He did not really know his cousin David but from what he had heard he was not one to take any misdemeanour lightly. It was all so damned unfair. He felt his eyes smart with despair. A warship would at least be tolerable. Where they were going sounded like the end of the earth.

The OC Troops winced as something very heavy crashed down on the upper desk and was followed by a stream of obscenities from one of the ship's petty officers. He could waste no more time.

'I have little to do with your Corps.' His tone was icy. 'But I can only advise you to think less of yourself and a bit more of your responsibility, *if* you have any!'

Ralf snapped his heels together and left the cabin, his face devoid of expression but inwardly seething.

The major in command of the marines saw him and shouted, 'And just where the bloody hell have you been?' Like the OC Troops, he was preoccupied with getting his own people settled in their overcrowded quarters. 'Report to the Adjutant at the double, sir!'

An artillery lieutenant touched Ralf's sleeve as the angry major strode away.

'Never mind him. I understand you're quite a hand at cards?'

Ralf was both surprised and flattered by the other officer's knowledge.

He thought of the General's Room, the great house which but for his parents' deaths might have been his.

They treated him like a child. Aunt Deirdre and her dreamy detachment from daily events. And his uncle, always on at him to remember the family, uphold the honour of the Corps. He was a fine one to lecture him. Ralf had heard things about the General's mother, about Harry Blackwood's own affairs with whores no better than she.

Ralf replied calmly, 'Any time.'

The artillery lieutenant grinned. 'As soon as we leave harbour.'

Ralf watched him go. This time his luck must change.

His sergeant found him and saluted.

'The men are waitin', sir.' He ran his eyes over the second lieutenant, critical and anxious. He would have to carry this one, he could see all the signs. Spoiled, arrogant, lazy. But if he let down the platoon and the adjutant became aware of it he knew who would get the blame.

'Let them wait, Sergeant. Can't you deal with them?'

The sergeant saw one of his corporals watching and

glared. His own wife was out there on the dockside. Two kids he might never see again.

Blackwood was a fine name in the Corps. The sergeant tightened his belt and grimaced. But there was usually a rotten apple in any barrel.

The *Aurora* slipped between Portsmouth Point and Fort Blockhouse just before dusk, her black and white hull shining in the steady rain like glass.

Her decks were crammed with scarlet and green, blue and khaki, the great anonymous mass of faces peering for someone dear or familiar as the band played its own farewell. Hundreds of troopships had sailed from here, and many more would follow. But it was a moment they would all remember.

2

The Letter

Private Swan took the sword and helmet and laid them carefully on a chest while he gauged his master's mood.

Outside the white-painted room the air still vibrated to the sorrowful drums and the slow marches of marines and soldiers, as dust swirled over the docks and parade ground and seemed to change colour in the sunshine.

David Blackwood allowed Swan to unfasten and remove his tunic. His shirt was plastered to his body like a second skin. After the marching and the drills the room felt almost cold.

No matter what was happening in other parts of the Queen's Empire the importance of ceremonial remained paramount. There had been several visits to Hong Kong by senior foreign dignitaries as well as senior British officers. It seemed as if almost overnight Hong Kong had become the hinge upon which the power in Whitehall extended to the Far East and beyond. In the spring it would be the ailing Queen's birthday, and that would mean even more drills and parades.

In South Africa what first had been scoffed at as a mere skirmish had changed into a full-scale and bloody war where British troops were too often getting the worst of it. That again was impossible to accept. Trained regular soldiers and marines against Boer farmers and renegades. More than once the enemy sharpshooters had proved a match for cavalry and tactics which had not altered since the Crimea.

Blackwood sighed and waited for Swan to tug off his

boots. It was now February 1900, and he had been in Hong Kong with little to occupy his time since he had arrived in the *Cocatrice*.

The harbour and dockyard were packed with men-of-war. Gleaming white hulls or black and buff, they represented the new iron navy. Here and there like reminders of a past era were still some of the old 'wooden walls', now mostly used as store and hospital ships.

Blackwood thought of his brother Neil who had been sent to South Africa. He had received one letter from him which had described the raids on Boer positions, the unending sniping which had caused heavy casualties amongst the British troops.

He had seemed extra bitter in that letter, scornful of the generals who had no idea of modern fighting conditions. He had described the perils of moving large numbers of men across open country without breaking formation even under fire.

David Blackwood could picture his father striding about his room at Hawks Hill, laying down the law on what they should be doing in the colony, demanding that he should be sent to take command. No wonder there was news of more trouble in China, he thought. The Empire seemed beset from every side while the great powers of France and Germany watched with unconcealed satisfaction. A real uprising in China would at least cement the relationships between these powers. But by the time they realized that danger like prosperity could be shared, it might be too late.

He heard Swan whispering at the door of his room and prayed that there was no further ceremonial for the day. After the relaxed atmosphere of Singapore this place was like an overcrowded beehive. Daily, men and guns moved along Queen's Road while the anchorage became full of vessels of every shape and class.

Swan returned, his round face disapproving.

'The major sends his compliments, sir, an' would you go over an' see him.'

Blackwood stood up while his faithful attendant went into the adjoining room to lay out a fresh uniform and shirt. Orders at last? He did not dare to hope. Anything was better than sweating it out here in Hong Kong. It had almost doubled in size since his first visit as a youthful lieutenant. New docks, larger barracks, a cricket field, he barely recognized the place. Likewise the harbour was flanked by bigger buildings. Prosperous merchants, warehouses and offices as the Empire's trade flowed further and further eastwards.

Twenty minutes later he was ushered into his commanding officer's little house which stood beside the barracks and yet was so much apart from it.

Major James Blair was standing by a wide window watching the harbour as Blackwood was shown into the room by a Chinese servant. He turned and nodded. 'Ah, David. Have a drink.' He did not wait for a reply. 'Parade went off extremely well, I thought, what?'

'Yes, sir.' Blackwood liked the major although he did not really understand him. Blair was described as an *old China hand*. One who loved the place and dreaded the thought of being sent home. It was said that he had a beautiful Chinese mistress. Today he looked worried, and it was unusual for him to suggest a drink before noon.

Blair gestured to his servant and waited for the door to close. Then he said abruptly, 'No easy way, David.' He watched him steadily. 'Just heard and thought you'd take it better from me than some idiot from the base.'

David Blackwood felt his fingers crushing the glass almost to breaking point. 'It's my brother Neil, isn't it, sir?'

Blair nodded. 'Killed in action. In some bloody place I've never heard of. A sniper.'

Blackwood let out his breath very slowly. In his heart he had known about it all the time. He had been closer to Neil than anyone. A lively friendly person. Without an enemy in the world. It would destroy their mother. The General would go and stand by the painting in his room. Pay homage to the family's dead.

He heard himself murmur, 'I'm glad you told me. I'd like to ask for a transfer immediately.' His fingers relaxed slightly and he placed the empty glass on a table. It was all he could think of. All he wanted. Revenge against those murderous, savage Boers.

Blair eyed him sadly. 'Impossible. You're appointed to Peking as soon as the arrangements are finalized.'

'China?' He stared at him. 'But what use will I be there, sir? Wiping carriage seats for the ladies of our legation and mounting guard for foreign ambassadors, is that all I'm worth?'

Blair poured another glass of whisky and waited for the captain to recover his composure.

Blackwood said, 'I'm sorry, sir.'

'Don't be.' He looked up searchingly. 'You've had a few hard knocks in your time. We're all proud of you. I'd not want you to think you're being wasted or pushed into an unimportant backwater. I know there has been little trouble with the mandarins since the *Arrow* War in fifty-eight, but there have been many changes since then. European governments are pushing hard for more concessions, getting greedy in some people's eyes, but as they say, China is a sleeping tiger. You can step on her tail once too often. If there *is* real trouble there must be some professional, experienced officers ready and available. Not here or in England, but on the spot.' He tried to smile but it would not come. 'You in fact.'

As if from a thousand miles away Blackwood heard the steady tramp of marching feet as the marines drilled in the unbroken sunlight. He could see them in his mind, still wearing their ceremonial scarlet tunics and their newly designed helmets. Just like his own men in the Niger expedition. Ready targets for any hidden marksmen. Only their blood had been concealed.

He thought of Neil's letter, his anger at the way they

were being sacrificed by minds totally outdated in a new
kind of war.

And there was his youngest brother. He felt his eyes
prick with sudden emotion. Jonathan was his only brother
now. How much worse it might seem to him at the very
beginning of his career with the Corps.

He asked dully, 'How many men, sir?'

'Ninety. I could give you more but the other legations
would kick up a fuss. Even ninety may be too many.'

Blair added, 'Go to your quarters, David. You are
relieved until I hear something final. You never know . . .'
He did not finish.

Outside the house Blackwood paused to recover himself.
An hour ago he had been cursing his luck. The news about
Neil made his own troubles seem infantile.

He thought of the girl Neil had brought home to Hawks
Hill. Like him, laughing and happy. He had wanted to
marry her and the General had said, 'When you've been
made up to captain, m'boy.' But even he had sounded
pleased.

Who would tell her? he wondered.

'*Sir!*'

He looked round and saw the tall, ramrod figure of Fox,
the sergeant major, striding after him. With so many new
recruits in the Corps veterans like Fox were worth more than
their weight in gold. How could he put his mind to duty?
What was it this time? Someone for promotion, a defaulter,
orders for tomorrow? It all seemed trivial.

'What is it, Sergeant Major?'

Fox slammed to a halt and saluted. Nothing wasted, not
a crease in his tunic to mark that he had been on the square
for several hours during the gloomy ceremonial.

'Just wanted to say I'm sorry, sir.' He watched him
calmly from beneath his helmet. 'Mr Neil, sir.'

Blackwood stared at him. Of course, Neil had served
with the tall sergeant major. Second lieutenant and sergeant
then. And Fox already knew. It was like that in the Corps.

In the family as they called it.

He said, 'Thank you.' He could not continue.

Fox fell in step beside him, his gloved fingers gripping his stick beneath one arm.

With unusual vehemence Fox said, 'I 'ates them bastards. We puts on a uniform. They shoots our lads in the back and then ˋpleads fer mercy when they're caught.' His fist tightened on the stick's silver knob. '*Mercy?* I'd give the poxy varmints mercy all right!'

They stood outside the officers' quarters not looking at each other.

Fox said, 'The old trooper *Aurora* is reported enterin' 'arbour, sir. I'd best get down there with a couple of sergeants and sort out the new arrivals.'

'I'll be there.'

Fox tightened his lips into a thin line. 'No, sir. I'll take young Mr Gravatt. Time 'e learned a thing or two.' He almost smiled. 'With respect, we'll be needin' *you* later on, sir.' His hand shot up to an immaculate salute and he marched away before Blackwood could protest.

Swan held the door open for him and he saw a glass and decanter already on the table.

Swan could not look at him either.

Blackwood sat down heavily. 'You've heard?'

'Aye, sir.' His hand shook as he poured a full measure of Scotch. 'Anything I can do, sir?'

'No!'

Swan paused at the door and saw the captain unfolding a letter. The one he had received from his brother in South Africa.

Blackwood did not hear the door shut but stared at the letter as a solitary tear splashed across his dead brother's writing. He swallowed the neat whisky and closed his eyes very tightly. What would those two nuns say if they could see him now?

'How was the family when you left England?'

David Blackwood offered his cousin a chair and watched him curiously. Ralf's arrival in Hong Kong had been a complete surprise, but his manner and attitude were even more astonishing.

He had not seen the youthful second lieutenant for a long time, since he had been a mere boy, but he had expected he would follow in the family mould, like the faces in the portraits at Hawks Hill.

He had grown a thin moustache on the passage from Portsmouth but it had made him look even younger and somehow vulnerable.

Ralf replied, 'I think they were all right, er, sir.' He was looking at him warily as if he expected a confrontation like the one he had had with his uncle.

Blackwood heard the other officers of his new detachment gathering in the mess nearby and decided that after this meeting he would treat the second lieutenant no differently from the rest. He wondered why his father had arranged Ralf's transfer. There must be a reason. He would soon discover what it was once they had worked properly together as a team.

But too many meetings like this would be seen as favouritism. Something he hated and which could disrupt any small unit.

Since the *Aurora*'s arrival in the harbour there had been many more signals and rumours about growing danger for the 'Foreign Devils' in Peking and around the various European and Japanese concessions along the coast. Major Blair had been correct. There would be trouble of vast proportions unless prompt action was taken.

For two weeks the new company had been drilling, marching and exercising together in the hills above Hong Kong, or from boats around Aberdeen harbour. It had already worked wonders, but there were too many new recruits amongst them to be certain of anything so soon.

Ralf Blackwood did not seem interested in anything. Of

Neil's terrible death he had muttered only a few words and then launched into his own list of complaints and requests for a transfer to one of the larger men-of-war in the harbour.

Major Blair had not even considered it. He had snapped, 'You *make* something of him, David. He might learn a bit about soldiering if he can set his mind to it.'

He tried again. 'How are you settling in, Ralf?'

The moustache turned down slightly. 'I don't think they like me.'

'Why not?' He was wrong even to ask. There was something not quite honest about this young man. Like a sulky child.

He shrugged. 'It's not my fault.' He looked up defiantly. 'I – I think it's because of the family. The name of Blackwood. They're jealous, I expect.'

Blackwood sat down and felt strangely satisfied that he had been right. Disappointed too for all their sakes.

'I don't want to hear that sort of trouble-making rubbish again, do you understand?'

He saw the sudden alarm in Ralf's eyes. And anger. That he had played his hand badly and too soon.

Blackwood tried again. He had always been sorry for the boy, and now that he was grown-up and an officer under his command he could appreciate what he must have suffered down the years.

'I never knew your father, Ralf. But he was a fine man, one to be proud of. Keep that memory alive.' He saw that he was making no impression. Ralf's eyes had the knack of becoming motionless and opaque. Like coloured glass. He said wearily, 'Dismiss. I'll see you when I speak to the others.'

Ralf marched from the room and shut the door as loudly as he dared.

Blackwood smiled gravely. He would have to watch that one very closely.

Later in the small private mess allotted to his newly formed company Blackwood ran his eyes over their expectant faces. The usual mixture, he thought. Excitement, anxiety, acceptance, it was all there. He could feel Ralf's eyes fixed on him as he ran briefly through his orders.

They would embark aboard the cruiser *Mediator* tomorrow and steam the thousand miles north-east along the coast of the mainland to Taku at the mouth of the Peiho river. There they would anchor and await instructions which would depend on the state of the emergency.

While he was speaking he was looking at his officers, the ones who would have to interpret them, to lead if he and others fell. The three lieutenants Gravatt, Bannatyre and de Courcy, the last from a very old marines family. Two second lieutenants, Ralf and a childlike youth named Earle. The three lieutenants had seen some action but on a very punitive and limited scale.

Blackwood continued, 'We shall be under the command of Captain Masterman of the *Mediator*. But *if* we are required to move inland to Peking we shall be taking orders from the military at the embassy.'

He saw a few grimaces. The Royal Marines tolerated being given orders by a ship's captain. There were plenty of second thoughts about the army.

Lieutenant Gravatt asked politely, 'How do we get to Peking, sir?'

It was a good question, Blackwood thought.

'Upriver as far as possible, then overland by train.' He had a stark picture of the armoured trains in South Africa. Neil had described them in his letter. He had probably been shot while he and his men were moving across country.

Gravatt, who was his second-in-command and acting adjutant, grinned. 'I shall sit with my back to the engine.'

They laughed. All except Ralf who barely seemed to blink.

'Just remember this.' His grave tone stilled the laughter like a closed door. 'We shall have to adapt to a new sort of warfare. Sentries and pickets in full marching order are perfect targets. Scarlet tunics have cost too many lives

already. At sea we stand-to with the sailors. Ashore we will
fight like the enemy. But on *our* terms.'

It was a beginning.

The *Mediator* was a second-class light cruiser of some three
thousand tons. As the marines had climbed aboard with
their piles of equipment and weapons Blackwood had found
time to admire her sleek and graceful lines. She was less
than a year old and a far cry from the old ironclads which
had once been the backbone of the fleet.

Now as he lay in his comfortable bunk Blackwood
wondered what had awakened him. He had been dreaming
about Neil, and had seen him walking away, glancing back
at him, his face incredibly sad.

Blackwood groaned and rolled over to find the bunk
light. It was still pitch dark, not even dawn.

As he gripped the side of the bunk he felt the *Mediator*
shivering under his touch, and as his mind pushed all
thoughts of sleep aside he heard the swish and plunge of the
light cruiser's hull as she increased speed.

They had been at sea for four days, but never exceeded ten
knots. Captain Masterman believed in conserving his stocks
of coal, just in case of some last-minute emergency.

Blackwood lowered himself to the deck and felt the
tremble pulsing through the steel plates. She was doing a
lot more than ten knots now.

As if to settle his uncertainty the whistle of a voice-pipe
shrilled above the bunk.

Blackwood snapped on the light and blinked at the
bulkhead clock. It was only four in the morning.

'Captain Blackwood.' He held the tube to his ear.

'Bridge, sir.' The sailor had a strong Cockney accent, like
the sergeant major. 'Cap'n Masterman's compliments an'
could you join 'im.'

'What's happening?' But the voice-pipe was dead again.

Blackwood scrambled into his uniform and smiled to

himself. He could not expect to hear any gossip with
Masterman on the bridge.

The cruiser's captain was tall and straight, as if every
ounce of unwanted fat and weight had been honed away. A
large beaked nose, dominated by deceptively mild blue eyes
and two sweeping sideburns iron grey against his sunburned
cheeks.

Blackwood had spoken to him only twice since he had
come aboard. Not a man to waste words. Like his coal. But
someone who would be like a rock in any kind of
emergency.

He climbed quickly to the upper bridge and soon saw
Masterman's tall outline framed against the white screen.
The bridge was full of people. Most of the ship's officers, the
yeoman of signals, lookouts, everyone.

Masterman glanced at him. 'Mornin', Soldier. Sorry to
get you up.'

'There, sir! Port bow!'

The lookout pointed above the screen with one arm.

Blackwood saw it. A rocket or flare, drifting lazily in the
far distance. Without any clouds to reflect the light it
looked puny, unreal.

Masterman breathed out very softly. To Blackwood he
remarked, 'Second one. Beginnin' to think the lookouts had
imagined it all.' He chuckled and some of the officers near
him visibly relaxed.

'Course to steer?'

The navigating officer was ready. He needed to be.

'North fifteen west, sir.'

'Alter course.'

Blackwood listened to the orders being passed down to
the quartermaster, the slight heel of the deck as the ship
changed course very slightly.

Masterman said offhandedly, 'Shanghai is about eighty
miles nor'-west of our present position. That ship is
somewhere in between.'

He made up his mind. 'Full ahead together. Close up

action stations.' He swivelled round as one of *Mediator*'s own Royal Marines stamped smartly to the rear of the bridge, moistening the mouth-piece of his bugle with his tongue.

'Not *that*, dammit!' He glared at the commander. 'I don't want the whole bloody world to hear us!'

The boatswains' mates scampered from the bridge and moments later seamen and marines poured up from below decks and ran to their stations while others manned the barbettes on either side.

Masterman said, 'She'll likely be the *Delhi Star*. Passengers and mail. She sailed two days before us.'

He did not attempt to hide the pride he had in his ship. Blackwood could picture her smashing through the water as she worked up to her impressive maximum of twenty knots. White hull and two buff funnels, she would look like a spectre in the pitch darkness. Light she might be but she carried six-inch guns as well as smaller weapons and could if required speak with authority.

Blackwood hesitated. Masterman did that to you. You felt obliged to honour his silence.

He asked, 'Shipwreck, sir?'

The captain shook his head. 'Unlikely. I know her master. A wily old chap.'

A voice called, 'Ship at action stations, sir!'

Masterman ignored him. 'My guess is pirates. This coast is rotten with 'em.'

The bridge was shaking so violently that it felt as if every rivet would burst loose. A great creaming wake carved a straight line astern and above it Blackwood could see the dense smoke belching low over the sea as evidence of the stokers' efforts far below the decks.

Pirates. They were in for a nasty surprise.

Masterman said abruptly, 'I want you to go with the boarding party, Blackwood. My people are pretty young and inexperienced.' He almost smiled but contained himself. 'Like *Mediator*. Do 'em good to have a real-life hero amongst 'em.'

Blackwood looked at him. There was neither sarcasm nor malice. He actually meant it.

He said awkwardly, 'I'll go below and change, sir.'

'Don't be too long. We'll be within range shortly. It will be first light by then. We'll need to bustle about a bit smartly. If there are any survivors aboard the *Delhi Star* they'll be in a bad way by now.'

Blackwood ran down a ladder and found Swan waiting beside the forward funnel.

'We goin' over, sir?'

'*I am.*' He relented immediately. To go without Swan would be like carrying an unloaded revolver. He grinned. 'Get our gear ready.'

It seemed unnaturally bright between decks. All the deadlights had been clamped shut across the scuttles and it was hard to imagine pirates so near. Masterman could be wrong, but that was even harder to believe.

The deck had been opened near the cabin flat and he saw some seamen by the tackles of a shell-hoist. He had not realized he had been sleeping directly above a magazine.

On the marines' messdeck Swan was dragging on his boots and buckling on belt and bayonet. He snatched his rifle from its rack and clattered up the ladder again to find the rest of the boarding party.

Blackwood dashed from his cabin and almost collided with Ralf. Like the rest of the new detachment he had no proper action station, and seemed at a loss.

'Is it true? About the pirates?'

Blackwood drew his heavy revolver and examined the chamber. There was no need. Swan had seen to that too.

'Yes, want to come?'

He had said it as a joke, something to steady his own nerves. But it was as if he had struck him.

'N-no, sir.'

A voice bellowed. 'A-way starboard whaler! Boardin' party to muster!'

Blackwood dashed by the men at the shell-hoist, oblivious to everything but Ralf's face.

He was terrified. And in a matter of weeks they might be fighting for their lives.

One of the light cruiser's lieutenants, pistol at his belt, saw him and grinned.

'Here we go, sir!'

The boat's crew were already in their places and there were more armed seamen in the sternsheets.

'Slip the gripes! Turns fer lowerin'!'

Blackwood climbed up and over the gunwale and saw the great seething wash begin to die away as *Mediator* reduced speed so that the boat could be dropped without danger of capsizing.

'Lower away, handsomely!' That was the commander. Masterman must have sent him to ensure there were no mistakes.

The boat dropped down the *Mediator*'s white plates, the sea lifting to meet them.

'Avast lowering!'

The pins were out and the boat swayed a foot or so above the water like an overloaded pod.

'Slip!' They were away, but as the oars dropped smartly into their crutches and the tiller was thrust hard over, all Blackwood could see was Ralf's terror.

3

Boarders Away!

Lieutenant Hudson, *Mediator*'s boarding officer, lurched to his feet to recover his bearings as the boat plunged and yawed in the short, choppy waves.

He rested one hand on Blackwood's shoulder, the only way he could remain upright, and shouted, 'I heard shots!'

Blackwood nodded. So there was still some resistance aboard the little steamer. How quickly the light was spreading down from the horizon, and how fast events were moving since the whaler had been lowered. He peered astern and saw that the ship had not moved and guessed that Captain Masterman was about to drop a second boat as additional support.

The lieutenant shouted, 'Watch the stroke, dammit!' But he sounded less confident without the *Mediator*'s authority at close quarters.

The boat seemed to fly across the water, spray rising from the oar blades as the seamen threw their weight on the looms, no easy task with the twenty-seven-foot hull packed with bodies and weapons.

Crack — crack — crack.

Blackwood licked his lips and unclipped the flap on his holster. He did it almost unconsciously, without even drawing the attention of the stroke oarsman.

The whaler's graceful hull lifted on an offshore roller and he saw the little steamer *Delhi Star* clearly for the first time. Masterman had been right about her too, he thought grimly.

And yet she was similar to dozens of an ever-growing fleet of such vessels. Small, single-screwed, able to carry passengers and light cargo for the benefit of the East's expanding trade and importance. He could see her white side glinting faintly in the early sunlight, her funnel smoke drifting downwind, and other smoke too, although whether from internal fires or explosions he could not say.

One of the seamen said hoarsely, 'Gawd! That'll please the Old Man, I don't think!'

Hudson snapped, 'Hold your tongue!' But he too stared astern where the second boat was in total confusion. She was the cruiser's cutter, and therefore double-banked for extra speed. But her oars were all mixed up and slashing at thin air, and Blackwood saw some men hanging over the boat's flat transom trying to re-ship the rudder which had obviously fallen off as the boat had been dropped from the davits.

The unknown sailor was correct. Masterman would be fuming.

He glanced at Hudson's tight profile. He looked scared to death. It was hard enough to board even a docile junk in these conditions. And there was fresh firing. Short and sharp. A last resistance. Perhaps the steamer's crew had sighted the light cruiser as sunlight swept over her like thin gold.

Blackwood turned his head towards the shore. He could not see the mainland, but there were several scattered groups of islets, some so small that they looked like basking whales, oblivious to the drama which was revealing itself more strongly every minute. There were fishing boats too amongst the islets, motionless like black sticks. Another hot day, he thought.

Hudson squatted down at his side, their faces an inch apart.

'Shall we wait for the cutter, d'you think?'

Blackwood could almost smell his fear. In a moment it would transmit itself through the boat with the speed of an arrow.

It was likely that the cutter was under the command of a midshipman, at best a sub-lieutenant. Hudson would still be in overall charge.

He replied, 'We'll go in as ordered.' He wished he knew the lieutenant's first name. It often helped in moments like these. He glanced at his attendant and knew that Swan was also recalling those other times. The fear changing to hate, the caution giving way to madness. Swan had already loosened his bayonet and as Blackwood nodded to him he jerked back the bolt of his rifle and slammed a bullet into the breech. It acted better than any bugle, and the oars seemed to blur as the boat surged forward. Blackwood peered over the swaying shoulders and saw the *Delhi Star*'s attacker rising above her opposite side like some nightmare bat.

Pirates and junks went together. The little steamer's master should know that. If not he was paying dearly for it.

A bullet hit the whaler's gunwale and threw a splinter at the stroke oarsman's feet. He barely blinked, but along the boat men were pulling in their heads as if that would help.

'Swan.'

Swan climbed deftly over the swaying looms and amongst the panting seamen until he was right in the bows.

He seemed to rise and fall like a figurehead, but Blackwood noted that the gleaming Lee-Metford rifle managed to remain steady.

There was a crack, and Swan remarked calmly, 'One down.'

'Keep firing, Swan. Drive them away from the rails!'

He did not need to be told but it would help to hold the discipline in the boat.

The air cringed as *Mediator*'s siren tore the morning apart with a raucous screech.

Birds rose flapping from the nearest islets, adding their protests to the din, and the whaler's coxswain exclaimed, 'She goin' to fire on the bastards, sir!'

There was a violent bang and from one of the light cruiser's long six-inch guns came a vivid orange flash.

They heard the shell rip overhead, like tearing a giant's canvas before exploding far beyond the fishing boats and islets in a solid tower of water.

Hudson said shakily, 'The junk's casting off!' He shook his fist in the air. 'We'll blow her sky-high!'

Blackwood kept his eyes on the steamer's hull, very aware of Hudson's relief, also that the junk's commander would use the *Delhi Star* as a shield until he was lost amongst the islets and the fishermen.

But it was too early for overconfidence. The junk must have cast off with such haste as the *Mediator* had announced her arrival that some of the pirates might still be aboard, and to all intents abandoned.

Hudson was yelling, 'Stand by bowman! Ready with grapnel!'

He looked elated, all his anxieties gone after the gun had fired.

The seamen boated their oars as best they could, and as the grapnel soared above the rails and held fast, they came alongside with a violent shudder.

'Boarders away!' Hudson had drawn his revolver and, with his men yelling and waving their cutlasses, scrambled up the ship's side. It was quite a low-hulled vessel, with just one line of scuttles before rising to a second deck beyond the bridge.

Blackwood darted a quick glance at the cutter; it was still a cable clear but pulling well, and there was a Maxim gun mounted above the stem.

He nodded to Swan and together they hauled themselves after the others.

The sudden silence was almost worse than a fusillade of shots.

Blackwood heard a man retching uncontrollably and saw a body by the scuppers so hacked about and mutilated that it was barely human. Blood filled the scuppers, surging this way and that as if to escape.

Hudson tore his eyes away. 'Bridge! Martin, take three men to the other side, lively now!'

From the corner of his eye Blackwood saw a movement by one of the companion-ways. He dragged out his sword, 'Swan, you come with me!'

It was useless to tell Hudson who was already charging towards a bridge ladder. It would delay things. Someone had run below. To do what? To blow up the whole ship perhaps?

He almost pitched down the ladder as he skidded on more blood.

He heard Swan gasp, *'Jesus Christ!'* It took a lot to impress Swan these days.

There was blood everywhere. Splashed on the sides of the long central passageway, up the sides, even on the deckhead. Corpses too, mutilated beyond belief, one even headless.

Blackwood said harshly, 'There's at least one of them down here!'

He almost ducked as *Mediator* fired again, the shell exploding in the sea with such force you could believe the ship had run aground.

A figure in white robes bounded from the cabin, a wide-bladed sword across his shoulder as he peered wildly at the two marines.

Blackwood felt Swan's bullet fan past his ear without remembering the sound of the shot. He heard it crack into the man's forehead, killing him instantly. But all Blackwood could recall was the blood pouring unheeded from the man's sword and down his arm before he dropped.

He kicked open the cabin door, his pistol held so tightly it hurt his fingers.

The contents of the drawers and luggage were all around but the cabin's occupants, a man, a woman and a small girl, were hacked to ribbons.

Blackwood looked meaningly at Swan. These people had

been butchered slowly. It was a scene from hell. But not by the man lying dead in the passageway. He had not had the time.

Swan said in a whisper, 'Reckon 'e was lookin' for a mate, sir.'

Blackwood pursed his lips. 'Another one then?'

Faintly overhead, from another world, they heard shouts and two shots. There was steel on steel as Hudson's men got busy with their cutlasses.

But this was here. Now. He could feel his heart thumping as if to break free, but when he glanced at his revolver his hand was as steady as Swan's rifle.

Two more cabins yet. Both doors shut. Not even a whimper.

Swan drew his bayonet deftly and snapped it into place.

He said almost casually, 'There's another of 'em in the shadows!' But as he lunged over a steel locker and swung the rifle down he gasped, 'This one's already done for.'

Blackwood pulled him backwards. There was a tiny hole in the cabin door where that one had fallen. A lucky shot perhaps but it had found its mark.

Swan gestured urgently to the other cabin. Its handle was moving very slowly. It would not even be noticed but for some blood which shone from the handle like cruel red eyes.

It was time to act. Blackwood pressed his back against the opposite side of the passageway and then hurled himself forward against the door just as it began to open.

He got a vague glimpse of another white-clad figure, the gleam of a swinging blade before he fell headlong into the cabin.

Swan fired from the hip, and using just his right hand parried the sword aside and drove his bayonet into the figure's chest almost to the hilt.

Blackwood peered at the body and then kicked the sword away.

They both looked up as feet stampeded across the deck above with sporadic firing coming from elsewhere, probably from the cutter.

There was a man sitting on the bunk, the body of a woman across his knees.

Blackwood murmured hoarsely. 'Take her from him and cover her up, for God's sake.' But the man tightened his grip, his whole body shaking to his grief. But no sound came from his lips as he held the dead woman in his arms.

Blackwood moved to the door, seeing it all in his mind. The last hope, then horror as the madman with the sword had burst in again.

'I'll be back!' But it made no impression.

Swan said tightly, 'Next door, sir. 'Eard a sound.'

'Right.' Blackwood felt hot and icy cold in turns. He looked at the cabin's door, the one with the small hole in it. Whoever had been in there might have killed one attacker but it could mean something else. More pirates. A last rally. After all they had nothing to lose. Once taken they would be hustled ashore and beheaded for their trade, and as a warning.

Blackwood had seen it before in China, could remember his own men standing around like uneasy spectators as a local mandarin's axeman had done his macabre works.

Blackwood heard himself say, 'I'm going in. These bloody doors are like cardboard.'

Swan grimaced, but kept his eyes on the door. 'Ready when you are, sir.' He brought his rifle to his waist. 'Good luck.'

Blackwood found a split second to look at him. The last time? Like it had been for Neil?

He drew aside and then flung himself at the door with Swan's bayonet almost brushing his shoulder as they burst through.

Light from the sun made a smoky beam across the cabin, and as Blackwood twisted round to get his back against a bulkhead he stared with astonishment at the woman who faced him. She stood absolutely motionless, her slim figure covered from neck to her bare feet by a dark blue dressing gown which shone in the sunlight like silk. Her hair was tangled across one shoulder and the gown had been badly torn; he could see the bare skin where a hand had tried to rip it from her.

A small Chinese girl crouched on her knees, her arms wrapped around the motionless figure. Blackwood noticed all and none of these things. He could only stare at the woman in blue, and at the tiny silver revolver she held in one hand, its muzzle levelled at his heart.

He said as steadily as he could, 'Don't be afraid. I am a British officer.' It sounded ridiculous, and he stared at her eyes which had not moved from his face.

There was a muffled crash as the cutter at last managed to get alongside, cheers and running feet, but somehow it meant nothing.

A body lay near the opposite end of the cabin, and for an instant he imagined it was a repeat of the terrible murders he had already seen.

Swan said, 'One of the pirates, sir.' He lowered his bayonet until it was aimed at the man in the white robe. 'Still alive.'

The woman slowly lowered the revolver and then, almost casually, tossed it on to the bunk.

'You were just in time.' She spoke with a foreign accent. 'I had but two bullets left. One for this foolish maid, Anna.' She seemed to realize he was looking at the bare skin below her shoulder. 'One for myself.'

Blackwood heard men charging through the ship, voices yelling orders, others vomiting as they discovered more butchered remains.

He took a step towards her, yet she seemed to get no nearer.

She said, 'I am the Countess von Heiser. I was — ' She hesitated and looked at the door as if expecting to see more attackers surging through. 'I *am* going to Shanghai to join my husband.'

Blackwood could feel himself shaking. It would not show

to others but it was there just the same. He slipped his
revolver into its holster and said, 'You are very brave,
Countess.' German. The name was familiar too. Her
husband was important. It explained why she had the best
cabin in the ship.

She waited for her quivering maid to release her hold and
then reached out one hand and said in the same level tone,
'Please. I think I am going to be sick.' She held his arm
with both hands, her nails biting through the tunic and
breaking his skin.

Close to she was not merely beautiful, she was entranc-
ing. Her hair was the colour of honey, her eyes, now tightly
closed, were violet.

Beside her Blackwood felt clumsy and unclean. He
wanted to hold her, to console her after what must have
been a terrible ordeal.

She said quietly, 'And your man is wrong. These are not
pirates. They are Boxers.' She made herself say it. 'The Big
Knife Society.'

He watched the pain moving from her face like a cloud.
She lifted her chin and looked at him curiously.

'I was in Hong Kong with my sister to buy some things.
I saw the British marines there. I know about the military,
you see.'

Figures loomed through the door and a petty officer said,
'Good God, sir. I thought you were done for!'

Blackwood replied, 'Carry on with the search. Any ship's
officers alive?'

'Two, sir.' The petty officer's eyes were fixed on the slim,
elegant woman as if he were mesmerized.

She said, 'The captain was a fool. He took on a deck cargo
of passengers. When the junk came near they rushed the
bridge. Only the mate had sense enough to hold the saloon
until he too was hacked to pieces.'

She slowly released her grip from his arm. 'In the next
cabin —' She looked at his eyes without flinching. 'Are they
killed?'

Somehow Blackwood knew the question was far more important than she had made it sound.

'I am afraid the lady is dead. The man with her is too stunned to move.'

She walked slowly to the scuttle and stared out at the clean, blue water.

'She is my sister.'

He saw her shoulders begin to shake, the pretence and the tenacity falling away like a loose robe.

He put his hands on her shoulders and said gently, 'I understand, Countess.'

She twisted round and stared up at him, her eyes brimming with tears.

'Do you? Do you indeed?'

He said, 'My brother was killed recently.'

She nodded and then reached up to touch his face. 'You are strong. Will you take me to her?'

Blackwood's mouth was dry like a kiln.

She saw his expression and laid her fingers flat on his mouth.

'I know what to expect, but I shall need your strength.'

Swan stood in the passageway and leaned on his rifle, one eye on the groaning figure inside the cabin.

Some seamen clattered along the bloodstained passageway and Swan jerked his head. 'In there. Wounded.' He thought of that tiny silver pistol. She had shot two of the bastards. They must have left her until last. There had to be a reason. The attack was no clumsy hit-or-miss affair. It had been managed like a military operation.

He saw one of the sailors pick up the fallen sword and felt a shiver at his spine.

Bloody hell. If all the Boxers were like these. He jerked to attention as Blackwood reappeared with his hand around the countess's arm.

Her face was ashen, but she had her chin lifted. She even tried to give Swan a smile as she passed.

Blackwood said, 'The boarding party has taken charge,

Countess. May I suggest that I have you carried across to the cruiser. It will take time to clean up this ship.'

She watched him thoughtfully. 'That is kind of you.' She beckoned to her tiny maid. 'Anna, lay out my things. Perhaps it would be possible to have a bath, yes?'

Blackwood looked at her with amazement. Her strength was returning even as he stood near her. One hand touched the torn gown, her fingers brushing over the bruise left on her skin.

Most women would have covered their faces and run through the horrific debris and not looked up until they were safely aboard the warship.

She felt his gaze on her and said, 'It would not do for your gallant captain to receive me looking like this, I think.'

He closed the door carefully and left Swan on guard outside. It would take an avalanche to shift Swan.

He found Hudson sitting on a bollard having his head bandaged by a young midshipman.

Hudson tried to grin but winced instead.

'Didn't lose a man. And *you* saved the German countess.'

Blackwood stared across at the ship. Of the junk there was no sign. Safe amongst the fishing boats and the crowded islets.

Masterman would not relish the prospect of risking his own ship's keel if he moved closer inshore. Anyway, he had done well. He watched a corpse being dragged across the deck. So they were Boxers. It explained the uniformity of their clothing. White robes and red turbans. Originally instituted as a powerful body-guard by Yu-Hsien, the Prefect of Tsau-Chaou, they now represented a force in their own right. Blackwood had heard from Major Blair of their fearful acts of barbarism, the inhuman killings of anyone who would not support their cause and their hatred for the 'Foreign Devils'.

Blair had said they were termed Boxers by the Europeans almost as a nickname because of their original title. *The Patriotic Harmony Fists*. He looked at the terrible pools of blood which were already drying in the sunlight. Big Knife Society seemed far the more suitable.

Hudson stiffened and stood up. 'Is that her?'

Blackwood turned and nodded. It was a picture he would never forget.

She was dressed in a cream, high-necked gown, her honey-coloured hair curled on the top of her head and shaded by a wide-brimmed hat which matched her gown perfectly.

It was like seeing an entirely different person from the one in the cabin with the pistol in her hand. Swan and the small Chinese maid followed her at a respectful distance, but Swan kept his eyes on his captain to watch the effect.

She walked slowly to the side where an accommodation ladder was already rigged, and Blackwood noticed that Masterman had even sent his steam pinnace to collect her. He felt suddenly shut out, and then angry with himself for his foolishness.

She paused and looked at him, her violet eyes almost hidden in shade.

She held out a white-gloved hand and he took it as she said gravely, 'Thank you, Captain Blackwood. We shall meet again.'

He raised her hand to his lips, seeing it as the one she had held out to him in that terrible cabin.

Around them the seamen and the engine-room crew who had survived the battle by sealing themselves in with the boilers stood motionless and spellbound.

She rested her hand on the midshipman's sleeve and he guided her carefully down the side to the swaying pinnace.

Blackwood watched the pinnace swing away from the ladder and searched for her but she had already been guided below to the cockpit.

She knew my name. She must have been speaking with Swan.

He removed his helmet and wiped his face with a crumpled handkerchief.

Swan joined him by the rails.

'Real lady, sir.' He nodded admiringly. ''Er 'usband must be proud to 'ave a lady like 'er, sir.' He watched the words go home like bullets.

Blackwood gave a great sigh and tried to return his mind to his immediate duties.

'Signal *Mediator* for a Royal Marines bugler. We shall have to bury all the remains before we can do anything else.'

He shaded his eyes to look for the pinnace but it had already vanished around the stern of the light cruiser.

He thought of her sister, and how the countess had held her until her husband had at last released his grip.

Courage was not the name for it.

Later as the two ships lay hove-to and the little marine bugler sounded the Last Post the pathetic bundles wrapped in canvas were dropped over the side.

Blackwood knew she would be watching and hoped she might find some comfort from the simple ceremony.

Then both ships got under way to leave the islets and the fishermen undisturbed.

4

A Bit of a Lark

Commander John Wilberforce, HMS *Mediator*'s second-in-command, handed Blackwood a glass of Scotch which he had taken from a passing steward and beamed at him.

'Exciting, eh, Soldier? I wish to God I'd been with you! When the Countess came up the side you could have heard a bloody pin drop on the quarterdeck!'

Blackwood smiled and glanced through one of the wardroom scuttles. Shanghai, crammed with ships, lighters, junks, even a few of the old trading schooners. The Waterfront of the World.

If Captain Masterman was annoyed at having to break his passage to the Peiho River in the north he had not shown it. There were some coal lighters being warped alongside already, so the captain was even using the occasion to replenish his supplies.

Blackwood could hear a petty officer bellowing threats at the coolies in the nearest lighter about standing away from the *Mediator*'s immaculate white paint.

Wilberforce was saying enthusiastically, 'What a lovely woman. God, no wonder they were after her.'

Blackwood asked, 'Her husband. Do you know about him?'

Wilberforce blinked as he tried to recover his train of thought.

'Count Manfred von Heiser. A sort of soldier-diplomat. Enormously rich, from an East Prussian family. Personal friend of the Kaiser. They say he is in China to decide which

German concessions and legations are worth keeping, and which should be bargained for.'

Once again Blackwood felt on the outside in his ignorance.

Across the big wardroom where the ship's officers were enjoying their first noon drinks since the anchor had splashed down, he saw some of his own subordinates, chatting and laughing like the rest. He tried not to consider how Ralf would have behaved if he had been with him and the boarding party.

Wilberforce said, 'The Old Man has been speaking with a couple of consulate officials for an hour at least. One German, the other one of our chaps. Not his line of country at all!'

Blackwood realized he had emptied his glass without noticing it.

We shall meet again, she had said. He imagined the feel of her gloved hand in his, the level gaze from those violet eyes. He shook himself. He must be more like his father than he had realized.

A messenger, cap in hand, hovered by the wardroom door.

Commander Wilberforce frowned. 'Here we go. They're all going ashore, I suppose.'

But the messenger's eyes rested on Blackwood.

'The Cap'n's compliments, sir, an' would you join 'im in 'is day cabin?'

The commander grinned but sounded disappointed. 'Lucky devil.'

Someone else shouted, 'Trust the Royals!'

Blackwood could sense the difference. That one brief action had broken down the barriers. They shared it with him, and wanted to show it.

The Royal Marines sentry stamped to attention at the door of Masterman's quarters. The sleeping and day cabins and the necessary offices filled a considerable part of the light cruiser's stern. As a steward opened the door for him

Blackwood realized he had only been in this place once since he had come aboard.

Blue curtains across the polished scuttles matched the furniture covers. *Mediator* was a new ship and the colours of some of the fittings had a woman's touch, he thought. Probably chosen by Masterman's wife after the commissioning ceremony. Strange, he had never thought of Masterman being married.

The man in question turned to face him, his tall figure impressive in white drill.

'Ah, Blackwood, may I introduce these gentlemen?' He gestured to a dispirited-looking man in a pale grey coat. 'Mr Pitt from the British consulate.' He waited for Blackwood to shake hands before adding, 'And Herr Westphal his German counterpart.'

Blackwood smiled and wanted to look at the countess who was standing right aft framed against the large open ports which were the captain's privilege.

She said quietly, 'Good-day, Captain Blackwood.'

He said, 'It is good to see you so well, Countess.'

They both sounded like total strangers.

Masterman grunted impatiently. 'There has been a lot of trouble along the coast as well as inland. Attacks on villages, even missionaries by these – ' He hesitated and cut back an adjective, ' – these *Boxers*.'

Blackwood waited. He sensed there had been some kind of argument.

Masterman continued, 'There is a steamship leaving for Hong Kong tomorrow. It is armed and able to beat off attack by such pirates, and I can think of them as nothing else.'

Mr Pitt said gently, 'The horse and stable door, er, Captain Blackwood, is it not?'

The German wiped his face and chin with his handkerchief, for in spite of an offshore breeze and the deckhead fans it felt like an oven.

He said, 'We have no ship of His Imperial Majesty's

Navy here.' He looked grimly at Masterman. 'Not yet. But
a cruiser is to join your ship off Taku. There is only an
Italian gunboat, a veritable relic, here in Shanghai which is
available for the Countess.'

Her voice cut across the cabin unhurried but very
definite.

'I am not setting foot on that thing!'

Blackwood could feel her watching him although she was
in dark silhouette.

'They are concerned for my safety, Captain Blackwood. I
should have met my husband here and accompanied him
inland to the most recent trading mission.' She gave a
shrug, as if it was of little importance. 'But he left without
waiting for me. I am *expected* to be with him. It is my
purpose for being.'

'Inland?' Blackwood could only think of her last sentence. What sort of man would leave his wife in a situation
like this anyway?

Masterman explained, 'The mission is fortified, and there
is a German river gunboat on regular patrol.' He hung on
the words. 'In truth I would be happier if the Countess
stayed aboard my ship, better still if she left the area
altogether.'

She moved down the centre of the cabin and looked
calmly at Blackwood.

'They are talking about me as if I were not here, as if I
were a piece of cargo, yes?'

The German named Westphal mopped his face even
harder. 'But, dear Countess, it is your safety which it is my
duty, my *honour* to uphold!'

He said something more in German but she cut him
short. 'In English if you please, Herr Westphal!'

She did not even raise her voice and yet Westphal seemed
to cringe.

Masterman said heavily, 'It's the Hoshun River, about
two hundred miles to the north-west of here. Impossible for
a ship this size.'

Blackwood said, 'But if there is a German gunboat, sir.'

She smiled gently. 'You see, gentlemen, the gallant young captain has faith.' Her eyes suddenly flashed. 'I loved my sister very much. Do you imagine I would take unnecessary risks after what they did to her!'

Masterman bit his lip. He obviously hated the complications of the land. He turned to Pitt.

'If you can obtain a steam vessel suitable to carry Countess von Heiser and whatever staff she requires, I will escort her to the Hoshun River, or as close as I can.' He saw Pitt give a relieved nod. 'Furthermore, I can guarantee a naval escort aboard the steamship.' He looked meaningly at Blackwood. 'Your company can easily supply a suitable detachment, right?'

Blackwood swallowed. 'Yes, sir.'

God, he thought, Count von Heiser must be influential. The countess had turned away their ideas with barely concealed contempt. Westphal had all but hinted that relations between *Mediator* and the German cruiser which was also expected off Taku might be damaged without Masterman's co-operation, and Pitt appeared as if he would agree to almost anything which might shift the responsibility elsewhere.

'That is settled then.' She looked at Blackwood. 'I make just one small request, gentlemen.' They froze, not knowing what to expect.

'I would wish that Captain Blackwood should command my escort. I feel certain that the Emperor would be grateful.'

Masterman beckoned to his steward who was standing with an empty tray, as if turned to stone.

He said, 'I could send *Mediator*'s own senior Royal Marines officer.'

She moved towards Blackwood until they were almost touching.

'Has your officer been decorated for gallantry, Captain?'

She reached up and very gently touched the blue ribbon on Blackwood's tunic. 'I believe this is the highest award your country can give, yes?'

Masterman spread his hands and gave a grudging smile.

'I admit defeat, Countess. Captain Blackwood it shall be.' He nodded. 'Carry on, if you please.'

Blackwood backed away and then found himself outside the cabin beside the marine sentry.

'I must be mad!'

The sentry stiffened even more. 'Sir?'

Blackwood looked at him with surprise. He had not even realized he had spoken aloud.

He found Swan in his cabin gathering up shirts for the Chinese dhobyman. He looked neat and contented, and it was impossible to picture him with his rifle balanced under his forearm as he had lanced the screaming Boxer with his bayonet.

Swan watched him warily and said, 'Sounds more interestin', sir. More our sort o' style. Bit of a lark to go inland, so to speak.'

Blackwood dropped his head in his hands. What was the point of questioning Swan about anything? The whole ship probably knew by now.

He could still feel where her finger had touched the VC ribbon on his breast. If he opened his tunic he could almost expect to see a mark or a sign there.

A bit of a lark. It would be more than that. A whole lot more.

Swan left the cabin with his bundle humming gentle to himself. Just like old times.

Sergeant Major Arthur Fox stood very erect beside the small desk in the Royal Marines office and watched as Blackwood leafed through a list of names. Beneath his polished boots the deck swayed very gently as if even *Mediator* respected his presence.

Blackwood could sense Fox watching him and knew what he was going to ask. Eventually.

'Why the Second Platoon?'

'Well, sir, you'll be needin' Mr Gravatt to stay aboard with 'is men, seein' as 'ow 'e's in command durin' your absence. The Third Platoon, well, sir, Mr de Courcy is fairly experienced too. So I thought you'd wish to take the Second an' Mr Bannatyre.'

Blackwood leaned back and listened to the confident thump of engines, the whirr of fans as *Mediator* ploughed her way through the smooth water. Fox was right, of course; he usually was. Bannatyre was a very likeable lieutenant but the least experienced of his officers. So if things went wrong he would be the least missed.

He looked at Fox. Unbending, reliable in any situation and yet still something of a mystery. He had offered him a chair, but Fox had politely declined. Come to think of it, Blackwood realized he had never seen the sergeant major sitting down.

It was strange to think that the countess was aft in Masterman's quarters while the captain had retreated to his sea cabin on the bridge. He had not seen her since that brief meeting in Shanghai and yet he could always feel her presence in the ship.

Perhaps she was playing with him. A game to amuse herself while she waited to rejoin her husband. But that was impossible after what she had seen and endured. *I am deluding myself. If she uses me then I am willing.*

Fox watched him narrowly. 'There is another reason, sir.'

'Well?'

'The platoon sergeant, sir, Kirby.' He waited for Blackwood to pick the man from his thoughts before adding, ''E's bin actin' a bit strange. Used to be a very calm bloke, sir. Good NCO.'

'Comes from your part of London if I remember?'

Fox grinned. 'Right, sir. Sunny Shoreditch. Just three streets from my lot. 'E enlisted about a year after me. A real Marine.'

There was no higher praise from Fox.

Fox added, ' 'E's put two men up for punishment since we come aboard *Mediator*. Not like 'im. A good thump round the ear when no officers are about is more 'is style.'

Blackwood smiled. 'Anything else?'

Fox pouted. 'No, sir. I've detailed the men, an' inspected the weapons an' equipment. Little as possible, like you said.'

Blackwood looked at the map by his elbow. As *Mediator*'s navigating officer had pointed out, the Hoshun River was narrow and twisting, and very low at this time of the year. A small coasting paddle-steamer named *Bajamar* had sailed from Shanghai three days ago. With luck they could leave it until the final rendezvous at the Hoshun before transferring their passengers and Royal Marines detachment.

'Good. There'll be little enough water under the keel without taking extra stores and ammunition.' He frowned. 'It *should* be simple enough.' The river was nothing to the ones they had tackled in Africa. If the German gunboat was already downriver they could make the transfer of passengers at once. He knew immediately that he was praying it would not be so. That he would meet and speak with the countess again. I must be mad, he thought. A million miles separate us. She is married to a powerful and successful man. She had a castle and great estates, according to Commander Wilberforce. Blackwood gave a rueful smile. He had almost begun to hate Wilberforce because of his knowledge about her.

He said, 'I want one of the second lieutenants to come with my detachment. Good experience.'

Even Fox flinched. 'One 'as already volunteered.' He hesitated. 'Mr Earle.'

'I see. Thank you.' He could not conceal his disappointment. He had been hoping it would be Ralf.

'So be it. You can carry on, Mr Fox.'

'One last thing, sir.'

Blackwood looked at him gravely. Here it comes. Perfectly timed as usual.

'I should like to come with you, sir. Colour Sar'nt Chittock is due for promotion if 'e keeps 'is nose clean, so I'd not be missed if things get a bit lively.'

It was easily said but Blackwood knew it was very important to Fox. And why not? Neil had been killed by an unknown sniper but how long would he have been missed? It was not the way in the Corps. Not until it happened to you. He had wanted Ralf to volunteer, but for whose sake? His own or Ralf's dead father's?

Fox persisted, 'You'll 'ave some good blokes, sir, but you'll need someone with service. Just to be on the safe side like.'

Blackwood stared at him. It had never occurred to him that the ramrod, taciturn sergeant major wanted to go because of *him*. He was suddenly moved, like that day on the square at Hong Kong when neither of them had been able to face each other.

'*Thank* you, Mr Fox. It will be an honour.'

Fox marched out and Blackwood heard him speaking with his crony, the colour sergeant. As thick as thieves, and yet Fox always kept his position, just that step apart from his comrades.

He glanced around the ship's office and tried to think if he had forgotten anything.

The rendezvous would be during the forenoon tomorrow. After that it was anyone's guess. He thought suddenly of Hawks Hill, of his mother and the General. He had written to them, but it was strange, it might be months before his letter reached the old house. He felt himself shiver. The General might even have died and Hawks Hill would be without the guiding hand it needed. He stood up and walked to a scuttle to watch some small fishing boats bobbing abeam. Like an old watercolour. What would he do then? Resign the Corps and take his place at Hawks Hill. He felt his lips tighten. Leave the Corps? That he would never do, unless he was kicked out.

He left the office and almost collided with his cousin

Ralf. The latter had managed to avoid him since his return from the *Delhi Star* except for matters of duty. But now he seemed unusually eager and pleased with himself.

Blackwood asked, 'Where have you been?'

Ralf touched his thin moustache and smiled gently.

'I have been taking tea with the Countess Friedrike von Heiser, er, sir. It was most enjoyable.'

Blackwood nodded. Ralf was watching him. Taunting him.

And why not? He had asked for it.

Blackwood turned on his heel. 'Something it appears you are better suited to.'

It was a childish remark but he felt strangely hurt and that angered him even more.

Fox saw him stride past and glanced at the slim second lieutenant. He was actually laughing.

You'll laugh on the other side of your face one of these days, Fox thought. When that time comes I want to be there.

Captain Masterman walked out on to the bridge wing and peered down at the small paddle-vessel alongside. She was narrow-beamed and of such shallow draft that her paddle-boxes were built high on either side, as if she was hunching her shoulders.

Masterman looked down at the water. With the ship riding to her anchor the sea looked very clear and unhealthily shallow. It was safe enough for the paddle-steamer. As he had heard the yeoman of signals explaining earlier to a young seaman, 'She draws so little water she can float in spit!'

The marine detachment were already climbing down, watched by their comrades and the unemployed hands along the guardrails. Further abeam the land was misty blue, and the narrow entrance to the river marked only by a sluggish ripple on the surface. The mainland looked solid and lifeless and yet Masterman felt that his ship had been watched since first light when they had exchanged signals with the anchored *Bajamar*. She was a real veteran of these waters. Commanded by a massive, untidy Norwegian, and crewed by the worst collection of rogues Masterman had ever laid eyes on, she was hardly what Masterman would have chosen.

But Pitt, the consul in Shanghai, had spoken highly of the vessel and her ability to drive off pirates on many occasions. There were some ancient swivel guns mounted in her bow and stern, probably loaded with rusty nails, Masterman thought, but deadly at close quarters.

Wilberforce stepped into the sunlight and saluted.

'Detachment all aboard, sir. Passengers about to leave.'

The captain grunted. There was no sign of a German gunboat, but there was no more time to wait. His ship might already be needed to help reinforce the legations or to evacuate refugees.

It was a great pity about the countess, he thought. Women always complicated things.

He said, 'I shall go down.'

The last of the luggage had been lowered to the *Bajamar* and had been taken below. Masterman walked slowly across his quarterdeck to the accommodation ladder. The countess was all in white, with another wide-brimmed hat with a matching ostrich feather. She looked ready for a reception at an embassy or Buckingham Palace rather than a cramped passage upriver in the little steamer.

He touched his cap. 'I hope that everything goes well for you, Countess.'

It was all wrong. The scruffy little vessel and the marines in their white rig instead of scarlet and blue. Masterman had definite standards no matter what the circumstances might be. But he had left the arrangements to Blackwood. He must know what he was doing.

She smiled. 'I thank you for your concern, Captain.' She held out her gloved hand. 'It will not go unnoticed, I think.'

She gestured to her maid. 'Go down, child.'

The maid looked at the smartly dressed side-party and the long-barrelled guns. Above it all the White Ensign rippled slightly in the offshore breeze. Security, power and safety. A stark contrast to the little hull alongside.

The man who had been married to the countess's sister was turning to leave. Masterman had learned that he was a commercial attaché to the German trade mission in Peking and had been sent to Hong Kong to attend a conference. But for that his wife, a good deal younger than himself, would still be alive. He had not spoken since Blackwood had brought him aboard. He seemed quite lost, as if unaware of what was happening about him.

Masterman brought her hand to his lips. He could smell a delicate perfume, and could sense her eyes watching him.

Suddenly he was glad he had agreed to send Blackwood. A gesture perhaps, but the right one.

He would get no thanks from the far-off Admiralty in London if he allowed any harm to come to the wife of someone so prominent. But then the Admiralty always laid the blame equally with the responsibility on the senior officer present. In this case, Captain Masterman.

Down on the *Bajamar*'s crowded deck Blackwood looked at the farewells on the light cruiser's quarterdeck.

He felt excited and yet apprehensive. The *Bajamar* might be of the right draught but there was little else in her favour once she was hemmed in by a narrow river. Most if not all her accommodation was above the waterline, even her engine, and her long boxlike superstructure with its thin black funnel was totally unprotected should they come under fire. It was unlikely that anything like that would occur, but if it did he would have to be ready.

He glanced at the *Bajamar*'s skipper, a great block of a man. He had skin like mahogany, and tufts of ginger hair which poked beneath his stained cap like spun yarn. It was doubtful if he had worn his gold-braided jacket for some while, Blackwood thought. The brass buttons were strained to bursting-point across the Norwegian's enormous belly.

He thought of Major Blair. Yet another *old China hand*.

His name was Lars Austad and Blackwood imagined he might look more at home in a longship and wearing a horned helmet.

Fox stood beside him and said, 'Comin' aboard now, sir.'

Blackwood watched her stepping carefully down the accommodation ladder, one hand on the rail, the other gripping a folded parasol.

Fox muttered, 'Strewth.'

Most of the marines had already been packed in sweating discomfort in the afterpart of the superstructure, their uniforms already crumpled in the humid air. Masterman might not approve, but Blackwood recalled hearing a story about his uncle in Africa, when he had made his men stain their shirts to conceal themselves when they were besieged in a trading post by both slavers and savage natives.

She allowed him to take her hand and guide her the last few paces on to the vessel's deck.

She smiled at the giant Norwegian and to Blackwood said, 'How quaint.'

He saw Swan's red apple-face split into a grin.

She nodded to the two Royal Marines officers, Lieutenant Bannatyre and Second Lieutenant Earle, and then paused by Fox who towered over her like a tree.

'I need have no fear with such as you to protect me, I think.'

She laughed, the sound fragile and out of place amongst the watching men and the neatly piled weapons.

Clank – clank – clank. *Mediator*'s cable was already jerking through the hawsepipe, and the accommodation ladder began to rise up her side even as her screws beat the placid water into a lively froth.

Blackwood looked at Austad. 'Get under way, Captain.'

The Norwegian's eyes were like saucers before he began to bellow orders at his ragged crew. It was doubtful if he had ever been addressed as captain before.

The deck swayed as *Mediator* moved slowly away, some of her people waving from the guardrails while Masterman's impressive figure stood on the bridge wing and saluted.

Austad cranked at a telegraph beside the wheel and the two paddles began to move, swinging the hull towards the shore.

Blackwood followed the countess to the cabin which had been prepared for her. It was not much larger than a cupboard. He watched her reaction, and expected her to explode.

He explained, 'I am sorry about this, Countess. But it is the safest one aboard in my opinion. Steel bulkhead at one end, and the storeroom just forrard. Your maid is in the adjoining cabin with your luggage.'

She turned and searched his face with her violet eyes. Then she tapped him gently on the shoulder with her parasol.

'You think of everything, Captain.'

Blackwood could feel her nearness and wanted to take hold of her. It was like physical pain. Worse, he knew that she understood exactly what he was thinking.

'A bath perhaps?'

Blackwood shrugged. 'I am afraid that is impossible, Countess.'

She watched him impassively. 'Two days in this craft and no bath? *That* is impossible.'

She touched her throat and dragged the high collar away from her skin. At any other time the gesture would have meant nothing, but Blackwood recalled with sudden clarity how she had looked in that other cabin, the blood on the deck, the tiny revolver in her hand. She had still had the strength, the will to take a bath after all that.

Feet thumped along the narrow side-decks. There was a lot to do before they reached the narrow river. The *Bajamar* might be quite at home in open waters. Once in the shallow river she would present an easy target.

She said, 'You may leave, Captain. Please send my maid to me.'

She waited until he had slid open the narrow door. 'I am grateful. You know that.' She was watching him without emotion, but her tone made her attitude a defence, a lie.

He replied, 'Thank you.' But he saw his cousin's face, the look of triumph and amusement. 'It is my duty.'

Outside the door he pressed his shoulders against the sun-heated metal and cursed himself for his stupidity.

Lieutenant Bannatyre hovered nearby. 'I have stationed the first section as ordered, sir.' He waited, suddenly alarmed by Blackwood's angry silence.

Blackwood clapped him on the shoulder. 'Very well, Ian, show me their positions, will you?'

He saw the little Chinese maid leave the cabin with her mistress's gown over one arm. It was the same one she had just been wearing when she had been plucking it from her skin.

He pictured her behind the door. Probably naked in the privacy of her cabin just a few yards away.

'Something wrong, sir?'

Blackwood sighed. 'It's the heat, I expect.'

Bannatyre nodded gravely. 'I see, sir.'

You don't, my lad. Blackwood turned to look for *Mediator* but she had already vanished around the headland leaving just a patch of funnel smoke to mark her passing.

Two days? It was going to seem a lifetime, he thought.

5

Just Ten Good Men

Blackwood stood by the starboard paddle-box and watched the night sky. The stars looked small and far away and added to the feeling of being shut in. Around and below him the *Bajamar* was very quiet after their first day crawling upriver. It was going to take longer than even the big Norwegian Austad had imagined. The river was extremely shallow and treacherous with uncharted sandbars and occasional clumps of rocks. Even a man of Austad's obvious experience and skill could not be expected to run his ship aground merely because he was under government orders.

Blackwood had just left him in his tiny chartroom. He had filled the space like a bear in a cave, the air thick with pungent smoke from a giant meerschaum pipe.

He had commented in his thick voice, 'You got your men posted, my ship is in dark, no more we can do.' It sounded final.

It was fortunate that such small craft should carry two boats, flat-bottomed sampans. Blackwood had sent one to either bank where the pickets would be crouching and listening to every creak and rustle.

Fox had made certain there was a fair sprinkling of old sweats amongst the recruits. All the same it must be nerve-racking to be landed in some unknown place with water at their backs. He nodded to the sentries, and continued right forward to where Lieutenant Bannatyre had sited the Maxim gun.

It would have been better to mount it amidships, but the

boxlike superstructure made that impossible unless you left it and its crew totally exposed on the upper deck.

He heard Sergeant Kirby mutter, 'All quiet, sir.'

'Good.' Blackwood stared at the black shoreline and wondered what had disturbed Fox about this stocky sergeant. He sounded normal enough. Blackwood had seen him in action when as a corporal he had rallied a handful of marines to charge a mob of savages and retrieve the flag from the grip of their dead colour sergeant.

'We'll relieve the pickets in half-an-hour. Men begin to imagine things after too long.' He touched the Maxim gun. Austad's cannon would be as much use in the dark.

He groped his way aft again and stared with surprise as he saw the countess standing by the guardrails, her figure shrouded in a long gown like a boatcloak.

'You should not be here, Countess!' He lowered his voice to a fierce whisper. 'It is not safe!'

She did not turn but stared intently at the shadows.

'China. The Tiger.' She spoke so softly Blackwood had to lower his head to hear.

She said, 'I could not sleep. I kept thinking – my sister – the sounds of those poor people screaming.'

Blackwood was afraid to move a muscle in case he broke the spell.

All the pent-up strain and outward poise were no longer enough. She was reliving it as she must have been ever since the attack on the *Delhi Star* had turned that night into an unforgettable horror.

Again he wanted to hold her but knew that her last reserves would turn her away from him.

He said quietly, 'And yet you risk this upriver passage, Countess. Must you go?' He sounded as if he was pleading, but he no longer cared.

She shrugged. 'You spoke of duty. I have mine also.'

She faced him through the gloom. 'That was unfair. Forgive me. But for you what would have happened to me?'

Blackwood listened to the soft footsteps of a native

crewman, the responding scrape of boots as a sentry came to the alert.

'You speak perfect English, Countess.' Why did he feel embarrassed?

She sounded as if she was smiling. 'I do travel a lot, Captain. My husband and I visit England whenever we can. He has relatives there. And there is Cowes, Henley and Ascot to enjoy, St James's too on occasions.'

Blackwood swallowed. It was another world, one controlled by the sort of people who decided where men like his marines, and like Neil and all who had gone before him, should be sent. Except that it would not show them as mere men on the plans. Units, ships, and the Flag. It was enough. Or was it? The thought of Neil could still wound him when he was unprepared.

She said, 'Was it wrong what I said?' She looked at him more closely. 'You are dismayed, hurt, yes?'

Blackwood shook his head. 'It was nothing. I thought of my brother. Just for a moment.'

'I understand. A comparison perhaps?' She saw him start. 'It is natural.' She seemed to sense danger in sharing her thoughts.

'This voyage is taking an eternity.'

Blackwood asked, 'Will you stay long at the trading mission?'

'I am not certain. Manfred will decide.' She sounded suddenly wistful. There was resentment too despite her outward calm.

'Do you have children, Countess? I expect you will be pleased – '

But she turned her face away and he could see her honey hair hanging down her spine in a long plait.

'No children.'

Just two words but they meant far more.

She said in a faraway voice. 'Naturally I wanted children. What woman does not?' She gave that same shrug again and the gesture touched Blackwood like a blade. 'It was not to be. But Manfred was generous. He accepts it.'

Blackwood tried to find the right words. 'There can be no blame.'

She swung round, the plait vanishing in the shadows.

'Blame? You astonish me, Captain. You act like a man. You speak like a child. *Blame!* I have just finished telling you, Manfred accepts it!'

Her words stung him like a blow to his face but he retorted hotly, 'You sound as if he had *forgiven* you, Countess! It might be his fault!' He had gone too far, and he could hear the regular thump of boots as the new pickets paraded for inspection.

He exclaimed, 'I – I am sorry, Countess. That was unpardonable. Please dismiss what I said – '

He looked down as she touched his forearm. In a small voice she said, 'There is nothing to forgive. What did you expect me to say?'

At any minute now Kirby would be coming to report to him.

He struggled with his words. 'I admire you so much, Countess. Your courage, everything about you – '

'You see, Captain? It is as I said. A childish dream.' But she did not remove her hand.

'Perhaps.' Blackwood covered her hand with his own. 'I suppose I am so involved with my profession. I have lost the ability to mix with civilized people.'

She smiled. 'Civilization counts for very little when a man sets his heart on personal gain.'

In the darkness Sergeant Kirby coughed politely and Blackwood hated him for it.

'I shall be there directly, Sergeant.'

She released her hand very gently. 'Go to him, Captain. He needs you.' She reached up impulsively and touched his face. In spite of the clinging humidity which enfolded the anchored vessel like a steam bath, her fingers were cool and very soft.

'We shall all need you soon.' Then she was gone,

swallowed up by the shadows like a phantom. He waited to hear her door slide and for his breathing to steady.

He found Second Lieutenant Earle and the next picket waiting to enter a sampan alongside.

'You know what to do?' Blackwood had to clear his throat. 'One sign of an attack and you will withdraw to the bank until we can give you covering fire with the Maxim. Stay together, and remove your helmets. You'll hear better that way.'

Earle nodded earnestly in time with his words as if memorizing every syllable.

'Yes, sir. I will, sir. You can trust me, sir.'

Kirby tore his mind away from his troubled thoughts and said harshly, 'I'll go with them, sir.'

Blackwood said, 'Very well.' He excluded the others as he added, 'No heroics, Charles.' He sensed the use of the youth's first name reaching its mark. 'I want this squad intact and ready for the next leg of the journey.'

Kirby groaned. It's all I need, he thought savagely. A second lieutenant who should still be in the bloody nursery, and a love-struck captain.

'Carry on, Mr Earle.' Blackwood watched the handful of men as they clambered down into the boat's paler outline. Then the sampan with its passengers merged with the river-bank and soon he thought he heard the returning marines climbing aboard. Thankful to be coming back. It was usually the way. The Royal Marines were soldiers and sailors too. But if there was a ship of any kind available he knew where their preference would lie.

Blackwood loosened his tunic and touched the bare skin beneath. Hot and sticky. Three hours yet to daybreak and then little relief as the *Bajamar* thrashed her way around the various obstacles and the sun pinned them down without mercy.

But he would speak with her again. He had to.

He sat down on a steel locker and stared hard across the rails. How did she see her husband? Respect, fear, admiration. There had been little hint of anything else, like the moments when she had spoken of her dead sister.

There was a sudden sharp crack, a momentary flash from the land and then a chilling silence.

Blackwood was on his feet as Lieutenant Bannatyre came running forward followed by the sergeant major.

Blackwood rapped, 'Silence on deck!' It was hopeless. The *Bajamar*'s crew were unused to discipline and voices called and echoed around the river in a mad chorus.

'Pistol shot, Ian.' Blackwood glanced at the lieutenant's motionless figure. '*Stand to, man!*'

Fox strode away, barely raising his voice and yet restoring instant order as his marines, some half-naked but grasping their rifles, bustled to their allotted positions on either side and up in the bows.

Blackwood strained his ears into the darkness but it was as if nothing had happened. It was on Earle's side of the river. He cursed himself for sending such an inexperienced officer. Maybe he had fired his pistol by accident. It was not unknown. He dismissed the idea instantly. He was looking for an easy way out. An explanation like the ones you heard at a court-martial. No. Earle was young and earnest but he was not a fool.

He felt the big Norwegian beside him.

'You want me go back?' He waited, the unlit pipe dragging at his jaw. 'Better going downstream.'

Blackwood swung on him, 'You have your orders. *Obey them!*' He realized with a start that the countess was on deck, her Chinese maid clinging to her arm.

'Please go to your cabin, Countess.'

She looked at him and said, 'Is it serious, Captain?'

Suddenly he wanted to throw his arms round her, to bury his face in her hair and tell her what it was like. Once the flood began he knew it would not stop. Faces flashed through his mind, his father the General, Neil and young Jonathan whom he barely knew. And all the other faces he had come to love. In the Corps you got to know people very well. Or you split wide open.

'Not bad, Countess.' He barely recognized his own voice. 'It will seem better when daylight comes. Try to – '

He heard the snap of a rifle-bolt and then Swan's round Hampshire voice. Its familiar tone did more to steady him than he could have believed.

'Boat's comin', sir.'

It was Sergeant Kirby. He dragged himself heavily over the guardrails and sought out Blackwood from the others.

Across that strip of dirty, sluggish current Sergeant Kirby's mind had stayed busy, ready for what was to come.

He said shortly, 'I've left Corporal Lyde in charge, sir.' Kirby had to grit his teeth together to control himself. Blackwood was like mustard and would see through any stupid lie. It was so bloody unfair on top of everything else. *But I should have known.* His own thoughts rang in his mind like an official reprimand. That stupid little bugger Earle. It was so *unfair*.

Blackwood asked quietly, 'In your own words, Sergeant. There may not be much time.'

Kirby fumbled inside his tunic and then dragged out a service revolver.

'Mr Earle's, sir.' He looked at the shadowy figures around him, quietly accusing. 'Weren't my fault! Must 'ave wandered off!'

Blackwood took the revolver and then handed it to Swan. He knew she was still there on deck watching him.

Swan said, 'It's 'is right enough, sir.'

Blackwood felt something like nausea as he recalled the mutilated gaping corpses, the great swinging swords and the blood.

He said, 'You go ashore, Ian.' He listened to his own voice and wondered how he could do it. 'Looks as if they've got him.'

The lieutenant nodded and hurried towards the boat.

To Fox he added, 'You take over here while I have a look at the map.' He gripped the nearest stanchion and murmured fiercely, 'Please God, let him be dead!'

The marines moved restlessly along either side as the news moved amongst them like an evil spectre.

Fox strode through the shadows and then paused by the slim figure with her maid.

'Would you please go to yer quarters, Ma'am.' He spoke very slowly and firmly as he always did when talking to foreigners. 'The Captain wants you to be safe. It's wot we're 'ere for, an' 'e's got enough on 'is plate at the moment without sweatin' about you, like.'

She only understood half of it but the man's genuine concern was clear in his rough voice.

'I shall do as you ask.' She hesitated, one hand on the door. 'You should be proud to serve him.'

Fox was taken aback. You did not discuss such things with women. 'I – I 'spect yer right, er, Countess.' He hurried away to look for Kirby and to force the truth out of him.

In the tiny, darkened chartroom Blackwood examined the map and compared it with a chart he had brought from *Mediator*. If nothing else happened in the next few hours they would up-anchor and proceed. He wiped his face with his sleeve. In the cramped space he could barely breathe. It was not helped by the stink of gin and stale pipesmoke.

Tomorrow. He blinked to clear his aching mind. *Today*. They would come to a great elbow-shaped bend in the river. High bank to starboard, a bit lower to port. If they got around that without incident they should be clear for a final run. The river was no deeper, but it was much wider. They could even anchor in midstream without the need to put pickets ashore.

But suppose this last terrible incident was a mere foretaste of what lay immediately ahead? He tried to keep his mind on an even keel, to shut out the pictures of what might be happening to Earle right at this moment. He *must* decide what to do. He tried again. If there was an attack or, worse, an ambush it would be there on the high ground.

The *Bajamar* would be too busy manoeuvring with her twin paddles to take evasive action, and she could not attempt it under cover of darkness.

They wanted the countess, whoever *they* were.

He measured the distances very carefully with some brass dividers, the sweat from his forehead dropping on his hands like hot rain. He thought of her cool fingers, the way she had looked at him as he had rapped out his orders. She would see him differently now. So would some of his men. The cold ruthless officer who did not even care about one of his own kind. Blackwood gripped the chart table until his fingers cracked. What the hell did they expect?

His breathing steadied and he slowly straightened his back. With unusual care he buttoned his tunic and adjusted his holster.

And it was only just beginning.

They crowded around Blackwood at one end of the *Bajamar*'s saloon, a place normally used by the vessel's rare passengers. Now it was littered with the marines' blankets and packs and some spare boxes of ammunition.

Blackwood looked at them, at their grim faces under a solitary deckhead oil lamp.

The sergeant major stooped even here between the overhead beams. Lieutenant Bannatyre had just returned from the shore. He had found Earle's white helmet tossed in some bushes. As with the revolver it was as if they wanted to be sure they knew they had captured the eighteen-year-old officer. Sergeant Kirby, lips compressed in a thin line, his eyes red from strain, and his two corporals, Lyde and O'Neil, both old campaigners.

Austad stood with but a little apart from them, his heavy face squinting through his own pipesmoke.

Blackwood said as evenly as he could manage, 'This is what I intend.' He gestured to a rough drawing he had made of the river bend they would have to pass. 'I believe an attack will be made here. If they delay, we can reach the trading mission and have the protection of a German gunboat. Or if they hoped to frighten us into turning back,' he sensed Austad's resentment at his words, 'they could try another attack closer to the sea. They've had plenty of time to prepare if they are as well informed as I think they must be.'

Kirby said bitterly, 'Looks like we're in a trap either way, sir.'

Blackwood placed his finger on the crudely drawn map. 'We shall land a small party there. It will soon be daylight and if Captain Austad can make plenty of smoke any lookouts will know his ship is approaching.' Austad made no comment and Blackwood continued in the same even tone, 'We shall have to rely on surprise.' They watched his finger as it moved in a straight line, inland to a point behind the salient which guarded the bend in the river. 'By my reckoning it should take an hour. Forced march, weapons and ammunition only.' He glanced at their intent faces. They knew what he meant all right. Kill or be killed. 'We'll take them from the rear.' Then he did look at Austad. 'If we fail you will turn back and return to Shanghai. Do not try to proceed any further unsupported.'

Fox said sharply, 'You goin' with 'em, sir?' He sounded as if he had misheard.

Blackwood eyed him gravely. What else can I do? Aloud he said, 'Mr Bannatyre will take command here, and you will, I know, Sergeant Major, give him every support.' He shifted his glance from Fox's unspoken protest to the young lieutenant. Bannatyre seemed surprised, or was it just relief?

'Your only task is to protect the Countess and deliver her into safe hands, right?'

'Sir.' Bannatyre's head bobbed as if the neck had been broken. He was probably thinking about Earle. They all were.

Blackwood said, 'Sergeant Kirby and his two corporals

will come with me. I want the best marksmen you can find.
I am *not* asking for volunteers. Just ten good men.'

Surprisingly Corporal O'Neil gave a deep guffaw.
'What's a volunteer, sorr?'

Blackwood found that he could smile. 'A deaf Marine.'
He wanted to dash the sweat from his face but needed to
appear calm and in control.

Fox asked, 'How long, sir?'

Austad reluctantly removed the meerschaum from his
mouth.

'Give me a half-hour. Then, very slow, I move.'

'Thank you.' Blackwood saw the Norwegian giant sigh.
He had already accepted they were as good as killed.

They left the saloon and Blackwood doused the lamp.
Then he opened one of the steel shutters which covered a
square port and stared into the darkness. He could smell the
land, still hot from the previous day. If only it would rain.
Anything was better than this crushing silence.

He heard Swan say, 'Can I have your gun, sir?'

Blackwood drew it from its leather holster and handed it
to him without turning round. Swan would check everything. It seemed wrong to drag him into danger yet again.
It would be insulting to leave him behind.

'Shan't be sorry to stretch my legs, sir.' Swan was feeling
the revolver in the darkness, removing each bullet and
making sure it was a perfect one before he refilled the
chamber.

'I could be wrong.' It was easy to admit doubt to Swan,
when he could share nothing with his officers. Fear was
something. To show it to those he had to lead was different
entirely. He half smiled into the darkness. He even *sounded*
like the old General. Then with Swan beside him he walked
to the side-deck where Kirby was explaining to his landing
party what was expected of them.

Kirby had picked his men well. It was almost as if he had
expected something like this to happen.

Suppose there were eyes still watching from the river-bank, waiting to hack them down even as they climbed from the boat? Blackwood moved his shoulders briskly beneath his tunic. He was suddenly quite cold. It was always the same. A hazy plan, the need to act before you had time to think it through or to weigh up the chances of failure.

He could feel it. The decision right or wrong was made. Now all he wanted to do was to get on with it.

'Into the boat.'

Several of the shadowy figures nearby whispered farewells to their friends as they vanished into the little sampan.

Fox said, 'Good luck, sir. I just wish – '

Blackwood touched his arm and felt the power of the man. 'I *know*. But it has to be this way.'

Fox grunted. 'I know that too, sir.'

Then he was in the sampan and the paddles guided the box-shaped hull swiftly clear of the side and into the deeper shadows of the bank. They paused within feet of the land, the paddles motionless while the marines peered and listened for any sign of sudden danger.

Blackwood swung his leg over the gunwale. Once he glanced over his shoulder but the anchored paddle-steamer was little more than a pale blur against the opposite bank.

As he waded from the shallows he heard his feet crunching on coarse grass and scrub. Like everything else, tinder-dry and smelling vaguely of rot. There were trees too, but not enough to provide cover.

They split into two squads, each in the charge of a corporal. Kirby, breathing hard, stayed with Blackwood.

The land climbed slowly but steeply and as Blackwood got his bearings and pointed towards the beginning of a ridge he sensed the uneasiness amongst his small party. One hillside had already shut off the river, and he could hear the faint hiss of a breeze as it stirred the dry grass like a hidden army of serpents.

Kirby had already sent two scouts ahead of the others and he could imagine their feelings as they occasionally lost

contact with their comrades. Few ever considered men like
those, he thought vaguely. The ones who spearheaded an
attack, and those who covered a retreat. The lonely ones.
The expendable. He stopped his wild thoughts with sudden
force. It was like the last time, only the country was
different.

Kirby peered at the sky. The rim of hillside was already
sharper, or were their eyes getting more used to the gloom?

One of the marines caught his foot in a root and fell on
his rifle with a clatter. Everyone froze, barely able to
breathe.

Kirby swore obscenely and snarled, 'Take that bugger's
name!' But like the rest he was thankful that nothing worse
had happened.

'Rest, Sergeant. Ten minutes. Pass the word to the
scouts.'

Blackwood threw himself down and saw Swan sitting
nearby, cross-legged like an Indian fakir. The sight made
him want to laugh out loud. They were creeping towards a
hill they knew nothing about, which they would probably
find deserted. Whoever had seized Earle possibly thought
that was enough. It might have been an accident more than
a planned attack. Austad would be raising steam now, he
thought. Shortening his cable in readiness to continue
upriver. How on earth had a man like him found his way
out here, he wondered.

He thought suddenly of the countess. She at least should
be safe. The reduced number of marines had nowhere else to
go. Even under Bannatyre's hesitant leadership they would
give a good account of themselves. Fox would see to that.

Blackwood rolled over on to his elbows and stared at the
hillside. What a place to end up. Only the river provided a
lifeline and it, like many of the others in China, was dotted
with trading missions, which in turn were protected by
gunboats from a half a dozen countries. It was a strange
impractical arrangement.

It was time to move.

He stood up and stifled a yawn. He could not remember exactly when he had last slept or eaten. 'Check your weapons.' Blackwood walked slowly amongst his men.

Private Kempster who came from Leeds, whose homely Yorkshire voice could usually be heard around the barracks. Trent, a swarthy-faced man who looked more like a Spaniard than anything. Even his friends called him Dago, and yet he came from four generations of marines. Corporal Lyde, who should have been a sergeant but had lost his stripes more times than he could remember for brawling ashore. Roberts, the ex-farm labourer from Sussex, amiable, slow, but probably the best shot in the company. They glanced at him as he passed without recognition. Each one was thinking of himself. If things go badly, how will I behave? Fight? Die?

'All correct, sir.'

Blackwood unclipped his holster and raised his arm to signal the advance. His arm seemed to stiffen in mid-air as if he had been paralysed. Then he heard it again. Surely nothing human could sound like that?

Kirby exclaimed thickly, 'Must be Mr Earle, fer Christ's sake!'

Blackwood wanted to press his hands to his ears. Anything to shut out those terrible agonized screams.

So they *were* there. He had been right. Waiting for the *Bajamar* while they tormented their victim yet denied him death.

Blackwood swallowed hard as somebody retched uncontrollably behind him. He knew that some of them were staring at him, pleading for him to attack and end the terrible cries.

It was too soon. If they ran all the way to the salient without knowing the strength of their enemy or waiting for Austad to appear, they would lose everything. But that would mean little enough to these men.

He said, 'Advance. Extend to right and left.' He heard their feet dragging, a gasp of horror as one terrible shriek scraped their minds like a hot wire. Then like the slamming of a great door it stopped.

Blackwood loosened his revolver and strode steadily through the coarse grass. As he had done before, as his ancestors had done in a hundred places and as many battles. It was what he had wanted, what everyone expected.

He felt the sweat running down his spine. It could have been Ralf up there.

Another half-hour passed and the sky became suddenly clearer. The marines rested amongst some bushes and in a low gully which must have once been cut by torrential rain.

Blackwood looked at them, their set expressions, their uniforms stained and torn as they clutched their rifles and peered at the skyline. The last horizon.

It was hard to picture these same men in scarlet and blue, the wheeling columns and hoarse commands across the barracks square. Even Corporal O'Neil had nothing to offer to break the tension. The screams still lingered in each man's mind.

Blackwood tugged out his watch and flicked open the guard. It had been given to him by his mother on his twenty-first birthday. It was light enough to see its face. He replaced it in his pocket and tried to appear calm. Where the hell was Austad?

A great screech made most of them start with alarm, but Blackwood was too thankful to notice. The Norwegian had kept his word. Right on time, even in the poor light he had picked his way up the river to play his part.

Blackwood said, 'Stand-to.' He glanced at Sergeant Kirby. 'Fix bayonets, if you please.' Then he drew his sword and felt Swan watching him. *His shadow*. Strangely enough it made him feel better. Stronger in some way, although he knew it might not last.

He shut Earle from his thoughts and said, 'Royal Marines will advance!'

The General would have been proud, he thought. Perhaps it would warrant another painting one day, to join all the others at Hawks Hill.

He saw pale sunlight touch the point of Swan's bayonet.
It was time.

6

A Walk in the Sun

From one corner of his eye Blackwood saw a swirling plume of dark smoke rise above the salient, proof of Austad's efforts to follow his orders. It was like moving up towards a cliff edge, he thought, the ground so steep that the land beyond as well as the river was completely hidden. To his right he could see a pyramid-shaped hill, still shrouded in early mist, and what looked like tiny dwellings scattered at its foot.

It was hard to imagine that over there people were living peacefully, probably hoping to be left undisturbed by Boxers and foreign troops alike.

It was all completely unreal, the slow-moving smoke, the swish of dry scrub against his feet and legs, and his men fanning out on either side of him in a ragged line, their bayonets glinting to mark their slow advance. *A walk in the sun.*

Blackwood found time to marvel, not for the first time, that training and tradition could hold them all together under any situation.

A figure burst from the ground almost at his feet. There was no place to hide and yet he was there as if he had broken out of hell itself.

Blackwood barely had time to think other than to realize that he was dressed in the same robes as the attackers aboard the *Delhi Star*. He felt the jarring pain in his arm as he parried the man's heavier blade with his own and used the force of his charge to take him off-balance. He heard him scream as he drove his sword under his guard and through his ribs. Swan silenced a last cry with the butt of his rifle.

They stared at each other, barely aware of the sporadic firing which came from the edge of the redoubt. It was the same madness. Blackwood could feel his mouth fixed in a wild grin.

'Together, lads! Charge!'

The marines gathered their strength and blundered up the remaining slope, their eyes slitted against the pungent smoke from the *Bajamar*'s funnel.

There were about twenty of them. Kneeling or lying along the rim of the land as the hidden paddle-wheeler pounded towards them. Some whirled round, eyes staring and wild as Corporal Lyde's squad poured a rapid volley from the right flank, followed instantly by the second party.

Blackwood held his revolver in his left fist although he did not recall drawing it from the holster.

'Advance!'

A wounded Boxer ran and hopped towards a discarded rifle and sprawled gasping as Kirby drove his bayonet through his chest. Not the crazy lunge of a recruit but the cool reaction of the old campaigner.

Blackwood yelled, 'Over there, O'Neil!' He gestured with his sword. 'The *gun!*'

It was carefully hidden in branches and dead leaves but there was no mistaking the ugly revolving snout of an old Hotchkiss cannon. Old perhaps, but if fired directly down on to the *Bajamar*'s helm and bridge it would have a devastating effect.

Blackwood aimed his revolver and saw one man fall, the other turning to cover his face with his arms as he realized for the first time that the marines were amongst them.

'First squad!' That was Lyde again. 'Kneel! Take aim! *Fire!*'

The figures around the Hotchkiss rolled away from the mounting and ammunition like rag puppets.

Kirby was yelling, 'At 'em!' Watch that bugger, Roberts!'

Private Roberts, the farm-boy from Sussex, did not appear to take aim. He waited until the running figure was right on the lip of the salient and then fired from the shoulder. He could have been despatching a rabbit.

Kirby almost kicked Private Trent aside as he gasped, 'No quarter! They'll cut you down, else!' His bayonet lunged and withdrew just as smartly, the blade edged in red.

Blackwood lowered his sword and stood sucking in great gulps of air. He hardly dared to look at his wild, breathless marines. One was staring at the sky, his face stiff with pain as Corporal Lyde expertly knotted a bandage around his arm.

Blackwood saw Kirby watching him and nodded. 'Well done, lads!' He walked slowly to the edge of the land and stood looking down at the curving river. It was yellow like the sun. He could feel his arms shaking, his whole body reacting to the swift attack. Not a man dead. It was still hard to believe. He removed his white helmet and waved it slowly from side to side. Far below Austad responded with another jubilant screech on his siren.

Kirby called, 'No sign of Mr Earle's body, sir.'

Blackwood watched the *Bajamar*'s anchor splash down, the two sampans already lowered to retrieve a landing-party which he doubted if anyone had ever expected to survive.

'Shall we bury this lot, sir?' The sergeant watched him curiously.

'No. Leave them. As a warning.'

He wiped his neck and face with a filthy handkerchief. 'Fall the men in. We'll *march* down to the river.'

He saw his weary, dazed men straighten their backs as if a silent order had been issued.

Corporal O'Neil shouted, 'Come along now, Dago! This is no time at all for slacking!'

Blackwood replaced his helmet and pulled the chinstrap into place. It was not exactly an army. He looked around at the sprawled corpses and an isolated patch of dried blood where they must have tortured Earle before killing him. But he knew he would not have exchanged them at this moment for a whole battalion of his own. Almost to himself he murmured, 'I'm sorry, Charles. I should never have sent you.'

Then he turned on his heel and followed his men down the slope towards the river.

Blackwood stood on the *Bajamar*'s open bridge and trained a borrowed telescope on the slow-moving river-bank and the blue hills beyond. The bridge was little more than a spidery catwalk which linked the two paddle-boxes on either beam together. In the fierce midday sun the rails were too hot to touch. Half of the marines stood guard along the bulwarks, helmets tilted to shield their eyes, their rifles resting on the rails ready for instant use.

But from the moment they had returned aboard and Austad had raised anchor again they had not sighted a living thing. Their return was something Blackwood would not forget. The anxious, grimy faces along the vessel's side, and then, suddenly, the tension had snapped like a taut mooring-wire and the marines had stood to wave and cheer despite every threat which Fox had hurled at them. Even Austad's villainous looking crew had joined in.

'I'm going below.' Blackwood glanced at the big Norwegian. His pipe was going well, and he seemed strangely content after what had happened.

Austad grunted. 'We shall reach the mission soon.' He chuckled. 'That German gunboat captain will be feeling very small, I think!' He was still laughing as Blackwood lowered himself to the deck.

He walked through the saloon his eyes almost blinded by the sun. The marines off-watch made to stand but he waved them down. They were amazing, he thought. In spite of all that had happened, Earle's capture and torture, and the

STRATFORD PUBLIC LIBRARY
19 ST. ANDREW ST.
STRATFORD, ONTARIO

swift savagery of their fight on the salient, he saw that his men had managed to shave and fold their blankets as neatly as in their barracks. There was a smell of coffee, and of something cooking in the tiny galley.

Swan was waiting for him at the forward end of the saloon, his rifle slung from one shoulder, his helmet on the back of his head. 'Beg pardon, sir, but the Countess would like to see you.'

'Yes.' Blackwood felt suddenly drained, the relief that they had somehow survived dragging at his last resources like claws. He wanted to see her, just as he knew he should stay away. Soon she would be reunited with her husband. He would become just a part of her memories.

Blackwood walked outside and tapped on her door. He knew he looked like a vagrant in his filthy uniform, streaks of dried blood on his sword-arm.

She opened the door and studied him gravely. 'Please enter, Captain.'

He noticed that the little Chinese maid was not present. He had barely been alone with her before. How did she manage to appear so cool, so elegant? She had changed her clothes again and was dressed in a pale yellow gown with an Oriental sash that revealed the smallness of her waist. She was about the same age as himself and yet so different. Distant in spite of her crowded surroundings. Like Royalty. It made him feel even less confident. Unclean.

She asked, 'Do you like what you see, Captain?'

He flushed. 'I was staring. I am sorry.'

She gestured to a chair. 'You apologize too much.' She watched him for several seconds. 'You did not come to see me when you returned.' It was an accusation. 'I was anxious. Worried for you.'

He looked at her. 'I am — '

She smiled gently. 'Sorry?'

He grinned. 'I suppose I was too concerned with getting the ship under way again. It seems quiet enough, but I'm not sure.'

She walked across the cabin and stared through an open scuttle. 'That poor young man. He died because of me. If I had not insisted on rejoining my husband it would never have happened.'

Blackwood twisted round to look at her but she gripped his shoulder tightly and exclaimed, '*Please*. Do not turn. I do not wish you to see me so.'

He could feel the emotion in her voice just as the strength of her grip told him something new about her.

He said, 'Mr Earle died doing his duty. If anyone is to blame it must be me. Ours can be a dangerous calling. Men die, some for no reason we can understand. We accept it.'

He saw her hand reach round and grope for his. 'You say that to protect me. To help me forget.' She shook her head, the piled crown of hair shining in reflected sunlight from the scuttle. 'I shall *never* forget.'

Blackwood felt the smoothness of her hand and could smell her perfume, her fragrance. What would she do if he took her in his arms here and now?

She turned and looked at him, her face in shadow.

'I know what you are thinking, my gallant young Captain. And I am ashamed of my own feelings towards you.' As he made to rise she pressed him back into the chair. 'But it cannot be. Such a secret is impossible to hide or to share.' She touched his face as she had that other time, as if to memorize every detail. 'Perhaps we shall meet again one day.' She smiled at him but it made her look incredibly sad. 'In the line of duty as you would call it, yes?'

There was a nervous tap at the door. It was Swan.

'Well?' Blackwood tried to sound calm. 'What is it?'

Swan glanced at a point between them.

'The Skipper sends 'is compliments and — '

'Spit it out, man!'

Swan looked at the countess. 'Well, sir — '

Blackwood said quietly, 'It's all right. You can speak in front of our passenger.'

Swan let out a sigh. 'The mission is round the next bend,

sir. But the river's so wide 'ere you can see it already with the glass.'

Blackwood reached out and took her hand. It seemed natural and easy in front of Swan.

Swan said wretchedly, 'There's *nothin'*, sir. The place is in ruins. Knocked to bloody hell, beggin' yer pardon, Ma'am.'

'No ship?'

Swan shook his head. 'All gone, sir.'

'Tell Austad I'll come up directly.' As the door shut he was conscious of the silence which hung over the vessel, so that the beat of her paddles seemed to intrude like muffled drums. He needed to think and act quickly.

She stepped closer and placed her hands on his shoulders. 'What will you do?'

He stood up. 'We shall anchor and stand off until I have gone ashore to investigate. Don't worry, I said I would protect you. So I shall.' Without realizing it he put his arm around her shoulders. He felt her stiffen as if about to pull away. Blackwood said, 'There may have been an attack.' He dismissed the idea instantly. 'No, the gunboat would not withdraw. She would be more than a match for a mob of Boxers.'

He felt her breast touching his tunic, the painful beat of his heart which she must feel. 'I have to go.' He lowered his arm. 'You will be safe here.' He was barely aware of what he was saying. 'Keep away from the ports and scuttles.'

She stayed where she was, watching his mouth as if to understand what was happening.

Then she said quietly, 'You see, Captain? What you have done? I am just a woman after all.'

He made to hold her again but she turned away. 'No. Do what you must but come back. To me.'

He watched her hands opening and closing as if she had lost control of them.

'You have my word, Countess.'

As he slid back the door she said quietly, 'Friedrike. It is my name.'

Blackwood barely remembered his climb to the bridge. He was aware of anxious, sun-reddened faces, of Lieutenant Bannatyre's relief as he appeared on the catwalk, of all these things and none of them.

Austad lowered his telescope and handed it to him.

'Burned out.' He watched Blackwood's profile. 'Some parts broken down with gunpowder, I think.'

Blackwood captured the scene of blackened desolation in the powerful lens. Austad was right. It was deliberate, not some frontal attack from outside.

Were they watching him right at this moment? Triumph and hatred, planning their next move against the foreign devils. He thought of her voice her hands in the cabin below. It made it suddenly personal and more dangerous because of it.

'Full landing party, Ian.' He moved the glass slightly. Humps in the rough ground by some trees. Graves. Crudely and hastily done. So there must have been an attack, but not so recently. Bannatyre was calling out his orders to the deck below, then he asked, 'What do you intend, sir?'

Blackwood did not look at him. If that Boxer lookout had been quicker with his great blade he might be lying dead back there. Then Bannatyre would be in command.

He replied, 'First we'll take a look. No chances. And be ready to fall back to the boats if we are attacked.' He lowered his voice and added sharply, 'I don't care if you are scared, Ian. We all get like that. But don't show it in front of the men!' He saw his words strike home and added more gently, 'The Germans may have had to leave overland.' It did not make sense. Where *was* the bloody gunboat?

Bannatyre said, 'Then we shall have to go back down-river, the way we came, sir.'

'It looks that way. At least we tried, eh?' But this time his words left Bannatyre untouched. He was remembering their slow, painful progress, and what the returning marines had told him about the Boxers and those hideous screams.

Blackwood looked past him as the paddles slowed for the final approach.

On the return passage the enemy would have all the time they needed. They would not be caught out again by a handful of marines.

The anchor clattered into shallow water and minutes later the two sampans were being warped alongside.

Blackwood nodded to Austad. 'Keep a close watch, Captain. Your old cannon are going to come in useful, I shouldn't wonder.'

Austad laughed, and the marines who were waiting to enter the boats heard him, and some even grinned as Blackwood strode through them. It couldn't be all that bad if their captain could joke about it. Fox did not smile. He knew the game of old, and understood all the rules better than most.

Blackwood said, 'You will be in charge until we return. Put what few men you have where they can be seen. The one who had his arm cut – '

Fox regarded him patiently. 'Farley, sir.'

'Have him move about the saloon and make it appear we have more men hidden below.'

'Yessir.' Fox shaded his eyes and peered at the shore. 'I'd issue Cap'n Austad with a uniform if I thought 'e could get into it!'

Blackwood eyed him fondly. 'The sooner we leave, the better chance we have of pulling out in daylight. Dawn tomorrow, with any luck.'

Fox stood at the rails and saluted as Blackwood jumped down amongst his men.

To himself he added, 'And we'll have to fight every bloody inch of the way, I shouldn't wonder.'

Blackwood stood quite still, one hand resting on his open holster as his landing party fanned out towards the trees and into the shattered mission. Near to it was even worse. It had been done with great care and deliberation to make certain that nothing of any use remained. There were scars on the burned walls, rifle and some musket fire. The first squad to return reported that there was evidence of shellfire, black holes in the ground to show where the gunboat had hit back from the river.

How many? he wondered. A handful of fanatics, or was the Boxer movement larger than anyone at home really understood. A full-scale rebellion would mark an end to any trade or colonial progress throughout the breadth of China.

Sergeant Kirby hurried down the slope while three of his men followed with what appeared to be some Chinese youths.

Lieutenant Bannatyre exclaimed, 'I'll see if they're armed!'

There were just two of them, both terrified as they were pushed towards Blackwood.

Kirby said dubiously, 'They say they're student interpreters who were employed 'ere by the Germans, sir. Can't be sure o' that neither.' He looked as if he would have killed them without thinking too much about it.

Bannatyre said, 'Could be true, sir. They use a lot of student interpreters at our legation in Peking.'

Blackwood asked quietly, 'What happened here?'

They both stared wild-eyed at him as if they still could not believe what was happening.

Blackwood continued in the same even tone. 'There was an attack.'

One of them nodded violently. 'Many Boxers, sir. Fighting for two days.' He made as if to look at the ruins but seemed to change his mind as if the memory was too vivid and terrible. 'We all ordered to leave in the ship.' He glanced at his friend. 'But we try to find our way across land. No want to go in ship.'

Blackwood could see it in his mind. But he had to know more.

'The German Count von Heiser, did you see him?'

'He go in ship too.'

Kirby muttered, 'Fer Chrissake!'

'D'you know if there are still any Boxers here?'

The youth looked at the ground. 'I think they go.' Once again the quick exchange of glances. 'They nearly found us. We heard them speak of river. They will try to block it.'

Bannatyre stared back at the sluggish current. 'My God, we'll be trapped!'

Blackwood tried to conceal his feelings. It was the only important thing he had discovered. They would know the old *Bajamar* was coming. How they knew was a mystery. But they obviously intended to cut their only line of escape. Perhaps they had forced something out of Earle before they allowed him to die.

He said, 'Send a boat for Austad. I want him here, now.'

He could sense the two Chinese youths shaking with fear. So great was the terror instilled by the Boxers they did not even feel safe with the marines.

The count had of course been under the impression that his wife had gone to Shanghai. They had not seen the gunboat so it seemed likely that the Germans had headed north perhaps with the intention of joining their legation in Peking. It was fast becoming a nightmare.

He said, 'Take these two on board.' In his heart he knew that the interpreters had been sent overland to carry news of the attack to Shanghai. Once they reached a fishing village the rest would have been easy.

Blackwood could find no other solution. One thing stood out above all else. Count von Heiser did not intend to let his wife's safety interfere with his duties.

Austad crunched up the beach and stared at the departing Chinese interpreters.

Blackwood said, 'We must lighten your ship, Captain. When we steer downriver I need you to be able to go as fast as you can.'

Austad removed his pipe and stared. 'Lighten the ship?'

Blackwood nodded. 'I believe the Boxers will try to block

our progress and launch an attack.' He saw his words going home.

Austad said, 'Not a dam, I think. The water would rise, and give my *Bajamar* more speed.'

'A boom then?' Blackwood controlled his impatience. The big Norwegian thought like he spoke, very slowly.

'*Boom?*' He pouted. 'More like.'

Blackwood looked across at the anchored paddle-steamer. She seemed totally at peace against the green backdrop of trees.

He said, 'How many anchors do you carry?'

Austad shrugged. 'Just two, Captain.' He sounded perplexed.

'Then I want one taken aft.' He looked for Kirby. 'Did you hear that? Get a party together and move the spare anchor right aft. Find a hawser of some sort and shackle it on. We may have to use a stream anchor.' The sergeant hurried away calling names. Orders he understood. He would carry them out to the letter.

'You can unload all your coal and burn wood instead. It is much lighter and we can use some of it as barricades.' He glanced at Bannatyre. 'See to it, Ian. I want the helm and Maxim gun protected.'

Austad struggled for words as if his collar was choking him.

'But my coal! I paid much money for it at Shanghai!'

'You'll get it back, Captain.' He eyed him impassively. 'But only if we escape from this bloody river!'

Within an hour the bulk of the marines, stripped and sweating with effort, and almost all of Austad's crew were hard at work. Spare cable, coal, some iron hatch covers, all were dragged or rolled over the side until the top of the pile showed above the surface like a tiny islet.

Blackwood watched from the shore. The waterline was already rising slightly. Just inches, but it would make all the difference. A dash downstream, dodging the worst of the big sandbars, and straight into the ambush. He rubbed his chin. A boom. It was the most likely. He had heard stories of such things from the *Arrow* Wars.

It would make even the unmovable Masterman sit up when the old *Bajamar* came puffing into view. He pictured *Mediator*, graceful and sleek as he had last seen her. And yet in this kind of situation she was as useless as a bow and arrow. Blackwood walked across to the crude graves. No name, no markers. They had probably been wondering why it had happened when death had cut them down.

He saw his pickets moving restlessly by the line of trees, their rifles and fixed bayonets at the ready. They needed no reminding now of what could happen.

Blackwood thought of the countess, hiding her feelings, few would ever guess what she was really enduring. He hoped that when she realized what had happened she would be equally strong.

He saw Swan watching him thoughtfully.

'We will ram the boom at full speed.' He found to his surprise that he could smile even now. The idea of the *Bajamar* managing even six knots was hard to believe.

Swan grimaced. 'We might broach-to, sir.' He waited warily. Blackwood took a few paces this way and that. 'We shall have to blow it first. The ship can ride on a stream anchor while we steer one of the sampans into the boom, barricade or whatever it turns out to be, and explode a charge against it.'

Swan persisted unhelpfully. 'The sampan might drift into the bank, sir. Or blow the backside out of our seagoing relic as we try to get past 'er.' He grinned broadly. 'You may 'ave to ask for volunteers this time, sir.'

Blackwood was grateful for Swan's trust or indifference, and not for the first time. He knew exactly how far he could go, but whatever it was it stayed between them, something private.

As soon as it was dark they would return aboard. It was no longer safe to leave isolated pickets on the land. Even now, no matter what the student interpreters had said, there might be hundreds of eyes watching them, gauging their readiness to move.

There was another great splash as some iron ballast was tipped into the river. If they ever got to sea the little *Bajamar* would toss about like a leaf on a millrace.

Timber from the burned-out mission was being hoisted from the sampans for Austad's boilers and for use as rough and ready barricades. It could make all the difference when bullets started to fly.

A strange bird squawked in the distance, but Blackwood chilled. It sounded like Earle. He could imagine the letter which the colonel commandant would eventually write to Earle's parents in Surrey. *Died bravely in the Service of his Queen and Country.* His own parents had doubtless had one at Hawks Hill for Neil. His mind shied away from it and he recalled instead a great marble bath he had shared with the army paymaster's young wife at Trincomalee. The thought made him feel even dirtier. Just to sink into a bath again. He touched his tunic beneath which the livid scar was another reminder.

He thought suddenly of the countess. Friedrike. Just to hold her like that, to take her –

Sergeant Kirby interrupted his thoughts. 'Anchor's in position aft, sir. Th' ship's drawin' five inches less as far as I can make out.'

'You've done well.' Blackwood looked away. The sky was changing to deep purple, the shadows from the trees looked like bars across the water.

'Recall all the working parties, Sergeant. See if Austad's cook can produce a good meal as soon as it's dark.'

Kirby understood. 'Long day termorrer.'

He marched off to gather up his sentries. A hard, embittered man, Blackwood thought.

He went over his plan again. It would be a long day right enough. He thought of men like these, Fox and Corporal O'Neil, Dago Trent, Lieutenant Bannatyre. They counted on him. It was no time for mistakes.

He closed his holster and glanced at his hand. He was surprised to discover he was completely unafraid and that unnerved him.

7

Under Fire

In the small cabin the imprisoned air was already hot and humid although it was not yet dawn.

Blackwood watched the countess as she sat on a small canvas chair and waited for her Chinese maid to finish dressing her hair.

Her eyes watched him in the mirror.

'We are leaving soon, Captain?'

Blackwood nodded. It seemed different with the maid here. A sort of formality had come between them.

He replied, 'My men have been fed. They are being mustered at their stations now.' He wished that he felt fresh and alert, but it had been a long night. The sampan to prepare, to transform into a floating bomb. Perhaps the interpreters were wrong, or the Boxers had changed their minds about a boom. But it was very unlikely they would escape downstream without an attack of some kind.

He thought of her face when he had described the scene ashore; he had expected some sign of disappointment, even anger, when he told her about her husband and the gunboat. All she had said was, 'He has a mission in life. Nothing ever obstructs that.'

On deck he heard the scrape of wire and a sudden rumble from the engine room. Soon now.

Blackwood also thought of his men's reactions when he had explained what he intended. They accepted it. The threat of more danger had pushed Earle's capture into the background for the present. They had piled logs and lengths

of timber around the gun in the bows to afford some
protection to its crew.

Sergeant Kirby had shown some of his own anxiety when
he had snapped, 'Bloody Maxim! Trust the Navy to give us
one o' them! I'll take the old Nordenfelt any time when it
comes to rapid-bloody-fire!'

Captain Masterman had probably offered the Maxim
because he thought it would be easier to mount in the
ancient *Bajamar*.

Other than that there had been little to reveal what his
men really felt.

She said, 'You may tell me, Captain.' Her eyes in the
mirror were quite steady. 'What chance do we have?'

Blackwood said, 'I believe we will have to fight our way
through.'

She turned on the chair to look at him, her hair gleaming
in the lamplight.

It was then that a memory stabbed at Blackwood like a
dagger. When he had joined his first ship he had been
serving with an old major who had seen a lot of service in
China. He had spoken of a hired surveying vessel named
Kite which had been wrecked on the Chinese mainland. Her
captain had been drowned, but his wife who had been on
board with him was taken prisoner and dragged by her long
red hair from village to village to be humiliated brutally
before being put in a small bamboo cage and carried on
display to Ningpo. To the Chinese rebels at the time she
must have symbolized the foreign invader if only because of
her hair. Her captors had carried her for many miles in the
cage where she could not sit or lie down. Neither she nor
the other survivors from the *Kite* had ever been seen again.

'You are staring, Captain.'

He looked away. 'I am sorry.' He forced a smile but his
mouth felt stiff. The Boxers wanted her for an important
hostage, but what might they do to her in the meantime?

'I am apologizing again.'

She stood up and faced him.

'I can read it in your eyes. Do not dismay, I will not show fear to *them*.'

He put his hands on her waist. 'In case anything should go wrong.' He hesitated and felt her body tense. 'I just want you to know that I have fallen in love with you.'

Her lips parted as if she would protest and he hurried on, 'I realize it is impossible. I *know* that.' He looked at her for several seconds and added, 'But nothing can change how I feel.'

A fist pounded the door. 'Cap'n Blackwood, *sir!*' It was Fox. Perhaps he knew too. Maybe they all did. It no longer seemed to matter.

'I'm coming right away, Sergeant Major!'

He let his arms drop to his sides. 'I have to go. They are raising the anchor. Time to leave.'

She moved closer, her face uplifted.

Blackwood could feel the maid staring at them, her eyes like saucers.

'May God guard you, my dear Captain.' Then she kissed him on the lips. It was more of a sensation than anything and in the next instant she was standing away from him. Unreachable.

Blackwood walked out to the side-deck and made his way forward to where the capstan clanked round in a cloud of rust.

Lieutenant Bannatyre drew himself to attention and said, 'All in position, sir.' Like the others he was wearing his field-service cap instead of the white helmet with its gleaming spike on the top. The marines might resent the order, but it made them smaller targets. Blackwood knew from bitter experience that a white helmet made a perfect aiming-mark for any marksman. He glanced aft and saw Austad's bulky silhouette on the bridge as he watched the anchor coming inboard. Behind him the smoke rolled downwind from the funnel and sparks too, as the boilers adjusted themselves to freshly cut wood.

Blackwood walked down the sloping deck and felt his

way past one of the great paddles. Figures crouched behind makeshift barricades, their eyes pale in the grey light as they turned to watch him. Corporal O'Neil was right aft by the taffrail, peering down at the sampan which was tied astern. The charge was concealed with canvas and more timber. It would not do to have a stray shot strike that pile of explosive, he thought.

O'Neil said cheerfully, 'Two fuses, sir, in case one misfires.' No questions, no doubts.

Blackwood smiled. 'You've done well.'

O'Neil chuckled. 'Learned a mite from my brother in the RMA, sir. A fine lad even if he is a gunner!'

Blackwood continued on his inspection. Even O'Neil's little joke seemed to symbolize something. The Corps. The *family*.

It was strange to think he had never seen Jonathan in uniform. He like O'Neil's brother was in the Royal Marine Artillery, the first gunner in the Blackwood family. A Blue Marine. That must have given the General a few doubtful moments.

The hull gave a shudder and a man yelled hoarsely from the bows as the anchor rose dripping against the hawsepipe. The great paddle-wheels thrashed round even as the helm went over, and belching more smoke the *Bajamar* pivoted in mid-stream like the old veteran she was.

It was already much lighter, and he could see the river-bank, the indistinct shadow of the ruined mission.

The paddles churned up sand and dirt from the bottom as with a leadsman in the bows she steadied on course. Austad left his little catwalk and stood near the helmsman. Austad looked over at Blackwood without a word and then put a match to his pipe. He reached out for the telegraph and Blackwood heard the bell jangle in the engine room, and the increasing beat of the paddles as they responded.

Corporal Lyde stood near the second anchor and eyed the tackle and slips with obvious contempt. It was a job for sailors, or coolie deckhands. Not Royal Marines.

He patted his ammunition pouches and checked that his Lee-Metford rifle was ready with the safety catch on. But if it had to be done, the Second Platoon would do it best, or he'd want to know why.

Midway between the machine gun and the oblong superstructure, Sergeant Kirby stood with his arms folded, his eyes apparently on the lieutenant in the bows. Bloody Bannatyre was already scared out of his wits and nothing had happened yet. But the thought failed to console him or shift his mind from his terrible secret.

He shouldn't have listened, then he wouldn't have known. Besides which, they could have sorted things out.

A *friend* at Forton Barracks had told him that he had seen Kirby's wife in a London ale house, she had been with a soldier, and they had apparently been aware of nothing but each other. Kirby had considered asking for leave, but with the whole company standing by for overseas he knew it would not be granted. Besides which, he had his pride, both in the Corps which he had entered as a boy, and in what he had achieved to get the chevrons on his sleeve.

He had spent all his money on a train fare to London. He did not really remember planning anything. It had just happened. Kirby could see her face right now, as if she was here on this ruddy steamer. He clutched the guardrail and felt the power running through his fingers.

The way they had stared at him from the bed. His bed. Both naked, and gaping at him in the doorway.

'Oh dear God!' He heard a man shuffle and knew he had spoken aloud.

The soldier had been quick. He had dived from the bed and had run frantically from the room. Kirby did not really care about him anyway. He could have been anyone. She had started to plead, to beg. With the same detached efficiency with which he might examine a recruit's rifle for a speck of dirt, he had strangled her. He could not even remember how long he had sat there after covering her contorted face with a blanket. *All his things*. Pictures of his past ships, fellow NCOs, even one of himself as a callow recruit.

Then he had left and had returned to the barracks on a milk train. Nobody had seen him leave or return. He was not even a minute adrift for reveille.

When her body was discovered the police would inform the barracks. Nobody else would care much. And the soldier? He would be careful to keep his mouth shut. He might well have been seen with her that night at the pub.

And yet. He felt the anxiety and despair closing round him like his fingers on her neck. *I know and I care*, his mind seemed to shout.

And supposing someone had seen him there?

Blackwood stood beside him. Kirby felt ice-cold. How long had he been watching him?

But Blackwood merely said, 'Ready for Rounds, Sergeant. Just to make sure we've forgotten nothing.' He looked at him in the gloom. 'Are you all right?'

Kirby nodded. 'Never better, sir.'

He followed the young captain, glad to be doing something, grateful to be a part of it all even if he had to die for it.

Blackwood walked past the saloon. In darkness but with each port wide open. Here and there a rifle muzzle showed itself. He pressed the white paintwork. The metal and wood beneath would not stop a bullet except at long range. But it was all they had.

He heard Kirby close on his heels. What the hell was the matter with him? he wondered.

Blackwood paused by the last door and thought of her on the other side. *Friedrike.* He touched his lips with the back of his hand and thought of her mouth, her nearness.

Nearby Fox saw his hesitation and allowed his stern features to relax. Then he glared at the crouching figures by the bulwark. In their stained whites they looked more like bloody convicts than marines. He would alter all that when they reached order and routine again. He looked up at the masthead, now clearly etched against the sky. Not even a flag. *Gawd*.

There was a sharp crack followed by the thud of a bullet hitting the hull on the port side.

Fox shouted, 'Stand-to! Face yer front but *keep down!*'

He stared at the lieutenant who was standing alone and framed against the sky. It went against Fox's instincts to shout at an officer. But in a few more seconds that marksman would see him and pick him out as a target.

'*Down*, Mr Bannatyre, if you please, sir!'

He sighed as the officer dropped to his knees.

Blackwood crouched beside him. Fox felt the captain's mind going like an engine.

'It's started, sir.'

'Sooner than I expected.' He grimaced as another shot clanged into the low hull. He said, 'No firing until I give the order.'

Fox watched him duck down and move to the opposite side. Sharp as a tack, that one. Blackwood knew that if they were allowed the marines would blaze away and use most of their ammunition before they had got halfway. Nobody liked to sit and take it without shooting back.

He looked at Sergeant Kirby who was kneeling behind a winch.

'All right, Jeff?'

Kirby glared at him. Why don't they all shut up and leave me alone?

But he answered readily, 'Never better, Sar'nt Major!'

The sun's rim shone like a gold halo above one of the pointed hills and with it came the attack.

'Hold yer fire!' Fox's voice carried like a trumpet above the sporadic crack of rifles and muskets which appeared to be coming from either bank.

Blackwood peered over the low bulwark and watched drifting smoke rising from some bushes, but of the marksmen there was no sign at all.

He shouted, 'More speed, Captain Austad!' He guessed the vessel was going as fast as she could, and the spray was flying from the churning paddle wheels like spindrift.

'There's Johnnie Chinaman!'

Blackwood saw the running figures as they broke from cover by some open ground.

'Two 'undred yards! Independent! *Fire!*'

The marines took careful aim and squeezed their triggers. Several of the running men tumbled down the slope, their red ribbons and loose white tunics like untidy bundles amongst the dried scrub.

'Cease firing!' Fox yelled, 'Reload magazines! Watch yer front!'

Blackwood glanced quickly at the nearest marines as they pressed eight more bullets into their rifles. Most of the heavy shooting had come from the port side. They would eventually have to steer closer to the salient where they had fought their swift, decisive battle. Blackwood saw that the dead Boxers had dropped their weapons, not swords this time but great shining blades mounted on staves like pikes. *The Big Knife Society*. It did not seem so bizarre now.

More white-clad figures broke from cover and ran recklessly towards the river, some firing, others brandishing their fearsome-looking blades, apparently oblivious to the danger.

'Commence firing!'

The Maxim gun came to life, *tak-tak-tak*, the ammunition belt jerking through a marine's fingers as the bullets made little spurts in the water, across the bank and then through the mob of yelling figures.

Blackwood recalled what Major Blair had told him in Hong Kong. That the Boxers were so fanatical that they really believed they were invulnerable to sword-cuts, even bullets.

More of them were flung down by the rapid fire, until the

Maxim jerked into silence and Kirby exclaimed, '*Jammed!* Wot did I tell you?'

But nobody listened as the river-bank and shallows swung even closer to the port-side paddle-wheel.

Bullets slammed into the hull and Blackwood heard glass shattering, the cry for assistance as one of his men was hit inside the saloon. The leadsman in the bows rose warily to his feet and flung his line over the side. He seemed to pivot on his heels, his mouth wide in a silent scream as a heavy ball smashed him in the chest and hurled him over the bulwark. Blackwood saw one of the marines shutting his eyes tightly as the leadsman was sucked into the great churning paddle-blades and ground to bloody fragments in seconds. Austad had drawn his old long-barrelled Colt revolver and was firing at some of the Boxers who stood waist-deep in the shallows. One fell, another waded closer, his rifle aimed at the bridge even as the stoppage was cleared from the Maxim and a hail of bullets tossed him aside within yards of the hull.

Blackwood strode to the bows, trying not to duck as several bullets struck sparks from the windlass or ploughed splinters from the deck. They were shooting down into the ship as the *Bajamar* steamed into the narrows at the start of the wide bend. Another marine fell on his back, gasping in agony as a red stain spread across his tunic and one of his comrades ran to drag him to safety.

Lieutenant Bannatyre, his revolver in his fist, stared at Blackwood without recognition.

Blackwood said sharply, 'They'll try and board us in a moment!'

'But – but – ' Bannatyre seemed unable to form his words. 'H-how can they?'

There was no time to explain. It would not help anyway. 'These people don't know what fear is!'

Crack – crack – crack! Shots clattered and ricocheted from the paddle-boxes and superstructure, and holes appeared in the sides of the saloon like brightly edged stars.

Corporal Lyde called hoarsely, 'Two men down, sir! I think Private Elmhirst is done for!'

Blackwood winced as a heavier bang shook the bridge. Probably an ancient Chinese gingall left over from the other wars. Like a giant duck-gun, it needed two men to carry and fire it.

A face intruded into his racing thoughts. Private Elmhirst, Lyde had said. Round and innocent, made more so by his carefully grown moustache. Like Ralf, he thought.

Running and ducking Blackwood hurried into the deeper shadow of a paddle-box and knelt beside the young marine. He looked so pale he could already have been dead. Elmhirst opened his eyes and stared up at him. His eyes seemed unable to focus properly as if he was barely aware of what was happening. More sharp cracks made the deck quiver and Blackwood could hear Fox calling for him. He took Elmhirst's hand in his. 'Easy, lad. Hold on.' Lyde had torn open his white tunic and was trying to staunch the blood with a dressing. It seemed to be everywhere.

'I – I got one of 'em, sir.' Elmhirst's voice was small, almost a whisper.

Lyde said roughly, ''*Course* you did. Two of the buggers more like, eh, sir?' He looked at Blackwood, his face saying it was hopeless.

Blackwood said, 'I'll tell them about it.' He saw the light go out in the youth's eyes and felt the grip on his hand slacken.

Lyde watched him stride forward again, then closed the marine's eyes. 'I hope you heard, that, my son.' Then he picked up his rifle, thumbed off the safety catch and fired over the rail. Lyde had already selected another zig-zagging target even as the first one dropped.

Fox beckoned to Blackwood and pointed at the hillside. 'Smoke, sir! They've got somethin' ready for us!'

A marine pounded the Maxim's breech until blood showed on his knuckles.

'*Bloody bastard!* 'Nother misfire!'

There was a muffled bang and then the early sunlight

vanished completely in a great ball of fire and dense smoke.

Fox rasped, 'Stink-pot, sir. It'll set the ship ablaze if they put one into us!'

Another bang and the hull shook violently as if it had run hard aground. The explosion was deafening, and within seconds the top of the saloon, the catwalk and even the mast flared up like torches.

'Fire party! At the double!'

Water splashed and hissed on the fires but the stink-pot had taken a firm hold. Blackwood could smell the seared paintwork, and heard flames fanning through the cabins, roaring like something alive.

Austad shouted, 'We soon reach the bend!' He stared at the damage with disbelief and anger. 'If we don't sink first!'

Another man dropped as a bullet flung him to the deck. One of Austad's crew this time. The flames licked along the deck and set the man ablaze so that he rolled and kicked while two marines tried to cover him with wet canvas.

Another fireball exploded right alongside, burning a great gash in the paddle-box before striking the river and hurling up a column of smoke and steam.

The Maxim came alive again and raked the nearest bank, back and forth like a reaper in a field. Bodies littered the ground and drifted in the shallows, but nothing stopped them. It was like a tide, Blackwood thought as he fired his revolver into a group behind some bushes, the gun kicking in his hand as if to fight him.

The smoke was thicker, pricking his eyes as it funnelled through the cabins and bridge. If they lost control now and ran into a sandbar they would be butchered without mercy. The lucky ones anyway.

'Put more men on the fires, Sergeant!' Blackwood struggled with his empty revolver then turned as Swan said calmly, 'Let me, sir.' He handed it back and wiped his face with his sleeve, leaving a black mark like a handprint.

Blackwood peered through the smoke and shouted, 'Mr Bannatyre, take charge here!' He did not wait for an answer but thrust his way into the saloon and saw flames darting through the bulkhead, consuming furniture and scattered clothing in an instant. More men followed him with slopping buckets of water, and Blackwood heard somebody screaming through the fires and guessed it was one of the stokers.

He kicked open a door and skidded to a halt as he saw the stooping figure of the countess's brother-in-law carrying a marine to safety behind some chests and upended foot lockers. He was in his shirt-sleeves and was murmuring gently to the sobbing marine who became suddenly quiet as he realized someone was trying to help. Blackwood knew that the marine did not understand a word of German, but the man's soothing voice and almost saintly countenance did more than any surgeon. Blackwood touched his shoulder as he hurried past. It was the first time since his wife had been murdered that he had heard him speak.

He blinked in smoky sunlight as he passed a big hole in the side, the edges bent inwards like wet cardboard. He saw the little Chinese maid crouching in a corner, her head in her hands, and for a moment he thought she had been killed or wounded. But she was sobbing very quietly, her small body rocking to the violent movement of the deck as the *Bajamar* swung on to a new leg of her dash downstream.

'Come along, Anna!' He seized her shoulder and pushed her to the last cabin.

The countess stared at him, her eyes wide and questioning.

Blackwood said, 'Take care of this one!' He ducked as a bullet or metal splinter came through the port and ricocheted across the cabin.

'*Down.*' He took her wrist and pulled her closer to a barricade of luggage which they had heaped against one bulkhead. She crouched beside him without protest as he tried to make her more comfortable. She put her hands over her ears as more crashes and thuds broke against the hull like fiery hammers.

'Sir! Sir! There's a boat ahead!' Swan peered in at them then swung round and fired from the hip as a figure loomed from the water right alongside. Blackwood tried to moisten his lips. God, there must only be a few inches under the keel.

He stood up and peered through the open port. The fires were under control, although he could hear demands for more water coming from aft. They had to keep the flames from reaching the sampan, or from burning the towline. The other sampan had been blasted to pieces by the stink-pots, and in any case time had run out.

She exclaimed suddenly, 'I must help! *Must* do something!' She watched him desperately, 'Dieter, my, my *vollbruder*, is out there, so please let me help him!'

Blackwood smiled. 'I'll send someone.' He heard shouts and the intermittent rattle of the machine-gun. He ran through the smoke catching stark glimpses of grim, determined faces, bolts being jerked, empty cartridge cases rattling in the scuppers to the swish and thunder of the racing paddles.

He found Bannatyre, hatless, with his revolver in his hand, standing beside two wounded marines while the rest of his party fired their rifles over the bulwark as fast as they could aim and reload. One of the wounded men, his head wrapped in a bloody bandage, was also busy reloading the discarded rifles, groaning to himself as he thrust in each new bullet.

Bannatyre looked wild. 'There, *look!*'

It was a large sampan, loaded with Chinese, and being propelled by poles from its stern, so that the men using them were concealed from the marines' rifle fire.

Someone cheered. 'It's aground! The bugger's hit the bottom!'

Fox shouted, 'Hold yer noise, damn you!'

Blackwood turned and looked at Austad's smoke-shrouded figure. The Norwegian made a chopping motion with his fist. The river was too narrow. They would have to keep going. Straight for the big sampan.

Blackwood cupped his hands. 'Stand by to repel boarders! Corporal Lyde, take your squad aft! It's the lowest point!'

The *Bajamar* was moving at full speed and yet it took an eternity to reach the other craft. The men at the poles were trying to thrust the sampan into deeper water, but she was too overloaded, and they were still shouting and screaming like fiends when the end of their boat took the full impact of the *Bajamar*'s blunt stem. Blackwood struggled with his sword hilt and dragged it from the scabbard.

'*Stand fast, Marines!*' The deck swayed over and a whole section of the Boxers' sampan reared up above the bows like something from the depths. Several of the Boxers were sucked bodily into the paddles, others were trapped in their shattered hull as it rolled along the bottom breaking up as it went. But there were many more who managed to climb over the rails unscathed, their teeth bared in unbelievable ferocity.

Blackwood waved his sword. 'At them, lads!'

The marines needed no urging now that the danger was right here, amongst them. Striding shoulder to shoulder, their boots catching and stumbling on fallen gear and ringbolts, they thrust at the Boxers with their bayonets, holding some against the guardrails, driving a few over the side into the frothing water.

Blackwood aimed his revolver as a great blade flashed in the sunshine and struck a marine on the shoulder. It was like an axe driving through a sapling. The revolver recoiled in his hand and he saw the yelling Boxer vanish amongst the gasping, stabbing figures. The marine fell and did not move, nor would he. The blade had all but severed his arm and shoulder from his body.

Bullets cracked amongst the Boxers who found themselves trapped in the narrow confines of the side-deck. Lyde and O'Neil were firing from aft with their men; they took their time to make each shot tell.

Blackwood saw a giant figure in white, his red headcloth

rising above his companions like a banner, hacking and stabbing his way through the marines. There were blood streaks over his clothing, and he must have been dying on his feet.

Kirby shouted, 'Watch out, sir!' Then he had to swing round to parry a blade aside with his bayonet before thrusting it into his attacker's chest.

The tall Boxer did not blink as he kept his eyes fastened on Blackwood. Like an enraged serpent, and making him even more terrible, he was frothing at the mouth.

Blackwood raised his revolver and levelled it on the giant's waist. He felt his heart jump as the hammer clicked on an empty chamber. He had fired every bullet without even noticing.

He saw the long blade glitter as it swung towards him, felt the pain in his wrist as he parried it aside with his sword. There was no change in the Boxer's expression nor did he falter as he pushed a marine aside to give himself space for another, final cut.

Swan darted forward and fired, Blackwood saw the Boxer stagger, the blood glinting like an eye in his shoulder. Then he fell. It was incredible. As he rolled on to his face Blackwood realized he must have been bayoneted or shot several times.

It was like a signal. Chased on by the battle-crazed marines the remaining Boxers were leaping over the bulwarks, floundering or wading in the shallows or falling to the rapid fire from aft. Blackwood dropped his arms to his sides and took several deep breaths.

He saw some of his men tipping the dead and wounded Boxers into the river, others frantically reloading in case of a fresh attack.

But when Blackwood looked at the nearest bank it was deserted. As if the running, chanting figures had been swallowed up. Bannatyre came over to him, his chest heaving as if he was in pain.

'We did it, sir!' He looked about to cheer, or weep.

Sergeant Major Fox joined them. 'Three dead, including young Elmhirst, sir. The others are Munro and Becket.'

Blackwood straightened his aching back. 'Wounded?'

Fox watched him calmly. 'Five, sir. I've 'ad 'em took below.'

Blackwood nodded and looked at the bloodstains on the deck. It was a miracle they had not lost half their number. But it was bad enough.

He tried to think more clearly, but all he could do was marvel they had survived. Behind him Swan was reloading his revolver and whistling quietly to himself. They were still together. He did not seem to need much more than that.

Bannatyre asked in a steadier tone, 'Will they come at us again?'

Blackwood stared past him at the land as it began to climb more steeply. It was not over. Perhaps it had not even begun. There was more smoke above the hill; if they had to anchor the Boxers would try to set the ship alight again with their fireballs and stink-pots.

Down aft he could see Corporal O'Neil and his squad hauling at the towline, making certain that their floating bomb was ready for immediate use. He heard a change in the paddles' beat and knew *Bajamar* was slowing down.

When he shaded his eyes to look for Austad he saw him framed against the sky, he was beckoning urgently with his telescope. Blackwood made himself walk to the bridge ladder. They were all watching him, looking for their fate in his eyes. Dirty, bloodied, ragged and red-eyed, they looked as if they had little more to give him.

He climbed swiftly up the ladder. The handrails were already hot in the sunlight. On the buckled catwalk he saw the extent of their damage, the charred deck and hatchways still smoking from the hastily flung buckets.

But they had done it. In spite of everything.

Even without the telescope he could see the boom. Supported on boats which they must have dragged from some nearby fishing village, the boom consisted of trees, long sharpened stakes of bamboo, the whole roped together from bank to bank. If they attempted to ram it they would lose control or put one of the paddles out of action.

He knew Sergeant Kirby was staring up at him from the foredeck. It was strange he had been so eager to volunteer for the job. Corporal O'Neil had also volunteered, but that made more sense. He was a superb swimmer, and just about mad enough for anything. They would have to swim upstream for about fifty yards after the *Bajamar* had dropped her stream anchor. It was unlikely either of them would survive.

He realized that Austad was staring at him, the telescope held out to him like a baton.

'Here. Look.'

Blackwood raised the glass and saw the crude barrier spring into focus, even a few figures scampering for cover as the vessel pounded towards them.

In the centre of the boom, on a pike, its empty eye-sockets watching their slow approach, was a severed head.

Blackwood handed the telescope back and allowed the hideous spectacle to fall into distance.

'Prepare to anchor. Tell Sergeant Kirby to be ready.'

There was no longer any mystery about Earle's fate. They must have been saving it for this very moment.

'Stop engine.' He felt desperately sick and knew he must not show it. Not now of all times.

'*Let go!*' He heard the anchor clatter down, the hawser just enough to hold them in midstream.

'Silence on deck!' That was Fox. As if he already knew.

It was like a tribute to their first casualty, respect for his final degradation.

8

A Bit of History

Sergeant Jeff Kirby put his shoulder to the long pole and heaved. A few feet away Corporal O'Neil lowered his rifle to watch as the sampan moved slowly away from the *Bajamar*'s bows where it had been hauled by the men on deck.

Kirby said, 'Probably the last time we see that lot, Paddy!'

O'Neil, whose name was Sean, gave a broad grin. Like the sergeant he was stripped to his white trousers and in spite of the tension appeared almost relaxed.

He grinned. 'A good swim will liven things up, eh, Sarge?'

Kirby thrust the pole into the bottom again. When he straightened his back he could see the boom across the river. The cunning bastards. At the narrowest point.

He glanced again at the anchored paddle-steamer. She already looked out of reach and he felt a twinge of panic. It was so deathly quiet after the swift battle, the feeling of hate and madness which had held them together as they had driven the enemy back into the water. He looked at his own rifle where it lay within his reach. There was dried blood on the bayonet, like black paint in the hard sunlight.

O'Neil raised his rifle and lowered it again. 'The buggers can't make us out, Sarge. There's two of 'em on that ridge, see?'

Kirby swallowed as the sweat poured down his body. The boat handled better than he had expected. Maybe there was still a chance. He winced as a sandbar swam to the surface like some sleeping fish. No, there was not a hope in hell. As Captain Blackwood had explained, if abandoned too soon the sampan might run aground or drift into the bank.

He peered at the boom again. It seemed no closer.

O'Neil was humming softly to himself and Kirby was torn between hate and envy.

He said brutally, 'You know what that bloody object is they've stuck on a pike?'

O'Neil regarded him curiously. 'To be sure. The little officer you left on his own, right?'

Kirby felt the blood pound in his veins. 'It wasn't my fault, *you know it!*'

There was a crack and a bullet hit the water several yards abeam. O'Neil lifted his rifle again and readjusted the backsight.

'Now there's a thing.' The rifle sounded twice as loud in the confines of the high banks, and O'Neil jerked open the bolt as a tiny figure rolled down the slope.

Several more shots cracked from the hillside, and from the anchored *Bajamar* came an overwhelming response. Machine-gun and rifle fire, and then one of Austad's little cannons which made the air shake. It probably sounded much more deadly than it was, Kirby thought. Why had he volunteered? To die perhaps in a blaze of glory? And now all he wanted to do was stay alive. It was so unfair.

A heavy shot burst through the side of the boat and made the canvas cover in the bows start to smoulder.

O'Neil was there in a flash and shouted, 'Must have been one o' them big muskets, Sarge!'

He snatched up his rifle and triggered two more shots as some men ran down a cleft in the hillside, firing as they came.

Kirby locked the pole in position and opened fire with his own rifle. He saw one of the bastards drop. But it gave him no satisfaction. Close-quarters, where you could see the enemy's strength or terror as you crossed blades with him, that was more like it. The rifle bucked hard into his bare shoulder and he saw another white-clad figure roll down amongst the scrub, one leg kicking for a full minute as if detached from its dead owner.

As he reloaded his magazine he glanced astern. The *Bajamar* was wreathed in smoke as every man who could pull a trigger laid down a barrage of fire across the salient.

The boom was nearer now, and more figures were thronging the nearest bank, some kneeling to shoot as the little boat drifted towards them.

Bullets slammed into and through the bulwarks, and others spurted water around the two crouching marines with barely a break. Kirby dashed the sweat from his eyes and tried to gauge the distance. He thought briefly of asking O'Neil's opinion but discarded the thought immediately. He was only a corporal and a bloody Irish one at that.

It must be now. Had to be. He felt something like a blow from an iron club and found himself on his back, his head on the bottom boards and one foot dangling from the gunwale.

'Bloody hell!' O'Neil stooped over him and stared at the blood which seemed to be pumping from Kirby's chest in an unstoppable torrent.

Kirby shut his eyes against the agony. He attempted to move but almost lost consciousness as the searing pain drove through him. He tried to speak clearly, but his voice sounded like a sob. 'Fuses! Light 'em now!' When the corporal's shadow remained over him he gasped, 'Do it, you Irish clod! Fer Christ's sake, light 'em!'

O'Neil stumbled towards the bows. He took time to fire and bring down a crouching marksman on the bank before he flung himself beside the fuses, his mind grappling with what he must do. He thought vaguely of Kirby's attempt to frighten and torment him over the severed head. It was just like him. Now he was probably dying. Like they all would unless he could blow the bloody boom. He recoiled, startled almost by the sudden spurt of life from the fuses.

Shots whined and cracked around him but he took time

to reload before struggling aft again to Kirby's sprawled body. It was probably hopeless anyway, he thought. But those fiends would never take him alive. Never.

In a steady voice he barely recognized he said, 'Right, Sarge, we're off then.'

He looked at the river and tried to shut out the sound of those two hissing fuses behind him. It would be a hard swim even without Kirby.

Kirby gasped thickly, 'You go. That's an order, damn you! Leave yer rifle. I'll take a few of the bastards with me!'

O'Neil ignored him. Instead he flung Kirby's rifle over the side and said, 'Give us yer arm. Lively then.' He waited for Kirby to hit the water and submerge, the blood trailing pink around him. Then he fired a full magazine of eight bullets and then with a kind of defiance hurled his own rifle into the river.

The water felt cool after the remorseless sunlight, and with his arm supporting the barely conscious sergeant he began to paddle slowly upstream.

The gunfire seemed to be over and around him as the marines opened rapid fire once again. Through the effort and the pain in his arm O'Neil heard the ship's siren give a loud toot as if to encourage him, to urge him on. He recalled the little pleasure steamers at Galway, on his own Ireland's west coast. Recalled too his dead father who had also been a corporal in the Corps.

'Come on, me boy!' His breath was bursting out in great gulps and once he swallowed some water. It tasted of salt and he thought of the sea. Safety. His pals around him.

Kirby had his eyes closed but knew what was happening. He tried to free himself from O'Neil's iron grip but heard him gasp, *'Together*, Sarge, or not at all!'

The explosion when it came was more of a sensation than a sound. O'Neil felt as if his whole body was being crushed and caressed at the same time as the exploding charge bowled a miniature tidal wave upstream and caught them both in a drunken dance. O'Neil could see it all in his dazed

mind, and wanted to laugh, to cheer for what they had
done. But his mouth was choked, and his body seemed to be
filling with water.

Dying was not so terrible after all.

'Rapid fire!' The remainder of Fox's words were lost as the
kneeling and prone marines took aim and squeezed their
triggers, oblivious to everything but the distant white
figures which were running towards the water.

Blackwood gripped a guardrail until the pain helped to
steady him. Set against the land, the sluggish river with the
crude boom across it like a gate, the sampan seemed puny.
A pointless gesture.

Austad held the telescope to his eye and said, 'The
sampan has been hit again, I think.'

Corporal Lyde was yelling, 'Train that gun to port!'

The belt began to jerk in time with the Maxim's laboured
stammer and Blackwood thought of Kirby and his sudden
anger over the machine-gun. Now he was up there with
O'Neil in company with enough explosive to blast them to
powder.

'Cease firing! Reload!' Fox strode behind his panting,
sweating men. Blackwood wondered how he could do it.
Fox's eyes were everywhere, and his voice never let his
marines falter or give in. They were hating him, but he got
the results he wanted.

Blackwood cupped his hands. 'Stand by to slip!' He saw
Austad's big hand close around the telegraph handle and
pictured the stokers crouching below in terrible heat,
wondering when a shot would burst in amongst them or
split open a boiler.

Lyde said harshly, 'One of 'em's down, sir.'

Blackwood nodded. It was obviously Kirby. Even at this
distance he could see the boat sway as the other figure
scrambled aft to assist him.

Fox muttered, 'Near enough.' He was speaking aloud but

to O'Neil. 'Get out while you can, dammit!'

Another said in a whisper, 'Gawd, Arthur, the mad bugger is bringing the sergeant with 'im!'

Blackwood shaded his eyes as more running figures rose like birds from cover.

'Take aim, rapid fire!'

A puff of smoke and Austad's squat cannon reared inboard on its tackles. Blackwood saw the packed charge scythe above the scrub and bushes, catching one of the Boxers and lifting him several feet in the air.

'Slip the stream anchor!' Blackwood could barely tear his eyes from the two bobbing heads in the water. He felt the deck shiver as the paddles began to churn slowly, almost gently, at the surface.

'All clear aft, sir!'

Blackwood ran to the side and leaned out to watch O'Neil's progress. Over his shoulder and in between sporadic bursts of rifle fire he shouted, 'Corporal Lyde! Warn Mr Bannatyre to stand by in the bows! It will have to be done quickly or we'll lose them in the paddles!'

There was a vivid flash from the boom, followed by a thunderclap of an explosion which seemed to push the *Bajamar* off course for just a few seconds. As a dense pall of smoke lifted and writhed across the river hundreds of fragments splashed down to throw feathers of spray from bank to bank.

Blackwood saw two of Austad's crew and Lieutenant Bannatyre leaning over the bulwark, while two half-naked marines were lowered down the rough plates on bowlines. It was touch and go. O'Neil would be protected by the hull on one side only, but bullets were still striking the rusty plating from the opposite beam.

'Second Section! Rapid fire to starboard!' Fox pushed a young marine with his boot. 'Take aim, you blockhead! Don't just blaze away!'

Austad bit hard on his pipe. 'I stop engine.' The paddles stilled as if seized by a giant's hand.

Through the din and bellowed orders Blackwood heard a wild cheer, and saw the head and shoulders of one of the marines in his bowline as he deftly made a line fast to Kirby's bloodsoaked body.

'Got both of 'em!'

Lyde grinned wildly. 'Deserve Victoria Crosses, th' pair of 'em!' He flushed. 'No disrespect, sir.'

Blackwood swung round as a great groan came from forward.

The smoke was slowly dispersing. Reluctant to go.

It was impossible. The boom was still there.

Fox snapped, 'Get those wounded men under cover.' But his eyes were on Blackwood.

Blackwood wiped his forehead with his sleeve and saw the glances. The utter despair on their faces. After all this. He felt like giving in, he had failed them.

Swan stood by his shoulder, his eyes slitted against the smoky glare.

'A bang like that, sir.' He waited for Blackwood to look at him. 'Chances are it'll 'ave weakened the thing anyway.' He ran his thumb along his rifle's backsight. 'We got nowhere else to go.'

Blackwood reached out and gripped Swan's shoulder. Swan was right. They could not retrace their course upstream. They would be hunted and ambushed at the first opportunity. The ammunition must be getting low anyway. But it was more than that. Certainly more than Swan could ever guess.

He said, 'Thank you.' He turned to Fox. 'Share out the ammunition, Sergeant Major.'

Fox understood. Only one way out. Fight or die. Probably both.

Blackwood glanced at Austad's untidy shape.

'Two minutes. Then full ahead.'

Austad grunted, his eyes fixed professionally beyond the bows, the slow drift as the paddle-wheels barely held the hull steady.

Blackwood raised the telescope and watched the little groups of figures on either bank, many of them struggling out along the boom. At least Earle's grisly remains had been hurled away.

'Nine rounds per man, sir!' That was Lyde.

It was precious little for what they were up against.

Blackwood placed the telescope on its rack by the helmsman.

'How's the sergeant?'

Lyde turned as several marines raised a cheer.

Blackwood stared as O'Neil lurched through a door and picked up one of the spare rifles. He looked dazed, drunk. He saw Blackwood and bared his teeth in a grin.

'I'll not be left out o' this, sir!'

Fox shook his head. 'Hell's bells! I don't bloody well believe it!'

Blackwood drew his revolver.

Here we go. 'Now, Captain Austad. Let us make a bit of history.'

It was soon obvious that Austad had taken Blackwood at his word. The *Bajamar* shook violently from keel to bridge, every plate and plank squeaking and protesting as the twin paddles worked up to full speed.

Blackwood stood on the port side just forward of a paddle-box and watched the boom, the pale figures which stood or crouched along it, and the occasional stab of rifle and musket fire. Someone had even hoisted a banner in the same position where Earle's head had been displayed. It was motionless, as if the air between the banks had been sucked away.

Beyond the high salient the sky was clear, and Blackwood knew that the sea would soon be in view if they managed to break through. When they hit the boom the greatest danger would be if the paddles became entangled, even for a moment. The enemy might try to board them again, and this time they would face less resistance. Nine rounds per head, and the Maxim could not train to the lowest part of *Bajamar*'s freeboard, midships to aft. Bannatyre had taken charge of the opposite side and Blackwood prayed that he would offer the example his weary men needed when the time came.

Shots hammered into the hull and superstructure or whined overhead. Blackwood saw some of the marines' rifles waver as their owners marked down enemy marksmen, and cursed the order not to retaliate.

He tried not to think of the countess as she waited behind the frail barricades with the wounded and the dying. After what she had already experienced it was a wonder she did not break down completely. At the same time he knew she had gained strength in some way. Did she still have her toylike silver pistol, he wondered, and the resolve to use it?

'Here they come!'

Blackwood thumbed back the hammer and stared at the nearest bank. Then he ducked down as the air exploded from another flaming ball hurled from the high bank, and held his breath. As the heat and stench enfolded the deck, he heard men coughing and retching, a solitary shot as one of the marines hit back without waiting for the order.

A tide of running, screaming figures had already reached the waterside and were shooting down at the churning, smoke-enshrouded *Bajamar*, their voices shrill and bonded together like a chorus from hell.

'Be ready! *Easy* there!' Blackwood needed all his strength to hold his voice level and outwardly calm. Like a trainer steadying a frightened horse.

A kneeling marine dropped his rifle and fell on his side, blood running between his fingers as he clutched at his stomach. Blackwood saw the man staring up at him, his eyes outraged and disbelieving even as another fusillade swept over the hull in a hail of splinters. When he looked again the man was dead.

The boom was sweeping towards them now, and he could identify the various figures, the reckless way they stood to fire at the oncoming steamship.

Austad was not even weaving his helm, and Blackwood saw that he had two men on the wheel, while he himself leaned against the binnacle, his long-barrelled Colt levelled towards the shore.

Blackwood watched the barrier rushing towards them and wondered briefly if anyone would ever hear about this day if the worst should happen. His parents, young Jonathan; it might even have some effect on Ralf.

'Stand by to ram!'

The telegraph jangled as Austad cut down the speed. Surely he must have served in the navy, his own country's or somebody else's. He was taking his battered command straight for the boom with all the dash of a torpedo boat destroyer.

Still the Boxers made no attempt to withdraw. Blackwood peered at one of them across the backsight of his revolver and waited for the collision. Maybe that was their only weakness. So fanatical and without fear that they could not recognize the courage of others. The impact was worse than he had expected. The bows seemed to rear right up, as if the hull had broken its back. Men were flung about like dolls, while the remnants of the charred mast plunged amongst them in pieces.

The paddles churned and frothed, forging ahead, catching and grinding at underwater fragments, now barely under control.

Blackwood saw the great pile of blackened timber and splintered fishing boats where the sampan had exploded. The whole boom was bending and lurching under the vessel's iron stem and he saw several Boxers leaping towards the bulwarks, some dropping, others clambering on to the deck to fall and die under the waiting bayonets.

'Take aim! *Fire!*' The rifles cracked out in a ragged volley, cutting down some of the nearest attackers, driving back others from the bows, each bullet aimed with care and desperation.

Blackwood shouted, 'To me, Marines!' Together they charged aft as faces appeared above the bulwark, some within inches of the thrashing paddle-blades.

Blackwood fired his revolver and then drew his sword as feet pounded on the stained planking and a knot of boarders rushed towards him. The hiss and clang of steel as sword met bayonet, the curses and yells of his men matched against the Boxers' blood-chilling screams blotted out all else. Beneath his feet Blackwood felt the deck jerking and sagging as Austad tried to hold her bows-on to the boom. But they were not forging ahead, and he heard one of the paddles grating and ripping at the piled logs like a fractured saw.

'Hold them!' Blackwood drove his blade through one of them, and heard him shriek as Swan, his magazine empty, finished him with his bayonet. But shoulder to shoulder the marines were falling back, pressed together in a tight group as more and more figures clambered over the rails, hampered only by their leaders with their glittering, deadly swords.

Lyde gasped, 'Can't-do-it, sir!' He fired point-blank into a Boxer's face and then lunged at another with his already reddened bayonet. Blackwood was dimly aware that one of the helmsmen was down, his head split open by a single blow, and that Austad, bleeding from a great slash on his cheek, was bellowing like a wild bull, his empty Colt rising and falling like a club.

A sword clattered by his feet and Swan shouted, 'Not this time, Johnnie!' Then he brought down his rifle-butt on the man's neck. His companions, wild-eyed and baring their teeth, stamped over the fallen man in their efforts to hold their advantage and hack down wounded and stragglers alike.

Blackwood felt the deck give one great lurch and saw the nearest barrier of sharpened bamboo stakes begin to fall aside. He heard some of his men cheering like demons, their strength renewed as the boom began to give way under the stem.

They were going through.

Blackwood caught a brief glimpse of a figure framed against the sun and realized he was taking aim. He felt the wind of the bullet and heard it hit the deckhouse beside him. It all took less than a second and he heard himself sob with agony as something like splinters cut into his eye, blinding him instantly. He was aware only that his men were cheering, that screams and splashes told him that most of the boarders were gone. He reeled about, his sense of position gone as the pain left him blinded and gasping. A shadow passed over his face and he heard Swan yell, 'Watch out, sir!'

Something struck him across the neck. He was barely aware that he was falling, or which way he was facing. Perhaps his head had been struck off like Earle's and there was merely a flash of understanding before the darkness came.

And yet he was conscious of a new voice rallying his victorious marines. Clipped and decisive. It was Bannatyre who had found strength through his fear. The hardest kind to discover.

He felt an arm under his shoulder, a shadow across him as the sun was extinguished. Then he seemed to be falling from a great height and tried to tense his limbs against the impact.

But instead there was oblivion.

When Blackwood eventually tried to open his eyes he found nothing but darkness. As his senses reluctantly returned he became aware that there was a cool bandage across his left eye, and that the other one pricked and smarted when he tried to focus it. The deck still swayed, but there was no feeling of movement. The paddles were stilled and for a moment more he imagined they were aground, that the enemy had somehow boarded and seized the ship.

He groped blindly for his holster but it had gone. So too had his tunic, and as his fingers moved across his ribs he felt another bandage although he could not remember being wounded there. In fact the pain in his skull was so intense he could barely think at all. And yet in spite of it his memory was returning. In his mind he could hear the fury of the battle, see the wild eyes, the flash of steel.

He made to move, but the pain held him motionless. Then he heard some empty cartridge cases rolling unheeded on the deck and knew the *Bajamar* was at anchor somewhere. He reached out gingerly and touched the bulkhead. It was cool, the heat of the day had gone. Or had it been more than one day? He felt something like despair while he strained his ears and fought to hold back the terrible throb in his head and neck.

He heard someone cry out. Just one short sound. It was close by, but separated by the bulkhead.

Blackwood moved his head on one side and tried not to catch the bandage on his eye. He was in a bunk and from the faint scent of perfume he knew it was hers.

Where the hell was Swan? He had to know what was happening. He would be needed. But when he tried to call out all he heard was a groan. There was an immediate response and he felt her come out of the darkness and sit beside him on the bunk.

'Rest easy, Captain.'

He felt her hand on his shoulder, her fingers gentle.

She said, 'We are safe. Thanks to you.' Her fingers reached the scar on his shoulder, the one he hated so much. They rested there, soothing him, holding him like someone under a spell.

'My – my men . . .'

The fingers did not move and he could sense that she was sharing his pain.

'Ten wounded.' Again the slight hesitation. 'Five dead.'

'God.' He lay back and peered at the darkness. 'My eyes.'

'You were fortunate. But you must rest.'

Her hand caressed the scar as if she was thinking of something else. Even her voice seemed far away.

'Did you take care of me?'

'Of course. I think your Mr Fox was unwilling to let me attend all the wounded.' He felt her give a little shrug. 'Besides, I wanted to.'

'But – but . . .' He could not form his words. She had undressed him. Washed and tended his injuries.

She said in the same quiet tone, 'Do not worry so much. Would you prefer that I stayed away? Hidden out of danger while you fought for me and nearly died because of it? Is that what you wanted?'

'You know it's not that.' She had stayed with him. Watched over him.

Blackwood struggled on to his elbow, aware of her closeness in spite of the pain, the turmoil in his mind.

'I have to get up. Must, go to them – ' He tried again. 'Could you send someone for Swan, please?' He knew he was pleading, but he had to make her understand.

But she did not argue and Blackwood heard her speaking quietly to her maid outside the door.

She returned and said, 'Close your eyes. I am going to light a lamp.' She stood between him and the small lamp and watched him without speaking as he opened his sound eye and blinked at the cabin. He could see shot and splinter holes in the side, and there were spots of blood on her clothes, his own or one of the wounded's, he did not know.

He peered down at his nakedness. 'Must look a mess.' It was all he could find to say.

Swan entered the cabin, his eyes moving swiftly between them, questioning and understanding.

'Sir?'

'I need to get up.'

Swan regarded him doubtfully. 'You took a real whack on the neck with a pike-'andle, sir. If it 'ad bin a blade – ' He did not finish.

She said, 'If you must, Captain.' She took his tunic from a chair and gently eased one of his arms into it. 'Now the other one.' He winced as the pain shot through him again, but he was very aware of her hair against his face, her breath on his skin.

'Now.' She looked at him gravely. 'Off we go.'

With Swan on one side and the countess on the other Blackwood staggered towards the door.

He gasped, 'Swan, boots and belt.'

Swan sighed. The captain would kill himself if he went on like this, but he knew he would never change, nor would he want him to.

She buttoned his tunic, her eyes averted from his as she said, 'Let me come.'

Swan thrust the door aside and clinging together they moved very slowly towards the saloon. There were several shaded lamps burning here, and the smell of blood and pain.

Those who were not asleep or too faint to care turned towards the trio in the entrance, their eyes flickering in the lamplight.

Blackwood saw it all. Pride, hostility perhaps towards her for throwing them at risk, and something more. They had survived. The victors.

Blackwood moved painfully along the saloon and felt her hand on his back. Somehow his tunic had caught on his belt and he could feel her fingers pressed into his skin like small extensions of her own emotion.

Fox loomed out of the shadows. 'You shouldn't be 'ere, sir.' But from his tone Blackwood knew he had done the right thing.

He paused and looked down at Sergeant Kirby. Even in the poor light he looked old and pale.

Fox said shortly, ''E'll live if we can get 'im to a surgeon in time.' He looked at the countess. 'She done wonders with 'im, sir.' He gave a rare smile. 'With you too, if you don't mind me sayin' so.'

Blackwood felt her fingers biting into his skin as a man cried out and another marine knelt down beside him with a water flask. He knew that some of the sentries were peering through the ports to see what was happening, and could smell the strong aroma of Austad's tobacco. He was glad the Norwegian had survived.

Blackwood said, 'I just want to tell you – ' He hesitated and looked at the deck. Tell them what? They knew well enough what they had achieved. What it had cost them. And this was just a beginning. He tried again. 'I am proud of all of you, grateful that I was given the honour to be with you.' He felt emotion in his unbandaged eye as he remembered the dying marine who had stared up at him. *Why me?* his eyes had asked. Of Corporal O'Neil who had staggered on deck again to fight in spite of everything. Not least of Kirby, so bitter, and yet too much of a marine not to volunteer. Of them all.

'Soon we shall be back aboard ship to await orders. Some of us will be parted.' Her hand stopped moving and lay flat on his spine. As if it, and not she, was listening to the meaning of his words.

Blackwood lifted his chin as he had seen his father do so many times when he had relived one of his experiences aboard ship or in some godforsaken battlefield. How right was the Corps's motto, he thought. *Per Mare, Per Terram.* Do anything, go anywhere. You were never supposed to ask questions.

'And some will never return.' He swayed and might have fallen but for Swan's powerful grip. 'But we shall not forget them. It is not our way.'

He turned with his supports to the door and saw Lieutenant Bannatyre smiling at him, his arms folded as if he hadn't a care in the world.

A voice came from the darkness, 'Good old Blackie, eh lads!' It had to be O'Neil. Nothing could disguise that brogue.

Outside the saloon the three of them stood by the

guardrails and stared abeam. There was no moon, and it was too dark to see how far out Austad had decided to anchor. But Blackwood could smell the land, and feel the power of the swell under the old keel which had somehow carried them to safety.

She said, 'You love those men, don't you?'

He looked at her and then slowly raised his arm around her shoulder. 'I'd never thought of it like that. I just did not know what to say. How to explain.'

He felt her shiver and her fingers bunch tightly against his back. He knew she was crying. Perhaps for all of them.

They returned to the cabin in silence, the ship rolling and creaking around them as if in a restless sleep after her moment of glory. Swan sat him on the bunk, removed his boots but stood aside as she said, 'Thank you, Herr Swan. I can do what is necessary.'

The door closed and Blackwood allowed her to remove his tunic and cradle his shoulders as he lay back on the bunk.

'You sleep now.' She watched him sadly, her cheek marked with tears. 'Tomorrow, who knows?'

He reached out and took her hand. 'I wish – ' Her hand moved in his grasp. In a moment she would pull away.

He persisted, 'If only – '

She grasped his hand in hers and without taking her gaze from his face pressed it beneath her breast and held it there.

'Do you think, my dear David, I am made of ice? That is my heart you can feel.'

He felt her breast against his fingers, the pressure as she leaned over him and kissed him. Not as a countess, but as a young girl.

She stood up, her face flushed, her calm momentarily gone. She said quietly, '*If only*, you said. What words, David. What might have been.'

She reached out suddenly and extinguished the lamp. 'I shall be near if you need me.' Then the door closed behind her.

He stared at the darkness again. She had called him by

name. Even the pain seemed less, the sting in his eyes of no importance. He thought of the way she had looked, the pressure of her breast against his hand.

He was still thinking of her when complete exhaustion carried him into a deep sleep.

9

Divided Loyalty

Captain Vere Masterman watched impassively as *Mediator*'s surgeon completed his examination. Only the fingers of his left hand which plucked at his white drill uniform gave any hint of his impatience and mounting irritation.

Eventually he could stand it no longer.

'Well, Doc, what's the verdict?'

The surgeon straightened his back and wound his hands together as if he was washing them.

'The eyes are excellent, sir. The blow on his head might be described as a serious concussion. There could be some trouble from it unless Captain Blackwood is allowed to rest, or at least undertake light duties.'

Blackwood sat on the edge of the bunk and controlled the desire to laugh. They were discussing him as if he were somewhere else, or did not really exist. Through the door of the sickbay he could see the gently swaying cots, everything spotless, glaring white.

He recalled his return to the *Mediator*, the unreality of it, the tremendous relief hitting him for the first time when he realized he had never expected to see the cruiser again. The poor little *Bajamar* had only just managed it. Even with Austad's skill, his threats and his pleas, they had still had to burn everything movable to get them here to Taku. It had been dusk and the evening air had been torn apart by the wild cheering which had greeted the listing paddle-steamer's arrival.

Now in the cool, ordered world of *Mediator*'s sickbay it

was impossible to accept what they had done. Even the anchorage was a surprise. He had expected to see *Mediator's* sleek outline, perhaps even a few support ships, but instead there seemed to be a whole fleet. Not just British either. German, Russian, Japanese and American, the vessels ranged from ponderous battleships to low, black-hulled torpedo boat destroyers.

Blackwood touched his head and felt both pairs of eyes turn towards him. If he was not careful he might be sent home to England. He thought of the past few days as the *Bajamar* had puffed and pounded her way north and around the Shantung Peninsula and into the vast Gulf of Chihli, to here off the Peiho River. Friedrike had rarely left his side. She had bathed his injured eye, changed his bandages, and refused to permit even Swan to take care of him. Now it was over and she was somewhere across the anchorage in the German cruiser which had been promised by the official called Westphal in Shanghai. He sighed. A million years ago.

The door slid shut and Masterman said abruptly, 'He's like an old woman.' He smiled, and Blackwood guessed that he probably knew that the surgeon was still listening outside the door. Masterman added, 'I am very glad to have you back aboard, although for how long – '

Blackwood struggled into his white tunic. 'I'm feeling much better, sir.'

Masterman continued wryly, 'I would not release you anyway. We are going to need experienced officers more than ever.' He sounded angry. 'I hate politicians. They seem to believe that a show of force is all that is needed to quell this uprising.' He snorted. 'Uprising? We'll have a full-scale bloody war on our hands if we're not careful!'

Blackwood stood up and glanced through the gleaming scuttle. Concussion, the surgeon had said. He could certainly feel the ache. Like blood pounding. He would have to be careful. He had known of a young lieutenant who had never recovered from a blow on the head. It had made him forgetful, only half aware of what was happening.

'What is the position, sir?'

Masterman shrugged. 'We and our allies have sent more troops by rail to Peking to protect the legations. They are getting very little aid from the Chinese government. Only these damned Boxers seem to have any power. Several outlying missions have been attacked, clergymen and nuns brutally treated. It must be stopped.' He studied Blackwood's grave features. 'It will be stopped. By the way, your new commanding officer has joined us. That chap Blair from Hong Kong.'

'Major Blair?'

Masterman was already thinking of something else. 'Lieutenant Colonel Blair now. That gives you some idea of the urgency. Damned politicians!'

There was a nervous tap at the door and a small midshipman peered at his captain with something like terror.

'Well, boy?' Masterman glared down at him from his great height.

'Th-the Commander sends his respects, sir, and would you repair on board the *Centurion*.'

'Hmm. Call away the pinnace.'

Blackwood pricked up his ears. *Centurion* was a battleship. It was that important.

Masterman saw his expression and nodded. 'Our lord and master, Sir Edward Seymour, is come amongst us.' He snorted again. 'Any captain worth his salt should be able to manage this affair.' Surprisingly he laughed. 'Of course, I won't take that view when *I'm* an admiral, eh?'

Muffled by steel and distance Blackwood heard a boatswain's mate bellow, 'Afternoon watchmen and relief boats' crews to dinner!'

A new anchorage, the very real chance of a war, but nothing changed the Royal Navy.

Masterman said over his shoulder, 'You may return to general duties as far as I'm concerned.' He looked round and added, 'Sorry you had to go through all that other business. You lost some good fellows by all accounts.'

It was the nearest Masterman would ever get to actual praise.

Swan flitted through the door within seconds of the captain's departure. 'I've got your cabin all sorted out, sir.' He bustled about, picking up odd garments and Blackwood's field-service cap, his eyes everywhere. 'You 'eard about 'Tenant Colonel Blair, sir?'

'Yes.' It would be good to see him again, although how Blair would like this sort of situation was something else. 'I'll report to him right away.'

Swan watched him rise to his feet, the way he waited to accustom himself to the gentle roll. This was more like it, he thought.

Swan replied, 'I'm afraid 'e's gone over to *Centurion* too, sir. All captains and senior officers from other ships to repair on board.'

Swan thought of the excitement their return had caused. Slaps on the back, more grog than any man could carry, and the whole ship was still buzzing with what they had done upriver. The German countess put just the right touch to the story, he thought. The beautiful woman in distress, rescued by the gallant Royals. It would read well if it ever reached the papers in Portsmouth.

She was probably over there with Admiral Seymour. Even that made him chuckle. He would never show disrespect for an officer in front of Captain Blackwood, not a senior one anyway, but he knew that right through fleet Admiral Seymour was nicknamed 'See-no-More'.

Blackwood walked slowly through the sickbay, glancing at the various faces as he passed. Most of them were sailors of the ship's company but in the end cots he found familiar ones, some of his own marines who were recovering from their injuries. He paused by one.

'Hello, Erskine, how are you feeling?' God, he thought, he looked such a boy, it was impossible to see him with rifle

and fixed bayonet when they had rammed the boom across
the Hoshun. He had been badly wounded in the foot and
Swan had brought him the news that *Mediator*'s surgeon had
amputated it to save his life. Private Erskine peered at him
seemingly without recognition. He was drugged but
probably still in great pain.

Then he shaded his eyes and said, 'Why did 'e do it, sir?'

Swan tried to move him away but Blackwood was
bending over the boy as he whispered, 'I'd rather be dead
than like this. I'll be like them others we used to see hangin''
around the gates at Forton Barracks.' He turned his face
away and said, 'I – I'm sorry, sir, it worn't your fault.' He
was sobbing uncontrollably.

Blackwood looked at the other. Sergeant Kirby, pale and
tight-lipped, refusing to die. Private Farley who had been
the first to be cut down. Now he was trying to play cards
with an injured seaman, his arm in a sling. But he was over
the worst. He would soon be back with his pals, cursing
Fox, and chasing the girls ashore.

Blackwood knew all about Erskine. His father had been
in the Corps, but had been drowned seven years ago when
his ship the *Victoria* had been accidentally rammed and sunk
by the *Camperdown* while on manoeuvres in the Mediterranean. Not only Erskine's father had been killed that day.
Victoria had been the flagship of Vice-Admiral Sir George
Tryon. The admiral and over three hundred others had died
because of a stupid miscalculation.

Erskine was the last Royal Marine in the family. Now he
was a cripple for the rest of his life.

Why did he do it? he had asked. There was no answer.
Men had been asking the same question since the Battle of
Hastings.

He touched the boy's shoulder. 'I'll do what I can.'

Swan followed his captain and wondered why he always
became so caught up with their affairs. It was the job. You
always thought it couldn't happen to you anyway. He
shrugged. But if it did, that was it.

Instead of going to the privacy of his cabin Blackwood went on deck, almost blinded by the sun despite the taut awnings above the after guns.

It was more like a fleet review than a preparation for war. He recognized several of the ships at anchor. Like the Corps the Navy was also a family. Ships came and went, old and new, happy ones and those which bred trouble like fever.

'You are looking so much better, sir.'

Blackwood turned and responded to his cousin's salute. Ralf looked wary, as if he expected to be criticized. To Blackwood he was one of the vague faces who had come and gone to visit him in the sick-quarters. The passage to Taku in the little paddle-steamer, to say nothing of the battle, had taken more out of him than he had realized. Even as he returned Ralf's salute he felt the sore tightness across his ribs. The wound he had not even felt in the heat of the fighting. Ralf looked pale. Perhaps he was the sort who never got sunburned.

'It's good to be back.' Was it? He remembered her replacing that dressing within hours of their arrival here. Her hands had been cool against his skin, her eyes downcast to avoid his gaze. He had watched his own hand as if it had belonged to someone else. A stranger. He had touched her shoulder, and as she had worked deftly with the bandage she had bent her head to rest her cheek on his wrist, still without looking at him.

Blackwood had heard some of the *Bajamar*'s crew shouting. They had sighted smoke. Help was close. It would soon all be finished.

Blackwood had raised her chin and had said, 'I love you, Friedrike. You know that – '

She had tried to smile. 'I adore your funny accent. The way you speak my name.' But instead of a smile only tears had come. They hugged each other, murmuring words that neither heard, holding, then touching with a boldness made from desperation.

She had forced herself away, her breasts rising and

falling, her eyes wanting him and yet holding him away.

'Please, David! Please help me! You know I cannot, *must* not!'

He had climbed from the bunk, the dangling bandage forgotten. 'And I love the way you say *my* name.' They had clung together, and she had kissed him again and again while his hand held her breast.

Blackwood looked past his cousin, the ache disturbing him as he knew it would.

'And I was terribly sorry to hear about Charles Earle.' Ralf was almost pleading. 'It should have been me.'

Blackwood smiled. 'It should not have been anyone.' He thought of the young marine with only one foot. 'Have you settled in now?' He almost said 'at last'.

Ralf shrugged easily, glad to be on safer ground.

'They're not a bad crowd. Some of them thought you weren't going to get back. I soon told them to mind their manners!'

A midshipman, the same one who had faced his captain, shouted to the officer-of-the-day, 'Boat coming from the German cruiser, sir! From SMS *Flensburg*, heading this way, sir!'

The lieutenant, who had been melting in the heat and thinking only of a drink before lunch, gripped his sword and snapped, 'Yes, there was a signal about it. Some important German count is coming to pay his respects or something.' He saw Blackwood and added in a calmer voice, 'Inform the Commander, Mr Lacy, and man the side.' He raised his telescope and then exclaimed loudly, 'And clear those idlers off the upper deck! The countess is aboard!'

Blackwood stared at the smart steam pinnace which was pushing up a moustache of foam as it swung in an arc towards the main gangway. He saw the familiar white ensign with its black cross and eagle streaming from the stern, but his eyes fixed on her, holding the brim of her wide hat as she stared up at the anchored cruiser.

Marines were falling into ranks by the gangway, with

Lieutenant de Courcy and Sergeant Greenaway of the Third Platoon making certain that everything was as it should be to receive foreigners.

Swan said quietly, 'I think you should go below an' change, sir.' He saw the curious glance from the second lieutenant. A snotty little bugger, Blackwood or not, Swan decided. It was like talking to a stone wall. His captain did not even hear him.

De Courcy drew his sword with a flourish. 'Royal Marines – '

Blackwood saw them tense, their white gloves gripping their rifles. A few paces inboard from the ship's brass nameplate Commander Wilberforce tipped his hat over his eyes, and dabbed his mouth with the back of his hand.

'Present – *arms!*'

Count Manfred von Heiser stood with his hat in his hand as the small marine band crashed out their version of 'Deutschland über Alles', while the guard of honour, bayonets at the present, and eyes fixed on some far-off point, waited for the din to cease.

Commander Wilberforce said, 'You do us a great honour, Count von Heiser. I regret that the Captain is aboard the flagship and he sends his apology.' He bowed slightly. 'We have of course had the additional honour of carrying the Countess as a passenger.'

The count was a big man, tall and straight-backed like Masterman. It was not difficult to picture him in uniform before he became a respected diplomat.

Blackwood watched and then heard the count reply. He had a deep voice, clear and not at all guttural. Powerful, like the man.

'We all have our duties, Commander. Now, perhaps more than ever.'

Blackwood saw her move slightly away from her husband so that he might see her. Beside him she looked like a very young girl playing a role. She had told Blackwood her husband was forty. He looked a lot older.

Blackwood tried not to think of him holding her, caressing her, wanting an heir. And he could tell from her eyes that she knew it was what he would be thinking.

'I cannot begin to thank you for all you have done, Commander. When I heard what had happened I believed that nothing could save the Countess. I will not waste your time or mine by making speeches. The purpose of my visit is to meet the officer responsible if that is possible?'

Blackwood saw the pain on her face. Perhaps he had brought her here to prove that nothing could ever alter.

'Of course, Count von Heiser.' Wilberforce glanced at a lieutenant and snapped his gloved fingers. 'My compliments to Captain Blackwood, and – '

Blackwood stepped forward and moved hesitatingly towards them. Several tiny images flashed across his mind. Lieutenant de Courcy's eyes filled with horror at the sight of his company commander, hatless and without his proper uniform. Sergeant Greenaway, sucking in his cheeks, but still able to remain motionless beside his men, and as for Wilberforce he seemed to have lost his usual urbane calm.

'So *this* is the man.' Von Heiser gripped his hand, his deep-set eyes exploring Blackwood's face as he continued, 'Blackwood. Victoria Cross. Now I understand.'

He stood aside as she held up her hand to Blackwood. She touched his so lightly with her gloved fingers he could barely feel it.

Blackwood kissed it and it was instantly withdrawn.

Wilberforce said rather too loudly, 'Well, now, we can go aft and take some sherry perhaps.'

Blackwood followed the others like a man in a trance. It would have been better never to see her again. Even as he watched her shoulders as she walked into the shadows of the quartermaster's lobby, he knew it was a lie.

They stood around in Masterman's day cabin like unrehearsed actors. The count's presence amongst them had brought an unnatural stiffness which only made things harder. As the stewards moved around with their trays of sherry Blackwood guessed that the other officers present already had a good idea of what was happening. *Mediator*'s own major of marines was here, two or three of the ship's lieutenants and a German officer who had accompanied Von Heiser as his escort.

Von Heiser studied Blackwood and raised his glass in salute. In his powerful hand it looked like a thimble.

'It was pointless to maintain the Hoshun trade mission. The river is too shallow for anything but local craft, and the roads are little better than goat-tracks.' He glanced at his wife. 'So if the Boxers intended to put pressure on my government by capturing the Countess as a hostage it was all to no purpose. Naturally I regret that her sister died in such terrible circumstances.'

It sounded like a carefully prepared speech, Blackwood thought, no matter what the count had said earlier.

He asked, 'What will you do now, sir?' He felt her watching him. It was all he could manage not to return her gaze.

'Proceed as arranged.' Von Heiser sounded mildly surprised at the question. 'Tomorrow we shall start our journey to Peking. By river to begin with, and then by train. The railway is quite safe, and I am assured by Baron von Ketteler in our Peking legation that more soldiers and marines are arriving to protect them. So you see, Captain Blackwood, there is nothing to fear.'

Blackwood stared at him. He knew from the sudden silence that the others were listening.

'I cannot agree, sir. The Boxers are united against all foreigners. There have been several confirmed reports of – '

Von Heiser smiled gently. 'You are a brave man. But you must leave diplomacy to others more experienced.'

The German officer glanced at the bulkhead clock and murmured something across Von Heiser's shoulder.

The count nodded. 'I must leave now.' He turned away to speak with Wilberforce and Blackwood whispered, 'You must not go with him! It is terribly dangerous.'

She flushed. 'Would you have me run away? I have possessions in Peking, and there are also those of my dead sister — ' She faltered and he saw her lip tremble. Although her husband had his back towards them he could sense that he was listening.

Blackwood exclaimed bitterly, 'It is wrong. A new uprising could sweep China from end to end. I may not be a diplomat, but I have seen good men die because of *their* complacency!'

Wilberforce shot him a warning glance but Blackwood could not stop. His head was aching badly, and he knew that he was saying all the wrong things.

She said insistently, 'I have to go, Captain.'

Blackwood could feel the gulf opening between them. What a fool he had been. She at least had tried to warn him. Now the moment was past.

They filed from the cabin, and *Mediator*'s gunnery officer glanced at his watch. 'Time to eat, thank God.' To Blackwood he whispered, 'Steady on, Soldier. It's not worth it.'

Blackwood swung away, blind to everything but his sense of loss. 'What the bloody hell d'you know about it!'

The gunnery officer watched him leave and then said to his companion, 'Well, well. More to him than meets the eye.'

On deck Blackwood stood in the shadows as the pinnace steamed away towards the German cruiser.

Wilberforce strode past and muttered, 'You can thank your lucky stars that I was here and not the Old Man. He'd have roasted you alive!' He paused and looked abeam at the fast-moving boat. 'All the same, I can't say I blame you.'

Swan appeared as if by magic.

God, the captain was taking it bad. Worse than he had ever seen before. Swan waited, gauging the moment. Then as Blackwood turned towards a companionway he said, 'I got somethin' for you, sir.' He held out a small velvet pouch no bigger than a badge. Blackwood opened it and then held the locket in his hand. It contained a perfect miniature of Friedrike, even the hair was exactly as it had been just now in the cabin.

Swan said nothing. It was not the right time. But Swan knew that the locket must have cost a fortune. It was not the kind of thing you handed out as a souvenir.

Blackwood replaced the locket in its velvet pouch and put it carefully in his pocket.

It was not over after all.

Lieutenant Colonel James Blair ran his eyes over a list of names and duties and remarked, 'You've done a good piece of work with your new company, David.' He glanced up from his desk and asked, 'Something wrong, old chap?'

Blackwood tore his eyes from the anchorage and the motionless warships which rested on their reflections like models. In spite of the deckhead fans he could feel the sweltering heat, the sense of apprehension in the ships as they and their companies waited, and waited.

It was a week since the Germans had left for Peking. They had been well supported by troops from several nations and a signal had been received that everyone had arrived safely and unmolested. It had all been too easy.

He replied, 'I wish we could be doing something, sir, and not just swinging round the anchor day after day.'

Blair said, 'It was bad luck about young Earle.' He did not seem to hear what Blackwood had said. As if half of his mind was elsewhere. 'Your Sergeant Kirby must be a strong character. The surgeon tells me he'll be able to walk before much longer.'

Blackwood looked away. In a way it was a miracle. The heavy, old-fashioned bullet which had smashed Kirby down had been deflected by the sampan's gunwale. But for that he would be back there still.

It was maddening the way that the ships were kept in the dark about the true situation ashore. It was said that the various legations, and especially Sir Claude MacDonald, the British minister in Peking, had tried to parley with the Chinese official government without success. But that was all they knew. One ominous note had been the arrival on board *Mediator* of several crates of the new long Lee-Enfield rifles for the marines, and some Nordenfeldt machine guns mounted on wheeled carriages which could only be used ashore.

It was evident that the Boxers were daily getting bolder. Masterman had received some news of a massacre of some seventy Chinese Christians only sixty miles from Peking itself and several savage attacks on foreign properties along the railway line, the last link with the capital.

As if from miles away Blackwood heard Fox drilling a detachment with their newly issued Lee-Enfields. It was a sign that perhaps at long last they were catching up with the army. It was always said by old Royal Marines that the Corps was five years behind the regular army in almost everything from weapons to uniforms. Maybe the necessity of the moment was about to speed the changes.

There was a polite tap at the door and Lieutenant Gravatt, the acting adjutant, stepped into the cabin and handed a piece of paper to the colonel.

Blair read the message slowly. Then he said, 'The Boxers have struck at Peking. They've burned the Racecourse down and sacked all the buildings around it. Our minister, Sir Claude MacDonald, has requested that a strong force of Marines and Bluejackets be sent immediately as reinforcements for the legations.' He looked up sharply. 'When did this signal arrive, Toby?'

'Yesterday, sir.'

'And nothing since?'

Gravatt glanced at Blackwood. 'The telegraph line from Peking has been cut. They're completely on their own.'

Blackwood bit his lip. It was worse even than he had expected.

Blair smoothed out the signal pad, his voice far away as

he said, 'Admiral Seymour will have to send a relief column right away. It'll be very difficult especially if the Boxers have torn up the railway.'

A seaman stood in the open doorway. 'Cap'n Masterman sends 'is compliments, sir. All senior officers to repair on board th' flagship immediately.'

Blair touched his neat moustache with one knuckle.

'It's started, David.' He groped for his cap. 'The bloody fools. They should have listened. Now it will be strength to meet strength. If only they'd *listened!*'

Blackwood wondered momentarily whom he meant by 'they'. The Chinese or the foreigners in their land? He remembered what they had said about Blair's Chinese mistress in Hong Kong and guessed the answer.

They left the small office and walked out into the passageway where some barefooted seamen were polishing the brass handrails.

Blackwood reached up unconsciously and touched the blue ribbon on his chest and remembered the way she had spoken of him to Masterman. How she had demanded his escort upriver.

Was there no end of it for her? He recalled her husband's stern features, the adamant way he had stated his reasons for returning to Peking. Blackwood clenched his fist. Well, he had been wrong about that too, and had put Friedrike directly into the line of fire.

Sergeant Major Fox brought the sweating marines to attention as they walked past to the main gangway. He watched Blackwood's face and understood. He did not need telling. These new rifles had come along at just the right moment.

Later, when the senior officers of the various ships and detachments were assembled in the flagship's spacious wardroom, Admiral Sir Edward Seymour came straight to the point.

'I have received an urgent request from our minister in Peking for us to advance on Peking with reinforcements.'

He was a mildly spoken man with a neat beard who appeared to be completely untroubled by the swift change of events.

The admiral continued, 'I intend to leave for Tientsin tomorrow at dawn and secure several special trains for a force of Royal Marines and Bluejackets. Certain other nations are sending their own support. Overall it will consist of some two thousand men. We shall be in Peking by the end of the day.'

Blackwood darted a quick glance at Blair but the colonel still had the same distant look. Surely Seymour's casual reference was a mistake? It was a hundred miles from Tientsin to Peking through country which was known to be patrolled by parties of Boxers who might even have torn up some of the railway track.

Blackwood had also heard that the Chinese Imperial Army was somewhere between Peking and the sea. When the cards were down it was likely that their general would throw in his hand with the Boxers, especially if he wished to retain the Dowager Empress's favour. She was openly opposed to any further negotiations with the foreigners and although some of her governors were against her alliance she remained firm.

'That is all, gentlemen.' The admiral gave a bleak smile. 'The Royal Marines will be the first to land. As usual.' That brought a few laughs as he had known it would.

Chairs scraped, aides picked up their maps and notebooks and they flowed out into the waiting sunshine to look for their boats.

Blackwood said, 'It's a very tall order, sir.'

Blair shrugged. 'We shall soon know, old chap. *We* are to lead.' He studied Blackwood for the first time since they had boarded the flagship.

'I seem to recall that when you were in Hong Kong you told me that this appointment meant little more than wiping carriage seats for the ladies of our legation, what? It's turning out to be somewhat more complicated, I'd have thought!' He laughed and looked about ten years younger.

Together they joined Captain Masterman by the gangway as the *Mediator*'s boat hooked on to receive them.

Masterman said almost to himself, 'Peking tomorrow, Colonel? That will be *the* day!'

10

No Pity

David Blackwood with Lieutenant Gravatt beside him walked slowly along the side of the railway track. It was a strange sensation, he thought, almost like a school outing. Gone was the apprehension and uncertainty. They had come ashore, ready if ordered to fight, but instead to find something of an anti-climax.

All the way to Tientsin the Royal Marines and Bluejackets had kept good marching distances between each unit, but most of the villages had appeared abandoned, some even derelict, and in the outskirts of the old city itself there had been more Chinese troops in evidence than civilians. Perhaps Von Heiser had been right to scoff at his concern after all.

The railway station to which his special detachment had marched was deserted but for a solitary train. It consisted of a squat, powerful-looking engine, which Private Kempster was quick to point out had been built in his home-town of Leeds.

The engine was to be preceded by a flat car protected by boiler plates, sandbags and heavy timber. This leading car carried a Nordenfeldt machine-gun and Blackwood saw Corporal O'Neil grin down at him as if it was a huge joke. He showed no sign of his ordeal whatsoever. Blackwood recalled his shout, *Good old Blackie.* He had never considered that he had a nickname, even such a mild one.

Gravatt said, 'I've detailed a section of marines for that truck, sir. It'll be a bit unhealthy if we get ambushed.' He dropped his eyes and flushed. 'I – I'm sorry, sir. I forgot.'

Blackwood shook his head. 'Not your fault.' The train's crude defences were typical of those used in Egypt and South Africa. Like the ones Neil had mentioned in his last letter.

Blackwood lifted his chin and walked further along the train. The driver and fireman were obviously Irish. O'Neil would feel quite at home in the vanguard of their advance.

The coaches behind the engine were for the rest of the detachment, some Bluejackets who would handle the two light field-pieces, and lastly another freight car with rails, ties and tools for making repairs to any damaged sections of the track. The rest of the company waited in the shadow of a sloping roof beside the train, leaning on their rifles, chatting and passing the time with some German sailors from the *Flensburg* who would be taking another train later on.

Blackwood touched his forehead and knew it was irritation which had roused his concussion again.

In spite of everything that had happened Seymour's flag-lieutenant had passed a message to Blair about the state and presentation of this company. 'They are amongst the forces of other foreign governments. The Royal Marines, no matter what might lie ahead, have to be properly turned out in their scarlet kerseys and blue trousers instead of their already crumpled whites.'

Blair had listened to Blackwood's protests and had agreed that as his detachment was to lead he must retain the choice. White uniforms could be boiled in tea if necessary. They had soon discovered that trick when fighting the Boers. Scarlet made a perfect target.

Seymour had apparently accepted this but had snapped back through his aide that the marines would take their proper uniforms with them anyway, so that when they marched through the gates of Peking there could not be a word of criticism aimed at them or their commander.

It was ridiculous, Blackwood thought. Like Seymour's

insistence that the trip would be over by nightfall. For the same reason he had ordered that only three days' rations would be carried.

As Fox had hinted darkly, ''E must 'ave better information than us, sir.'

It had been almost sad to leave the *Mediator*. Masterman's company had made all the extra marines welcome and comfortable in spite of the overcrowding between deck.

As they had been ferried ashore Austad's little *Bajamar* had given a final salute on her siren. She was returning to safer waters and her old habits, but Blackwood doubted if things would ever seem quite the same again for the big Norwegian and his crew.

On the way across the blue water Blackwood had watched the crouching forts which protected the entrance to the Peiho River. Through his powerful binoculars, a present from his mother before he had left England, Blackwood had studied the forts with great care. It was hard to tell where the Taku forts ended and the land began. Ageless. But they could hold back an armada if they fell into the wrong hands.

'Colonel's coming, sir.'

That was Swan, always close by when you needed him. He had already been aboard the train and had doubtless selected a place in the leading compartment for Blackwood and his capacious bag in which he usually carried some whisky for emergencies.

Blair returned their salutes and regarded the train without much enthusiasm.

'Some bloody command, eh?'

Blackwood stared. 'Are you coming with us, sir?'

'Well of course I am, dammit!' He glared along the track towards the sea as if he expected to recognize the admiral amongst the milling troops and sailors.

'I'd not leave it to these – ' he sought for a suitable word, ' – bloody amateurs!'

Blackwood smiled. 'I've brought the two student interpreters we found at the mission, sir. They might try to run, but they'd be invaluable if we meet with an argument.'

Blair nodded. 'Good thinking. Tell them – ' He gave a sad smile. 'No, I shall tell them, that one goes up the front and the other remains in the last carriage with our men. One sign of treachery and I'll blow their heads off! Not that they'll believe it of course.'

He was about to turn away when he added, 'I've detailed Second Lieutenant Blackwood to act as my aide, right? I'll try and keep him out of trouble.'

A runner panted along the track and saluted.

'Signal, sir. Time to move off!'

Blair looked at the engine, shrouded in steam, as if it too was eager to leave.

'Better get them mounted, or whatever you do in a bloody train!' He was desperately worried. You could feel it like a fever.

Blackwood waved to the sergeant major. 'First Platoon!'

Three days' rations, Seymour had decided. It did not seem much. Even when they got to Peking they might find supplies very short. But he would see her again. No matter what she thought, or which way her loyalty directed her, she would know he was there, within call. He found himself smiling as he thought of Hawks Hill, of what his father would say about his lovesick behaviour.

A lot of damned nonsense. A woman is just a woman, boy. Leave it at that. No wonder his mother had aged so noticeably.

It would be high-summer now. The smell of fields and hedgerows, good earth and farmyards. Hampshire.

Blackwood saw Swan swing himself easily into the first compartment, his new rifle already an extension of himself. Did he ever think of home, of the Hampshire they both knew so well?

'Second Platoon?' Fox marched beside the train, his stick at right-angles beneath his arm. He would be missing Sergeant Kirby. They lived only a street apart before they had enlisted. And what of Kirby, still in pain in *Mediator*'s sickbay, but far worse off now that his world had deserted him. Fox paused as someone spoke from one of the windows. It was Private Kempster, telling him about the locomotive.

Fox snarled, '*Leeds?* I thought you all lived in bleedin' caves up there! Now pull yer 'ead inside, man, or they'll be thinkin' it's a cattle truck!'

Ralf Blackwood said quietly, 'I'm glad I'm coming this time, sir.'

Blackwood looked at him and wanted more than anything in the world to like him. Especially now that Neil had gone.

'I am too, Ralf. Keep with the old hands. Don't try to outsmart the NCOs. Most of them have been through it several times.'

'Yes, sir.' Ralf looked up at the leading truck with the machine-gun and jutting rifle muzzles.

O'Neil was standing with his hands on his hips exchanging cheerful insults with the driver and his mate. Ralf tried to hide his contempt. A drunken lout. He had heard Fox telling Gravatt that the Irish corporal was to get his third stripe, a decoration too if he lived through this escapade.

Gravatt had replied seriously, 'A VC I shouldn't wonder. It will look good back at the depot.'

Was that all that mattered to them? He could barely contain his feelings. There was no point to it. He did not belong here. Ralf thought of London, of the girl named Helen. The daughter of a cabinet minister. She understood what he wanted, and taunted him about his family tradition, the Corps, or the Regiment as she called it. Summer balls, bare shoulders and gowns swinging to the orchestra. His stomach contracted. With him overseas she might find someone else. When they had first met her dance-card had always been filled.

Blair snapped, '*Ready*, Mr Blackwood?'

Ralf clambered up the steps, hating Blair for drawing attention to him, for the grins from the marines.

Blackwood watched him and then looked at his colonel. 'Right on the half-hour, sir.' It was strange. The bustle and frantic preparations, and now this station was deserted, all his men and their hopes gathered into carriages like fish in boxes.

Blair still hesitated. 'I expect we shall be too busy to gossip later on, David. I've felt that I can always talk to you.'

Blackwood waited. 'Thank you. Like the day you took it on yourself to tell me about my brother. I appreciated it.'

Blair looked at him searchingly. 'Did you?' He sounded vague. 'Yes, I'm sure.' He turned away so that Blackwood could only see his profile, the neat moustache, a mask for the man behind it.

Blair said, 'I don't have any relatives who count. Not any more. I've left a letter aboard *Mediator* which you can give to a lady in Hong Kong if you would.' His mouth twitched in a smile. 'I'd be grateful.'

Blackwood waited for him to climb aboard. What was there to say? Blackwood was only twenty-seven but he had seen and done enough to know the signs. Blair was old for his rank and he would know too. It was pointless to utter some pretence.

Blackwood hung on the short ladder and waved to the engine driver. The train shuddered and gave a lurch forward as it took the weight of its load.

It was as obvious as a shouted command. Blair was not coming back.

The train rattled along the tracks, the speed held down in case of damage or hidden mines.

Blackwood sat in one corner of the compartment, the window lowered to its full extent to encourage a flow of air. With the sun getting higher above the flat landscape the carriage was already an oven, and he knew they would all have to guard against dozing or falling asleep. *Clack-clack-*

clack-clack, even the wheels on the rails seemed to lull him away from any sort of vigilance.

Occasionally he saw a tiny village or perhaps a farm. Low, yellow buildings almost lost in the heat haze and the train's drifting dust. They always seemed to be a long way from the railway tracks, as if the inhabitants had never really trusted its invasion, another invention of the foreigners.

Private Dago Trent was on the opposite side, his eyes slitted against the glare, his rifle propped on the window ledge. It reminded Blackwood of the youth Erskine who had lost a foot. He and Dago had been friends. The veteran and the wide-eyed recruit. They had been inseparable. Trent was probably thinking of him right now, that he would be better dead than a cripple for all those years to come.

Sergeant Major Fox came through from the rear of the carriage. Blackwood wondered how he always managed to appear neat and tidy no matter what the conditions were like. Even his tunic was whiter than anyone else's.

'All quiet?'

Fox glanced at Blair who was apparently fast asleep, arms folded, his legs thrust out amongst the piled ammunition as if it was the first good rest he had had in weeks.

He replied, 'Corporal Lyde reckons he just spotted some 'orsemen to th' right of us, sir.' He smiled. He had almost said 'starboard'.

Blackwood said, 'Pass the word to the machine-gun section. They might have been some of our people, I suppose.' That was another unsettling thing about the haste of Seymour's actions. There had been no proper information about who was doing what. It was rumoured that the Russians had landed some Cossacks, that the Germans too were to use their cavalry for the relief of Peking. But nobody really knew anything for certain. Corporal Lyde might be a brawler and a natural fighter, but he was a very reliable NCO. If he said he had seen mounted men then there was no doubting him. But if the horsemen stayed out of contact with the slow-moving train it seemed very likely that they were either Chinese regulars or Boxers.

Fox climbed through the little door in the front of the carriage and over a pile of hastily filled sandbags.

Without opening his eyes Blair murmured, 'Boxers. Must be. The whole damned countryside will know we're coming.'

Blackwood grinned. 'Thought you were asleep, sir.'

'Never asleep. Not any more. Getting old. Past it.'

Swan appeared with two steaming mugs. 'Tea, sir.' He saw their surprise. 'One o' th' interpreters 'as brewed up, sir.'

The tea was surprisingly good and refreshing, and once again Blackwood drifted into his thought of Friedrike von Heiser, what she was doing, how she might receive him when they arrived. Her husband would soon suspect something, if he did not already.

Blackwood shook himself. He was deluding himself all over again. The estates in East Prussia, the tradition and the power of the family would not allow such an intrusion. And yet – He touched the locket which hung around his neck, hidden beneath his tunic. Even that made him feel guilty as he glanced quickly at his drowsing companions. Gravatt and de Courcy were too weary to care, but Ralf's eyes were wide open, opaque as he stared through the open window. It must mean something more than a farewell or a paid-off gesture surely?

Blair sat bolt upright. 'Train's slowing down!' He glared at the others. 'Are you all bloody deaf?'

Blackwood leaned out of the window. Here there was a slight curve in the track and he could see the front of the train, the sandbags on the leading car, someone, probably Bannatyre, gesturing with his arm. Blackwood fumbled with his binoculars. Blair's harsh comment had been directed at him also. That made him feel more guilty, as he knew he had earned it.

The train sighed to a halt, steam belching from beneath the engine in a white cloud.

He levelled the binoculars and held his breath. 'The track's been broken, sir.'

Blair grunted testily. 'Didn't imagine we'd stopped to buy souvenirs!'

Blackwood glanced at de Courcy. 'Two sections, Edmund. Tell the others to cover them all the way.' He shaded his eyes. 'At least there's not much shelter. Not enough for an ambush.' He stared beyond the haze to the vague ridge of blue mountains. They never got any nearer. Like the horizon at sea.

Blair said, 'I'm going to take a look. Get the repairs moving. I don't want Admiral Seymour's advance train to catch up with us.' It had obviously become something personal.

Blair strode away from the train, his orderly having to run to keep up with his neat, lithe figure.

Gravatt muttered, 'So much for Peking in a day, sir. I doubt if we've made a good thirty miles.'

Pickets were sent out, rations were served as well as a tot of rum per man to keep up their spirits.

It did not take as long as Blackwood had expected to repair the broken tracks, and much of the credit went to a stoker petty officer from *Mediator*'s engine room. He soon had his working parties sweating back and forth in the boiling heat, laying down rails, and beating them into position.

It was true what they said about sailors, Blackwood thought. They could turn their hands to anything.

In the afternoon the train moved forward again. There was still no sign of an enemy, but all the while Blackwood had the feeling they were being watched by unseen eyes.

Blair unfolded his map and studied it for several minutes as the train clattered unhurriedly through the barren countryside.

'There's this village about ten miles ahead. We'll stop there for the night.' He sounded bitter. 'I shall *have* to wait for Seymour now. Another day at least. But I'm not pushing ahead in the dark.'

Blackwood leaned his back against the worn seat. He felt unusually tense. The feeling he had once had in Africa. It was often like that in the Royal Marines. A river, even a tiny stream, was better than nothing. But here they were cut off from the sea, and each turn of the wheels was carrying them further and further into the unknown.

Blackwood said, 'Tell the Sergeant Major, Toby, half-rations from now on.'

Gravatt grinned. 'They won't like that, sir.'

Blair waited for him to leave and said quietly, 'We may get supplies at the village, but I doubt it.' He ran his finger around his collar. 'I've a nasty intuition about all this. I can see you've got it too.'

Blackwood nodded. The colonel made him feel transparent.

'You're like a naked man out here, sir.'

'Hmm.' He stood up abruptly as a voice shouted, 'Stand-to, lads!' The train rolled to a standstill and while the resting marines snatched up their weapons again, Blackwood climbed through the little hatch and stood on the coal in the tender.

He used levelled binoculars and to his astonishment saw a solitary horseman trotting down the track towards them. He was a white man, and swayed back and forth in the saddle as if he were drunk. The horse too was streaked in sweat and almost done for.

'Go and help him! Corporal Lyde, take six men to that gully, at the double!'

As the marines bounded across the open ground their torpor forgotten, the five-barrelled machine-gun swung round to follow their progress.

There were more shouts as a few shots echoed across the track, but they had been fired at extreme range and whimpered overhead like dying hornets.

The horseman toppled from his saddle even as two marines ran to catch him. They carried him to the train and laid him carefully on one of the seats while Swan moistened his lips with a water flask. Blackwood had expected him to be wounded but he was unhurt. As his strength began to return he stammered out his unbelievable story.

His name was John Twiss and he had been a riding instructor in Peking and used regularly by civilian members of the various legations. He was English, and as he described the realization of the Boxers' intentions and their savage attack on the Peking Racecourse his eyes grew brighter, as if he relived the nightmare.

The legation quarter was surrounded by the Boxers and several large units of the Chinese army who had thrown in their lot with them. Prince Tuan now openly supported the Boxers and held the real power in Peking. It was just a matter of time before a full-scale attack supported by artillery was launched against the legations. Without reinforcements they had no chance of survival.

Blackwood watched as Twiss spoke to the colonel. He seemed to exclude the rest of them. Perhaps even in his distress he had recognized in Blair another old China hand. One whose trust and hope had been hacked aside by the bloody uprising.

The British minister had asked for volunteers to attempt to get through the enemy lines and carry word to Admiral Seymour about the mounting danger. Without telegraph or mail, there was no other way. This man Twiss, and he was nobody you would even notice under ordinary circumstances, had offered to ride along the track until he found help. He had left with two others, both of whom were excellent horsemen. One had been captured when his horse had fallen. The other had been shot dead just this morning near the village up ahead.

Twiss looked at his hands. 'He was the lucky one.'

Blackwood glanced at Swan and saw his grim expression. He too was thinking of Earle's terrible screams.

Blair said, 'Recall the pickets. We'll move on as soon as that horse has been properly watered. Detail someone to ride it beside the train. Might come in handy sooner than we think.' He was scheming ahead, creating obstacles only to find a way around them.

He looked at Twiss. 'You have achieved what you set out to do. You're a brave fellow. I shall tell Admiral Seymour exactly what we all owe to your courage.'

Twiss watched him, his eyes glazed with fatigue. 'He'll never get through, you know. The Boxers will cut the railway ahead of him, and then behind at Tientsin. I heard one of the officers say as much at the legation.'

'Well, we shall have to see about that.' Blair straightened his back and stared through the window at the dust which had begun to settle again. But not before Blackwood had seen the understanding in his eyes. The whole force could be cut off and destroyed piecemeal. It would be Seymour who needed help then.

Eventually the train began to move forward again with many eyes probing the landscape and peering at the glittering rails ahead until they were almost blinded in the glare.

It felt like an age before they sighted the village. Just a few small dwellings on either side of the track, and a water-tower on stilts.

The marines crouched on either side of the train, rifles wavering as they searched for danger.

Private Knowles, who had been raised on a Dorset farm, struggled to control the horse as it reared and kicked when moments earlier it had been trotting quite happily with its new rider.

Blair said quietly, 'Trouble, David. I can smell it. So can the horse.'

The train halted and in sections the first marines fanned out on either side of the train, bayonets fixed in case of a sudden attack.

Lieutenant Gravatt shouted, 'Sar'nt Davis! Use the water-tower to refill all the flasks and canteens!'

Blair snapped, 'Belay that!' He gestured towards a

building beside the track. A marine was leaning against it vomiting helplessly.

Blair said, 'Come on. De Courcy, take charge here!'

You would not really have known they were human, just that they had once been white-skinned. Headless and disembowelled the two corpses hung from a roof like obscene meat.

Fox exclaimed hoarsely, 'An' one of 'em was already dead, yet they still did that to 'im!'

Blair did not sound as if he had heard. 'Send someone to the water-tower. Tell him to watch out for snipers.' He made himself look at the dangling horror. 'Cut those down and bury them.'

It was not then the end of it. The Boxers must have struck the village like a tornado, murdering anyone they could find, men, women, even children in an orgy of horror.

Blackwood walked through the small village, and forced himself to join his men as they searched for any survivors. The village was poor, but with the new railway running right through it, prosperity might one day have been theirs. Perhaps that too was a sin to the puritanical Boxers. A foreign infection which must be stamped out.

He thought of Friedrike that night in her cabin with her little pistol, the terrible scenes of mutilation and death he had seen aboard the *Delhi Star*.

In one dwelling, little more than a hut, he found a young Chinese mother, her eyes wide with terror, but her arms locked protectively around the child which had been feeding at her breast. Mercifully they must both have died together, but what sort of monster could see this young girl with her baby and feel no pity as he swung his great blade.

He leaned against a wall, sick of the stench, the busy murmur of flies. Blair joined him. 'As I thought. The water's poisoned. Full of corpses.' He spoke without any emotion and yet Blackwood imagined he might be near to breaking-point.

He saw some of his men staring around as if shocked out

of their minds. The Boxers had achieved what they had set out to do. These men, even the recruits, would stand and fight, die if need be, if so ordered. But they were no match for such scenes as these, and Blackwood could feel their despair as it moved amongst them like a spectre.

Gravatt crunched across the tracks and asked, 'Orders, sir?' He was as pale as death.

Blackwood looked at the colonel. 'No sense in pushing forward any further, sir.'

'No. Twiss says there could be twenty thousand of the enemy converging on Peking. How many of us?' He looked round at the silent, listless marines. 'A hundred? Even for the Royals I fear we may be outmatched.' He became brisk and businesslike just as quickly. 'There is a siding of some kind here. Change the trucks around, we will reverse the train back to Tientsin, or as near as we can get to it.'

Blackwood passed his orders and then asked, 'What will the admiral do, sir?'

'Do?' Blair's eyes settled on his and Blackwood saw the pain deep inside them for the first time. 'He'll run for the sea. At least I hope he does. If I meet him face to face I shall probably shoot him!'

All that night the train stood beside the poisoned water-tower, surrounded by silence and the smell of death. Nobody slept, not even the sentries when they were relieved.

At first light they found the heads of the two murdered riders, propped on stakes and within yards of where two sentries had been posted. They were as close as that.

The wheels spun, and smoke belched from the funnel and then with the horse trotting beside it the train backed slowly along the tracks.

Blackwood climbed through the carriages, speaking to his men, or just letting them know he was there.

He heard one marine say, 'One thing, Fred, we *are* goin' towards the sea this time, eh?'

Blackwood felt a lump in his throat. Was it that simple?

He thought of the girl with the baby at her breast and pushed the sentiment from his mind.

There was a hell of a lot to do before they found the sea again.

11

The Hero

Captain Vere Masterman put down his empty teacup and stared impassively through the stern ports of his spacious quarters. Separated from *Mediator*'s busy routine by steel bulkheads he could still hear the shrill of the boatswain's calls, and the cry, 'Hands to breakfast and clean!' Seven in the morning although the light cruiser's people or a large part of them had been up and about for an hour and a half already.

Masterman prepared himself for the many tasks he had to attend to. In another hour the Colours would be hoisted to mark the official start of another day, but to Masterman this was always the best part, the early morning when a man's mind was crisp like the air. He stared at the nearest anchored warships, the German *Flensburg*, and beyond her an elderly French steam sloop. Like some of the other foreign men-of-war they had their guns trained on the shore. Masterman was irritated by what he saw. Things were quite serious enough without this pointless show of force.

Aboard his ship at least things would remain normal until he decided otherwise. When the time came *Mediator* would respond without any fuss or bravado.

He could see two of the Chinese forts through the morning mist, biscuit-coloured in the frail sunlight. There would be another series of useless parleys with the Chinese garrison commanders, but nothing would happen. The Chinese knew that the Allies would not open fire with

Seymour's force still trapped ashore. And every captain knew he would not shoot. So what was the point?

There was a tap at the door. Time to make decisions.

'Come!'

It was Commander Wilberforce as he knew it would be, his arm wrapped around a bundle of lists, requests, and the usual signal pad. Wilberforce took his time as he laid down his papers, it was his usual ploy while he gauged the captain's mood. The signs were not good.

Wilberforce said, 'Signal from Flag, sir. A report has got through to say that Admiral Seymour's force is falling back as planned.'

'Falling back?' He did not hide his anger. 'It's a bloody rout!'

'Yes, sir.'

Masterman glared at the throngs of junks and small Chinese boats which hovered around the anchored warships like moths. Some of them would be pirates, the sweepings of the China Seas, he thought. They probably hated the Boxers more than anyone, as a criminal hates a man who murders a policeman. They knew that while the crime was unavenged they would get no peace to go about their affairs, unlawful or not.

'The sloop *Caistor* has anchored, sir. From Hong Kong with despatches for the flagship.' He held out a signal. 'This came over in the guard-boat, sir.'

Masterman did not look at it immediately. He kept thinking of the Royal Marines he had landed at this godforsaken place. A day to reach Peking the admiral had proclaimed. It was already five days, and Seymour's force was in full retreat, ridding itself of stores and equipment in its haste to reach the sea.

And things were getting steadily worse, backed up by terrible rumours which had spread through the Allied squadron like a forest-fire.

The Boxers had stormed and seized the Native City of Tientsin and were now preparing an attack on the International Settlement there. Word had filtered through that the Japanese Chancellor Sugiyama had been murdered in Peking by Chinese troops, so any hope of some last-minute parley was gone.

He read through the signal and then realized what it said.

'Sergeant Kirby, does he know?'

'No, sir.'

'Well, better get it done as quickly as possible. I'll go and see him myself after Colours.'

As if to measure the time a boatswain's mate called again, 'Guard and Band to muster on the quarterdeck!'

Masterman glanced at the deckhead just inches above him. Some captains hated the tramp of marching above their private quarters, the clatter of weapons and the blare of a Royal Marines band. Not Masterman, he loved every part of it, just as he knew the name and face of every man under his command.

Wilberforce said, 'It's strange you should say that, sir, but Sergeant Kirby has already put in a request to see you. He's walking quite well, considering.'

'Very well. This is bad luck after what he's been through.'

A midshipman tapped on the outer door and Masterman's steward called, 'For the Commander, sir. Two minutes to Colours.'

Wilberforce picked up his cap and withdrew.

The stern swung slightly as the inshore current began to move the anchored warships around their cables. Masterman was glad when that happened, and the land vanished from his vision for a few hours at least.

He picked up the photograph of his wife which stood in a silver frame on a polished cabinet. He was always close to her at this time of the day.

Through the open skylight he heard a voice call, 'Colours, sir!' And Wilberforce's reply, calm, unruffled, 'Make it so!'

'Royal Marines! Pre-*sent arms*!'

The rest was drowned in the blare of bugles and rattle of drums but Masterman did not need to be there. He had seen it in every major harbour around the world, the White Ensign rising in time to the salute. It never failed to move him.

He spoke aloud, 'If only we could get those men off.' Where was Blackwood and his men? Cut off and abandoned by the rest of the landing force. It was unthinkable. Outrageous.

Masterman sat down at his table and contained his sudden rage. It was not the right time.

The outer door opened and he saw Wilberforce again, followed by the wounded sergeant with a sickberth attendant hovering anxiously in the rear.

The sergeant looked very pale, but was moving well, and doing his best not to show the pain he must feel.

Kirby brought his heels together and looked at the captain squarely. He had known it was coming, but the shock seemed somehow worse now that he was away from the company, from his fellow NCOs.

Masterman eyed him gravely, measuring the moment, hating it.

'I have bad news, I'm afraid, Sergeant Kirby.'

'Sir?' He had half expected to be placed under immediate arrest.

'I have just received word from Hong Kong that your wife is dead.'

He snapped his fingers. 'Chair, man!'

The sickberth attendant snatched a chair and held it for Kirby as he slumped down.

'Dead, sir?' Kirby barely recognized his own voice. He was going mad. All the weeks of worrying and tormenting himself and now the captain was acting as if he was sorry for him. Of course she was bloody dead! He felt like screaming, or throwing himself on the deck.

Masterman nodded. 'There was, *is* a street lamp outside your house it seems. There was a gas explosion and I fear that your wife perished in the fire which followed.'

Kirby tried to speak but nothing came. In his reeling thoughts he could see that solitary street lamp. They had often undressed by its glow to save money when they had first got married. An explosion? A fire? Masterman's voice scattered his memories as he continued.

'I have to tell you, Sergeant Kirby, and I hope it may be of some consolation, that I received confirmation from the flagship that your recommendation for an award has been approved. For your gallantry under fire, well over and above the line of duty, you will in due course be decorated with the Victoria Cross, and I am instructed to offer my congratulations.'

Masterman saw the sergeant sway on the chair. He must not prolong it any more.

He said in a gentle voice which Wilberforce would not have recognized had he not been staring at the scene which he would always remember. 'Remember this, Kirby. She would have been proud of you.' He turned away, embarrassed by his own sincerity. 'As we all are.'

Wilberforce gestured to the steward. 'Help the SBA to take Sergeant Kirby down to the sickbay.'

As the door closed behind the two white-coated figures and the tall, bent shape of the sergeant, Masterman said, 'I know how I'd feel.' He glanced at the photograph again, hearing her voice calling the dog, waking him in time to catch the train back to his ship.

'Now, John, about this retreat. What is our state of readiness?'

Wilberforce tried to relax, but he knew that he would never see Masterman as quite the same again.

Safely laid in his cot once more Kirby stared at the revolving deckhead fan and tried to assemble his thoughts. It was hard to believe it had happened. His secret had tortured him for weeks; now because of some impossible act of fate the burden was lifted. He peered over the edge of the cot, but he was alone. Even Private Erskine who had lost a foot had been carried on deck to benefit from the air and the sunshine.

He thought of the medal, of Masterman's words. Of what Fox would say when he heard about it. The Victoria Cross. Just like Captain Blackwood and his father.

Jeff Kirby, born and raised in a London slum, respected and often feared by his men, was suddenly aware of something which had never happened before. He was shocked beyond reason to discover that tears were pouring uncontrollably down his face. He tried to stop, to stifle his terrible sobs in the pillow and to shut out the picture of her terror as she had pleaded with him.

'Oh, Nance!' He crushed the pillow into a ball against his face but he only saw her more clearly. *'Nance!* I – I'm so sorry, love!'

It was worse than any secret.

'Stop the train!' Lieutenant Colonel Blair clambered through the little door at the end of the carriage which was now in the front of the train. 'Quickly.' He blinked at Blackwood, his chest heaving from exertion and the oppressive heat. He had been squatting like a wiry bird on the roof of the carriage for most of the journey. Blackwood heard the warning being shouted from carriage to carriage as the driver applied the brakes.

Blair said, 'They've broken the track again.' He nodded gratefully to Swan as he swallowed a mug of water. 'A mile ahead of us.'

Blackwood wanted to ask why they had stopped here, but knew Blair would have a good reason.

'Not just Boxers this time. Imperial soldiers too.' Blair added quietly, 'I could see the buggers through my glasses. They're waiting for us to stop. They could kill or wound half of our people before we could hit back. They know this territory, we don't.' He unfolded his map and Blackwood saw that his hand was shaking from the strain he was under.

Blair sounded absorbed. 'According to this there's a small river beyond those hills to our right. It joins the Peiho after a mile or so, down to the sea after that, eh?'

Blackwood waited seeing the excitement returning to Blair's thin features.

'If we tried to reach the hills the Boxers would cut us down before we got halfway. I want our men ready to fight, not to die like bloody scavengers!'

Fight? Blackwood pictured their dispirited, weary faces.

Blair glanced up as the lieutenants climbed into the carriage, their faces full of questions.

Blair said, 'We shall detrain here, gentlemen. By platoons as before. Mr Gravatt, go with the Sergeant Major and start the ball rolling.' He spoke lightly, as if it was an exercise rather than a walk into probable death.

Gravatt swallowed hard. 'In the *open*, sir?'

'Yes. There is an army of Boxers and soldiers up there where they've ripped up the tracks. They will expect us to make a stand or break out from there while they shoot us down from cover, right?'

Gravatt nodded. 'I see, sir.'

Blair smiled. 'You don't but never mind. When the Boxers see us leave the train *here* they'll have to leave their cover to cut us off.' He looked at Blackwood. 'The machine-gun sections will remain on the train. We shall have to leave the two field-pieces behind, I'm afraid. Have them spiked before you follow me. Tell the engine driver to go like hell. I want to catch those bastards out in the open with their trousers down for once!'

Blackwood nodded. 'I'll tell him.'

Blair touched his arm. 'It's up to you really. Reverse back here when you're ready and don't leave it too late.' He looked at the others. 'Leave no one behind.' His eyes rested momentarily on Ralf. 'We take care of our own in the Corps.' He nodded curtly. 'So let us be about it, eh?'

Outside Blackwood could hear the bark of commands, the sudden bustle and stamp of feet as the marines jumped from the train, dragging their packs and ammunition with them.

'Fall them in, Sergeant Major.'

By the time Blackwood reached the engine the marines were standing in sections beside the train. He could sense their sudden reluctance to leave the train's frail protection.

Blair stood in front of them and raised his voice. 'Now listen to me, all of you. We shall march to those hills, and I mean *march*. I don't give a damn what you've seen or done in the past, this is bloody now! So stop feeling sorry for yourselves!'

Blackwood saw the hurt and resentment on their faces, the way they held their rifles as if they wanted to kill the man who was flaying them with his insults.

'Remember that you are Royal Marines, not a lot of mummy's boys!'

As Blackwood walked back along the train Blair looked at him and grinned. 'I'm a real bastard, aren't I?' He returned Fox's salute and at a shouted command the first platoon marched away from the train.

Blair's grin widened. 'But it's working.'

Blackwood took a deep breath. The arms were swinging, the dusty boots moved as one, and the sloped rifles would have done credit to Forton Barracks.

Blair lifted his glasses and stared along the line. 'It's working with them too. Now get your men under cover.'

A door squeaked and Blair nodded with satisfaction as the other Nordenfeldt machine-gun poked through the gap. Then he strode briskly after the winding column of marines and did not look back.

Blackwood climbed over the sandbags and boiler plates on the leading car and knelt down with the small squad of marines there.

Corporal O'Neil stared at him. 'Is it yourself, sir?'

Blackwood found he could smile in spite of the tension which held him like claws.

When he trained his binoculars over the barrier he saw

the horde of figures breaking from their hiding places and charging across the flat ground towards the slow-moving column.

Suppose the engine failed to move, or the driver got into a panic and ran for his life?

The men moved around restlessly and dragged up more ammunition to be in easy reach.

O'Neil rested his hand on the machine-gun and murmured, 'And if you jam, me boyo, I'll not forgive you!'

One of the marines said sharply, 'Some of 'em are headin' for the train, sir.'

Blackwood saw Swan nestle his rifle against his cheek while he adjusted his sights with great care. The Boxers on the track were probably coming to loot rather than to fight. They would get a rude surprise.

A few shots cracked across the ground, but the Boxers were too eager to get to grips with the column to take proper aim.

It was almost time. Blackwood felt the sweat trickle down his spine. He made himself count up to twenty and then stood upright on the top of the sandbags so that the driver could see him above the roofs of the carriages.

He yelled, '*Now!*' To his surprise he saw the stoker petty officer and two sailors in their wide-brimmed sennets on the footplate with the driver. He had forgotten all about the stokers. They would make sure that the engine kept going with or without the driver.

The car gave a great lurch and Blackwood almost fell over the side. He looked at O'Neil. *Good old Blackie.* 'Here we go.'

Whatever the Boxers thought was happening they showed no sign of slowing down or changing direction.

Blackwood drew his revolver. 'Open fire!'

The sandbags were rolled aside and the machine-gun clattered into life even as the other one poured a long burst into the charging mob of Boxers and troops. A few rifles joined in, and Blackwood wondered if the marching marines would dare to turn their heads to watch.

Back and forth the five-barrelled gun ripped above the track until the figures which had been running towards the train were either hurled down or had turned to flee.

The train gathered momentum, the bright wheels cutting through the fallen corpses and bringing screams from the wounded before they too were smashed aside.

Blackwood tried to concentrate on the bulk of the attackers. As O'Neil's gun joined forces with the other one, the running figures seemed to become confused, like a sea caught between wind and tide. Many were falling, others ran on, and a few swayed back again against their companions.

'Reload! *Steady*, lads!' A sight like this one was enough to make any man shoot without aiming or caring.

It was unreal and terrible, and Blackwood flinched as two of the marching marines fell from the ranks. They were gathered up into the column as if it was the living being and the marines merely incidental.

We take care of our own, Blair had said. What officers in the Corps had probably said at the Nile and Trafalgar.

Blackwood peered at the torn-up rails. They would never be repaired in time. Blair was right about that also.

'Stop the train! Back up!' It was far enough. The engine shuddered to a halt and Swan vaulted over the side to snatch up a fallen pike with its fearsome blade attached and was back with it even as the wheels spun into reverse.

Blackwood said hoarsely, 'You bloody fool! I should put you on a charge for that!'

Swan hung his head. 'Souvenir, sir.'

They stared at each other, both knowing the real reason for Blackwood's concern.

O'Neil watched impatiently as the gun was reloaded. 'You're a terrible chap, Private Swan, desertin' your train in the face o' the enemy!'

Blackwood stared at his crouching, smoke-grimed men. They were rocking about and laughing as if it was the greatest joke in the world.

'*Open fire!*'

Along the train the few remaining rifles cracked out, while the two machine-guns scythed back and forth with deadly effect.

O'Neil said over his shoulder. 'Nearly out of ammo', sir.' He glanced at his mate. 'Sergeant Kirby wouldn't be happy about that, eh, Willy?'

'They're in full retreat, the bloody hounds!' The man ducked and swore as a stray bullet sang past his head.

The train stopped at the exact spot where Blair had made his brief speech.

It was a strange feeling to climb down without anything happening. There was a slow, hot wind across the open ground and it stirred the white and bloodied garments of the fallen Boxers so that it appeared as if they really were invulnerable and returning to life.

The marching column was completely hidden in dust and haze, as if it too had been swallowed up.

They piled up their spare kit and ammunition on the two Nordenfeldt carriages, and then, pushing and pulling the ungainly wheels, they hurried after the others.

Blackwood saw the engine driver pause to stare back at the abandoned train. Like a master leaving his ship, he thought. The train looked forlorn as it stood with its doors open, and steam still trickling from the boiler.

Blackwood said, 'Come on. There'll be other trains.'

The driver shook his head. Suddenly his whole life was in ruins and he still did not understand why.

'Not like her,' was all he said.

Swan fell into step beside him, his rifle slung, the great blade shining across his other shoulder.

The captain had been afraid for him. It touched Swan more deeply than any bloody medal.

Blackwood lay beside the colonel, his elbows wedged into

some pebbles as they trained their glasses on the scene
below. The hill, like the others which rolled away on either
side, was not very high, but compared to the flat countryside it still offered a good vantage point.

'There's the river anyway.' Blair moved his glasses with
great care. It was sunset and the sky was fiery red, but still
strong enough to reflect from a lens if you moved too
sharply.

The river was narrow and probably quite shallow like the
other one had been. At the point where it joined the Peiho
was a long squat building like an ancient fortress. They had
seen it earlier when they had been placing the sentries and
setting up the machine-guns.

The two marines who had been wounded were only
suffering from flesh injuries and with luck would soon
recover.

Blair remarked, 'You notice that wide road coming from
the rear of the building. Odd, that. It's the end of nowhere,
I'd have thought.'

Blair stiffened and readjusted his glasses as a tiny figure
appeared on top of the wall.

He said softly, as if the far-off man might hear, 'Soldier,
Imperial Army.' He lowered his glasses and studied
Blackwood thoughtfully. 'No Boxers in sight. You know
what I think, David, this is an arsenal. That would explain
the size of the road.' He snapped open his pocket compass.
'Which by my reckoning goes straight into Tientsin.' He
nodded to confirm his ideas. 'There are several big arsenals
around the city. I was just thinking, it's a pity we had to
leave the two field-guns on the train. Still, they'd have
slowed us down even more.'

Blackwood waited, it was fascinating just to watch his
mind work.

The two little cannon had been rendered useless before
they had left, their breech-blocks thrown into the engine's
furnace. Even a first-class gun would be so much scrap after
that. But surely Blair was not even considering an attack on

the arsenal? They would have to cross the river, and even though there did not appear to be any heavy defences it would be an almost impossible task.

Blair twisted on to his side and looked at Swan who lay behind them, his rifle to his shoulder. Just in case.

'How much drinking water have you got, Swan?'

Swan sounded surprised. ''Bout an inch, sir.'

'You see, David? Swan is a veteran and even he's only got a swallow left in his flask. The younger ones will have drunk the lot by now, no matter what threats the NCOs hurl at 'em!' He looked again at the long building which was already falling into deep shadow. 'There's fresh water and rations galore over there, or I'm a Dutchman. The whole countryside is obviously raised against us, so we must act accordingly. They'll need us badly in Tientsin. That's where we'll go.'

'And Admiral Seymour?'

Blair gave his impish grin. 'Who?'

He became serious instantly. 'Fetch the petty officer and one of the student interpreters.' He tapped his teeth with the strap of his binocular case. 'A diversion is what we need.'

He slithered a few yards down the slope. 'I'm going to tell the PO what I want.'

Blackwood peered at the building until his eyes throbbed. They had come all this way and had suffered only two casualties. As far as they could tell there was no pursuit, not yet anyway. Perhaps the other Boxers had changed their minds and had gone to join their army massing in Tientsin as they were in Peking.

He heard Blair say, 'There are several abandoned boats down by the river. Ran like hell when they knew the Boxers were coming, I expect.' His tone sharpened. 'I want you to take one as soon as it's dark and make your way downstream. It shouldn't be difficult. I'll give you a message for Captain Masterman, how about that?'

The petty officer's voice rumbled, 'I'll 'ave a go, sir.' The mention of his captain's name had knocked his defences aside like a battering ram.

'You'll do better than that, Petty Officer.' Blair's voice was incisive. 'We're all depending on you.' He swung round before the man could say anything more. 'David, muster the sailors and see that they're armed.'

As Blackwood walked downhill towards the hidden marines he tried not to think about the beheaded, mutilated corpses. It was lucky that the petty officer had remained inside the train.

Gravatt and the others were waiting for him, while Fox stood just the required number of paces to one side.

Blackwood told them briefly what Blair intended and stressed the vital importance of the food and drink they would find in the arsenal.

Nobody spoke, but their shocked silence made it worse.

Blackwood finished by saying, 'As soon as it's dark I want the men to get as much rest as they can.' He saw them stare as he added, 'The colonel wants the horse led down and watered at the river as soon as we're sure it's safe.'

Gravatt said politely, 'Did he say why, sir?'

Blackwood grinned, the colonel's mood was infectious. 'He's going to ride the bloody thing when he leads us into Tientsin, because *that's* where we're going next!'

Gravatt looked at Lieutenant Bannatyre. ''Pon my soul, Ian, I do believe he means it!'

Blackwood found the colonel sitting alone, his back propped against a huge rock which had been split in equal halves, like an egg. Without the others near him he seemed tense, on edge.

Blair said, 'It's the only way, David. If the trap closes around us this time, it's over.'

'I know.' Blackwood sat down beside him. He found that he was touching the locket beneath his tunic.

Was she safe? he wondered. Did she think of him sometimes?

His head lolled and then he was asleep.

12

The Last Bugle

The silver calls trilled in salute as Captain Masterman stepped on to *Mediator*'s quarterdeck and touched the peak of his cap in acknowledgement to the flag.

Commander Wilberforce hurried forward to greet him but did not get a chance to speak.

Masterman said, 'Bloody hopeless. Allies indeed? You would think we were all on opposite sides!' He glared across at the other warships. 'The Japanese want to go in and attack, the Russians want to wait here off the Taku bar, the Germans are keen to bombard the forts, and the Americans won't do a damn thing. Their Admiral Kempff has his hands tied by a directive from Washington which forbids him from taking part in any hostile acts against the Chinese. The fact that the Americans have their own marines cut off in Peking too, and that we are in a state of war to all intents and purposes with Johnnie Chinaman seems to matter not!' He lowered his voice with an effort. 'I might as well have stayed here. Seymour's second-in-command will do nothing until his master returns. *If* he returns!' He peered over the side. 'And what is that object doing tied to the boom?'

Wilberforce tugged at his collar. It was all going wrong, and Masterman was in no mood for mistakes today.

'I was going to tell you, sir. Stoker Petty Officer Gooch arrived aboard just after you'd gone across to the flagship.'

'*What* did you say?'

Two seamen who were polishing the brass nameplate

stiffened to listen, their cloths motionless.

Wilberforce tried to explain. 'He got downriver in that boat, sir. He has a signal from Lieutenant Colonel Blair.' He wilted under Masterman's angry stare.

Masterman strode to the quarterdeck companionway leaving the officer-of-the-day and his midshipman gaping after him.

The stoker petty officer was found in his mess and bustled aft to the day cabin where his captain was still studying Blair's message. The petty officer had been greeted as something of a conqueror by his messmates, and had even found time to down a large tot of rum after his escape from the river. Masterman soon changed all that.

'How long has *this* man been back aboard, Commander?' Wilberforce replied unhappily, 'Since eight bells, sir.'

Masterman looked at the petty officer and asked almost gently, 'Why did it take you so long, Gooch? According to this message, you left the others as soon as it was dark.'

'We 'ad trouble, sir. The boat ran aground twice, it were that shallow. Then when we reached the main river we 'ad to 'ide in some rushes. There were Chinese soljers on th' bank. An' further downstream they was layin' mines, least I think they was.'

Masterman frowned. He had heard as much aboard the flagship. If the Chinese succeeded in mining the Peiho's entrance not only would Seymour and his men be done for, but also the last chance of relieving Peking would be gone.

He stared hard at the petty officer. But for him they would know very little. Blackwood and his men were still together, and whereas the petty officer could only thank his lucky stars that he was safely back in his ship, Blair was planning an attack. The Allies would have to act within forty-eight hours at the very latest.

They had to capture the forts, and open a passage for future reinforcements. If they achieved neither they might as well up-anchor and leave the Taku bar for good.

'How were the marines when you left them?'

Petty Officer Gooch tried not to drop his eyes under that remorseless stare.

'Tired, sir, 'ungry too, an' there's no water left.' He flushed. 'They give the last of it to my lads.'

'They would.' Masterman looked away. Over the years he had taught himself to stay calm while he considered his plans, item by item. The poor devils could die out there for nothing.

He said quietly, 'Fetch the Chief Engineer and Gunnery Officer. At once.' To the petty officer he added, 'If by the Grace of God you still have that rank on your sleeve at the end of the day, Gooch, you will know I have intervened with Providence on your behalf. Now get out of my sight!'

Wilberforce was almost knocked over by the petty officer as he ran from the cabin.

'I've sent for them, sir.'

The captain moved to the stern ports and stared across the placid water. The tide had turned again, and the land, apart from some small islets, was hidden.

Wilberforce said carefully, 'I suppose we can't really blame Gooch, sir. It was quite a responsibility for him.'

'I'm not. I blame you for not making a signal directly he came on board.' He relented slightly. 'Now get the chart of the Peiho and those forts.'

The chief engineer entered the cabin and waited, his eyes flitting from one to the other.

'How long to raise steam, Chief?'

The engineer shrugged. 'I'm ready any time, more or less. When you ordered a state of readiness, well, I know your standards by now, sir.'

Masterman smiled. 'So you do, Chief.'

The gunnery officer, some breadcrumbs on his chest, hurried into the cabin.

Masterman eyed him gravely. 'I am going to get under way, Guns. We shall go to the bridge and compare Blair's little map with the chart. As we cross the river-mouth you will have to fire on a difficult bearing, but it must be accurate.'

The gunnery officer glanced at Wilberforce who quickly shook his head. Masterman added, 'The Royal Marines are going to attack and capture an arsenal, Guns. We will keep the enemy occupied, although – ' he glanced at the bulkhead clock, 'I fear we are already too late.'

He snatched up his cap. 'Clear lower decks, John. Steam on the capstan and hoist all boats inboard.'

He looked at them and smiled. 'And later, John, you may clear for action.'

Wilberforce hurried after him beckoning to boatswain's mates and messengers as he tried to keep up.

'Are you sure, sir? I – I mean, is it our responsibility?'

Masterman paused, framed against the blue sky above the ladder. The question would ensure that Wilberforce would never hold any real responsibility.

'It's mine, John. It's called initiative.' He ran up the last steps. 'Now get the people moving!'

He strode into the wheelhouse and aft to the chartroom. Men were bustling everywhere, and already he could hear the dull clank from the capstan as the cable was hove short.

He paused and glanced at the wheel, with the gleaming binnacle and telegraphs. He really loved this ship more than any other, and he could remember how proud his wife had been when he had been given *Mediator*. In a matter of hours his career could easily be in ruins. Then he thought of Blackwood, how young he had looked when the German countess had asked for his escort. When you compared him with Wilberforce's hesitancy – he shook himself. There was no comparison.

'Special sea dutymen to your stations! First part o' starboard watch muster on th' fo'c'sle!'

Mediator seemed to stir beneath his white shoes.

'Signal from flagship, sir.' The lieutenant sounded confused. '*What do you intend to do?*'

Masterman eyed him thoughtfully. Nelson would have known what to say. He always did.

'Make to Flag. *My duty.*'

'Aye, sir.' The lieutenant hurried to the flag deck, convinced that the captain was going mad.

The bridge party had closed up now. Quartermaster, telegraphsmen, yeoman of signals. Masterman's tools.

'Anchor's weigh, sir.'

'Slow ahead together.'

The light cruiser moved quietly ahead, her dripping anchor still being hoisted as she turned towards the open water.

The lieutenant was muttering to the yeoman of signals. Then he said uncertainly, 'From flagship, sir. *Your signal not understood.*'

Wilberforce entered the bridge in time to see his captain burst out laughing.

Masterman said, 'The truest words we've heard yet!'

He saw Wilberforce and said more calmly, 'When we pass abeam of the last fort I want you to sound Action Stations.' He walked out on to the sun-blistered wing and stared at the land. 'They might hear it. From one of their own.'

Blackwood scrambled up the slope and dropped beside the colonel. Blair was peering through his binoculars and said, 'Dawn any minute now.' He sounded quite calm again. In control.

Blackwood peered through the rough gorse towards the arsenal. How he had managed to sleep he could not begin to understand. It was behind him now. This was another day. Perhaps the last.

'I've checked with the pickets, sir, and re-sited the machine-gun where it will perform best.' He had ordered all the Nordenfeldt ammunition to be taken to just the one gun. The other one would have to be abandoned like the field-pieces.

Blair never asked him where or what he had been doing,

and he liked him for that. He trusted and he delegated, unlike some field officers Blackwood had known.

He watched the growing light seeping across the top of the arsenal, and wondered if the stoker petty officer and his party had reached safety. What could Masterman do anyway?

Blackwood had spoken to most of the marines while they were munching the last of their meagre rations. Without water or tea to wash it down it was an unhappy way to begin a day like this.

Fox had awakened him during the night after the pickets had found two white-clad sailors stumbling about in the dark. It was a miracle they had not been bayoneted before they had identified themselves. They were both Austro-Hungarian sailors who had become separated and lost from Seymour's column. One spoke a little English, and with the aid of gestures and a crude map they had explained how the column was in full retreat, dropping weapons and equipment to make as much speed as possible. They did not know how far Seymour had reached, but they had told a gruesome story about another massacred village, and about the Boxer flags flying over Tientsin's Native City. The International Settlement there was obviously their goal.

Blair had remarked, 'Well it's two more rifles. That's something, I suppose.'

'Look!' Blair touched his arm. 'Now there's a sight!'

Blackwood imagined he had seen an enemy movement but realized that the sea had suddenly become visible. It was like a dark blue barrier beyond the jutting land which supported the arsenal. Blackwood thought it was the most beautiful thing he had ever seen.

'There's the other fort. Just beyond the bend. Must have been built to command the main river. They have good modern artillery in those forts, I'm told.' He shot Blackwood a grin. 'But they all point out to sea. Bit of luck, eh?'

Blair removed his helmet and crawled to the lip of the hill. 'The boats are still there, and unguarded. We'll have to jump about a bit when we cross the river.' He gauged the distance with his eyes. 'Once across, the machine-gun section can offer covering fire. That'll keep their heads down for a bit.' Surprisingly he rolled on to his back and stared up at the paling sky.

'I've been really happy during my time out here. I suppose I've been getting past it for some time.' He turned his head and looked at Blackwood. 'I'm about twenty years older than you, and I feel it.'

Blackwood watched him in the faint glow. Without his helmet he looked unshaven and tired. For some reason he wanted to talk. To while away the time or to ease the tension, he could not tell.

Blair continued, 'To begin with I was like any other young officer. You learn the jargon and the right postures. The rest comes easily. One ship after the other. Captains with different whims and fancies, and always you're separate from the rest, no matter how crowded the ship might be. I suppose I grew tired of it. Even leave in England had nothing to offer. I've no family to speak of, whereas in Hong Kong . . .' He sighed and rolled over on to his elbows again.

'But all that is far away. We are here.' He became businesslike and brisk once more. 'Order a runner to de Courcy's sector. Tell him to send a squad down to the boats, but keep them hidden.'

Swan said, 'I'll do it, sir.'

Blackwood licked his lips. They were beginning to crack. In an hour the land would start to throw back the heat. They could not go through another day. Even as he thought it, he knew they would if need be. And another, and another until the sun smashed them down.

'Good chap, your man Swan.' Blair yawned hugely. 'A few thousand like him and I could take the whole of China!' But the smile would not come. Blackwood looked at the river as the growing light gave it colour and movement again.

Just to have a drink. Was that all that mattered in the
end?

Hidden in the fold of an adjoining hill Lieutenant
Edmund de Courcy listened to Swan's message and said,
'Right away.' He beckoned to Greenaway, his sergeant. 'Job
for you. Take a squad down to the boats. You should be
hidden from the arsenal, but keep a weather eye on that
bloody fort.'

Sergeant Tom Greenaway was the oldest man in the
whole company and had been in the Corps since he was
fifteen. He had fought in most of the big campaigns in
Africa and Egypt, and several of the little bush wars as well.
He was old enough to be the lieutenant's father and then
some, but he liked de Courcy all the same. He had the
ability to make quick decisions and act on them, unlike
poor young Mr Bannatyre. He came from a good old Royal
Marines family too. That carried more weight than de
Courcy's lack of experience.

Greenaway detailed off his small squad and picked up his
rifle. Some of the youngsters were worried, on edge. But
Greenaway had grown out of all that. Curiously enough he
had never even got a scratch, except once in a brawl with
some soldiers in Southsea.

He heard de Courcy say, 'You go along with them, Ralf.
Get the lie of the land.'

Greenaway dropped his eyes to hide his irritation. The
second lieutenant might be a Blackwood but he was bloody
useless.

He looked up. 'Ready to move off, sir.'

Ralf nodded. 'Very well. Carry on.'

Greenaway gritted his teeth. That was all the little snob
ever said. *Carry on.*

'Poole, take the point. Adams, bring up the rear.'

Ralf said, 'Have them fix bayonets, Sergeant.'

Greenaway pushed his lower lip up into his big, bushy
moustache.

'Too risky. The sun'll be up soon. It'll reflect off 'em.'

De Courcy heard him, but walked away rattling a warm pebble around his tongue and teeth to hold his terrible thirst at bay. Ralf Blackwood would get little change out of Greenaway, he thought.

The squad slithered and crawled amongst some bushes, feeling their way, eyes everywhere as they headed for the river.

How inviting the sea had looked from the hillside, Ralf thought. It was all so unfair. They should have been got out of it at the first sign of danger.

He thought of *Mediator*. Probably lying safe and snug around the next spur of land. Surely they would not be left to die here in a wilderness? The thought unnerved him and for a moment he felt on the verge of panic.

'Far enough, sir.' Greenaway signalled the others to take cover as he flopped down behind a barrier of stones. Perhaps there had once been a terrible flood here, and only the stones remained to mark its passing.

Ralf glared at the sergeant as he studied the boats which had been abandoned on the bank. Big, coarse and ugly, with thick hair on the backs of his hands.

Ralf turned away as the anger swept through him.

The sun touched his face and he dreaded the heat to come. There was a dark patch in the sky which had not been there before. From the direction of Tientsin. Part of it must be on fire. He thought of the mutilated and headless corpses when they had stopped the train and almost vomited.

Here there was no train, no sign of help, and he had heard that only one of the machine-guns was serviceable. Even that fool Blair must see it was hopeless.

An hour dragged past and Ralf's anxiety mounted with each minute. It was as if they had been left behind, that nothing else lived here.

Greenaway sucked on a piece of grass, his rifle pushed through the scrub and resting on the little stones as he watched the opposite bank. After this little lot he would be out of the Corps for good. But it was all he remembered, all he knew. What would he and Beth do when he quit the

barracks for the last time? He had two daughters, but no
son to carry on the tradition. Still, perhaps one of the girls
would give him a grandson.

He heard someone creeping down beside him and tensed
as if he expected a blow from one of those terrible knives.
But it was Corporal Addis from the platoon.

'Gawd, you gave me a start, creepin' up like that, Percy!'

The corporal peered past him at the river. 'We're goin' to
attack. Just 'ad word from Cap'n Blackwood.'

Even with the shock of his announcement Greenaway was
able to hiss, 'Tell the *officer* then!'

Addis glanced contemptuously at the second lieutenant,
'Fifteen minutes, sir. Mr de Courcy's runner 'as reported a
force of Boxers coming from the sou'-west.'

Greenaway grimaced. 'That's torn it. There's only one
way, an' that's through that ruddy arsenal.'

Ralf floundered for words. 'But − but what about the
ship? I thought we were getting support?'

Greenaway frowned. He shouldn't talk like that in front
of a corporal. Percy Addis was well known for his big mouth
and lower-deck gossip.

He growled, 'Tell 'm we're standin' fast until he comes.'
He pulled back his rifle-bolt with extreme care and thrust a
bullet into the breech.

Ralf stood up and stared wildly at the hillside. Addis had
already vanished.

'I'll go and see Mr de Courcy.' He nodded jerkily, only
vaguely aware of the sprawled marines who were staring at
him, their eyes like glass in the sunshine.

Greenaway said, 'It won't do no good, sir.' He reached
out to encourage the young officer back into cover, but as he
touched his sleeve he seemed to trigger off all of his pent-up
fears and emotions.

'Don't you dare to touch me, you − you − ' He ripped
open his holster and made to drag out his revolver. 'You
think you know everything − '

In his agitation Ralf had holstered his revolver while it

was still cocked. Now as he jerked it, his mind blank to everything but their hostility, the hammer caught in his belt and the revolver swung heavily against Greenaway's rifle and exploded.

Nobody saw where the bullet went but the sound of the single shot echoed across the sluggish river like a thunderclap.

Unware of what had provoked someone to open fire Blair jumped to his feet and shouted, 'At the double!' The marines, who had already been mustered in their various sections, came to life like puppets. With grim faces and rifles at the high-port they trotted down the hillside towards the river.

Most of them had no idea of what might be expected of them. And those who had knew they would now do it alone without even the smallest hope of having surprise on their side.

Blackwood waved his arm and saw the men fan out, keeping their proper distance in spite of the swift change of events. He heard the distant sound of a horn, and knew an alarm was being raised.

It was suddenly desperate and they had not even begun.

He yelled, 'Colour Sergeant! The flag!'

Some of the running marines turned to stare as the burly colour sergeant uncased the flag, and swung it through the air to clear its folds.

Blackwood heard Blair panting beside him. It was only a gesture. But battles had been won on less.

Lieutenant de Courcy paused only to stare across at the arsenal's high wall, his eyes blazing as he shouted, 'First Section into the boats!' He pulled out his revolver and waited for the marines to run the last few yards to the water.

A few shots whimpered and cracked around them, some hitting the river, others thudding into the boats.

Sergeant Greenaway waved his men on. 'Pole 'em over,

lads!' One man spun round, his mouth wide in a silent cry as a heavy bullet hit him in the throat.

More marines hurried past, their bodies bent as if carrying great loads, eyes startled at the sight of the dead man in their own uniform.

De Courcy emitted a sigh as the hidden machine-gun clattered into life and cut little spurts of dust from the high parapet where the Chinese bullets had come from.

He glared at Ralf. 'Take charge of the MG section and the wounded!' He seized him and shook his arm. 'Control yourself, man! They'll be looking even to you in a moment.'

Ralf stared at him, his eyes wide. 'But — but the Boxers are coming this way!'

'Second Section!' De Courcy winced as another man cried out in agony. But he had to make Ralf understand. 'I shall signal you to cross the river. Cover us 'til then!' He bounded over the stones and joined the second boat which was already being poled across the river, while some of the marines fired at the heads on the parapet.

Blackwood saw the leading boats grind ashore, their occupants only too glad to leave and run for the hillside which sloped towards the arsenal. But for that single shot they would have had some small benefit. He saw a marine fall, clutching his stomach even as he vaulted from one of the boats. It was all going wrong, but if they stayed here they would be surrounded by the Boxers who were about a mile away and approaching fast.

More men ran for the boats, while Blackwood saw his cousin climbing back up the hill, his revolver still dangling from its lanyard. In his heart he had known it had been Ralf.

Blair joined him and paused to train his binoculars on the arsenal. The whole countryside would have heard the firing by now.

He said, 'Time to go.' He shot him a twisted smile. 'Separate boats, I think.'

Blackwood ran over the last strip of land and saw the

earth spurt beside him as some invisible marksman marked him down. Swan kept pace with him and dropped his rifle only to seize one of the long poles with Corporal Addis.

A snail's pace, Blackwood thought. He cocked his head to listen as the machine-gun fell silent. But it restarted and he pictured the dwindling pile of ammunition beside it.

On, on, on, with the flag adding a touch of vivid colour above their lowered heads and taut faces.

'Re-form!' Blair limped up the last few yards and leaned against the rocks below the arsenal. 'Get those wounded off the bank!'

Blackwood glanced along the line of men nearest him. Some were feverishly reloading their magazines from their pouches, others stood with their eyes closed as they sucked in great gulps of air.

Sergeant Major Fox bellowed, 'Remember, lads, there's food and drink over that wall! Come on, smarten yerselves up, goddammit!'

Blackwood saw some of the men glaring at his squared shoulders, loathing him, but still managing to react as Fox knew they would.

Blackwood heard someone give a groan as bullets hammered into one of the crude fishing boats while it was still in mid-stream. He saw several marines fall, one completely out of the boat. Another, probably his friend, tried to reach him but the current carried the dead man away. He looked strangely peaceful.

Blair said sharply, 'Mr Gravatt, have your men fire on the parapet. We shall go around to the gates on the road. It's the weakest point.'

Whistles shrilled and NCOs shouted names. Blair added between his teeth, 'God, what a bloody mess!'

Swan whispered, 'The Colonel's been 'it, sir.'

Blackwood realized that Blair was keeping his left elbow jammed against his side. There were flecks of blood on his sleeve. He seemed to sense Blackwood's concern through his pain and gasped, 'Say nothing, David. Not a bloody thing!'

Blackwood cocked his revolver and saw the bugler watching him, his eyes horrified as a marine bounced from the wall, his face a mass of blood.

He thought suddenly of Ralf, back there with the machine-gun section. It would be too much for him to deal with. The machine-gunners, a riding instructor, the engine driver and his mate, and the horse.

It was not much of a threat to the oncoming Boxers. They were all caught in a trap. There was no way out this time.

He forced his mind to respond. If he showed the slightest hint of anxiety or worse, they might break and run. Back to the boats, anywhere.

He nodded to the bugler and realized he was not afraid, he was not even angry any more.

'Sound the Advance, Oates!' Blackwood's grandfather's old servant had been called Oates, and this callow-looking private was related to him. Nothing changed.

Oates raised his instrument, and Blackwood saw his eyes widen as another bugle call echoed faintly above the firing.

Sergeant Greenaway wiped his streaming face with his forearm and said hoarsely, 'Jesus, will you look at *her!*'

Blackwood swung round and heard the others calling to each other as *Mediator*'s long, graceful hull crossed very slowly from left to right beyond the fort.

Splashes marked the sea around her white sides, but Blackwood saw the guns swinging towards the shore, as if they were pointing directly at him.

He said to the bugler, 'Your turn, Oates.' It was all he could do to keep his voice steady. Masterman had made his gesture too, only he would have kept his bugler for this precise moment.

Blair shouted, 'Now, *at them*, Marines!'

The blare of the bugle, the sudden crash of gunfire from *Mediator*'s six-inch armament were almost drowned by the wild cheers as the marines swept towards the adjoining wall and across the road which Blackwood and the colonel had watched from the hilltop.

Huge gouts of fire and earth shot skywards as the first shell exploded on the land. *Mediator*'s gunnery officer was first-class, Blackwood thought, although through his powerful rangefinder the forts and the arsenal probably looked at arm's length.

The lieutenants shouted wildly to restrain their men from breaking cover until they were ready to attack.

Fox pointed and showed a rare excitement. 'Look, the buggers are comin' out!'

The arsenal's gates were opening even as the marines knelt down to take aim. Just a handful of Imperial soldiers in their strange smocks and dark mandarin hats were crowding each other through the gap, ducking as another salvo blasted into the hillside. Masterman's guns were firing well clear of the arsenal, but these Chinese soldiers were not to know that. One of those six-inch shells exploding inside the ancient arsenal would have blasted them to pieces.

'*Take aim!*'

Blair gasped, 'Belay that, Gravatt! Let 'em run. There's been enough slaughter.'

Gravatt lowered his revolver, the light of wildness still in his eyes. 'Inside the arsenal, Sergeant! Jump about!'

Blackwood watched the colonel anxiously. He was bleeding badly, but showed no sign of collapse. He heard de Courcy order his runner to recall the machine-gun section, for the Third Platoon to give them covering fire as they crossed the narrow river.

When he turned again most of the others had already vanished through the gates, bayonets ready, nerves brittle in case of a trick or ambush.

A few moments later the Chinese standard above the wall was hauled down and the bright Union Flag appeared in its place. Blackwood stared up at it. But for Masterman he doubted if any of them would have survived to see it.

Swan muttered, 'Close thing.'

There was no more opposition, and while the wounded were carried into the protection of a cool cellar, the dead were dragged to the wall for a hasty burial.

The last boat, with the horse swimming and wading beside it, grated into the bank and Blackwood saw his cousin amongst the small rearguard. They all ducked as another salvo ripped noisily overhead to explode beyond the low hills. The gunnery officer and his spotters could probably see the advancing Boxers. At such range and exposed as they were on open ground, the Boxers would stand no chance at all.

Blair sat down very carefully on an upended ammunition case, his orderly steadying his arm.

Blair asked, 'How are the supplies, David?'

Blackwood began to unbutton Blair's tunic with the aid of his orderly.

'Just as you said, sir. Food, water, ammunition, everything. It must be one of Tientsin's main arsenals.'

Blair nodded dully. 'The road. I knew it was a clue if only we could use it.'

Swan hissed. 'Gawd, sir. That's a bad 'un.'

The bullet had hit Blair in the side and had made a black-rimmed hole which revealed at least one shattered rib. How he had managed to carry on in such terrible agony was beyond understanding.

Blair sat very upright as they tied a thick dressing around his body. Even that was soon sodden with blood. In the shadowy gloom of the building it looked black.

Gravatt whispered, 'We'll get him back to the ship if she comes further inshore, sir.'

Blair heard him despite his low voice. 'No. We keep together. My orders are to reinforce Peking, but first we have to protect our rear and supplies by holding Tientsin, *do you understand?*'

Blackwood nodded sadly. 'Yes, sir.'

Blair peered at him searchingly. 'You're a good chap, David. Now get round the sentries and see that our people are fed.' He seemed to think of something. 'Where's the horse. I want to see it.'

Blackwood climbed some narrow stone stairs, how many he could not guess. When he reached the high parapet he saw the dead soldiers who had been caught by their machine-gun, the exhausted marines leaning behind the wall as they watched the white-hulled cruiser.

Gravatt and the sergeant major had everything in hand; there was even woodsmoke rising from a spindly chimney as they broke open some rations.

Swan handed him a full canteen. ''Ere, sir.'

It was water from an internal well. It tasted like champagne.

There was more gunfire, but intermittent and further along the coast. The Allied admirals had been driven to action at long last against the other fort. But for *Mediator*'s example he doubted if they would have quit the Peiho bar.

Blackwood walked down the stairs again where after the parapet and the river it seemed almost icy.

He saw the horse standing in the centre of the courtyard, drinking from a bucket and apparently unharmed by the battle.

Blackwood crossed to the main building and saw several marines resting on their rifles, and Blair still sitting on the box.

Blackwood said, 'The horse is here, sir.'

Sergeant Greenaway leaned over. ''E don't 'ear you, sir.' He closed Blair's eyes, his big hand surprisingly gentle. ''E won't get no ride after all.'

Blackwood looked at Blair's upright figure. It was as if he was still with them. He felt it like a personal loss, as if they had all been cheated in the face of victory.

They were all watching him. Gravatt and de Courcy, the colour sergeant Nat Chittock, and the bugler whose grandfather had been related to a Blackwood servant.

He heard himself say, 'We'll bury him with the others. Tomorrow we move on. To Tientsin.'

He glanced again at the watching colonel.

I hope you heard that, old friend.

Another salvo shook the hillside. It sounded like a last tribute.

13

Soldiering

As the last notes of the bugle died away Blackwood handed the small prayer book to Lieutenant Gravatt. He looked at the six crude graves and hoped they would be left unmolested. It already seemed strange without Blair. Later it would dim like the other memories. But now . . . he sighed and then drove Blair's sword into the head of the grave.

De Courcy said in a hushed tone, 'More firing downriver, sir.' Blackwood nodded. He had already heard it. A machine-gun too. But it seemed excluded from the place, this moment.

He saw his cousin watching him from the far side of the courtyard. So far they had not spoken since the incident. Sergeant Greenaway had said nothing, nor would he unless it was dragged out of him.

A sentry shouted from the ramparts, 'Boat comin', sir!' His voice seemed too bright and cheerful after the burial, and Blackwood guessed that it was one of *Mediator*'s boats.

'Take charge here, Toby. Have the wounded ready to be moved.'

Some of the marines heard what he said, and he saw one of the wounded move into the ranks of the others. He did not want to leave. Blackwood saw it was a private called Carver, the one who had tried to save his friend when he had fallen overboard.

The sentries opened the big gate and Blackwood walked down towards the river. Apart from the abandoned boats and some blood-stains in the dirt there was nothing to show of their wild, desperate attack. He shaded his eyes to watch the boat as it manoeuvred awkwardly amongst the sandbars and treacherous rushes. Smoke gushed from the brass funnel, and it appeared to be crammed with men, and there was a machine-gun in the cockpit.

He recognized the lieutenant in charge of the boat and saw the man's astonishment as he waded ashore, his eyes taking in the marines in their crumpled uniforms, the stains which told their own story.

'My God, David, you are full of surprises!'

Blackwood shook his head. Two Englishmen meeting in the middle of nowhere. He wanted to laugh, but needed to cry.

'The Colonel's dead, Harry.' He could feel the naval officer's concern, his inability to grasp what they had all endured.

The lieutenant said, 'The Old Man intends to land his own marines and some Bluejackets as soon as the other captains agree. They are shelling the other forts, and once we've driven them back we shall occupy the port.' It sounded easy. He added, 'We received word that Admiral Seymour's force have taken another big arsenal, and are staying put until relief arrives.' It seemed to amuse him. 'The rescuers awaiting rescue, so to speak. The message said that his men were starving when they took the arsenal.' He watched Blackwood's strained features and said, 'You must have been on your last legs too.'

Blackwood said, 'Him and his three days' rations!' He did not hide his anger and bitterness.

'By the way, I've brought some of your chaps with me. The Surgeon says they are recovered from their injuries up to a point. Anyway, they pretty well insisted.' He turned his head as more shots echoed from the main river. 'We were fired on by Chinese soldiers on our way here. It's war as far as they're concerned.'

Blackwood heard the returning marines being greeted by

ironic cheers. With men like these . . . Blair had said.

The lieutenant wanted to go. Not because he was afraid, but because it was not his world.

'Tell Captain Masterman, thank you from me. It was a near thing.' He pulled out a hastily written message and handed it to him. 'This will explain about a letter which the Colonel left on board. Perhaps Captain Masterman will deal with it if – ' *If* – the word hung between them like a threat.

The lieutenant thrust the message into his pocket and shouted to his coxswain, 'Get those wounded on board, Thomas! Fast as you like.' He turned to Blackwood again. 'There's something else, sir.'

Blackwood saw his eyes move towards the boat and when he looked he saw Sergeant Kirby marching purposefully towards him.

'I don't believe it!'

It was unreal. Even the way Kirby was holding back his shoulders, the set of his jaw, his attempt to conceal his pain and discomfort. The fact that he was dressed from top to toe in clean, fresh whites made it even harder to accept.

Kirby stamped to a halt and saluted. 'The NCOs in *Mediator*'s barracks kitted me out, sir.' He sounded very calm, but his eyes were anxious.

Blackwood knew he should not be here. Men in battle could often stand up to almost anything as Blair had proved. But sooner or later they broke.

He said, 'I'm glad to have you back again.' He held out his hand. 'You're more than welcome.'

Kirby stared at the proffered hand. He must be going mad. Then he seized it and walked up the slope to where Fox was waiting to greet him.

The naval lieutenant said softly, 'We had news. His wife died in a fire.'

Blackwood looked at the marines who were gathered by the gates.

'Poor devil. No wonder he wants to get back with the company. I know I would.'

The lieutenant nodded. 'But he's been put up for the VC I hear.'

Blackwood thought of his dead brother in South Africa, of his frail mother and the pretty girl he had left behind. No decoration on earth could fill that gap.

He walked across to a stretcher as Twiss was carried to the boat.

'Don't worry, I'll take care of the horse.' He had not even seen the riding instructor struck down.

The man grinned up at him, his face pale with pain. '*You* ride him. You're in command now.' He waved to the marines as he was lifted over the gunwale. The engine driver shook Blackwood's hand but said nothing. It was all too much for him.

Corporal Lyde said, 'He misses 'is engine!'

Sergeant Owen Davis of the First Platoon exclaimed, 'Well, there's sorry I am indeed, Corporal, but *he's* still alive, look you!'

The coxswain touched his hat. 'All aboard, sir. The sooner we gets one of 'em to the Surgeon the better, I'm thinkin'.'

'Wait.' Blackwood waded through the yellow water and clung to the gunwale. Without their spiked helmets how young they seemed. The man referred to by the coxswain was a private named Campbell. He looked as if he was dying even while one of the Bluejackets supported his head on his lap.

'Good luck, lads.'

Blackwood heard someone give a weak cheer. 'You too, Blackie!'

Blackwood strode up the bank, afraid they would see his face. *Good God Almighty, what have we done to them?*

The lieutenant held out his hand. 'The Old Man would quite understand if you decide to return to the ship, David. Even if we take the forts we've still got a bloody great army to smash through before we can lift the siege on Tientsin. You'll be stuck there with a mixed garrison, to all intents on your own.'

Return to *Mediator*? It was strange but Blackwood had never even considered it. If the new attacks were repulsed by the Chinese Army, which had obviously joined forces with the Boxers, there was an even greater need for reinforcing the International Settlement in Tientsin.

A small figure dashed past him from the boat and he saw it was the other interpreter who had gone downriver with his message for Masterman. The one who had remained with the marines broke through the group by the gates, his face split in a great grin as his friend ran to meet him and threw his arms around him.

The lieutenant said, 'They must be pretty fond of one another, what?'

Blackwood smiled. 'You must have been at sea a long time, Harry.' No wonder they had not wanted to be separated. 'If you've forgotten what a girl looks like!'

The girl had removed her pointed straw hat and her long hair hung down her back like black silk.

'I stay.' She stepped between Blackwood and her friend. 'We work for you.' She gave Blackwood a coy smile. 'I born in Tientsin. I know secret way through wall.'

Gravatt murmured anxiously, 'It's a big risk, sir. Can she be trusted?'

Blackwood put his fingers under her chin and lifted it gently.

'I believe her.' To the other interpreter, who was also about sixteen, he added, 'Lucky chap.'

He heard the boat churning astern away from the land, and hoped it got back to the cruiser without more pain and damage.

Inside the courtyard it was as if the boat had never been, and the graves were the only reminder of this long day.

A marine was feeding the horse. Blackwood was reminded of its last owner's simple statement. *You're in command now.*

He crossed to the horse and patted it, his eyes distant as

he remembered Blair, his divided affections for the Corps and this mysterious land.

Ralf was waiting by the stairway. He said, 'It wasn't my fault!'

Blackwood studied him calmly. 'What happened exactly?'

Ralf looked startled. 'Did Sergeant Greenaway – '

'Nobody's said anything. What did you expect?'

Ralf replied, 'Greenaway was trying to make me look a fool in front of the men. I am quite capable of doing my job without interference from his sort.'

Blackwood felt sickened by it as he watched the petulant strength returning to Ralf's features. He gestured towards the rough graves, and the one with the sword glittering in the filtered sunlight.

'We lost some good men today. But for your stupid, intolerant behaviour we might have escaped with fewer casualties, so think of that for a change!'

Ralf hung his head. 'I thought you would stand up for me.'

'So I will.' Blackwood knew Fox was waiting for him. There were plans to be made, a route to be discussed with the interpreters. There was not much time to rest. If half of what the naval lieutenant had told him was true most of the Boxers would be rallying to withstand a possible landing. It would be their only chance to get into the city before they too were cut off by the enemy.

He added, 'Even at a court-martial. Now be off to your duties and see that your people eat and rest in turns. Show that you are interested in them, that they can rely on you.' He touched Ralf's shoulder but felt more like hitting him. 'That you've got the gut for it.'

He walked away, knowing that as before Ralf had seen right through him.

Blackwood spread his map carefully on the table while the officers and senior NCOs pressed closer around him. In the light from a solitary lantern the room was spartan like most of the arsenal; there were even some half-consumed dishes of tea left by the small detachment of soldiers when Ralf's revolver had raised the alarm.

It would be dawn again very soon, but it was difficult to believe they had been here since yesterday. Outside the little room he could hear the marines being mustered by their corporals, the horse stamping its newly muffled hooves on the cobbles. Each man would be carrying a full pack which they had recovered from the opposite bank during the night. Blackwood half expected an attack, but Bannatyre's scouting party had found nothing. *Mediator*'s unexpected bombardment had worked. Only corpses lay beyond the humped hill.

Blackwood was sorry they had thrown the second machine-gun into the river. There was three-oh-three ammunition in plenty for it and any other weapon stacked within the arsenal. There was ample food too, but if the marines were required to fight without warning they would have to rid themselves of their overweight packs and equipment.

It was amazing what a good meal and a few gallons of tea had done for his depleted company. In spite of their losses and what still lay ahead they were able to joke about it, to impress the returned wounded who had been the original heroes until now.

Blackwood pointed at the map. 'We shall skirt round the city and make our approach from the south-west. That way we shall avoid the more crowded parts and another big arsenal which will be heavily guarded. It appears that Admiral Seymour's forces have occupied the Hsiku arsenal to the north, that too will be under siege by now. So if our ships are attacking the forts most attention will be concentrated on the places mentioned.' He saw Sergeant Kirby sway forward as if to study the map more closely.

Incredibly brave, foolish too. It was hard to know which he admired most. Kirby knew exactly what he was doing. Reason had flown out of the window.

'I intend to leave at first light, and enter the city at dusk.' He glanced around their intent faces. So much depended on the interpreters' information. He had spent over an hour discussing his tactics with them, and it was remarkable how quickly they had grasped his ideas. The girl, who had been born in Tientsin, had even changed his plan from his original one. She had described a long, empty gully which ran from the south-west wall of the city, intended originally to deal with rare but overwhelming rainfalls in the area.

Madness, just the place the enemy would be guarding? But why should they? The defenders were penned inside the various concessions and could not break out, and the only real danger came from the sea. He half smiled. It was just about the craziest plan he had ever heard, let alone created.

Fox said, 'I laid 'ands on a cart, sir. Useful fer ferryin' wounded an' the like.' He was only concerned with details. The chances of risk and survival were not his to question.

De Courcy remarked, 'We'll need some good scouts for this one.'

He glanced at Sergeant Greenaway who nodded and said, 'Taken care of, sir.'

Chittock, the colour sergeant, said, 'I borrowed a spare flag from the boat, sir. Don't want to damage our own.'

Several of them laughed. They all knew what Chittock meant by 'borrow'.

Blackwood straightened his back and looked at each of them in turn. 'You may think this is a waste of time, perhaps a waste of lives. But think of yourselves under fire in Tientsin, hoping and praying for a relief which never comes. You've all seen what the Boxers are capable of. When we enter the city it will give them new heart.' He had almost said *if* instead of *when*.

'One thing, and it has to be said. There will be no surrender. It would only prolong the agony.' He made himself grin. 'So be prepared to move.'

When the others had left Gravatt said, 'Will we blow the arsenal, sir?'

'No. We would lose any chance of surprise. At the moment the enemy seems to think we left in *Mediator*.'

Gravatt laughed. 'It *would* seem the sensible thing to do!'

Blackwood glanced at the empty room. 'You are second-in-command now, Toby, you may need a plan all of your own!'

'A sobering thought, sir.'

Blackwood clapped him on the shoulder. 'Take my – er, Mr Blackwood with you.' He saw Gravatt's surprise. 'And watch him, for all our sakes.'

Gravatt nodded, his mood changed. He probably guessed what it had cost Blackwood to say it. But there was far more at stake now than family ties.

Gravatt looked down at his uniform and groaned. 'God, look at us!' Like the rest of the men his tunic and trousers had been soaked in a vat of boiled tea, so that they had a dirty mottled appearance. But Blackwood knew from the past it offered some cover and disguise.

Gravatt was unimpressed. 'Lord knows what my chap in Savile Row would say!'

They left the room. Blackwood felt like his adjutant. It was a shame to abandon the arsenal intact. All those weapons and ammunition might one day be used against them. Perhaps Masterman's guns would finish the job once they had moved inland again.

In the courtyard the air still felt cool and damp.

He glanced at the scouting party which Greenaway had hand-picked himself. He thought suddenly of Blair and his trust in others. It worked. They were all there. Corporal O'Neil, Dago Trent, Roberts, the crack shot who said he came from a farm. A poacher more likely. There were a few others too, faces as familiar as his own in a mirror.

Sergeant Greenaway strode towards him, ungainly and heavy.

'Ready, sir.' He hesitated. 'Will an officer be comin' with us?'

'No, Sergeant.' It was painful to see his relief. 'It's up to you.'

O'Neil called to his friend the Nordenfeldt gunner. 'Will you be safe without me, Willy? I'll try not to be too long!'

Kirby's harsh voice echoed from the wall. 'Quiet, you bog-trottin' madman!'

Blackwood looked away. Kirby had changed again in some way. There was no malice in the sergeant's voice. He was glad to be back, more than that, he *needed* to be here.

'Open the gates.'

The scouting party drifted through the gap and vanished into the gloom. From the parapet a sentry called in a hushed voice, 'All's well, sir!'

Blackwood crossed to the graves. What did they always say? No goodbyes, never go back.

'Withdraw the sentries, Mr Bannatyre, and take command of the rearguard.' He stopped him in his tracks. 'No heroics this time, Ian. We'll try and stay together.'

In sections the marines began to move towards the gate, rifles slung, shoulders bowed under their packs, extra ammunition, food and all that went to make them independent of the land.

Swan coughed politely. ''Ere we are, sir.' His teeth were very white in the darkness. ''Is name's Trooper.'

Blackwood smiled. He could almost feel Blair watching and listening. It was what he would have done.

Blackwood raised his foot to the stirrup and heaved himself into the saddle. It reminded him of those keen mornings at Hawks Hill, the copse sweeping past in that first gallop.

Swan stood back and looked at him. 'Wish I 'ad one of them new camera-things, sir. The General'd be right proud of you!'

Blackwood spurred the horse after Fox's handcart. 'Come on then, Trooper, let's see what you can do.'

As he trotted along the lines of marines he saw them glance at him, some to nudge their companions and grin. *A bit of soldiering*, as Fox would put it. What it was all about.

At the rear of the thin column Private Jack Swan placed his captured pike on the cart and fell in step behind the others. His belly was full, his throat was no longer like a kiln, and he had enough ammo to last him quite a while.

When you considered it, he thought, you didn't need much else.

The gully was about ten feet deep and lined with crudely cut stone blocks which looked as old as time.

For most of the day the marines had trudged along the gully's curved base, some gasping for breath as the sun made the airless heat unbearable.

Every so often Blackwood had signalled them to pause and take a rest. Weighed down as they were, they could not be expected to keep up a good pace. And all the time they had heard the distant bark of light artillery, the crack of rifle fire, where or whose it was Blackwood did not know, he was just thankful it was away from their gully. There was smoke too which as dusk closed in looked solid against the sky.

A runner came back along the straggling column, jumping to avoid the cracks between the stones and the great tufts of grass which had somehow survived in the searing heat.

'Beg pardon, sir.' He paused for breath. 'Mr de Courcy's respects, an' we're in sight of the wall.'

'Tell the advance guard to stand-to.'

Sergeant Greenaway would keep his scouts hidden; he always seemed to know what to do.

Blackwood hurried after the runner and heard Swan calling somebody to lead the horse in his place. Even here, Swan trusted nobody to guard him.

He found Gravatt and de Courcy sprawled amongst some stones which had collapsed over the side of the gully.

Neither of them was wearing his helmet as he peered over the side. Another lesson learned, thought Blackwood.

'What is it?' He noticed that Gravatt had Blair's binoculars slung around his neck and saw dried blood on the leather case.

He dragged out his own glasses and wriggled up beside the others. The land was quite flat, and he could see the smouldering buildings of the Native City, and clouds of drifting sparks from the more substantial European houses.

He trained his glasses with great care and saw the wall and sand-bagged defences of the south-west corner. The girl had been right about everything so far.

The gunfire seemed to be coming from the other sector, and he heard someone shouting as more shots cracked amongst the ruins.

He said quietly, 'Most of the fighting seems to be on the far side near the canal. Maybe some of our people are trying to reach the city from the Peiho itself. If so they're getting a hot reception.'

Gravatt pointed at another low wall which crossed diagonally in front of the city. It had obviously been the first line of defence for the various legation guards, but they had been forced back into the city itself. The low wall was pockmarked with white stars where hundreds of bullets had left their mark. In the centre of the wall, almost opposite the barricaded gates, was a great V-shaped gap. A shell must have done it, but it looked as if some giant beast had gnawed it out.

Gravatt waited for him to see the occasional movements where the attackers were now using the same wall for their own cover.

White smocks criss-crossed with bandoliers of ammunition and the now familiar red head scarves.

'No more than a dozen of them, sir.'

Blackwood measured the distance with his eyes. Once they left the gully there was over a hundred yards to the gates. A lot depended on the intelligence of the defenders, and the strength of enemy forces nearby.

They could proceed no further in the gully. Most of the sides had fallen down to block it nearer the city, or had been detonated to prevent a surprise attack.

The sky was getting darker. It was the colour of blood towards the west. He bit his lip. Hopefully not an omen.

'Firing's getting heavier, sir.' De Courcy watched him patiently. 'Another attack before nightfall maybe?'

Gravatt slid down and replaced his helmet. 'We'll not get a better chance, sir.'

'I agree.' Blackwood levelled his glasses again. The Boxers behind the low wall were so confident that only two were watching the city wall, the others had their backs to it, their weapons propped or lying nearby.

One Boxer looked straight at him, his face stark and cruel in the lens. For an instant Blackwood thought he had seen him, but the man's eyes moved on, impassive once again.

'We shall attack in two prongs from left to right. One section only will remain in the centre with the MG carriage and Sergeant Major Fox's cart.' Like the others he always saw the cart as Fox's personal property.

De Courcy eyed him doubtfully. 'They could still pin us down while they call for reinforcements. There are probably others in those ruins over yonder.'

'We must have what our late Colonel would call a *diversion*.' He looked for Swan. 'Lead Trooper up here and fetch the Colour Sergeant and a bugler.'

It was a strange unnerving feeling. As if his whole body had suddenly become weightless. The tension was the biggest drain on men's nerves. It was now or never.

He heard the horse thudding past the crouching marines and saw Chittock with his sheathed flag following close behind.

'Get to your positions.' He glanced at the lieutenants and tried to smile. But his muscles were so hard that he could barely manage it. It was like that other time when he had thought he was about to die. When he had won his VC.

'Good luck. Tell your people to *trot* when they hear the bugle. They'll drop like flies before they've covered half the distance otherwise.'

They nodded, their faces stiff, like strangers.

To Swan he added, 'Take those rags off Trooper's hooves.' He loosened his sword and did the same with his revolver.

Swan stared at him. 'You're not goin' over on '*im?*'

'Watch me.' Blackwood turned to the others. 'When I come past, sound the Charge, and keep on, no matter what.' To Swan he said quietly, 'Listen. The firing is getting less. Soon it will be too late. Try to understand. It's what I'm here for.'

Swan opened his mouth to protest but closed it again. Then he said, 'I'll be with you, sir. All the bloody way.'

Blackwood pulled himself into the saddle and felt the horse flinch nervously, Perhaps it knew, or could smell the blood.

He replied, 'I know that, you rascal.' Then he cantered back down the gully where the NCOs were hissing instructions to their men.

'Fix bayonets!' In the red glow from the sky the blades looked as if they had already been used.

They watched him pass and then Blackwood saw Ralf waiting for him by the cart and the men with the machine-gun carriage. Pity they couldn't use that now, he thought vaguely. But they would need it later on. If they survived.

He wheeled his horse and faced the end of the gully which he had just left. All movement had ceased and the marines crouched or lay along the side, some chewing on their chinstraps, others looking at him as he gauged the moment.

'What is it, Ralf?' It came out sharper than he intended.

'The interpreters, sir. They want to leave.' He sounded on the edge of real fear. 'They'll betray us!'

The two interpreters came and stood beside the horse, the girl soothing the animal with her small hand.

'We leave now.' She was not pleading. 'We go to my home.'

Blackwood thought of the dense smoke and flattened buildings. Home. He tried to control his body. It must be shaking for everyone to see.

He asked, 'Is it safe?'

She touched his stirrup. 'Where is safe?'

Where is safe? Its very simplicity seemed to sum up every campaign he had ever seen.

He tugged down his helmet and then drew his sword. As he bit on his chinstrap he managed to say, 'Pass them through. And good luck.' Then he spurred the horse into a trot, his sword over his shoulder as the waiting marines seemed to flash past him.

Round the long curve and there were the fallen stones, the bugler and the others staring at him as if they would never move again.

'Sound the Charge!' As the bugle blared across the gully Blackwood spurred the horse into a gallop, straight for the fallen barrier. For an instant he thought Trooper was going to rear up and throw him, but he dragged at the reins and felt the powerful body lift beneath him and they were suddenly thundering across open ground. It was all moving like a wild dream, the bugle seemed to go on and on, and in his mind he could see the two halves of his company bursting from cover and pounding along behind him.

And here was the wall, with more gaping faces, and the sudden crack of a rifle. One Boxer ran straight for him but slithered away with a terrible shriek as Blackwood's blade hacked him across the neck. Up again, and through the gap in the wall. There were more shots now, but they were coming from the advancing marines who fired from the hip without even taking aim in the confusion. Pinned against the wall the remaining Boxers stood ready to fight, but those who did not fall reeled before the glittering bayonets as the marines charged through them.

Protected by the centre section the colour sergeant

managed to hold the flag high, his bright scarlet sash at odds with his crumpled tea-stained clothing.

Two marines on the right flank fell in the dust, and as another section opened covering fire they were dragged on to the cart and rushed towards the wall.

Blackwood galloped along the barricades and shell-pitted wall and saw startled faces peering down at him. Their uniforms all seemed to be different, like the flags which flew over Seymour's ships.

'*Open the gate!*' Blackwood waved his sword. 'Move your bloody breeches!'

The gates swung inwards and Blackwood reined back as his breathless wild-eyed men charged through.

A few shots whimpered overhead but Blackwood barely noticed them.

Somewhere a voice shouted, 'The relief's here! My God they've got through! Who are you, lads?'

And Fox's harsh voice as loud as on any parade ground. '*The Royal Marines*, that's who, mate!'

But Blackwood patted the horse and waited for Swan to join him. Only when the gates crashed together behind him did he really understand what they had done.

As he allowed the horse to carry him beneath the overhang of the wall he heard a marine exclaim, 'You should'er seen 'im! Talk abaht the Charge o' the bleedin' Light Brigade!'

Blair would have approved.

14

Love and Hate

Blackwood sat uncomfortably on a straightbacked chair which seemed to have been placed about ten feet from the desk. It made him feel isolated from the man behind it, and he guessed that was probably the intention.

Colonel Sir John Hay of the Foot Guards had sent for him as soon as the Royal Marines had arrived at their temporary quarters, a long stone building which had been stables. At least Trooper would feel at home there.

The thought made him smile. It was like everything else, unreal, larger than life. Sergeant Kirby's return, the mad dash on horseback, the cheers of his men.

It had taken a toll of his own strength. He could feel the hammers beating inside his skull and recalled what the naval surgeon had hinted about concussion.

Colonel Hay was almost the strangest person you might expect to find in this situation, he thought.

He was tall, square-shouldered, with an upturned ginger moustache, and bright, pale eyes which were almost colourless. On the rare occasions Blackwood had seen him smile he changed entirely. His grin, like his voice, was fierce, so that he looked slightly unhinged.

Blackwood recalled Hay's first words as the exhausted marines had waited patiently in a square which was littered with debris from the surrounding buildings, and which stank of corpses still buried under the bricks and charred beams.

After what they had done to reach Tientsin, and the

many pitched battles since their arrival in China, Blackwood had expected a brief speech of welcome at least.

Hay had seemed almost beside himself with disbelief. 'Is this *all*? What happened to the relief?' He had glared at Blackwood accusingly. 'How many have you got, for God's sake?'

Blackwood had answered as calmly as he could. 'Seventy officers and marines, sir.' He had forced a smile. 'And two Austro-Hungarian sailors we gathered on the way.'

Hay had not been amused. 'They promised reinforcements.' He had glared at the marines in their tea-stained uniforms and filthy boots. 'God, they look like – ' He had not said any more. Then as now Hay made a stark contrast in his red tunic and gold shoulder straps. There was not a speck of dust on his uniform in spite of the irregular explosions around the city, the occasional whiplash crack of sniper fire.

Blackwood shifted in the chair. His body felt restricted in his scarlet tunic which Swan had hastily unpacked and brushed for him.

Hay had said hotly, 'We represent the British authorities here. As senior officer in Tientsin I expect, no, demand, a proper turnout at all times. It is the only way to retain these people's respect.'

Blackwood was still not certain whom he had meant by 'these people'. The Chinese, or the Allied troops who made up most of the city's defenders.

Hay turned his head and stared at the heavily shuttered window. 'We've about two thousand soldiers here. Russians, French, Americans, Japanese and of course my own men. We've a perimeter of some five miles to defend, and the barricades make up much of the protection along the river and canal. Some American engineer named Hoover did most of the planning. Quite a fair job.'

It sounded condescending. As if it was of no real importance.

His head was getting worse and he knew he needed sleep

more than anything. It was incredible to accept that they had marched from the arsenal that morning. Now it was midnight or near enough and it was all he could do to concentrate on Hay's sharp, irritated voice.

'Pity you didn't blow up that magazine. The enemy have enough looted weapons as it is. It's been absolute hell here, and we've all the civilians, women and children to care for.'

Blackwood made himself ask, 'How many of the enemy, sir?'

Hay glared at him as if he expected a trap. 'They estimate about ten thousand, with more coming every day. Unless reinforcements can break through there'll soon be nothing to defend. Somebody should try to negotiate again with the Chinese government. This kind of uprising ought to be stamped out immediately.'

There was no point in telling Hay it was no longer just an uprising. At Hawks Hill the General with his maps and his memories would probably agree with him and describe it as a 'skirmish'.

Instead he said, 'The whole countryside is terrified of the Boxers.'

'You would know of course.' Again the fierce grin. 'I've heard about the Royal Marines.'

'I've lost my colonel, another officer and twenty-three others killed and wounded. Some of the latter have voluntarily rejoined the detachment.' He added bitterly, 'They can still give a good account when called for.'

Hay changed tack. 'I shall give your men the south-west sector. Some fortifications, several good strong buildings, and one of the hotels which we use for civilians.' He dropped his pale stare. 'Ours, of course.'

Of course. What was the real cause of his dislike? Blackwood wondered. He thought of the marines' expressions when Hay had criticized their appearance. For an instant he had feared that some wild man might yell something from the safety of the ranks. But as had happened before it had acted as a challenge to the marines.

Within the hour they were paraded again in their scarlet kerseys with buttons as bright as ever.

He had heard Fox saying in a voice just a bit too loud, 'And any Royal Marine who lets me down in front of a bloody Foot Guard will know what my temper can be like!'

Perhaps because of their calling they had hated the dirt, the sweat and torn clothing which they had carried with them all the way from *Mediator*'s gleaming messdecks.

'I've heard that you have seen quite a bit of service, Captain Blackwood.'

Blackwood said nothing. How different from Blair. The day that Hay calls me by my first name will be *the*day.

Hay studied him severely. 'Nowadays I am more used to diplomats than the Brigade.'

A small Chinese girl in a white smock entered the room with a silver tray. On it were two large glasses of whisky.

Blackwood could not remember asking for it, but he was so drained he could hardly recall any sequence of events.

The room gave a shiver as some shells fell somewhere in the city. He saw the servant's eyes widen with alarm and wondered how the two interpreters were getting on, and if they were still alive. The whisky was good and he felt its strength warming him.

Hay said, 'The officers here are a mixed bunch naturally.' He frowned. 'Some of them lost their kit in the first attacks, so there's no need to dress for dinner.'

'I don't have mess kit either, sir.'

'I understand.'

He went off at a tangent again. 'I believe they will mount a big attack tomorrow or the day after. They need to occupy the whole city and destroy the defenders before they can join together at Peking.'

'We are in the same position, sir.'

'Really?' He sounded distant. 'So long as we can hold the perimeter things should get better.'

Blackwood tried not to look at him. At this stage of the game it seemed inconceivable that anyone could ignore the problems of shortages which would soon bear down on them all. Food, ammunition, survival.

Hay said, 'The Boxers never attack at night. Perhaps their invulnerability only works in daylight, eh?' He gave a short laugh, like a dog barking.

He added, 'It was a pity you were not sent directly here in the first place.' Again it sounded like an accusation. 'That business upriver was a waste of time. That's where you lost a subaltern, right?'

'Yes, sir.' Blackwood placed his empty glass on a table and saw that Hay had not drunk any of his. What was the matter with him? One minute he acted towards him with total indifference, and the next he had released some information which he must have gathered from someone else.

'Oh yes, brave enough, no doubt of that, but not thought through.'

Blackwood asked abruptly, 'Who told you about the Hoshun, sir?'

Hay stood up and squared his shoulders. 'I heard something about it when you and Admiral Seymour's advance party went through Tientsin. I also met quite a few of the people who were trying to get back to Peking before you arrived.'

'Did you meet any of the Germans who returned to their Peking legation?' Without noticing it he was leaning forward in the chair.

'Oh yes. Count von Heiser of course.'

Why did he always add *of course*? He tried again, 'I heard they arrived safely.'

'Did you?'

He wants me to beg, but how could he know or guess?

Hay remarked offhandedly, 'They went in separate parties in case the railway was torn up. As it happened, the Chinese closed the city to the Allies the day they arrived. But the second party turned back.' His eyes glittered in the lamplight. 'These Germans don't know everything. It will do them good to have their tails between their legs for a change!' Again the short, humourless laugh.

The colonel pulled a watch from his pocket. 'You'd better get back to your sector. Don't forget, double the sentries. All looters will be shot on sight. Stand-to at first light.' It was dismissal.

Blackwood walked through an outer room where a tired-looking servant was busy polishing the colonel's boots.

Sir John Hay was a strange bird, he thought. Was his comment about dressing for dinner merely to cover something else? He seemed very confident, perhaps too much so.

The warm night air made him yawn. He would have to go round the sentries before speaking to Gravatt.

It was deathly quiet, but in the sky he could still see the reflected fires, drifting smoke.

As he strode towards the sector where they had burst through the gates just a few hours ago he saw Swan's shadow detach itself from the side of a low building.

'You ought to get some rest, Swan. That's one privilege at least your job gives you.'

Swan studied him in the darkness. 'A Chinese girl brought you a letter, sir.' He could not hold the pretence any longer and Blackwood saw his grin splitting his face as he added. 'It was our little Anna.'

Blackwood took the small envelope and turned it over in his hands.

'Tell Mr Gravatt I want him.' He waited for Swan to hurry away and then ducked into the low doorway of the abandoned building. By the light of a shaded lamp he opened the envelope and held a single sheet of notepaper in the glow.

It said, *Please come*, and it was sighed with an *F*.

She is here. Hay had known the reason for his questions, or he soon would. He must be careful for her sake.

Gravatt crunched out of the darkness. 'I've been round our posts, sir. I had the machine-gun mounted on a low building. The men there will be protected by a barricade of sandbags and sacks of grain. Best we can do.'

'Stand-to at first light, Toby.'

'I know, sir.'

Blackwood did not ask him how he knew.

He said, 'Call me if you need me.'

Gravatt watched him go. No wonder the men liked him so much. He had seen Anna give the letter to Swan. The rest was easy to fathom out.

He removed his helmet and dragged his finger around his tunic collar. First light and they would stand and fight. Suddenly he envied Blackwood. Just to hold a woman's hand again, to blurt out your fears, to pretend there was a future.

He sighed and walked around the corner to seek out the last picket.

The hotel which Hay had described in their brief interview was at the rear of the marines' sector, hemmed in on either side by sturdy, barricaded buildings. One of the latter was where Gravatt had sited their only machine-gun. If he lived he would one day make a good field officer Blackwood thought.

If the enemy forced the gates and drove the marines back to their next line of defence, the gun could cover them from the flat roof and still be able to fire above the defences without being moved. The hotel was shuttered and cur-tained and smelt of musty carpets and decay. The last place on earth where any European might expect to end up.

A British soldier in a white jacket watched Blackwood with obvious suspicion as he explained who he had come to see.

''S like this, sir, we're not supposed to let service people in 'ere after dark. Regulations, sir.'

'Colonel Hay said it was perfectly all right.'

The man looked relieved. 'In that case, sir.' He gestured with his tray. 'Up them stairs, second right.' He hesitated.

'If you're sure, sir?'

Blackwood hurried up the curved staircase. The soldier might call his superior officer, but he doubted it. He guessed that sleep was a bonus around here; it would take a strong heart to wake an officer. He saw a small figure huddled in an armchair outside a door.

'Hello, Anna.'

The girl took his hands in hers and rocked from side to side, as she had aboard the old *Bajamar*, a million years ago.

She whispered, 'Bye um bye we all finish, Sah. Boxer come um choppum head. All gone!'

Blackwood could feel her terror, also the loyalty which held her to her German mistress.

He released his hands and tapped gently on the door.

It opened instantly, as if she had been listening, waiting.

He closed the door quietly and followed her through vague shadow to an adjoining room. There was a small glow from a lamp, but otherwise the place was in darkness, the air humid and without life.

She was wearing the same dark blue robe as when he had burst into her cabin with Swan's shoulder beside him. Her hair too hung down her back, more like gold than honey in the faint glow.

She did not resist as he took her shoulders and pulled her against him.

She said, 'When I heard the excitement and the cheering I knew it was you. It had to be.' She looked up and searched his face. 'You are not hurt? I heard that you had a bad time, that men were killed.'

'Some were. Thank God you are safe, Friedrike.' How easy it was to speak her name. 'When Colonel Hay told me, I could not believe you might be here too.'

Her mouth quivered. 'That man Hay. He is in the wrong army, I think. He should be a Prussian Guard!'

Blackwood held her closer and touched her hair, her soft warmth, and allowed the dream to become reality.

'And you are alone here?'

She rested her head on his shoulder. 'Yes. Manfred had to go to Peking. He will be needed, I think. There is a rumour that Baron von Ketteler has been murdered there by Chinese troops. Nothing is certain.' She looked at him again. 'Except that you came. To me.'

Somewhere in the musty hotel a clock chimed. It sounded doleful, like a dirge. One o'clock.

She said suddenly, 'I need air. I shall open the window. There can be no danger if the light is out.'

He released her reluctantly. Had she done that deliberately but was now once again in control of herself?

He turned off the lamp as she opened the long curtains and pushed the heavy shutters away from the windows.

'Look at the moon, David.' She sounded excited, like a child.

He stood behind her, his hands on her small waist as he stared across the beleaguered city. *Tomorrow.* What was the use of thinking about any tomorrow? It might be pointless.

She asked, 'Will help come, David?'

He felt her shiver, but when he touched her neck it was hot, as if she had a fever.

'They will come. They must.' He thought of Masterman's determination, his example to the others who had waited too long.

'My men are nearest to you. We will protect you, no matter what.'

She spoke with great care and deliberation. 'But if the Boxers come here, David, it will mean – '

'It will mean that we have failed, and have paid for it.' He forced the picture of the murdered Chinese girl and her baby from his mind. 'But we shall make our stand here, you can depend on it.'

She turned easily in his arms and studied him although Blackwood could not see her face in the darkness.

'I feel safe now.'

She did not resist as he lowered his mouth to hers and kissed her very gently. It was like touching something

STRATFORD PUBLIC LIBRARY
19 ST. ANDREW ST.
STRATFORD, ONTARIO

fragile, or saying the wrong word when it counted most. She did not pull away but kissed him in return, her heart pounding to match his own. Only when he slipped his hand through the robe and touched her breast did she exclaim, 'Oh, my God, David, I can't, must not!'

But he held her breast in his hand. It was alive, warm and beating as if it would burst free.

She leaned against him, her hair brushing his mouth as she gasped, 'I can't!' Then she struggled free of his arms and stood a few paces away. 'What am I saying to you, David? We are deluding ourselves, I saw it on your face when you came in. We shall not survive!' She tugged at the cord about her throat and allowed the robe to drop on the floor. Framed against the pale moonlight Blackwood saw her beautiful body as clearly as if she had been naked.

He took her to him again and soothed her sudden despair, the violent trembling which seemed to run right through her.

He said huskily, 'I want you, Friedrike. I want you now. Then tomorrow can do what it will.'

She nodded against his chest. 'I know. But it has been so long for me. I am afraid, just a little bit.'

Blackwood could feel her shivering, and guessed what it was costing her to reveal her feelings to him.

He heard himself murmur, 'I'll lock the outer door.' He saw her watching him as he unbuckled his sword and revolver. The trappings of war which could reach neither of them, until as in the fairy-story the daylight came.

Blackwood placed them carefully on a chair and unbuttoned his tunic. His fingers were all thumbs, his mind blank to the consequences if there was an attack, if the belief that Boxers would not storm the city by night was just a legend.

He turned and for an instant he thought he had imagined all of it. She had gone.

Then he heard her voice from the darkness. 'David.'

He moved into the deeper shadows and saw her arms

rising from the bed to embrace him. His foot caught on the night-dress where she had thrown it, and the next second he was standing over her. In the moonlight, so faint here in one corner of the room, her body stood out like a fallen statue, her hair in disorder around her shoulders. She bunched her hands tightly into fists as he touched her and caressed her breasts, the gentle curve of her stomach and further still. She cried out and shook her head from side to side as if to defy some silent warning.

Blackwood threw his clothes on the floor and sat beside her. It was perfect, and it was torture. He kissed her mouth, and felt her lips part, her tongue on his as he kissed her harder. Only when he knelt above her did she show real fear.

She reached out for him, her hands frantic as they gripped his body.

'Please, be gentle!'

It was like falling, he had known nothing like it. He felt her hand lose its fear as it reached out to guide him. Then she gasped just once as she arched her back to receive and to hold him.

When they had finished it was a long while before they moved. When he made to leave her she seized his hair in both hands and whispered, 'No, stay. I can still feel you. Try to sleep. I will hold you.'

And so it was. When the window became edged with grey they stirred, as did their want of each other. They made love again, with the quiet desperation of wrongdoers.

Blackwood found himself half-running to the staircase, buckling on his weapons as he went. He should be totally exhausted, he could not remember sleeping at all. Only her voice calling his name, and the passion of her body which had been released like a trapped animal.

For a few moments longer he stood outside in the littered street and stared up at the vanishing stars.

He felt as if he could do anything.

Sergeant Tom Greenaway gripped part of the rough
barricade and tried to shake it. It did not budge in spite of
the mixture of things which had gone in to its construction.
Iron rails, boulders, upended waggons and carts and sacks of
grain. It might do the trick. He glanced at the two sentries
who stood together like twins.

'All quiet, Sarge.'

'Good.' Greenaway stood on a cartwheel and peered
across at the shadows. It would be light in no time, he
thought. In these parts the sun came up like a fireball. No
hanging about.

He saw the pale shapes of Boxer corpses lying like
discarded bundles of dhobying. He had laid two of them
low himself on that charge from the gully. Yesterday. Was
that all it had been?

Dago Trent chuckled. 'They brought round some more
grub in the night, Sarge. This billet'll suit me proper!'

The other marine, a new recruit called Vicary, asked,
'You reckon them buggers'll come for us today, Sergeant?'

Greenaway thought about it. 'Likely, I'd say. They've got
everythin' to lose by stayin' put. 'Side which they may be
gettin' short o' rations like we was.' Poor little sod, he
thought. He'd done well this far, but he was still green and
needed more time.

Dago Trent hissed, 'Officer comin'!'

Greenaway tensed. It was the second lieutenant. He
would watch his tongue. Inspect every word before he let it
go.

He said smartly, 'All's well, sir.'

Ralf peered at the sentries. 'Keep your eyes open.' He
turned to the younger man, 'What's your name?'

'V-Vicary, sir.' The young private had a stammer which
showed itself when he was upset.

Greenaway tore his eyes away and stared over at the wall
where Captain Blackwood's horse had made such a fine leap.
How could he and his cousin be so different?

Ralf said, 'Well then, Private V-Vicary, you should

know by now that when you're on sentry-duty you'll – '

Dago Trent said rudely, 'He's not been in the Corps that long, sir.'

'Hold your tongue! Is this what you allow, Sergeant?' He stared at Greenaway who was still standing on the cartwheel and apparently excluding himself completely. 'Pay *attention*, Sergeant!'

Greenaway hissed, 'Quiet, everybody!' He did not hear the officer's furious exclamation. 'Somethin' wrong. I think, no, I'm certain that one o' them corpses 'as moved.'

'Don't be such a blithering idiot, Sergeant!' It suddenly hit him what Greenaway had said. 'It's absurd, you're seeing things!'

Absurd is it, you little maggot. Aloud Greenaway muttered, 'Look, fifty yards. By them torn sandbags.'

Ralf peered blankly into the shadows. 'You must be mistaken!' But his voice lacked conviction this time.

A soft breeze moved one of the corpse's clothing and Ralf added, 'See that? It's what you saw just now, right?'

'*Wrong.*' Greenaway could barely control his breathing. He added, 'Sir.'

'Why don't you go and see?' Ralf was confused.

Dago Trent asked, 'Why don't you, sir?'

Greenaway barked, 'Cut it out, Dago!' Trent usually managed to go just that bit too far.

'I'll see that you regret this, Trent! Don't forget we come under the Army Discipline Act here, a bit of field punishment might teach you to show respect for your betters!'

Greenaway could see the danger. It could go right through his platoon like the pox.

He said heavily, 'You're ordering me to go, sir, is that it?'

Greenaway's sudden challenge took Ralf off-balance, but not for long.

'Yes, I bloody well am!'

'Suits me.' Greenaway picked up his rifle and climbed on

to the barricade. As Trent made to follow he said, 'You stay. Cover me.' He glanced at the youth. 'You come with me, Private Vicary.' He grinned although he knew he was acting foolishly, out of anger. 'An' no stutterin', see?' He did not even glance at the second lieutenant. 'It's not respectful.'

The youth grinned. 'I'm with you, Sarge!' He blushed in the gloom. He was not that much a veteran yet. 'I mean Sergeant.'

Dago Trent threw himself into a niche between the sandbags and levelled his rifle.

Under his breath he murmured softly, 'If they get it, so will you, you little bastard!'

Boots scraped on sand and Blackwood, with Swan behind him, walked along the barricade.

'Where's Vicary?' Blackwood stared at his cousin. 'What the hell's going on here?'

Ralf said, 'He's with Sergeant Greenaway, sir. They're looking at a corpse.' He sounded less sure again. 'Greenaway thought he saw it move.'

'Fetch them back at once.' Blackwood turned to Swan. 'Bugler, *fast!*'

Ralf jumped down from the barricade and hurried after the two marines. For a moment or two he lost his bearings and when he looked back he could not see the point where he had left cover.

'Oh bloody hell!' He drew his revolver carefully, the memory of that moment on the river-bank still painful in his mind.

There they were. That lump Greenaway groping about like an old woman. He shouted, 'Fall back, Sergeant!'

Greenaway turned and stared. 'You'll wake the 'ole of bloody China!' Greenaway swung round and saw Vicary struggling with his rifle as one of the corpses bounded to its feet, and another rolled over before running away at a tangent.

Greenaway almost vomited as the great blade swung

mercilessly across the young marine's neck. Vicary's head seemed to fall to his chest as the force of the blow almost cut it from his body.

Greenaway threw up his rifle and fired. As he jammed home the bolt again he yelled, 'Get the other one! *Shoot*, fer Chrissake!'

Ralf raised his revolver and fired, the flash momentarily blinding him. 'I can't see him!'

He felt the sergeant seize his arm, then as he turned to fire once more Greenaway said harshly, 'Get back! Run while you still can!'

Blackwood saw most of it and guessed the rest. Other pale shapes were emerging from the shadows. Flitting about like spectres on a battlefield.

Swan reappeared on the barricade and threw himself down beside Trent.

The latter was repeating over and over again. 'He's just a kid. A poor bloody kid!'

Blackwood snapped, *'Bugler, sound the Alarm!'*

As the bugle cut through the still air Blackwood heard the bark of orders as the marines ran from their stables where they were being mustered for stand-to.

Blackwood gritted his teeth as more figures darted towards the main wall. 'Send a runner to the colonel's HQ.'

Gravatt stood beside him breathing fast. 'I reckon he'll know, sir.'

'Stand-to! Fix bayonets an' face yer front!'

Blackwood heard Ralf and Greenaway being hoisted over the barricade. Ralf should have known better. So should Greenaway.

As silence settled once again around the crouching marines most of them heard the awful sounds of the long blades hacking at Vicary's corpse.

'Hold yer fire!' That was Fox. 'They *want*you ter get riled up!'

The explosion when it came caught everybody unprepared. It must have been a mine of some kind. To his left

Blackwood saw the high gates through which they had made their entry were blasted completely away. Blackwood's ears rang to the explosion, and all around him men were coughing and spitting out dust and sand.

There was another sound. A great baying noise as if a gigantic throat was making one terrifying chorus of hate.

'*Here they come!*'

'Take aim! Fifty yards!'

Blackwood drew his sword and noticed that it was shining in the frail dawn light.

It was true. The Boxers had kept their word.

15

Stand and Fight

A quick glance to left and right told Blackwood that all of his men were in position at the wall and along the barricades. In the frail sunlight the scene could have been one from the paintings at Hawks Hill. Only the helmets with their glittering spikes were different. The scarlet tunics and the grim faces could be from any of a hundred battles in an expanding Empire.

The noise was deafening and when he looked again he saw the charging mass of Boxers and Imperial soldiers spreading away on either side in a human tide.

Their combined chanting of *Sha! Sha!* was deafening and made any sort of thought or plan impossible. Kill! Kill!

Blackwood raised his sword. 'Ready, lads!' He saw the bayonets waver and then settle as each man selected a target. Not that it mattered, it was impossible to miss.

'Fire!'

The rifles stabbed flame along the barricade, but even as they jerked their bolts and reloaded the oncoming horde had already overrun the ones who had fallen.

'Steady!' Gravatt looked at him despairingly. 'We can't stop them!'

Blackwood trained his revolver. 'Rapid fire!'

The rifles cracked out in response, so fast that when the Nordenfeldt gun joined in it sounded slow by comparison.

The Chinese attack wavered as the steady fusillade of bullets tore through their packed ranks. The new bullets cut down two, sometimes three men at a time, and still they came on.

The machine-gun stilled and as Blackwood stared up at the flat roof he saw the gun's five muzzles being depressed towards the broken gates.

The leading Boxers were pouring through them. Blackwood thought suddenly of the hotel somewhere behind him, what the roar of voices and rifle-fire would be doing to those who sheltered there. Her words seemed to murmur inside his reeling mind as the first Boxers to his right reached the barricade, their wild eyes and piercing screams enough to make the strongest heart falter.

Some of the marines had jumped on the barricade to meet the challenge face to face. As swords and axes flashed, the bayonets lunged and withdrew like steel tongues, urged on by Fox and the other NCOs.

A Boxer's head-dress appeared directly opposite Blackwood, but his yell was checked short as the revolver's heavy bullet cracked through his forehead.

The machine-gun rattled into life again and caught the attackers in a tight wedge of struggling bodies inside and beyond the high gateway. Some tried to retreat, but were cut down as the mass behind them continued to press forward.

The machine-gun moved remorselessly back and forth, Corporal O'Neil and his friend Willy Hudson taking their time and fighting their own anxiety while they concentrated on the gates.

'They're pulling back, sir!' Gravatt was frantically reloading his revolver, his eyes almost blinded by the sweat of battle.

The marines fired a last volley and brought down another file of retreating figures before Blackwood signalled to them to cease fire.

Other sounds intruded in the brutal silence. Another bugle in a different part of the city was calling a retreat. Perhaps one of the barricades had collapsed and the defenders were falling back to another line.

'Stretcher bearer!' Blackwood checked his revolver and thrust it into his holster. How familiar was that cry on any battlefield. He heard a man gasping with pain and saw Corporal Lyde trying to staunch the bleeding in a marine's neck.

Along the serried line there were one or two with minor wounds. It was a miracle and nothing less that they had stemmed the first attack.

The sun was already hotter. He wondered if the marines could stand it after their forced march along the gully under full packs. Many had been close to fainting then as the heat had followed them over the hot stones like a fireball.

An army runner came panting along the barricade. He saluted and handed a message to Blackwood.

Blackwood said, 'The French troops have had to pull back from the railway station, Toby. The Boxers are burning some more of the European property, they're killing and looting as they go.' He looked at the young lieutenant. 'We're to hold this sector.' He recalled his words to Friedrike. No matter what.

Gravatt mopped his face and throat with a grubby handkerchief.

'The Japanese infantry and some cavalry are on our left, sir. They'll not give in easily.'

Blackwood scribbled on a pad and handed it to the army runner.

Colonel Sir John Hay needed the marines now all right, he thought bitterly.

He recalled what he had learned about the Boxers and how they hated the Japanese as a race. All foreign devils were inferior, but the land of Nippon was the lowest of all in their beliefs.

'They're gettin' ready to rush us again.'

Blackwood licked his lips. Why did he always get so thirsty? He turned to look at the defences, the corpses scattered untidily below the barricade. The Boxers who had feigned death must have been the ones who had prepared

the mine to blow down the gates. Only Greenaway's
experience, and some argument which had held him there
with the sentries had prevented a much worse disaster.

'We *must* repair the gates, Toby. As soon as it's dark we'll
send out a squad.'

'Yes, sir.' Gravatt pulled Blair's binoculars from their
case and watched the great pall of dust which swirled above
the Chinese soldiers and Boxers. Here and there a Boxer
standard waved amidst the shining blades and long bayoneted rifles. If we last that long, he thought.

The defences which had been sited and planned by the
American engineer named Herbert Hoover were shaped like
a great oblong box. Their strength depended on the tenacity
of the defenders in any one sector. With the Japanese on the
left, the US Marine Corps somewhere to the south by the
old mud wall, and the French to the east by the river, the
whole force was extended to its limit. Perhaps beyond it.

Blackwood watched the assembling Chinese. There were
no obvious leaders. It was as if the combined army had a
mind all of its own.

He saw the marines nearest him pulling in their heads
and tucking their Lee-Enfields against their cheeks as the
leaderless mob began to sway towards them. He noticed too
that the marine who had been wounded in the neck lay
behind the barricade, his arms to his side as if on parade,
but with his face covered with his helmet.

Sergeant Davis of the First Platoon saw his glance and
explained simply, 'Private Frost, sir.' His strong Welsh
accent seemed out of place amidst the dust and the scent of
death.

Blackwood hardly knew the dead man. He was one of
those quiet ones, a countryman like Private Roberts, but
whose family connection with the Royals went back further
than his own.

Davis added as an afterthought, 'His Da's the Colour
Sergeant in the old *Trafalgar*, sir. He'll not take this
kindly.'

Blackwood drew his revolver again. The sun was so hot now that the pistol felt as if he had just fired it.

He saw Sergeant Davis wet his thumb and put a clearer edge on his rifle's foresight. He did not miss a trick.

Blackwood said, 'They're coming more slowly this time. Saving their wind for the last few yards.' He saw his words ripple along the tensed shoulders. 'We'll hold our fire to twenty-five yards. Pass the word to the MG.'

It took nerves of steel to stand motionless as a screaming horde came charging towards you. It also required discipline which was every bit as strong as steel.

Once again the rifles steadied along the sand and grain bags, the carts and the pieces of timber.

Blackwood saw a Boxer standard bearer capering from side to side and keeping well ahead of the others. He was a massively built man, like the one who had beaten him unconscious aboard the *Bajamar*.

'Swan, you see him?'

Swan nodded slightly and moved his rifle an inch to his right.

'No one else is to fire.' He counted the seconds. 'Now!'

The rifle bucked into Swan's shoulder and the yellow standard flew through the air like a dying bird.

It seemed to spur the attack forward, with some hanging back as they had been ordered; others maddened by the insult to their standard broke ranks and ran like madmen towards the rifles.

'Take aim! Rapid fire!'

The Nordenfeldt gun sent a hail of bullets through the packed gateway and then swung across to the right where the nearest Boxers were almost at the barricade.

Blackwood squeezed the trigger and felt the recoil jar up his arm. He could have hit several of the enemy, but nothing seemed to make any difference. He found he was pulling in his stomach muscles as if to anticipate a blow or a bullet, but tried to concentrate on his defences, faces and names committed to close-action on the right of the line.

There was a lot of smoke and leaping flames in the next sector, and he wondered if the enemy had already burst through at that point. Once inside both the perimeter defences they would be hard to stop.

The rifles cracked and flashed, and as men reloaded their magazines some of the slightly wounded were dragging up fresh boxes of ammunition.

'God, here they come!' Blackwood hauled himself on to the barricade as a mass of Boxers charged into it like a battering ram. He felt it shake as yelling faces and corpses were jammed together below his feet, hacking and stabbing while the marines met them again blade to blade. Further to the left near the gates some Boxers had broken through and were splitting up as they ran towards the next line of obstacles. Rapid fire swept through their flanks and Blackwood realized the Japanese were hurling in a counter-attack with their usual frenzied disregard for casualties.

'Second Platoon extend to the left!' Blackwood parried a bayonet aside with his sword and blasted its owner down with a single bullet. Another marine fell headlong over the barricade. He was hacked to pieces before he hit the ground. The marine nearest him emptied his rifle into the swaying mob and then lunged at a Boxer as he trampled on corpses to cross the barricade. The Boxer slashed out with his blade, his arm scything back and forth even as the marine's bayonet plunged through his bared teeth.

The attack turned to the sound of a horn like the one at the arsenal. As one they surged clear of the barricade, some falling headlong over dead and wounded and pursued by a hail of bullets.

'Cease firing!'

Behind him Blackwood heard individual shots as the infiltrators were hunted down in the narrow side-streets. It would be an unenviable task, Blackwood thought. In some of the streets a man could reach out and touch both sides at once.

He turned to see some white-helmeted troops in khaki

uniforms hurrying down the rear of the barricade carrying cases of wine. One of them, an officer, paused and beamed up at him.

'Good morning, Herr Kapitän!' He handed Blackwood a bottle and some goblets. 'We were told you were here.' His grin broadened. 'Royal Marines, ja?'

Blackwood realized that these were German marines of their *Seebataillon*.

Gravatt poured three full goblets, some of the wine slopping over his wrist like blood.

Blackwood smiled, 'Many thanks, Herr Leutnant.' He raised his goblet. He found it strange, unnerving that he could share a joke with this unknown German marine, probably his opposite number in Tientsin, with the enemy only half a cable away and massing again for another attack.

The German glanced at the sweating marines. 'Hot vork, ja?'

Blackwood thought of the discarded white uniforms. They were paying for it now.

He waited for Gravatt to scribble something for his runner and asked quietly, 'You know that the Countess von Heiser is in the hotel?'

The German took the proffered goblet. 'I do. I know all about her, Kapitän.'

Blackwood waited for his goblet to be refilled and saw more wine being handed out to his men. Perhaps all marines were in the same family?

The German asked politely, 'Do you know her?'

'Yes. Quite well.'

'Quite well.' The German repeated the words carefully. He was not fully aware of their use. He nodded. 'I understand.'

Sergeant Major Fox shouted, 'They're comin' back, sir!'

Blackwood wiped his mouth with his wrist. You don't understand at all, my friend. He said, 'If you see her — '

He saw the immediate curiosity in the lieutenant's eyes and added, 'Nothing.'

The German clicked his heels and yelled at his NCO to recall his men.

He smiled. 'I shall tell her, Herr Kapitän.'

The roar of voices intruded and Blackwood drew his revolver and watched as his men gripped their rifles and waited. The wine had been a good gesture. It would be the last drink for some of these same men, he thought.

'Commence firing!' The bugle blared and the machine-gun kicked and clattered from its rooftop. Was it never going to end? There appeared to be thousands of them, but they all had to get through the barricade or the gate if they were to extend their advance.

At a guess there were barely sixty marines still able to fight.

He thought of her in his arms, just hours ago.

Then he fired his revolver at point-blank range at a Chinese soldier who had thrown himself bodily into a gap between some upended carts. We must hold on. We must hold on. The words were like a prayer or an epitaph.

His arms were throbbing with exhaustion, and the revolver was empty. This time they were not falling back, and nothing seemed able to stem the attack.

A hoarse voice boomed from the right. It was Kirby, rallying his men better than any fanfare.

'Come on, you mothers' boys!' He sounded crazy and was obviously in tremendous pain. 'Stand and fight the bastards!'

The marines had been falling back but Kirby's strength seemed to spread to them so that they charged at the Boxers in a solid scarlet line.

The horn boomed again and reluctantly the Boxers started to withdraw. They must have lost hundreds, Blackwood thought, and yet they could still advance without hesitation, eyes dilated, teeth bared and with froth on their lips. No wonder the ordinary Chinese people were terrified of them.

Blackwood felt the lanyard on his revolver jerk and knew

Swan was checking it before reloading for him.

His head was beating like iron on an anvil, and his whole body shook as if it would never stop.

Several marines were stretched out on the dirt and having their wounds dressed; another lay as if asleep, his dead eyes watching his friends and comrades as they prepared to meet another assault.

The bugle shattered the stillness. Blackwood heard Gravatt murmur, 'Dear God, don't fail me now!'

He wondered how Ralf was managing, what he would do if anything happened to de Courcy.

Then his thoughts were scattered by that same overwhelming chant. *Sha! Sha!* The urge to kill the foreign devils or drive them out.

'Commence firing!'

This must be what Hell is like, Blackwood thought. Only the dream had been Heaven.

Sergeant Major Arthur Fox ducked through the door of the small airless room and regarded his officers impassively.

Blackwood put down his pen and looked at him. 'All quiet?'

'Sir.' Fox glanced at the others. De Courcy lay on his back on a blanket, his arms across his face as if the tiny lamp was blinding him. Bannatyre sat on an empty box, an untouched glass of whisky gripped in both hands as he stared into nothing. Gravatt looked calm enough, his breathing regular as he made his whisky last. Only his eyes told the truth. He was reliving each terrible minute and hour of the day. The insane charges, the crash and bang of rifle fire, the impartial clatter of the machine-gun.

Now it was dark once again, and the city seemed at peace.

Fox said, 'Three dead, sir, twelve wounded, six badly.' He saw the pain on Blackwood's face. 'It could 'ave bin much worse, sir.'

'I suppose so.' Fox always made it sound like routine. But
Blackwood had seen them die, or fall in agony. Some good
men, some valuable ones. Corporal Bill Handley had died in
the last attack, Corporal Lyde had been bayoneted in the
stomach. He would not last out the night. Lyde would be
sorely missed. What the General would call a *proper marine.*
He could have had Fox's rank if he'd wanted it. But he had
been broken to the ranks more times than he could
remember, usually for brawling in a foreign port, or
smashing up an alehouse in Portsmouth.

I have not slept for days. I am like a machine.

Blackwood said, 'Have you made sure that the rations are
getting to them?' It was a pointless question. Fox, for all his
threats and fury, always looked after his men before
anything else.

'Yessir.' Fox gave a grim smile. 'One good bit er news,
sir, I got a Chinese dhobyman to wash out an' repair our
whites.'

Blackwood stared at him. Fox was a marvel. Colonel Hay
could fume and bluster if he wanted to, but at least the
marines would face a new day in clean comfort.

'Have a drink, Mr Fox.'

Fox grinned, 'Ta, sir.' He took the mug in his hand but
as always seemed to remain at attention.

'What is our strength?'

Fox pouted. 'Sixty fit men, more or less. Sar'nt Kirby 'as
bin an example to the wounded, I must say, sir. They all
knows 'ow bad 'e is, so they just carries on like.'

Swan peered through the door and waited for Fox to see
him.

'Corporal Lyde's gone, Sar'nt Major.'

Fox sighed. 'A good 'un. The best.'

Blackwood poured some more whisky into Fox's mug.
'You're not too bad yourself, as a matter of fact.'

Gravatt said, 'About tonight, sir.'

Fox said, 'I can muster a squad in a few minutes, sir.'

Blackwood glanced at de Courcy and Bannatyre. They

had done so well, but they were paying for it. That gate had to be blocked. There was no shortage of material. It would have to be soon, before the moon became too strong. He tried not to think of her beautiful body framed in the silver light. She was just yards away and yet it could have been on the other side of the globe.

'I want Mr Blackwood to select his own squad.'

He saw Gravatt start, and even de Courcy dropped his arms to stare at him.

Only Fox seemed to understand. Kill or cure. It was a fair trade. 'I'll see to it, sir. Young Mr Blackwood is doin' Rounds with Sar'nt Davis at the moment.'

'Good. You attend to it. Have the First Platoon stand-to while they're fixing the gates. The remainder are to get some sleep while there's still time. Issue the whites as each post is relieved.'

'Good as done, sir.'

Fox strode away, his mind busy and with no outward sign of fatigue.

Gravatt yawned, 'I sometimes think old Fox must be related to God.'

Blackwood looked at his diary and felt his head loll forward. What was the point anyway? Would anyone ever read his report of their exploits?

He tried again. Supplies, ammunition, fit and wounded marines, those who could still fight or at least assist in loading spare weapons. Those who would never fight again.

Swan stood by the door. 'Second Lieutenant Blackwood to see you, sir.'

Blackwood thrust his weariness aside. 'I'll come.' Ralf obviously wanted to speak to him alone.

He ducked through the door, his eyes instantly adjusting to the darkness, and the high pale stars. He could smell the burned woodwork, the clinging stench of gunsmoke and death.

Ralf was waiting by a barricade and exclaimed, 'I've just heard. You want me to go out with a patrol.'

'That's true.' Blackwood glanced over the barricade. It was easy to see the corpses between it and the gates. Everything was so still. It was impossible to believe that this was the same place where men had fought and died. He said, 'You can select your own men. There should be no danger. If you keep your wits about you, that is.'

Ralf looked away. 'What about you? Will you be in charge here while I'm gone?'

Blackwood answered calmly, 'I shall be here.'

'I mean, that is, I'd not like to think one of the others is left responsible for the safety of my party.'

'What the hell do you mean by that, exactly?'

Ralf shrugged. 'Last night you were at the hotel.' He flinched as Blackwood took half a pace towards him. 'I'm only repeating what someone told me.'

Blackwood replied, 'Tomorrow, the next day, any time I might be killed. So might the others. Then you'll be in command, have you thought about that?'

Ralf faced him with surprising confidence. 'And have you thought what Aunt Deirdre or the General would think if they knew about your affair? I don't suppose that Count von Heiser would be too pleased, either!'

Blackwood clenched his fists but controlled himself with a supreme effort.

'Are you threatening me, Ralf? If so you've picked the wrong chap.'

Ralf sounded as if he was smiling. 'I just wanted you to think about it, *sir*. I'll not face a court-martial because of you. Or anyone else.'

'Have it your way, Ralf. Now go and muster your squad. The Sergeant Major will prepare the necessary gear for you.'

'I don't need him either, thank you.'

Blackwood watched his slim figure melt into the darkness. Fear did strange things to people. Unfortunately in this case Ralf held all the cards. Also he knew he was right. The fact that the General had a wild reputation where women were concerned would not prevent a scandal over Friedrike.

He walked slowly along the battered defence line, pausing occasionally to speak with a sentry, or to peer across at the enemy's campfires which seemed to surround the city like far-off beacons.

If they had more men, preferably cavalry, they could have attacked the Boxers and their comrades in the Imperial Army and cut a corridor right through them.

He thought of Friedrike in her airless room, the little maid combing her hair, or helping her to cleanse her body with the rationed supply of fresh water.

She would be thinking of him. Or was she already regretting her actions, the wanton way she had given herself to him? Someone of her background and breeding might discover how fine the margin between love and disgust could become.

He kicked at a loose stone. No, it was not just an act. The thought gave him strength, and made Ralf's threats seem pathetic and somehow sad.

He found Sergeant Greenaway at the place where the barricade met the old city wall.

The bulky sergeant said, 'All's well, sir. Seems nice an' quiet for the patrol.' He hesitated and added, 'I'm rare sorry about Private Vicary, sir. It weren't 'is fault. It were mine more than anyone's.'

Blackwood nodded. 'Try and forget it. It could have been any one of us.'

'An' about young Mr Blackwood, sir, I'm sure 'e'll be all right given 'alf th' chance.' He fumbled for words. ' 'E's got the *makin's*, sir.'

Blackwood was glad the darkness hid his face. 'Probably.'

He moved on, knowing that Greenaway was still staring after him. Swan followed at a discreet distance, his rifle in the crook of his arm like a gamekeeper going round his traps.

He had heard most of it. Poor old Greenaway, he thought. Doing his best to spare the captain's feelings. The night-patrol might be very interesting and in a way he wished he was going too.

Sergeant Owen Davis said, 'I've got the men ready, sir.'

Ralf tried to relax as he moved nearer to the small squad of marines by the barricade. He saw the sergeant major's handcart already loaded with ropes and lengths of timber, just enough to block the gateway, to give the rifles and machine-gun a chance to hold back the next attack, and the one after that.

He said, 'Listen to me, all of you. This has to be done quickly.' He turned to the sergeant, 'Where's Corporal Lyde?'

Davis stared at him. 'He died, sir.'

Ralf touched his moustache and tried to remain calm.

Corporal Percy Addis said, 'So *I* stood in for 'im, sir.'

Ralf could sense the sneer in Addis's tone, even though his face was hidden in the darkness. Addis had been there with that ox Greenaway when his revolver had accidentally fired and roused the Chinese garrison at the arsenal. Addis was here for a purpose.

He snapped, 'Very commendable, Corporal. Try not to foul things up this time.'

It was gratifying the way some of the others chuckled. Addis was not from their platoon anyway. It made all the difference.

Davis whispered, 'We'd better leave now, sir.'

'When I'm ready, *Sergeant*.' Ralf fidgeted with his belt and holster. What had happened to him? He felt completely at ease, untroubled even by the task ahead.

'Remove your tunics and leave them behind with your helmets.' He unbuttoned his own and handed it to Davis while he refastened his belt. He had seen his cousin give this kind of order, the way the men always accepted it without question. Now he could sense their resentment, and even that gave him a kind of strength. 'Now, tell the sentry, and we'll move out directly.'

He clambered over the dip in the barricade where a working party had made a space for the handcart.

One officer, a sergeant, a corporal and six privates. They had seemed like a crowd behind the barricade but as soon as they moved beyond it Ralf thought it was like walking naked into a lion's den.

How near the enemy campfires looked, and each sprawled corpse appeared as if it would suddenly leap up and try to hack them to pieces. He heard Sergeant Davis mutter a warning as one of the cartwheels emitted a loud squeak, but they moved on, apparently unheard and undetected.

The gate suddenly towered over them, the ground littered with broken beams across which Boxer corpses lay like exhausted runners.

'Corporal, stand guard.' Ralf walked carefully through the gate and stared over at the twinkling fires. Apart from the flames nothing moved. Probably sleeping after their terrifying charges, he thought.

'Get on with it, Sergeant.' Ralf heard the cautious scrape of timber and fallen stones as the men got to work with ropes and levers. It should not take long. Ralf loosened the revolver and touched its hammer with his thumb. Safe but ready.

He thought of his cousin's quietness when he had attacked him over the German countess, and how it would affect Aunt Deirdre. It had been so easy. Laughable. He recalled when he had joined the countess for tea aboard *Mediator*, and David's pathetic jealousy when he had told him about it.

David was brave and had all the qualities he would have liked. Ralf was surprised to discover he did not mind admitting it, at least to himself. But Victoria Cross or not he was a fool where women were concerned. Surely he did not believe that the German aristocrat would let him touch her; he only made himself ridiculous by deluding his mind with such ideas.

Ralf thought suddenly of the girl in England, Helen. With her at his side things would be very different. In the Corps or released from its code and tradition, he would soon rise to the top. Her father seemed to like him, even if he did keep going on about the splendid Blackwood heritage.

He felt his lips lift in a smile. That too could be used to advantage once the old General had passed on.

He started as Addis said, 'Did you 'ear that, sir?'

'What, man?' Ralf hated the corporal. His cocky self-confidence, the smell of his sweat.

Addis gripped his rifle and peered into the darkness. 'I dunno, sir.'

Bloody idiot! Why must I be plagued by such mindless fools? Ralf tensed as he heard the sound himself. It was the sound of wheels. 'Come with me.' He moved further to the right with Addis crouching along behind him. Wheels, but where and what? He continued to move along parallel with the broken walls and paler-coloured barricades. It would be just like some nervous sentry to fire on him, he thought savagely. Soon now. Whatever it was sounded heavy and should therefore be visible against the lines of campfires. The simplicity of it made him grin. Bannatyre or de Courcy would have probably retreated to the defences at the gallop.

'Still.' Ralf groped in his pocket and pulled out a small collapsible telescope. It only measured five inches but when extended was still as powerful as some binoculars. He had never shown it to anyone. It had belonged to his father. The one he had used in the Crimea. He thought of the great painting in the General's room. The fire and thunder of the Russian redoubt. Even the General had admitted that Philip Blackwood should have been awarded the VC instead of him.

He opened the small telescope and heard Addis's sharp breathing. It was not just sweat, he decided. It was the sweat of fear. Like the others Addis thought him useless. He would bloody well change his ideas soon.

Addis asked nervously, 'See anythin', sir?'

'Hold your noise.' Ralf moved the telescope slowly and with great care. If some of the corpses were really live Boxers he would be hard put to get back to the barricade before they cut him down. His hand shook slightly as he recalled what they had said about Second Lieutenant Earle's awful screams. When he had been tortured before they had hacked off his head and stuck it on a pole as an obscene trophy. He forgot Earle as he moved the glass back again. Only one figure moved by the nearest fires, a black shadow framed occasionally against the flames as he flung on more wood. But there was nothing else moving between the fires and himself. *There was nobody.* He could feel the hair rising on his neck, as if a chill wind had somehow invaded this desolate place.

He listened, his hair falling across his eyes as he leaned forward. The noise continued as before, a very slow rumbling like iron wheels. He stared round wildly, stunned by his discovery. It was artillery, it had to be.

God, it had been a near thing all the previous day. With heavy guns the Boxers could smash down the defences before attacking at full strength. Nothing would stop them.

Addis watched him, much as a rabbit watches a fox.

'I can't see nothin', sir.'

'It's the gully.' He was startled by his own understanding, his grasp of what was happening. The Boxers must be dragging their guns along that same gully. No wonder they were invisible, just as the marines had been until they had burst from cover to surprise the enemy from their rear.

Sergeant Davis loomed out of the darkness. 'There's done we are, sir.' He looked at the officer and added, 'You heard it too, sir.'

Addis said, 'Artillery, Sarge.'

Davis rubbed his chin. It made a rasping noise. 'We'd better tell the commanding officer.'

Ralf raised his telescope again. No wonder there was no movement around the enemy's fires. They were all hauling the guns. It had to be that.

'We have to be certain. A reconnaissance.'

Addis swallowed hard. 'Who's goin', sir?'

Davis said, 'It'd be a terrible risk, sir.'

Ralf had intended to send Davis and one other while a runner was sent back to alert his cousin.

Addis's dismay that he might be sent because of his insolence by the river, the fact that his was the mouth which was always ready to smear him with gossip was enough. Even the reliable Sergeant Davis was doubtful and would prefer any other officer to be here. Ralf looked at the squad who waited by the barricade, their work done.

There was one marine called Adams, a quiet, modest youth who was often mocked goodheartedly by the seasoned members of his platoon because of his manner. He never swore or complained, and was obviously glad to be in the Corps. Shown on the records as eighteen he seemed nearer to sixteen, he was so keen to better himself. Unlike so many of the others he was a first-time marine, a new recruit with no family connections in the Corps.

'I shall go.' It came out quite easily. 'You too, Adams.'

That would hit Davis and the others where it hurt most. Their pride, and their contempt for any new officer.

By contrast Adams was delighted. Ralf tried not to think of Vicary's pleasure at being selected by Greenaway before he had been killed, beheaded just a few yards from here.

Davis said firmly, 'If you want my advice, sir.'

'I don't.' He thrust the telescope into his pocket and carefully drew his sword. It would make less noise if they stumbled on a Boxer guard. 'You withdraw with the squad, Sergeant. *Try* not to make too much noise about it, eh?'

He trembled with chilled excitement. It was easy. An act, but it worked. Why had he never realized it?

They melted into the shadows and Ralf glanced up as a shaft of moonlight touched the scarred gateway like silver paint.

Adams, his rifle across his body, its bayonet already fixed, trod quietly after the second lieutenant.

Adams's family came from Exeter, where his father was a shoe-maker. His was a large family and times were hard, otherwise his mother would have prevented him from enlisting. Adams had always wanted to join the Corps, and had never lost an opportunity to visit Plymouth to watch the Royal Marines at drill, the men-of-war proud and beflagged in the Sound.

When a recruiting party had visited Exeter Adams had pleaded with his parents and they had reluctantly agreed to his going, and to keeping quiet about his age. He had been just sixteen on that day. The recruiting sergeant had been a jovial fellow, with a big yellow moustache and a breast full of medals.

Adams had never mentioned that his father was also a lay-preacher. That would have got some of the old sweats going, he thought. As it was he still found it difficult not to blush when he heard some of their jokes and stories of past exploits.

Now Private John Adams of the RMLI was here in the middle of danger, fighting his country's enemies just as the recruiting sergeant in his red sash had described in such gory detail.

He was glad to be with the second lieutenant. He too was young, a year or so older than himself, and a Blackwood. It was hard not to hear that family name in Forton Barracks.

He had heard the others saying terrible things about him, but he had ignored it. From his own experience he knew that they always used their brutal humour on new faces, officers and privates alike.

Oblivious to Adams's admiration Ralf glanced at the strengthening moonlight and then paused to listen to the sound of wheels. It was unnerving. As if an enormous underground monster was about to burst from its lair at any moment and devour them.

He gave a thin smile. Goliath.

It was very bright. He looked back at the wall. They had come a long way. His stomach rebelled against the stench of corpses. Why the hell didn't they bury them?

He heard Adams behind him. I must have been mad to bring him. He'd stand no chance at all if things went wrong.

Sergeant Davis would have run to David by now, he thought. All hell would break loose when he found out.

He should go back now. Let the others finish what he alone had begun. He looked at his young companion. 'We shall stroll over and take a look. What d'you say?'

Adams's eyes were like saucers. 'Gosh, sir. Just us two!'

Ralf sighed. If Adams had not been here he knew he would probably have gone back with the others.

'If we see anyone, stand absolutely still.' Ralf eyed him bleakly. 'D'you *understand?*'

Adams bobbed his head, 'Yessir. We'll show 'em, eh, sir?'

Ralf turned and walked slowly towards the noise. It was strangely menacing. He thought only briefly of Adams. For once it seemed he had found someone who looked up to him.

16

Never the Right Words

Second Lieutenant Ralf Blackwood raised himself on his elbows and stared fixedly at the pile of rocks at the end of the gully. The ground was very hard and uncomfortable and he could feel small spiky stones jabbing through his shirt as he tried to discover what was happening.

Once when he looked back over his shoulder he was amazed how far they had come. When they had burst from this same gully for that wild charge towards the old city wall it had seemed to pass in a flash. Now he was very conscious of the gap between him and safety. *Safety*. Even the word was a mockery. He felt his lips twist into a smile.

Private Adams, who was lying nearby, saw the smile in the moonlight and drew comfort from it.

The noise of the wheels had ceased. Maybe they were merely wagons of food or ammunition, Ralf thought. He dismissed it instantly. There would be little need for secrecy with the city surrounded. It had to be something worthwhile, worth this risk of stripping the camp of every available man.

He said quietly, 'You stay here, Adams, and watch the rear. If anyone looks like cutting us off from the main defences *tell me*.'

'What about you, sir?'

'I'm going a bit closer. Have to.' He had a mental picture of their sneers if he failed what he had started out to do. *Show them you've got the gut for it*. He twisted his head to the right. It was a solitary figure crossing the camp fires again.

Even in the strange glacier light he saw the red head-dress and felt his stomach muscles tighten.

He began to crawl forward, rolling from side to side on his elbows as he had been trained to do.

God they were making a din. The wheels had stopped but there were other sounds now. His brain examined them and he realized it was like a ship under sail, the creak of ropes and tackles.

He held his breath as some figures clambered over the gully's lip and scuttled away into the shadows. They appeared to be hauling ropes behind them, and soon he heard the thud of hammers as the Chinese prepared to fasten their blocks and shouted for the others to help them.

Within a couple of minutes there were hundreds of them, ducking and groping through the shadows to take their places along the taut ropes. It was unnerving to see so many. The nearest was about fifty yards away. One, a tall figure with a long halberd, called out an order and the whole column of men threw its weight on the tackles. Ralf wanted to leave but felt mesmerized and unable to move as a gun-muzzle, very slowly at first and then with gathering momentum, lurched out of the gully.

It was a sizeable cannon. Old perhaps but breech-loading. Probably one of the Krupp guns from the forts. It would be able to smash the defenders into oblivion even as they lined the flimsy barricades for the dawn stand-to.

He wriggled backwards, his eyes still fixed on the long human rope.

'I was right, Adams. Time to get out of here.' He almost grinned. 'Not a bloody sentry anywhere.' He rested his hand on the youth's shoulder. 'No chances, all the same. I could be wrong, so take it nice and slowly.'

Adams nodded jerkily and tried to hold his rifle clear of the rough stones. How did the officer behave so calmly? He would never forget it.

Ralf said, 'We'll head for the break in the wall.' Again he fixed a picture in his mind. His cousin flying through the same gap, his sword in the air as the horse lifted him clear.

They reached the wall. The corpses were still where they had fallen. Ralf swallowed hard. He could smell them. Could feel their eyes on him.

He pulled out the little telescope and tried to focus it on the camp, and the edge of the gully. But all of it was lost in shadows, or distorted by silver shafts of moonlight. He could not see the cannon at all. But he heard the tackles squeaking. There must be a second cannon. Not that it mattered. One was all they needed. He closed the telescope and thought of his dead father, how he must have used the telescope in the Crimea.

'Right, Adams, over you go – ' He seized his arm. '*Still!*' Even a whisper sounded too loud.

Adams stared at him but did not move.

Ralf watched the sentry. He must have been resting somewhere, hidden from view.

Now he was walking very slowly towards them, his chin on his chest, asleep on his feet.

'Bloody hell.' Ralf knew there was no chance of not being seen. There were hundreds of armed men near the gully. Neither he nor Adams would make the crossing in time.

'Give me your bayonet.' He kept his hand on Adams's shoulder. Holding him, calming him like a frightened mount.

'Easy now.'

He watched the sentry moving nearer. He was probably grateful to be spared the harder work with the cannon.

'When I drop my hand, Adams.' He spoke very evenly even though every nerve in his body was screaming. 'Stand up. Keep your hands to your sides. All right?'

Adams bobbed his head. 'I think so, sir.'

'You'll do better than that, man.' Ralf gripped the bayonet and tested its weight. Where had he heard those words before?

Then he pressed himself amongst the stones which had been blasted from the wall and as the sentry's shadow flowed across the ground like some black serpent he dropped his hand.

Adams scrambled to his feet, his mind reeling with sudden fear as he saw the sentry stare at him with utter astonishment, then with understanding as he began to unsling his rifle from his shoulder.

Adams did not really know what happened next. The second lieutenant just seemed to appear from the ground a pace behind the Boxer with the levelled rifle.

Ralf wrapped his forearm around the man's throat, tugging him backwards even though he knew the Boxer was taller and far stronger. It had to be quick. With all his strength he drove the bayonet inwards and upwards, the point catching only momentarily on his bandolier before thrusting into his body. Ralf dragged with his forearm and felt the man's strangled cry change to a horrible rattle as he slipped from his grasp and lay between them.

Ralf held his breath. 'Better make certain.' But the corpse did not move as the bayonet found its mark once again.

Ralf handed the blade back to Adams and hoped he had not seen how near he had been to vomiting.

'Right, Adams, off we go. You first.' He drew his revolver and wiped his face with his sleeve. *God Almighty.*

Adams vaulted over the gap and Ralf heard a sharp metallic snap. He clambered into the gap and saw the young marine holding his leg and writhing on the ground in terrible agony. He had trodden on a pile of straw. But beneath it had been a steel-jawed man-trap which he had sprung like a mouse after cheese.

Ralf knelt beside him. It was bad. He felt blood on his fingers as he tested the strength of the trap. But for his boot, it would have taken his foot off.

He groped in his pocket and pulled out a cigar case. 'Here, bite on this.' At any moment Adams would scream. You could hardly blame him.

Ralf tried again, but each time Adams rocked about in

agony, his teeth already half through the case in his jaws.

Ralf wedged a stone into the trap. That would prevent it from closing even tighter. He felt his way to the left and found where the trap was fastened. He could sense Adams terrified eyes watching him. He was almost choking on the gag.

It was no good. The chain was fixed beneath several large stones. It would take a squad to lift them clear.

Ralf peered through the gap to give himself time to think.

Christ in Heaven. There were five figures moving unhurriedly towards the wall. Probably to relieve the other sentries.

One of them called to his companions and Adams must have heard him. He spat out the case and gasped, 'Please, sir! Don't leave me to them!' He was sobbing uncontrollably like a child. 'Kill me, sir, for God's sake, *kill me* first!'

Ralf thumbed back the hammer on his revolver and listened to the distant voices.

'Keep still.' He realized with a start that Adams had closed his eyes. He really expected him to shoot him. One shot. There was no margin for error. He held the muzzle as close as he dared to a link by Adams's foot.

Now or never. He squeezed the trigger and heard Adams cry out as the chain was blasted from the trap.

'Hang on to your rifle!' He did not know why he had said it. Maybe to give Adams something to keep his mind occupied. Thank God he was only a youth. Even so with his rifle and ammunition he was heavy enough.

He hauled him up and over his shoulder, holding him in position with one arm, leaving the other free for his revolver. If he fell he would make sure that neither of them was taken.

Voices yelled, strengthened and faded as the Boxers ran to discover what was happening. A few shots whined dangerously close overhead, and one spat sand against his leg. He felt more blood running from Adams's leg and thought one of the bullets had hit him, that he was carrying a dead man.

He gasped between breaths. 'Hold on, Adams!' His heart must surely burst. 'You must, you're my trophy!'

Adams's voice seemed to come from miles away. 'I – I'm all right, sir.'

They're gaining on me. Ralf tried to blink the sweat from his eyes. Any second now. He saw the gateway where they had built the barricade. So near, so far.

A voice shattered the silence. 'Platoon, *steady!* Take aim, *fire!*'

The bullets tore past Ralf and his sobbing burden like a swarm of hornets. Out of the shadows pale figures ran to lift Adams from his back, others fired into the shadows. At nothing. It was as if the Boxers had never been.

He heard Sergeant Davis exclaim, 'Carry this boy to the Surgeon.'

Adams reached out, his arm flailing about with the pain.

Ralf ran beside him, and seized his hand.

'What's your name?'

'John, sir.'

'Right, John, when you're up and about I'll want you in my platoon.'

The boy nodded, unable to speak as they hustled him away.

Sergeant Davis stared at him, as if he could not believe what he saw.

Ralf said, 'I must see the commanding officer. At once.'

Blackwood walked to meet him. 'I'm here.'

'I saw the guns. One, more likely two.'

'And I saw you, Ralf, just now with that lad.'

Ralf took his tunic and helmet from Davis.

Blackwood said, 'I take back what I said.'

Ralf regarded him calmly. 'Measure up, do I? Good enough at last?'

Blackwood smiled. 'Well let's go and see the Colonel. Together.'

Gravatt said, 'Bloody marvellous.'

Ralf shrugged. 'It won't matter anyway. They'll blow us all to hell. If not today, then tomorrow.'

They found Colonel Sir John Hay wide awake in his small headquarters, roused from his brief rest by the platoon's covering fire. He was wearing his breeches and highly polished boots, doubtless the ones Blackwood had seen being cared for by his servant. But above that he wore only his shirt. It looked almost indecent, Blackwood thought.

Hay listened to his report impassively. Nodding every so often with a grunt. 'Go on then.'

Gravatt said, 'The marine should be all right, sir. He'll not lose a foot, thanks to young Mr Blackwood here.'

'Yes, yes, I daresay,' Hay said impatiently. 'I heard much the same report from the American sector. A withdrawal of Boxers and Imperial troops at dusk. We had no real idea why, of course, but we can't afford to waste chances. An English officer and an escort of two or three Cossacks from the Russian detachment have been sent through the enemy lines. The Chinese will be around us again at dawn. It was a chance which had to be taken. The telegraph has been cut again. We have to let them know at Taku just how serious our position has become.'

Blackwood thought of the English horseman. Another Twiss perhaps? They would need all the luck to reach the Taku forts with their heads on their shoulders. In this strangely mixed assortment of soldiers and sailors from several nations there had already been incredible acts of courage and co-operation, which a few weeks ago would have been thought impossible.

Hay said, 'Even if they get through it will take time. We shall have to withdraw to the second line of barricades. We must.' For the first time he shot Ralf a fierce grin. 'But for you, young fellow, all your people and some of mine would have been on the receiving end of those guns without knowing what had hit them.'

The grin vanished just as quickly. 'We shall evacuate the

hotel immediately. Women, children, and wounded unable to walk will be moved to the Catholic Mission. I do not believe in miracles, gentlemen, but I happen to know that the mission's walls are the thickest in the city.'

Blackwood watched fascinated. After Blair's quiet confidence and occasional uncertainties, Hay was like a tiger. It was incredible but either he was really looking forward to the last battle, or he was a damned good actor.

'My men and some of the Germans are evacuating the hotel and adjoining buildings. I suggest you move your machine-gun, Captain Blackwood. It's the only one we have, and I think it will be a prime target where it stands at present.' His mind veered away. 'I see that you are back in your white uniforms again.' He allowed his servant to ease his arms into his perfectly fitting tunic. 'At least they *appear* cleaner.'

That was probably the nearest he ever got to praise, Blackwood thought.

'See you all at first light, gentlemen.'

His hard voice held them in the doorway. 'I thought you might like to know, China has officially declared war on us.' He smiled at their expressions. 'I know. I thought much the same!'

Blackwood strode into the shadows and bridges of moonlight.

'I want the gateway mined right away, Toby. We've no more fuses, so make sure we have two good marksmen ready to mark down the charges.' He turned to Ralf. 'Have the First Platoon relieved and see they're properly fed and have full canteens. It may be a while before we get another chance.'

Ralf walked away without even a word or a glance.

Gravatt hurried back, 'Mr de Courcy's dealing with that, sir.'

They fell in step, Gravatt remaining silent as Blackwood's mind jumped and sidestepped past obstacles he could only guess at. Somewhere he could hear a baby crying, and a muffled bang as a Boxer sentry fired his musket towards the city in the hope of a lucky shot. They walked along the deserted barricade which would be their new, and last, line of defence. It was shorter, but that was all you could say for it.

He thought of Ralf. He had certainly shown what he could do. But what had induced him to make such a gesture? But for him the defences would be running with blood when the dawn found them.

He heard someone whistling a cheerful jig and knew it was O'Neil as he supervised the re-siting of his Nordenfeldt.

He said, 'Swan, stay with the adjutant. If I'm needed come at once.'

'Yes, sir.' Swan ignored Gravatt's curious stare. He never needed to be told.

Blackwood closed one of the heavy mission doors behind him and looked at the scene of crowded disorder. Along one wall many children who had arrived earlier were already mercifully asleep, while others clung to their mothers and stared around with obvious anxiety. At the opposite side there were small desks and bench seats, occupied now by weary women and some of the wounded servicemen. In stark contrast along the wall behind them were children's drawings, Chinese characters, and beside a large picture of the Virgin Mary one of a fearsome green dragon.

The nuns who served the mission moved sedately amongst the new arrivals, ready to share their sparse rations or to answer the many questions which were fired at them.

It was a cruel twist of fate, Blackwood thought, that these same gentle nuns were one of the main targets for Boxer hatred. Foreign missionaries of any kind represented a threat to their beliefs, to the very roots of their religion. Missionaries, men and women, had been among the first to fall victim to the long knives of the Righteous Harmonious Fists.

Above the head and shoulders of a nun who was kneeling

to placate a small sobbing girl Blackwood suddenly saw Friedrike. She looked very calm or would appear so to anyone who did not know her, and seemed withdrawn from the bustle around her.

She looked straight at him, and as Blackwood pushed his way across the room he marvelled at the way she managed to appear so unafraid. He made to seize her hands but something in her violet eyes signalled a caution. He realized that several women were standing nearby, and although they were apparently speaking to each other, he had the feeling they were watching and listening.

Blackwood said awkwardly, 'I'm so sorry about this — ' He faltered. 'Countess.'

He saw the pain and the relief in her eyes. She understood what it was costing him. Both of them.

She said, 'You must not always apologize, Captain. I think the war is *not* of your doing.' She tried to smile, but it only made her look more sad.

It was like saying goodbye minutes before a troopship casts off, and the thin path of water widens to an impossible gulf. Never the right words when you needed them most. It was always too late.

Blackwood said quietly, 'You look wonderful. I want to hold you, to touch you — '

She dropped her eyes and he saw her breasts moving quickly despite her guard, her pretence.

'Please, David. I cannot bear it. To have you so close, and yet — '

He said, 'I am wearing the locket.' He looked round at the milling figures, his voice despairing. 'I love you.'

She forgot her caution and reached up to touch his mouth. 'Shh. Do not torture yourself.' She could barely hold back the tears.

'I have to go, Friedrike.' He could smell perfume or soap on her fingers and wanted all the more to hold her, to shut out the others, the war, everything.

She glanced quickly at the other women, probably the

wives of German officials and traders.

'Together yet so apart, David.' She looked up, startled as a stray bullet cracked amongst the buildings. 'I must be strong.'

Blackwood knew he had to leave but found it almost impossible.

She whispered, 'Our night together, my dearest. I shall never, *never* forget no matter what happens.'

He started to protest. 'It's not over, Friedrike!'

She smiled at him but did not speak as she studied his face. As if they would never see each other again.

A solider stood beside them, his arm in a sling. 'Pardon, sir, but one of your men is here.'

Blackwood turned towards the door, knowing it would be Swan.

Swan was wearing his blue field-service cap. Blackwood had ordered his men to discard their helmets. It was just possible that the enemy might think there were fresh, unused troops on the barricade, but now as Swan looked across at him it seemed a pitiful deception. Against the cannon they would need more than party-tricks.

He said, 'I'm needed.' He moved slightly towards her so that her back was towards the other women. 'I hate to go. I want you so much.'

Her eyes glistened in the full lamplight. 'I *know*.' She bit her lip to hold back the emotion. 'I *know*.'

Blackwood took her hand and kissed it. Then he released it and looked at her. 'Until we meet – '

She lifted her chin as he had seen her do many times. 'Take care, David.'

Oblivious to the watching eyes Blackwood hurried from the room. He did not look back. He did not dare.

Swan held the door for him and shot the countess a quick glance. Had they? he wondered. God she was a fair treat to look at.

'Mr Gravatt's musterin' the men now, sir.'

He glanced at Blackwood's stern profile.

'Think we'll 'old the buggers off, sir?'

Blackwood tried not to think of her at the mercy of the Boxers.

'Of course.' It was what Hay would have said.

Blackwood paused by the machine-gun and lowered his head to peer along its five barrels. The old Nordenfeldt might be hand-operated but a good gun-layer like Private Hudson could still get off some three-hundred and-fifty rounds a minute.

Corporal O'Neil followed his glance and said, 'When they come over the outer barricade we'll give them a right welcome, sir.' His face was blistered from the sun after all his hours on the flat roof which he had now abandoned.

Blackwood looked at the gates, the rough and ready defences. De Courcy had used his common sense again and had painted two large aiming marks so that the marksmen could fire off the explosion.

He saw the two sharpshooters, Roberts and Dago Trent, in their sandbagged positions, each with extra ammunition pouches opened and within reach. Colour Sergeant Chittock had unrolled his Colours although in the morning gloom the red looked black. Before they had fallen back to the second defence line Chittock had hoisted his borrowed Union Jack above the gateway. That more than anything would attract the enemy's anger and attention.

Blackwood walked slowly down the line. He saw Sergeant Kirby leaning on some old steel plates and gripping them with both hands. It looked as if he was taking slow, deep breaths, but before he saw Blackwood's approach and straightened his back, the pain on his heavy face was only too apparent.

'Morning, Sergeant.'

'Sir.'

'How's the wound?' Blackwood watched the sudden wariness in Kirby's eyes. What was the matter with him? If he was afraid of being sent back to the *Mediator* or a field dressing station he could put it from his mind. Nobody would leave Tientsin until the battle was fought and won, or the city was relieved.

'Never better, sir.' Kirby stared at a point above Blackwood's shoulder.

'Good, I'm glad to hear it.' He saw the relief on the sergeant's face. What did he expect him to say?

The sergeant major stood near the colour sergeant, his features calm, as if he had accepted the reality of defeat.

Blackwood said, 'Have you spoken to Mr Bannatyre?'

'Yessir.' Fox looked at him squarely and added, ''E'll be a good 'un, after this, sir.'

It was the worse part of it. But they had to make a show of defending the outer barricades until the last moment. Twenty men including Bannatyre and the sergeant major, and that was more than they could really spare.

Somewhere a voice yelled a command. The Japanese were preparing for their own dawn. Blackwood had met their major only briefly, a stocky little man in blue cap and tunic, with a sword which seemed far too large for him. A dangerous adversary to meet in battle.

He found Gravatt with de Courcy and a runner, drinking tea from giant mugs which they had carried from their quarters.

Gravatt put down his mug. 'Sorry to call you so soon, sir. It's all quiet now, but the pickets saw some movement on our left front. It could be they're moving a cannon, and making sure we can't see where it's hidden.' He peered forward. 'Have you had any sleep, sir?' He sounded concerned.

Blackwood climbed over the barricade and walked across the open ground to the outer defence line.

'I don't need sleep.'

He found the same box he had used before and stood on it to peer towards the enemy's camp. Most of the fires were out now, and even the stars had almost faded away. He shivered in spite of the fact he knew he was prepared for what must come. He did not feel afraid, at least he did not recognize it. Committed, resigned, it was an empty ache like hunger.

It would soon be dawn. He glanced at the gateway's battered silhouette. It would serve him right if the enemy fired first because they already knew the packed charges were there. He would be blown to pieces in the blink of an eye.

Lieutenant Bannatyre turned to face him. He had removed his field-service cap and had tucked it in his belt.

Blackwood said, 'They may gather behind the old wall where Adams was caught in the trap. It would give them cover until the gun is brought to bear.' He recalled Ralf's description, the hostility in his voice, Blackwood could almost see the gun for himself.

He heard the careful tread of feet as the marines who were to man these defences approached from the rear.

He said, 'God, Ian, you've not brought Sergeant Kirby here with you?'

Bannatyre shrugged. 'I tried to dissuade him, sir. But he *is* my platoon sergeant, and sick or not the men respect him.'

'I see.' Blackwood thought of Kirby's anxious eyes. It was like the last time when he had volunteered to go with O'Neil to blow up the boom across the river. He had been eager then. It had been far more than bravado. Kirby was too professional a Royal Marine for that.

'In position, sir.'

'Very well, Sergeant.' Bannatyre sounded as if he wanted to yawn. A bad sign. Men who were afraid often needed to yawn; Blackwood had known the feeling but had never understood it.

A marine who stood with his back to the enemy said, 'Looks good, dunnit, sir?'

Blackwood followed his gaze and saw Chittock's borrowed flag lift lazily in a tiny breeze above the gateway. The red no longer looked black, and the white crosses were as clear as a marine's belts.

'Permission to sound Stand-To, sir?'

'Not yet. I want every man under cover first. Tell Mr Gravatt to pass the word.' He knew that Fox was standing nearby although he had not heard his approach.

'It's time, Sergeant Major.' Blackwood looked at his tall figure with affection, and recalled his words about Neil when he had received the news of his death. At times like these Fox was like a rock, and yet Blackwood felt he knew as little about him as when they had first met.

Swan glanced up at the gateway. The whole of the Union Jack and its staff were now clearly visible. But the small breeze had expended itself, and the flag had no movement. It was as if the whole area including the scattered corpses was holding its breath.

Bannatyre said, 'Good luck, sir.'

Blackwood nodded as he glanced at the extended line of pale uniforms. 'You too. Keep those men down and out of the way until the signal.'

He walked slowly across the open stretch of churned-up ground and thought of the injured marine with the vicious trap still clamped to his leg, of Ralf, aloof, defiant, but changed for all that. The General might approve now, he decided.

Gravatt reached down to assist him over the barricade. He saw the nearest marines looking at him. They trusted him, and yet he had nothing to offer. They needed him more than ever, and would never understand that he needed them more.

Sergeant Greenaway, his rifle like a stick in his massive fists. Private Kempster, the lad from Leeds who had been so excited at seeing the engine from his home-town. Oates, the bugler, Corporal Addis, the barrack-room lawyer who had been strangely subdued since Ralf's return with the injured marine. But there were too many missing faces. There would be more.

He took out his handkerchief and unbuttoned his collar

to wipe his throat. He felt the locket-chain warm against his skin and thought of that one night when they had loved so fiercely and with such need.

He heard a man whisper, ''Ere comes 'is lordship!'

Blackwood pretended he had not heard and turned to greet Colonel Hay who was to his surprise riding the horse Trooper.

Hay looked along the defences. 'All ready, I see.' The horse sidestepped but Hay brought it instantly under control. 'These animals need exercise. I hope you don't object to my borrowing him, what?'

'Not at all, sir. He doesn't belong to me either.'

'I see.' Hay made even trivialities sound important. 'I shall visit you later on.' He looked at Blackwood and lowered his voice. 'This line will be held, d'you understand?'

'I do, sir.'

'Good.' Hay nodded to Gravatt and spurred the horse on towards the other sector beyond the mission.

Gravatt emitted a deep sigh. 'I was just thinking, sir. Summer in England. It's hard to believe, isn't it? I don't suppose anyones knows about Tientsin, or cares for that matter.'

Blackwood smiled grimly. 'Well I care and so must you.' He tugged out his watch and held it up to his eyes. He saw Gravatt and Swan watching him, and pictured de Courcy and Ralf at the other end of the line which would act as a hinge if the defences were forced back.

This line will be held, Hay had said. The *buts* and the *if onlys* no longer counted for anything.

Blackwood licked his lips and tried to shut out the memories and the hopes. They never helped.

'Bugler! Sound off!'

He stepped down from the barricade and watched the retreating shadows as the bugle's clear notes put an end to the night and its protection.

Along the outer line of barricades he heard the hoarse

shouts from Bannatyre's small detachment, calling along the line as if it were fully manned as usual, so that it would sound more like a battalion than a mere handful of men.

Blackwood watched the sky and remembered how he had torn himself from her when dawn had been near. The heat of her body, the curve of her breasts in his hands. Everything.

There was a violent bang, very loud and without an echo, and seconds later the shell landed inside the defences with a deafening explosion.

'*Keep down!*' Not that they needed telling. The aiming shot. The next would be more accurate. Blackwood saw a young marine press his face against some sandbags, his fingers locked into them like claws.

Crash. The next shell hit the centre of the open space where Blackwood had just been walking. He felt the air sucked from his lungs, the hiss and crack of steel splinters as they scythed wall and barricade alike. But for Ralf's unexpected act of courage that one shell alone would have killed and wounded a third of their strength.

Gravatt muttered, 'Here comes another bastard!'

Blackwood turned his face away. He wanted to yawn, and the discovery was worse than any wound.

17

Roll-Call

The bombardment of the south-western defences continued for an hour. Each explosion was deafening to the men crouching and hiding behind their barricades or inside collapsed buildings, but by some miracle none of the marines had been seriously hurt.

Lieutenant Ian Bannatyre counted each shot. The bang, the abbreviated whistle followed instantly by the crash of an exploding shell seemed to scrape the inside of his skull like hot claws. There was a ten-minute interval between each shot. Either the Boxers were short of ammunition, which seemed unlikely, or they were having to carry it some distance to the gun, probably from that same gully, he thought despairingly.

When he looked back at the nearest buildings there was smoke everywhere. A few reluctant coolies had been ordered to douse the fires, and to carry more material to the barricades, but they were more afraid of the Boxers than of the marines.

Sergeant Major Fox peered over the sandbags as the dust swirled overhead from the last shell.

'They're massin' for a charge, sir.'

Bannatyre raised his head and saw the vague groups of Boxers and troops beginning to merge into a solid wedge of men and weapons. Like that last time. He shuddered.

Fox watched him grimly. 'We just makes a show, then we falls back to the second line, sir. We should catch a few 'undred of 'em 'til they catches on wot we're up to.'

Bannatyre worried him. For one who had never seen any real combat before, the young lieutenant had done fairly well, he thought. But his strength was running away like sand.

Bannatyre gripped his revolver until his fingers ached. 'God, how long can we hold out?'

Fox thought, as long as it bloody well takes. He said, 'They've only got one gun anyway. The other wheels must 'ave been a limber for the ammo.'

Bannatyre looked along his stretched line of men. He could only see the occasional cap, or the gleam of a bayonet.

There was a dull roar of voices which rose to a terrifying crescendo as the enemy began to lope forward. They were moving more slowly than before. It only added to the menace. Bannatyre tried to moisten his lips but they were hard and dry like leather.

Fox snapped, 'They can't understand.' What was the use. Bannatyre was too frightened to give the order.

'Open fire!' He snatched up a rifle and poked it through the sandbags. '*Rapid fire*, damn you!'

Along the barricade the rifles cracked and spat flame at the oncoming horde. Some of the enemy must have fallen but they were trampled underfoot so that it appeared as if the yelling, screaming ranks were unstoppable.

Fox felt the butt kick into his shoulder and jerked the bolt even as he took aim on one of the leaders. He groped for fresh bullets before his target had hit the ground.

He thought of Blackwood and all the others watching and waiting. It would have to be perfectly timed. He thought too of Blackwood's behaviour in the past, his ability to think of everyone but himself.

Fox took careful aim and fired again.

Bannatyre emptied his revolver over the barricade, his breath rasping aloud like an old man's.

Some of the Boxers were almost at the barricade where it joined the broken wall. Above the old gateway the Union Jack moved only occasionally as a bullet or musket ball cut it into defiant ribbons. It seemed to draw the enemy like a magnet, a symbol of all they hated.

The bugle bleated above the crackle of rifles and the roar of voices. 'Retreat! Fall back!'

Bannatyre was trying to reload his revolver, his mind reeling to the din. More than anything he wanted to run with his men as they scrambled or fell from the barricades and pelted for the second line.

Fox shouted, 'Come on, sir!' He gave a mad grin. 'No time for a picnic!'

The surging mass of Boxers and Imperial soldiers seemed to sway as one and change direction towards the gates as they realized that the defenders were running for their lives.

A bullet slammed into the barricade and Bannatyre clapped his hand to his eye as some grit spurted into it. He tried to climb down to the ground but stumbled over a corpse and pitched headlong.

Fox believed that Bannatyre was behind him and only realized what had happened when he turned and saw some jubilant Boxers on top of the abandoned barricade.

Two figures charged from the right, one was Private Carver, the other was Sergeant Kirby. As one of the Boxers jumped down towards Bannatyre, his bayoneted rifle ready to pin him to the ground, Kirby gave a great, inhuman bellow.

In those split seconds Fox saw it all, the veins bulging from Kirby's head and neck, the great bloody patch on his tunic where his terrible wound had burst open. Kirby swung his rifle and caught the Boxer off-balance with the heel-plate then as the man toppled sideways he drove his bayonet into his side, almost to the hilt.

Fox ran towards them, firing from his hip as more of the enemy bobbed over the barricade. The main force of attackers were at the gates now and he could hear them tearing the makeshift defences apart with their bare hands.

Bullets whistled across the clearing, and Private Carver fell dead, blood pouring from his mouth. Another Boxer dropped to the ground as lightly as a cat. Fox saw the blade swing in his hands and retched as it cleaved Bannatyre across the neck and shoulder.

Fox's last bullet brought the Boxer down. He did not wait any longer but thrust his arm about Kirby's waist and together they ran and staggered towards the next barricade.

Fox was only vaguely aware of some shouted commands, the heads and levelled rifles rising above the defences as the marines poured a devastating volley into the men below the wall. Two other shots were aimed at the packed explosives in the gateway, and even as the barricade there collapsed under the weight of bodies and the enemy surged through the air was rent apart by one thunderous explosion.

Fox heard Kirby gasping in agony. Nothing could save him now. Hands reached out to haul him to safety and Fox shouted, 'Easy! Carry 'im to the army dressin' station!'

Some last reserve of strength seemed to rouse Kirby from his terrible pain.

'*No!* Just put me down!'

Fox reloaded his rifle and nodded to the grim faces around him.

'All right, Jeff. You'll be good as new soon.'

Surprisingly Kirby managed a weak grin. 'You always was a bloody good liar!' Then his face twisted in agony again and he fell silent.

Corporal O'Neil waited until the Boxers already inside the defences were trapped by the gateway which was choked with corpses and the remains of a stone arch which had crossed above the original gates. The machine-gun rattled into life, the bullets knocking the confused Boxers from their feet like an invisible arm.

'They're running!'

Blackwood strode along the barricade, the bugler hurrying behind him.

'Cease firing!' He saw Kirby lying on his back, a blanket folded beneath his head.

Fox said heavily. ''E tried to save Mr Bannatyre, sir.'

Blackwood watched him gravely. 'I know. I saw it. I saw what you did too.' He knelt down beside the dying sergeant, knowing in his heart he should not be wasting time. He was needed everywhere. His mind still quaked from the roar of firing and the crash of those great shells. Bannatyre was dead, and for what? He was wrong to let his mind drift like this. Bannatyre had been doing his job. Because of his desperate rearguard action at least two hundred Boxers had been killed or badly wounded. It might blunt the edge of their next attack. It was all they could hope for.

Kirby opened his eyes and peered up at him. 'Sorry 'bout this, sir.'

'Don't talk.'

Kirby tried to shake his head but the pain made him whimper like a child.

'Must talk. 'Ave to.'

Fox said uneasily, 'Stow it, Jeff.'

Kirby glared at him. 'I bin in the Corps almost as long as you. I knows me rights. Dyin' declaration, that's wot.'

Fox knelt beside Blackwood. ''E's goin' fast, sir. Losin' 'is mind.'

Kirby gritted his teeth. 'My wife,' he groaned. 'Nance, she's dead.'

Blackwood said gently, 'I know.'

'I killed 'er! The fire was later. Oh, Nance, forgive me!'

He opened his mouth wide as if to shout, but it remained open, and his eyes were fixed and without understanding.

Fox stood up. 'Wot's he talking about, sir?' He shook his head. 'Poor sod. 'E was a good mate.'

Blackwood walked along his men, and waited for de Courcy to lead a party of marines to the outer defences again. There was no point in trying to barricade the gate. If they did, the Boxers would use their gun to blow it down. He saw a wounded Boxer rise up on his elbow and aim a musket at a passing marine. Sergeant Greenaway kicked the weapon aside and brought his bayonet down in a straight lunge.

'No you don't, matey.'

He found Gravatt and Ralf in the centre of the line staring after the retreating enemy.

Gravatt said, 'They'll be back.' He saw Blackwood. 'I heard about Ian, sir. Bad luck.'

They looked at each other. It was always the way. Any one of them could have been killed. As it was they had hardly lost a man. Poor Bannatyre and Private Carver. And now Kirby who had acted like a lion right to the end.

Had he been delirious, or did he really murder his wife?

Blackwood discovered he did not care. Kirby had shown remarkable courage. As if, like the time on the river, he had wanted to die. But who would ever know for certain? Even fewer would care.

Gravatt watched his face and said, 'I wonder if Colonel Hay's messenger got through the Chinese lines, sir.'

Blackwood winced as the cannon fired again, then ducked as a shell exploded on the top of a nearby building. Where O'Neil and his machine-gun would have been. Maybe the Boxers did not realize it had been moved. Not yet.

He said, 'I think we have to assume he didn't get through, Toby. So until a relief does reach us we must hold on.' He stared bitterly at the dust above the enemy camp. 'But for that damned gun – '

Ralf said, 'Is there no way of destroying it, or knocking it out of action?'

Blackwood studied him thoughtfully. Ralf had certainly changed since he had carried the injured Private Adams to safety.

'Impossible.' He saw the shutter drop instantly behind Ralf's opaque stare. He added, 'The gun will be in the centre of their camp. There are thousands of the enemy out there, night or day. It would be suicide.' He saw Swan leaning on his rifle, his eyes closed as if he was asleep on his feet. 'But I agree with you, Ralf. It's the *only* way.'

They ducked again as another explosion made the ground jump beneath them and pebbles and broken beams were flung into the air almost where the previous shell had landed.

'Ten minutes between each shot or near enough. They must be frightened we'll produce some artillery of our own and blow up their ammunition store.'

Gravatt grimaced. 'Some hopes.'

Blackwood tried not to measure their limit of existence. Two more days? At the most. But not with the shells crashing down every few minutes. It seemed likely that even if the Boxers did not attack at night, they would keep up a bombardment around the clock. Then even rest would be denied to his men.

He tried to think it out, but his head was aching unmercifully.

Gravatt lowered his binoculars. 'They don't look as if they're going to attack for a while, sir.'

'No. They'll try to soften us with shellfire first.' He looked at the scattered corpses, some already grotesque in the strong sunlight. 'Have that lot cleared away from our lines, Toby. Things are bad enough without the stench.'

Gravatt nodded. 'I'll get Ian Bannatyre to – ' Their eyes met and he left the rest unsaid. It was often impossible to accept the loss of a man in such a close-knit body.

Blackwood nudged Swan. 'Come on, man, I have to see the Colonel.'

Ralf blocked his way. 'I want to do it.' He dropped his eyes. 'Sir.'

They ducked as another shell ploughed amongst some hovels near the mission. Somewhere a voice shouted, 'Stretcher bearer, this way!'

Blackwood eyed his cousin and said, 'It would mean blowing up their supply of shells. Without them, the gun is just scrap-iron.'

Ralf fell in step beside him, his hands moving jerkily as he said, 'The General told me often enough about my father in the Crimea, and the way they blew up the Russian guns.'

Blackwood replied, 'I'll speak with Sir John Hay. Then

we'll see.' He smiled sadly. 'I'm supposed to be looking after you, remember?'

Ralf shrugged. 'I can manage.'

Blackwood found Hay in his battered command post, sitting on a canvas chair and sipping a glass of wine. He was studying a map and looked up when he saw Blackwood's shadow.

'Holding out?'

Blackwood sighed. There was no wastage with Hay. Not even with words.

'We're under heavy fire, sir.'

'I know that, dammit. But can you hold?'

'No, sir. Not with that gun out there.'

Hay glared at him. 'If we try to attack it, they'll cut us into pieces! Dammit, Blackwood, they outnumber us twenty times over. I've heard that Chinese resistance is stiffening, by the way. So it may take even longer to force a relief column through to us.'

Blackwood gauged the moment. It was not easy for Hay. No amount of bluster could change the cruel facts.

Blackwood said, 'I think we should try to blow up the enemy's magazine or limber, sir. It's in the gully, I'm certain of it.'

A shell exploded somewhere, the sound muffled here. Blackwood saw dust fall from the roof and sprinkle Hay's immaculate red tunic. He did not appear to notice. 'It sounds like madness.' For the first time he gave his maniac grin. 'But I suppose if you've earned the VC you must be crazy enough for anything, what?' He shook with soundless laughter.

He became suddenly serious. 'Volunteers of course.'

'Of course, sir.'

'And you can forget any idea of going yourself. You're here to *command*, not to lead some death-or-glory escapade, see?'

Blackwood smiled. What did Hay expect? Whoever volunteered would be unlikely to return. This was not the Crimea as described by the General at Hawks Hill. No great

armies this time. A handful of men against an unknown
force of fanatics. Surrounded, and probably already listed as
missing, it was a terrible responsibility to ask men to throw
away their lives because of some hazy idea.

Hay added. 'I'll try to get some support for you of
course.'

Blackwood walked out into the sunlight and saw Swan
waiting for him.

'Tonight, sir?'

'It has to be.'

Swan slung his rifle and waited for the dust to settle from
the last shellburst. 'Rather them than me.'

Blackwood found Gravatt at his post and told him. The
adjutant listened without comment then said quietly, 'I'll
go.'

He saw the colour sergeant standing back from the ruined
gateway staring up at the bullet-riddled flag which he had
obviously replaced in spite of the bursting shells.

Sergeant Greenaway shouted, 'I think they're coming at
us again, sir!'

Blackwood looked at Gravatt. 'I shall decide later, Toby.'
You may be in command by then.

Gravatt bit his lip. 'Very well, sir.' He drew his revolver
and examined it automatically.

'Until then, Toby, we must hold this line.'

'Stand-to!' Fox came striding along the barricade, Kirby
momentarily forgotten. 'Face yer front! Give the bastards
'ell!'

Blackwood walked away from Gravatt. They were too few
in number now to be caught together.

He leaned on the rough parapet and levelled his revolver
with both hands.

She would be listening. Packed in the mission with all
those women and children. He shivered in spite of his taut
nerves.

'Fifty yards! Independent! *Fire!*'

It was never-ending.

Inside the stone-built stables where the marines were housed, where they rested or fretted with anxiety while they waited for daylight, it was almost dark.

Ralf Blackwood glanced around the spartan surroundings where some marines were lying exhausted beside their kit and was amazed that he felt so self-controlled.

It had been a terrible day. The bombardment, then the wild charges to the barricades. It had sounded as if the Japanese troops were under equal pressure too. It could not last. The realization gave him a strange sensation of power and inner strength.

They had lost three more marines killed, and several wounded; Ralf was not certain how many. Or maybe he did not really care. It could not help to dwell on weakness, he thought.

And soon he would be going out into the darkness. It was sheer, utter madness.

But when the fighting had died down, and they had stood gasping at their posts like stricken animals, his cousin David had told them about the proposed raid into the enemy's territory. The others had volunteered, and Ralf had seen from the pain in his cousin's eyes that he wanted to go himself.

Ralf had watched their faces when he had said, 'I'm the one. I've been out there in the dark before, remember?'

He had expected an argument and he had been surprised by their acceptance. Perhaps they believed his simple explanation. Unlikely. They needed to keep together when the end came, it was obvious.

By contrast Ralf hated the stand-and-die sentiment. But he needed two volunteers to accompany him. He could see them now watching him from the shadows.

His cousin had asked if they were genuine volunteers. Ralf almost smiled. How could they refuse in front of their *mates*?

Corporal Addis was one. It would be interesting to discover if he could still sneer behind his back on this

impossible mission. And Private Roberts, the Sussex
countryman who never missed with any sort of rifle. He had
been brought up in the fields and hedgerows, and could
move like a ghost when need be. He would have detailed
Sergeant Greenaway but his size and age would only
jeopardize the raid. It would have taught him a lesson too.

The sergeant major was already present, as Ralf knew he
would be.

'Six grenades, sir, two each.'

'I can count, Sergeant Major.' It was easy when you knew
how. Fox was no better than a hotel porter when you learned
his weakness, his instant obedience.

There was an uncomfortable silence, broken only by the
horse Trooper who was munching contentedly from a feed-
bag. Trooper was apparently untroubled by the stench of
death and charred buildings, the day's chorus of gunfire and
yells.

Ralf said, 'Now, you two, pay attention.' He saw some of
the resting marines propping themselves on their elbows,
hating him for disturbing them rather than for what he was
saying.

'I want you to strip to your trousers.' He gestured
towards an old unused fireplace, perhaps where a blacksmith
had worked in safer times. 'Rub yourselves all over with
soot. I want you as black as boots.' David would have made
a joke about it, even though his mind told him otherwise.
There was no point in it, any more than there was with Fox.

I don't need them. I don't need anyone.

He thought momentarily of the German countess and
wondered if they had made love. He had watched his cousin
since that night, but if he had acted with dishonour he was
hiding it well.

He recalled that afternoon, during an attack when the
centre of the line had almost collapsed. There had been
Chinese everywhere, and the marines' bayonets had shone
with blood.

In the weakest part of the line he had seen David waving

his sword, his teeth white in the smoky sunshine as he had urged, encouraged, and forced his men back and the enemy with them.

Once as David had turned towards him he had seen the real man, spent, sickened at what was happening, knowing he had to keep them all going. Like a state of shock, Ralf thought, he had looked right through him.

Enough of this. It was time to make a move.

He unbuttoned his tunic and threw it with his shirt on the ground. He saw the youthful Private Adams staring at him from a rough stretcher, his injured foot a mass of bandages.

'Here, sir, let me.'

Ralf smiled and sat beside the youth as he leaned over to slap the wet soot all over his naked back. It was wet because at one stage of the battle the roof of the stable had taken fire. Several buildings were still blazing but to the marines this wretched slum was a temporary barracks and they had quickly doused the flames.

They stood and looked at each other. Roberts was unconcerned about going on the raid. For, apart from his genuine pride in the Corps and its comradeship, he was in fact a loner. On leave in Portsmouth, or runs ashore from one ship or another, he always went by himself.

Corporal Addis on the other hand was almost shaking with anxiety and worse. He still could not really believe it. When the second lieutenant had put the idea of volunteering to him it had been in earshot of several other marines. Men he had known and had often dominated with his apparent knowledge of the law and his inside-information about their officers.

Fox said, 'Cap'n Blackwood is comin', sir.' He sounded wary, which was unusual.

Ralf faced the doorway as Blackwood and Private Swan ducked through a rough sacking curtain.

'Good luck, all of you. If you get sighted before you reach an objective return immediately. There's been enough waste of life already.'

Ralf watched him. That was what Blair might have said.

Ralf said, 'I intend to make a wide detour. Longer but safer.'

Blackwood nodded. He felt like dropping, and every nerve and muscle screamed out for sleep. He tried not to think of that afternoon. The relentless attacks, his men fighting them back again and again. He thought of the faces which had fallen. Private Knowles, the one who had ridden Trooper. Hacked to death as a shot had brought him down. Davis, the Welsh sergeant, killed while fighting three Boxers single-handed, and Private McCulloch, whose father was a sergeant major at Forton Barracks. So many faces that they became mixed up in his aching mind.

There seemed to be no more cannon-fire. The enemy were probably saving their strength for the next morning. Perhaps the last one. He watched his young cousin and wanted to say something which might bridge the gulf. At the same time he knew Ralf would resent it. Perhaps his total independence was all he had to sustain him.

Blackwood said simply, 'I shall miss you.' It came out unintentionally. Just like that. He was surprised to discover that he meant it.

Ralf looked up, his eyes very pale in his nigger-black face.

'Don't. It'll be over for all of us soon.' He tightened his belt and waited for the others to pick up the grenades. Then he said, 'I hope the General will be satisfied.' Then he turned on his heel and walked out. He did not even look back to see if Addis and Roberts were following.

At the outer barricade de Courcy and the colour sergeant waited to see them through the shattered gateway.

Ralf noticed that many of the corpses had been dragged away. As if a dead army had risen and marched from the killing-ground.

The night breeze was warm on his bare shoulders and he was grateful for the cup of whisky which Swan had got for him.

Ralf touched his trousers pocket and felt the brass telescope hot against his thigh.

He wished he had really known his father. From the portrait which hung at Hawks Hill he had looked more like David, he thought. He tightened his jaw. Maybe it was David he was really trying to impress.

Ralf glanced angrily at the first pale stars.

'This way. Follow me.'

He thought suddenly of the boy Adams, the way he wanted to help and serve him.

The realization hit him like a fist. It was not just Adams. Like it or not they all depended on him now.

'Wake up, sir. It's time.'

Blackwood rolled over and groaned as Swan released his grip on his shoulder. As his senses returned he wished he had not given in to sleep. It made him feel weak, vulnerable, his whole body protesting. It was very dark. Not for long.

Swan held out a mug of tea. 'Best I could do, sir.'

Blackwood nodded thankfully. 'Any news of my cousin?'

Swan eyed him steadily. 'No. Probably too early.'

Blackwood said, 'I'd like to have a shave.' Swan got to his feet. The request did not surprise him. It was odd the way blokes made the effort before a last battle. He had already seen some of the marines rolling and packing their kit, their faces strangely dedicated, as if nothing else mattered.

He had heard that it had been common enough in the great days of sail. Clean shirt and a good meal before hell broke loose.

Blackwood stared up at the sky as he sipped the scalding tea. There was more hot water than tea leaves, he thought. Everything was suddenly in short supply.

He wondered if Ralf was still safe or out there unable to move in either direction. A wide detour, he had said. If he was too long he and his two volunteers might be the only survivors.

He looked round as Swan returned with his shaving kit. Ralf might already be a prisoner, gasping out his life, praying for death. He heard a dog barking somewhere, a few hasty footsteps as the remaining coolies were released from their work removing enemy corpses. What did they think about it? They surely could not believe the Boxers to be invulnerable to foreign bullets any more?

He thought too of Friedrike at the mission building. Gravatt had told him that it was now being defended by the German marines, the *Seebataillon*. It might comfort her to hear her own language around her.

Swan handed him a towel and he cleaned his face, the skin tender after a quick shave. Bravado, another gesture, what did it matter? He got to his feet and stared at the horizon. There was still smoke and a few sparks across the sky, but he could see the outline of the buildings, a gradual lightening which meant an early dawn.

'I want you to go to Mr Gravatt.'

Swan checked his rifle. 'No bother, sir. 'E's taken care of everythin'.'

Blackwood ran his fingers through his hair. It felt full of grit, dirtied by gunsmoke and sweat.

He heard Gravatt approaching and straightened his back.

Swan saw his composure return, the outer confidence which the other took for granted. He felt moved by what he saw, to know he had always shared it.

Gravatt reported, 'All available men are in position, sir. Some of the wounded have joined them. They can keep the spare rifles loaded.' He added with sudden bitterness, 'There are enough of them!'

Blackwood climbed on to a slab of stone and lifted his glasses. It was still too dark to see much. If he was wrong about the Boxers they might rush the outer wall and use it as a defence while they fired directly on to the inner barricades.

There was a sudden bang and seconds later the first shell exploded at the foot of the wall. Blackwood did not need to see it; he could hear the worn stones crashing down, splinters whining overhead or cracking into the barricades.

He had been right. The enemy intended to make so many breaks in the wall that they could attack several places at once.

Crash.

Blackwood said, 'Tell them to keep down. The Boxers are firing more often this time.'

A gold rim of sunlight touched one of the tallest buildings then vanished momentarily in a cloud of smoke and fragments as another shell exploded.

He felt Swan remove his revolver and then murmur, 'Only three shots left in it, sir.'

Blackwood loosened his sword and said nothing. He no longer trusted his voice. He would feel better when action was joined. It was always like that. The madness. The wild excitement which could preserve or kill with equal indifference.

He heard O'Neil dragging an ammunition box beside the machine-gun, and Sergeant Chittock unsheathing the Colours. Individual acts of defiance but with little hope left.

The cannon fired once again and Blackwood felt the ground vibrate as more stones and bricks rained down. The wall had been built a long time ago, strong enough to withstand muskets and pikes. It was no match for shellfire.

The sunlight continued remorselessly to lay bare the battlefield, the other lower wall where they had made their first appearance at Tientsin. Blackwood thought of Admiral Seymour's anticipated arrival in Peking in a single day. That was two weeks ago, a century.

He levelled his glasses. 'Bugler, sound the alarm!'

On either side of him he heard the marines preparing themselves. The click of rifle-bolts, the nervous movements along the sandbags as each man tried to find the best vantage point.

He heard the Boxers' horn, mournful but threatening, and pictured the mass of men beginning to form up, to move towards the hated foreigners with gathering momentum.

'*Stand-to!*' Fox was everywhere as usual. Eventually he planted his boots at the place where the barricade had almost collapsed. He would not move unless he fell dead.

Sergeant Greenaway was on the left of the line, and Blackwood found time to notice he had chosen a position amongst some of the youngest marines, new recruits such a short while ago. An ancient warrior to most of them, but he could give them strength when they most needed it. That was now.

Blackwood shouted, 'Hold your fire until I give the order!'

If they fired too soon the first wave of attackers would take cover behind the wall. As the light continued to strengthen he saw the great holes and gaps in the outer wall. Impossible to defend, but still good cover for the advancing enemy.

Hidden on the other side of some sand and grain bags he heard someone repeating over and over again, 'Oh God, oh God' – like that time on the mad dash downriver.

He balanced his revolver in his left hand and drew his sword with the other. Three bullets Swan had said.

He wiped his face with his sleeve.

Come on, you bastards! He glanced quickly at Swan. He had imagined he had shouted the words aloud. But Swan was concentrating on a gap in the wall directly opposite the barricade. There were lots of fallen stones on the inside. The enemy might stumble, others would certainly be thrusting them from the rear. It would give him time to bring several of them down, he thought.

The noise was deafening, and dust from thousands of running feet drove towards the waiting marines like a desert sandstorm.

'*Ready!*'

The rifles moved slightly and then settled on their selected targets.

'*Fire!*'

The charging figures were pouring through the shattered gateway and the gaps along the wall, others knelt on the outer barricade and fired across the shell-pitted ground.

Blackwood waved his sword. 'Again, lads!' He yelled at the nearest marine, the one who had been sobbing prayers. 'Take aim, man, don't waste them!'

'*Fire!*' The order was almost lost in the lethal clatter of the machine-gun. The front ranks seemed to bend and fall or were stamped underfoot by the press of figures behind.

It was hopeless. They were almost here. Blackwood saw two marines step back from the barricade, as if unable to face the onslaught.

It was now or never.

He climbed on to the barricade and shouted above the din, 'Meet them! Come on, the Royals!'

The madness gripped all of them as they leapt from their hiding places and met the oncoming mob out in the open.

Blackwood parried a pike to one side and drove his blade through an Imperial soldier's neck. As he tore the sword free he swung it across the front of a marine who had dropped to one knee, his fingers locked around his thigh as the blood shone to match his fallen bayonet.

Oates sounded his bugle again and again, it was the only sound to carry from one end of the embattled line to the other. The Boxers surged against the barricade, and tried to pull the marines down amongst them. The bayonets darted and lunged, and here and there a marine found time to reload his rifle and fire into the screaming mass of faces which could not move forward or back.

Corporal O'Neil yelled, 'Quick, me boy! Put your weight on this wheel, we'll give the gateway a burst.' He stared horrified as his friend the gun-layer fell backwards, a gaping hole punched between his eyes. O'Neil sobbed, 'Oh, Willy! Not you too!'

Then he dragged his friend aside and threw himself at the machine-gun yelling curses and obscenities as he worked the firing-handle until his hand seemed blurred. Once a bullet cut across his forearm and left a livid, black scar, but O'Neil barely noticed.

At the centre of the line some of the Boxers, one carrying a yellow standard, hurled themselves over the top. Some were impaled on bayonets, another shot down by one of the marines who had been wounded earlier.

Lieutenant de Courcy shouted, 'Can't hold 'em, sir!' He fired his revolver until it was empty and then charged into the fight with only his sword.

Blackwood saw the colour sergeant clinging to his staff, his eyes squinting with pain as blood ran from two wounds in his shoulder. But he clung to the flag, for it was what he had always done. When the truth came to him at last he managed to pass the flag to a wild-eyed marine and gasp, 'Don't let go, Dago! Not fer nothing!' Then he died.

The explosion when it came felt like an earthquake, as if it was many miles away and did not concern them at all.

Blackwood locked swords with a yelling Chinese officer, pushed him against the barricade and then drove the blade into his stomach. The dying officer was still shouting as he dropped. Hate, surrender, Blackwood did not care which. In his mind all he could recognize was the gigantic explosion. Ralf and his men had done it. It must have taken more than mere courage to wait for daylight and the first shots from the cannon. Every available Boxer and soldier must have gathered for the attack after the shells had done their work.

'*Cease firing!*' That was Gravatt, instantly supported by the bugler.

Blackwood stared dazedly as the enemy melted back towards the wall, over the dead and dying and through the gaps without firing another shot.

Blackwood sheathed his sword. It clung to the scabbard, sticky with blood.

Gravatt shouted wildly, 'They're on the run!' He waved his cap in the air. 'Look at 'em go!'

The explosion must have caught the enemy completely off-balance, Blackwood thought. Then he looked along his line of breathless, bleeding marines. Fox still a ramrod amidst chaos and horror. De Courcy gritting his teeth as a marine bandaged his wounded hand. He had seized a Chinese blade to push it away and might lose all his fingers. But his face said it all. *I am alive.*

Blackwood walked slowly amongst his men. Several were dead, and more wounded than otherwise.

The Boxers would come back. They had to. Without Tientsin in their hands they would be in the same position as Seymour.

Blackwood saw O'Neil carrying Private Willy Hudson away from the machine-gun. He glanced briefly at Blackwood who was moved by the tears on his battered face. He carried his friend to the nearest building and laid him to rest there. Then he snatched up a rifle and said brokenly. 'No more ammo for th' Nordenfeldt, sir. I'll stand with you.'

Sergeant Greenaway yelled, ''Ere come three o' th' bastards!'

A few rifles lifted and steadied as the figures tumbled through a smashed barricade.

Blackwood held up his hand. 'Belay that!'

In their stolen clothing, their faces still liberally smeared with soot, Ralf and his two marines walked slowly through the dead Boxers. They stopped at the barricade where the battle-shocked marines peered despairingly at the rising dust above the enemy camp.

Ralf said huskily, 'I thought we were too late.' He looked across at Colour Sergeant Nat Chittock who lay with one arm outflung, unwilling to the last to release his precious flag.

Blackwood grasped his cousin by the shoulders. 'You were bloody marvellous, Ralf. It knocked the stuffing out of them.'

Ralf studied him emptily. 'They'll be back.' He tore off the Boxer smock and threw it to one side. 'We laid all night with the other corpses.' It seemed to amuse him. 'I stink.'

Blackwood dropped his arms to his sides. They were like lead. But Ralf was right. Gun or no gun they would be back. He looked at the marines who stood along the barricade. There were great gaps between them. He doubted if there were more than thirty who were still able to fight. But at least Ralf's action had given them time to regroup, then to fall back to the city-centre, or wherever Hay intended to see it through to a bloody conclusion.

'Get the wounded under cover, Toby.' He nodded gratefully as Swan handed him a canteen of water. It was like wine. Perhaps it was; Swan could do anything.

Blackwood took another grip on himself. If he cracked now – He swung round and said, 'Share out the ammunition.' He realized he had spoken sharply and saw Gravatt watching him.

Ralf said, 'I'll see to it.' He looked at him and added, 'Then I'll be back.'

Blackwood walked to the barricade. They would be together when it happened.

Sergeant Greenaway said, 'Private Smith is signallin', sir!'

Blackwood wanted to weep. So soon? The enemy were wasting no time to take their revenge on the ragged flag and those who continued to defend it.

'*Up, lads!*' Fox picked up a rifle. 'Move yerselves!' But when his eyes met Blackwood's they told the truth. It was already finished.

Blackwood raised his glasses and saw the solid mass of Chinese surging about in the dusty sunlight, a few banners still waving here and there; it was like something from a nightmare.

The sun touched on gleaming sabres and suddenly as he watched spellbound Blackwood saw the horses for the first time. Cavalry, a solid wedge of them charging straight for the stampeding mass of Boxers and troops.

I must be going mad. Blackwood recognized the tall headgear of the riders, Cossacks, their heavy sabres slashing a path right through the enemy. He blinked to clear the mist from his eyes. Troops too. Bayonets fixed. He could even hear the raucous call of a bugle.

Gravatt whispered, 'Dear God, it's the relief!'

Blackwood lowered his binoculars and pressed his hands on the empty machine-gun. The enemy was in full retreat. First their shells had been destroyed, and now they were caught between two fires.

It seemed to take an eternity for the first of the relief force to reach them. The Cossacks remained at a distance, or galloped after a few groups of Boxers, their sabres more than a match for the Long Knives.

Fox bellowed, 'Fall in there! Smarten yerselves up!' He sounded angry that soldiers should see them like this.

The first to arrive in the gateway was an army lieutenant colonel mounted on a fine grey stallion. He reined up just a few yards from the Royal Marines and looked at them for what seemed like an age before he said anything. Then he dismounted and returned Blackwood's salute.

He said quietly, 'I've seen a lot of battles in my service, Captain Blackwood.' He glanced along the swaying line of filthy marines, and saw their determination to hold on. 'But never anything like this. We thought you were already dead.' He faced the marines and saluted them stiffly. 'Now I must find Colonel Hay.' He seemed strangely unwilling to leave a scene which he knew he could never forget.

Blackwood said, 'Then on to Peking, sir.'

The officer eyed him sadly. 'You are relieved, Captain Blackwood. You and your men have done more than enough.' He glanced towards the drifting smoke. 'Where are the rest of your company?'

Blackwood bunched his hands into fists to control his sudden emotion.

'These are all of them, sir.'

The lieutenant colonel looked at Sergeant Major Fox, at Ralf, his young features a mask of disapproval even now, at Swan, and Oates, and all the survivors.

He said half to himself. 'What do they say about your Corps? *The first to land*, right?'

Blackwood thought of the others who were not there. Of Bannatyre and young Earle, Sergeants Kirby and Davis, Corporals Lyde and Handley, Chittock, the colour sergeant. And all the other rough graves which had marked their course to this place.

He heard himself say, 'And the last to leave.'

Epilogue

Captain David Blackwood leaned back in a comfortable leather chair and stared through the open French windows. Inside the great house nothing seemed to have changed, he thought. Only when the carriage had carried him through the high gates of Hawks Hill three days ago had he noticed any difference. The big gates needed painting badly, and the lodge-house looked unkempt.

Later after an emotional welcome, Trent, the estate steward, had told him that two of the small farms had been sold off in an effort to pay for some of the General's extravagances.

But that could wait. It was good to be back in England and in time for another summer. Through the windows he could see the neatly trimmed bushes, the swaying masses of colour from the well-tended flower-beds.

Upon his return to Portsmouth in a slow troopship he had heard the news of the Allies finally lifting the siege of Peking, and the end of the Boxers' Society. The damage to Chinese trade and finances was almost crippling with millions of pounds' indemnity to be paid to the European powers and their allies.

Now, looking at the gardens and the green Hampshire countryside beyond, it was hard to believe that it was exactly a year since he and his men had stood together for the final attack which never came.

Most of the survivors of his company had also returned to England, some to their homes, others to the naval hospital at Haslar. Blackwood had made a point of visiting the wounded before he had left Portsmouth for Hawks Hill. They had seemed cheerful enough, but Blackwood doubted if their nights were so peaceful. But now that he was home again perhaps the nightmares would leave him alone. The distorted, screaming faces, the terrible chant *Sha! Sha!* Even in the troopship he had awakened in a cold sweat night after night.

He thought of the General and his mother. They seemed to have got over Neil's death, or at least they were able to accept it. His return and Ralf's impulsive gallantry in that final battle had made up for a lot.

Blackwood often recalled the last time he had seen Friedrike. Almost as soon as the relief force had occupied the city, and the weary defenders relieved, he had hurried to the mission to see her. He had been in time to see her being assisted to a carriage with a full escort of German marines.

They had touched hands and he had seen the tears in her eyes before a black-coated official had coughed politely and guided her into the carriage. It all seemed like a dream. Something which had happened and which he could not accept or understand.

Like the news which had greeted his return to home waters. The Queen was dead. The end of an era. A personality they had all come to take for granted. Perhaps the affairs of state, the wars in China and South Africa, Egypt and the Crimea during her long reign had finally been too much for her.

But the memory of Friedrike and their one night of love together rarely left his thoughts. When he walked round the estate to meet new faces and renew old acquaintances he had touched the locket around his neck, and had wondered about her.

He saw Trooper, the ubiquitous horse, being led by Swan towards the stables. A very adaptable animal, he thought, who seemed as much at home here as in Tientsin. How much younger Swan looked out of uniform. If he was surprised to have survived he kept it a secret.

He heard a door open and watched his father settle himself in one of the big chairs. If he had changed at all it was only that he no longer bothered about the servants seeing him wearing spectacles in the house.

He would want to hear it all over again. The events which had led up to the battle, pieced together with names and faces, strength and weakness.

When Blackwood had told him about Ralf he had chuckled. 'Young puppy. Up in London now chasin' some filly or other.' His severe features had relaxed. 'God, Philip would have been *proud* of him. I am.'

There was to be a special dinner in David Blackwood's honour tonight. He hoped his stomach could cope after all the bad food and coarse rations of the campaign.

And there was Sarah, the girl Neil had hoped to marry. *A nice sensible girl*, as his mother had described her. But there was a lot more to her than that. She would be here too. She had seemed pleased to meet him, with a sort of questioning shyness. Perhaps she was searching for Neil in him?

He smiled to himself. His mother had taken the girl with her to Alresford, their nearest village. Perhaps she was match-making in her quiet way.

He glanced at the headlines on his father's newspaper. *The Kaiser demands massive rearmament. German Fleet to be reinforced.*

His father looked over his glasses.

'There was a piece about your German countess in the paper a few weeks back. I meant to mention it, but what with your return and the news about – '

'What was it?' He found himself on the edge of his chair.

The General eyed him curiously. 'On the society page. The Countess von Heiser had a baby, a boy as it turns out. So the old family line will continue after all. Strange, I heard at the Club that the Count was supposed to be impotent.'

He went back to his newspaper.

Blackwood stood up and walked slowly into the clean June air.

They had both wanted an heir more than anything. They would tell nobody. Only he knew the truth. He touched the locket beneath his shirt. *Our son.*

The old General looked up and watched him cross the terrace to speak with Swan.

Then he gave a slow smile. He had not yet forgotten what it was like to be young.

C

recover his breath, one juror called out: "Could you enlighten us as to why Dumouriez failed to pursue the Prussians during their retreat?"

Danton sidestepped this allusion to the mystery of Valmy by saying: "I was only concerned with the war in its political aspects. Military operations as such were a closed book to me." Herman stepped in and took over from the juror, but was no more successful in pinning Danton down to an explanation. Exhausted by the strain of defending himself, but resolute in his determination not to reveal the truth, Danton pulled out a handkerchief and mopped his forehead. With a certain sly duplicity, Herman suggested adjourning till the next day, so that he could "continue his apologia in greater calm and tranquillity."

Danton accepted, and this was his undoing. Before he sat down, he asked the Court not to forget to summon his witnesses for the next hearing. He then supplied a list of them. His fellow prisoners supported such a move. Herman raised various objections. This gave rise to an argument, which soon degenerated into noisy chaos. Some of those present thought they heard Danton exclaim, amid the uproar: "If they refuse me my witnesses, there's no point in my defending myself any longer."

The first scene of the third act took place that same evening, 14 Germinal, in the Pavillon de l'Égalité. Robespierre, Couthon, and Saint-Just—that famous triumvirate—were at work with their colleagues, when one of Fouquier-Tinville's messengers delivered the following hastily scribbled note by Herman: "We have had an extremely stormy session from the moment it started. The accused are insisting, in the most violent manner, on having witnesses examined for the defense. They have listed the following Deputies: Simon, Courtois, Laignelot, Fréron, Panis, Lindet, Calon, Merlin [the member for Douai], Gossuin, Legendre, Robin, Goupilleau, Lecointre [the member for Versailles], Brival, and Merlin [the member for Thionville]. They are calling the public to witness what they term the refusal of their just claims. Despite the firm stand taken by the President and the entire Tribunal, their reiterated demands are holding up the case. Furthermore, they openly declare that until their

trol over the proceedings. Danton, by his fiery eloquence, had usurped the President's position and held the floor uninterrupted throughout. His skillful blend of wit and seriousness captivated the spectators. He recalled his past triumphs before the Jacobins and the Cordeliers, as a Minister, in the Riding School. He evoked the trust which his fellow Deputies had placed in him. With nice irony he concluded: "How odd that the Convention remained so blind to my faults until now! And how truly miraculous this sudden collective delusion concerning me!"

As he paused for a moment to draw breath, Herman cut in: "Your irony is no answer to the charge that you used patriotism as a mask, behind which you gave secret support to the monarchy!"

With still heavier irony Danton sneered: "Ah yes, indeed, I remember. Now how did I promote the restoration of the monarchy and safeguard the tyrant's attempted flight? As I recall it, by doing everything in my power to prevent his trip to Saint-Cloud, by hedging him about with a forest of pikes and bayonets. If that is to prove oneself a dedicated Royalist, then I must plead guilty to the charge!"

This statement drew laughter and applause from the gallery. With a flash of pride he exclaimed: "You are the people, and when I have presented my case it is you who will judge me! My voice should not be heard by you alone, but by all France!" The applause redoubled.

The word that Danton was gaining the upper hand over his opponents rapidly spread throughout the Law Courts, from mouth to mouth, down corridor and staircase, until at last it penetrated the Conciergerie. Full of anxious hope, the prisoners waited, sure that Danton's victory, if he achieved it, would secure their own release.

He came within a hairsbreadth of success. The whole Tribunal, President, judges, jury, Public Prosecutor, everyone, seemed overwhelmed by his onslaught. Herman passed a note to Fouquier-Tinville which read: "In half an hour I shall adjourn the hearing." Meanwhile Danton himself was beginning to tire. He had been speaking for over an hour, and his voice had lost its strength. Despite everything, he feared for his life, and the terror he felt made a drain on his reserves of energy. As he paused to

ple's behalf," Danton told them, "supporting and defending their interests. It should have little difficulty now in refuting mere slander. Would my cowardly persecutors dare to attack me to my face? I doubt it. Let them but show themselves, and soon enough I will cover them with the ignominy and opprobrium which are their fitting lot in life. . . . I insist that the Convention appoint Commissioners to investigate my exposure of dictatorial practices. Yes, I, Danton, will strip the mask from this shameless and naked dictatorship! I, Danton—"

At this point Herman interrupted him. "Audacity," he said, "is a characteristic of guilt. Innocence keeps a cool head."

"If you will let me—"

"Self-defense is a legitimate privilege. But it must contain itself within limits. The defendant must show proper respect for everything and everybody—even his accusers."

"*Individual* audacity is, doubtless, reprehensible," Danton thundered, "but *national* audacity, which I have used time and again to serve the public weal, is a different, and quite legitimate, human characteristic. Besides, when I find myself faced with so grievous and unjust an accusation, how am I to control the anger and resentment which boil up in me? And is a revolutionary extremist such as myself the kind of person from whom you expect a frigid, unemotional defense?"

Indeed, his speech was more of a fiery diatribe. The charge of conspiracy he swept aside with the joking remark: "Me a conspirator? I'm too busy kissing my wife every night!" Complaints of his venality he rebutted with another historical aphorism: "*I sell my allegiance? Why, there is no price high enough for a man of my caliber!*" He went on to demand that the prosecution furnish "proof, or part proof, or any evidence whatsoever" of his supposed corruption. If he had been bought by Mirabeau or the Duke of Orléans or the Court, then let his accusers provide chapter and verse to prove it. "Bring these creatures before me, and I will hurl them back into the obscurity from which they never should have emerged! Vile imposters, stand forth, and let me strip off the mask you wear to protect yourselves against public obloquy!"

His voice was drowned in applause, and he had to stop. From this point until the adjournment Herman had no effective con-

lot d'Herbois, Saint-Just, Jagot, C. A. Prieur, Couthon, Dubarran, Voulland, Moyse Bayle, Amar, Élie Lacoste, Robespierre, and Lavicomterie.

Not all these despots could match Saint-Just and Vadier for implacability, or Billaud-Varennes and Collot d'Herbois for bloodthirstiness, or Le Bas and Robespierre for ambition. If men as estimable as Carnot, Louis, Prieur, and Lacoste (who could meet the Incorruptible on his own ground) were prepared to sign what virtually amounted to a death warrant, they must have believed Danton guilty of the charges against him.

Only two Committee members refused to append their names at the foot of the document: the aged Rühl, of the Committee of General Security, and Robert Lindet, of the Committee of Public Safety. The former was a onetime Presbyterian minister who owed what fame he possessed to the so-called Massacre of the Sacred Ampulla at Rheims. The Ampulla was the vessel that held the holy oil, and Rühl had smashed it before an enthusiastic crowd. Lindet, who had been elected to the Robespierre Committee several months before, could not forget his earlier membership of the same Committee under Danton.

Both of them deputed Panis (a former member of the Commune of August 10) to go without delay and attempt to rouse Danton from his lethargy. Panis reached the rue Marat between midnight and one o'clock. Louise opened the door to him; the servants were all asleep. Somewhat alarmed, she took the visitor to her husband. Panis found him sitting by the fireside in his dressing gown, sunk deep in his own thoughts. To the somewhat vague report of Fabricius Pâris he added one concrete and indisputable fact: the warrant for Danton's arrest had been issued. Danton got up and poked at the fire. "I can't believe it," he said.

Robert Lindet appeared in person to confirm the truth of Panis's statement. There was no longer room for doubt; the arrest had been planned for that very night. "You've still got time to get away," Danton's friend urged him. But Danton made evasive replies, and after a while Lindet took himself off, aghast at the lack of interest which his old comrade showed in saving his own skin. Was he still hoping against hope that all would be well?

would come in occasionally and the lovers would exchange a kiss. When Danton's two children went scampering through with their cousin, he called them over and dandled them on his knee. It is hard to understand this persistent mood of apathy and inaction. Why did he not go straight to the Convention? Had he forgotten that the Committees were bent on destroying him? Was he unaware that Vouland, Amar, Couthon, Collot d'Herbois, and Barère were all behind Billaud-Varennes and Vadier, and that Robespierre had authorized the terrible Saint-Just to draw up the indictment against him?

On the evening of March 30 the street bell rang once more. A servant showed in Fabricius Pâris, the copying clerk who was now both a member of the jury and Clerk of the Court to the Revolutionary Tribunal—a post he had secured through Danton's offices. Every day he went over from the Law Courts to the Tuileries, to collect the Committee of Public Safety's latest orders and deliver them to Fouquier-Tinville. That evening, however, the chamber in which France's masters conducted their deliberations had been locked. Intrigued, he hurried through the other rooms of the Pavillon de l'Égalité (he knew the layout of the building very well), and found a keyhole through which he could see Saint-Just, who had a series of papers in his hand and was reading their contents aloud to the members of both Committees. Fabricius Pâris then applied his ear to the keyhole, and what he heard boded ill for his patron. The very next day, it transpired, Saint-Just intended to ask the Convention to approve' Danton's arrest and trial.

Danton's only response to this revelation was a shrug of the shoulders. "They would never dare," he said. But Pâris had failed to discover one vital piece of evidence, the draft decree still preserved in the Musée des Archives: "The Committees of Public Safety and of General Security hereby decree that Danton, Lacroix (of the Eure-et-Loire *département*), Camille Desmoulins, and Philippeaux, all members of the National Convention, shall be arrested and taken to the Luxembourg Prison, there to be kept in solitary and secret confinement. And they do command the Mayor of Paris to execute this present decree immediately on receipt thereof." The document was signed, in that order, by Billaud-Varennes, Vadier, Carnot, Le Bas, Louis, Col-

CHAPTER XVIII

Famous Last Words

ROBESPIERRE'S BEHAVIOR SUGGESTS that all he wanted was Danton's political elimination. If Danton, exhausted by partisan struggles and (as he was often fond of saying) "sick of his fellow men," had retired to plant cabbages in Arcis-sur-Aube, doubtless Robespierre would have spared his life. But Billaud-Varennes and Vadier were implacably set on having him executed. Billaud —that "foursquare Republican and choleric patriot," as Desmoulins called him—regarded Danton's "moderatism" as a plot against the régime and his dealings with the *affairistes* as part of an intrigue to undermine the nation's finances. As for Vadier —the other Incorruptible—this impotent old ex-rake, this Republican puritan would never forgive the virility of which Danton made such abundant demonstration. He envied him his size, his strength, his eloquence. He was jealous of his successes with women—not least his possession, at thirty-four, of a wife who had barely reached adolescence. Later, after his downfall, Vadier declared: "Little Louise was our most useful assistant during this crisis. It was her fresh complexion and melting eyes that disarmed the circus strong man for us."

Disarmed Danton seemed to be indeed, in sober earnest, after his return from Sèvres. Though he reached Paris on the evening of 9 Germinal, he did not do what he should have done, which was to hurry to the Jacobin Club without a moment's delay and make his voice heard there. All next day he spent in dressing gown and slippers, drowsing in front of the fire, only leaving his armchair from time to time to throw on more logs. Louise

number of the *Vieux Cordelier*. Desmoulins, faithful to the pact concluded on that evening beside the Seine, had opened his campaign in favor of mercy. This inaugural issue was a very clever piece of work; it carefully avoided any call for leniency toward real or supposed opponents of the régime. On the contrary, the *Vieux Cordelier* went out of its way to sing Robespierre's praises. However, it did not neglect to bestow a like tribute upon "his rival in patriotic virtue, the permanent President of the Old Cordeliers." Before having this issue run off, Desmoulins made sure that Robespierre got, and read, a set of proofs.

Five days later, on December 10, the second number of this periodical appeared, again with the Incorruptible's *imprimatur*. This time the seal of approval covered an attack on Hébert and Anacharsis Clootz—a German baron who had plunged enthusiastically into the French Revolution and was now preaching paganism on behalf of Père Duchesne. The success of the *Vieux Cordelier*—it had a print order of fifty thousand copies —began to worry Robespierre. Desmoulins's views were very much in agreement with his own, but the journalist's eloquent pen seemed as though it might divert some of Robespierre's own popular acclaim.

When the third number was published, on December 15, the moving spirit behind the Committee of Public Safety held his breath. This time he had not read the proofs; if he had, he would have exploded with fury. Desmoulins had turned historian and satirist, with a sketch of Rome under the Caesars —its tyranny and excesses and victims. There could hardly have been a more pointed allusion to the *régime des suspects*.

Yet Robespierre made no move. He needed the *Vieux Cordelier* too badly, as a weapon with which to destroy *Le Père Duchesne*. Since Desmoulins waited ten days before publishing the fourth number, the Incorruptible took advantage of the delay to make it appear that he shared the views expressed in the third. While taking care to uphold "the sacred cause of justice," he announced the discussion of a measure which, by making all verdicts subject to confirmation and approval, would keep a check on "excesses committed in the name of patriotism."

This gave Desmoulins an admirable opening. In his fourth

the oratorical genius of the other, so recently allied to create the Terror, joined forces that evening to plot its overthrow.

The first essential step was the elimination of Hébert's more fanatical supporters. A fresh opportunity to attack them occurred on 13 Frimaire, at the Jacobin Club—though as it turned out it was Danton himself who very nearly became the victim. That day (December 3) it was proposed that the Club should invite the Convention to make the rents of popular clubs a charge on the Treasury. Danton spoke against such a suggestion. In his view, its realization would have taken the people "beyond the limits of the Revolution." This was the first time he had publicly attacked the "ultra-revolutionists," and his audience reacted strongly. There were whistles and catcalls, followed by accusations of "aiding and abetting the traitors."

Robespierre, who was relying on Danton to purge Paris of *hébertistes,* had no option but to defend him vigorously. "Patriots and tyrants," he declared, "have one thing in common: their cause unites them all. Perhaps I am mistaken about Danton the man; but viewed in his family context he deserves unqualified praise. I have observed his political attitudes; a difference of opinion between us led me to study this aspect of him closely, and often with anger. He was, I know, too slow in suspecting Dumouriez, and he did not show himself implacable enough toward Brissot and his accomplices. But because he has not always seen eye to eye with me, must I conclude from this that he was betraying his country? Indeed not; he has always, to the best of my knowledge, served France with devoted zeal. If there is any person here present who has some criticism to make against Danton, let him do so now!"

No one dared take up this invitation; the prophet had spoken. Better still, Momoro—who had some while previously transferred his allegiance from Danton to Hébert—was heard remarking, in the hush: "Well, there's nothing to be said against Danton—that proves it." He went on to suggest that the President of the Club should give him "the brotherly accolade," i.e. a kiss of peace. This short-lived reconciliation took place amid applause.

The following day, December 5, there appeared the first

enemy was approaching Paris, who had inspired and built up the new system of government and judicial administration, who had declared that "a nation in the midst of a revolution is nearer to vanquishing its neighbors than being vanquished by them"—this coarse, muscular figure, whose final achievement was the Terror, could now stand back and observe the outcome of his labors. Everywhere the Republic was either victorious or well on the road to victory. Thanks to Carnot, the conscription of some 600,000 men had produced the most formidable army in Europe. French troops fought to defend their rights or their fields, whereas the soldiers of other nations were still mercenaries, campaigning for pay. There was all the difference in the world between them. The patriotic ardor of the French army proved more than a match for the cash-based discipline of their opponents. This being so, why should heads continue to roll under the guillotine?

One evening Danton and Desmoulins were on their way home after a meeting of the Convention. As they strolled along beside the Seine, the reflected rays of the setting sun stained the surface of the water a bright crimson. The two friends happened to meet Souberbielle (the surgeon summoned by decree to leave his hospital and act as juror on the Revolutionary Tribunal), who had just come from the Law Courts. Fifteen heads had rolled that afternoon, and twenty-seven more were due to do so the following morning. On hearing this news Danton said: "Look at the Seine; it's flowing blood."

"It's true," the doctor remarked. "The sky's red. . . ." He paused. "They asked for inflexible judges. What they want now are obliging executioners. If we save some innocent head from that chopping machine of theirs, they tax us with royalism. But what can *I* do about it? I'm just an ordinary citizen. Ah, if only I were Danton—"

"Danton is returning to the fray. He has slept too long." Then the demagogue turned to Desmoulins and said: "There has been too much blood spilled. Camille, take up your pen again—appeal to them to be more merciful. I'll back you up. You can see my hand, you know its strength—"

And Desmoulins promised. The literary skill of the one and

strode down from the rostrum he glanced contemptuously at Hébert. As always, he had managed to talk his way back into public favor.

Throughout September he was the idol of the Convention. To list all his many interventions would be a tedious task; let us restrict ourselves to one characteristic example, his plea that every citizen should be provided with a firearm for the defense of his country, and that the Treasury should earmark 100,000,000 francs for their manufacture. In this famous speech he proclaimed, with fulsome pomposity: "All homage to you, O sublime People! To your greatness you add the capacity for endurance; nothing can daunt you in the pursuit of liberty. To achieve that goal you have shed your blood, and accepted many privations. You must and shall win through! We shall march shoulder to shoulder with you! Your enemies will be confounded, freedom shall be yours!"

Newspapers reporting this speech asserted that at its close hats were thrown in the air, and the applause was so thunderous that it nearly brought the house down.

Prieur de la Côte-d'Or, a member of the Committee of Public Safety, afterward wrote in his *Mémoires sur Carnot:* "Billaud and Collot d'Herbois kept up a constant stream of criticism against everything we did. Finally we agreed that the only way to silence them was to make them members of the Committee." The Committee duly proposed this measure to the Convention, but received a shock when not only Billaud-Varennes and Collot d'Herbois were elected, but Danton and Granet, too. Both the latter refused to serve, however. Danton's words were: "I swear by the liberty of my country that I will never accept a place on the Committee!"

Coming from him, this might be thought a somewhat surprising oath. But in his heart of hearts he was fed up with the whole political game. These tub-thumping triumphs had begun to pall on him. Since his defeat he had not been able to spend a single undisturbed day with Louise. What was more, he felt ill, or perhaps just thoroughly exhausted: a sudden overwhelming sense of depression and fatigue, which he found it impossible to

Paré, Danton's boyhood friend and former chief clerk, and Hébert, the editor of *Le Père Duchesne* and Danton's successor as Deputy Public Prosecutor to the Commune. Naturally Danton backed Paré, who was duly elected Minister. This produced some angry invective in *Le Père Duchesne,* which described Danton and Paré as "thick as thieves—just as Danton was with Dumouriez." By this oblique reference to the Belgian mission, Hébert revived the old charges of fleecing and extortion. Delving still further into the past, he also accused Danton of having obtained compensation for his advocateship far in excess of the post's real value. Thanks to his various financial malversations, Hébert claimed, the former Minister had been able to settle 14,000,000 francs on his wife at the time of their marriage.

Danton, who detested writing but was unsurpassed as a speaker, did not reply to Hébert in print. Knowing that the latter would be present at the Jacobin Club on August 26, he appeared there himself to conduct his own defense. The 14,000,-000 francs Hébert had mentioned were in fact a mere 40,000 *livres.* And since when had it been considered reprehensible for a widower with a family to remarry so as to give his children a mother again? Since when had it been a crime for a husband to safeguard his wife's future? In any case, Danton's private life was his own affair. Descending from indignation to self-abasement, this independent character then admitted his dependence on the opposite sex. "I must have women," he declared tearfully, with a touch of farcical inspiration. But he had restricted himself to one, so there was no reason for people to persecute him like this. The 40,000 *livres* which his enemies were so skeptical about—though the figure could be checked from his marriage contract—had been earned by the sweat of his brow. "I am proud that I was born a *sans-culotte,*" he declared, "and that nature endowed me with sufficient physical strength to provide for my sustenance."

As he said this, he drew himself up, so that he looked even taller, threw out his chest, which added to his already formidable bulk, and rounded his big arms, as though the swelling muscles were visible through the stuff of his coat sleeves. Everyone burst out laughing. He had won again; he had got his audience where he wanted them. His speech was loudly applauded, and as he

bers dozed off and the spectators up in the galleries began to fidget irritably. If Danton did nothing else, he woke everyone up. His trumpet sounded the charge, and the public brightened visibly. When word went around that he was about to make an intervention, crowds of people would hurry across to the Tuileries Theater.

Louise was now officially established as the great man's wife. On certain fixed days she was "at home" in the Cour du Commerce. A "domestic official" in knee breeches (the word "valet" had been dropped) helped the two "female domestic officials" to serve *petits fours*. (By way of a small economy, the same man also acted as coachman.) Gabrielle had played the clavichord, but Louise offered her guests the chance to enjoy a somewhat more striking talent. Her instrument was the guitar, and she sang to her own accompaniment. Danton went in for musically minded wives.

Like Gabrielle, too, Louise preferred to keep away from the Convention. Her marriage and the love she bore her husband had made no difference either to her religious beliefs or to her Royalist opinions. Like her parents, she detested the rabble-rousing atmosphere of the "national circus," and her appearances there were rare in the extreme. But being the wife of a man such as Danton had its drawbacks no less than its advantages. Through no fault of her own, Louise found herself the bone of contention during a public debate—not in the Assembly, but at that scarcely less influential (if unofficial) institution the Jacobin Club.

Nevertheless it was in the Convention that the incident really began, when Danton was still President. Garat, the Minister of the Interior, came within an ace of losing his head after that sinister ex-actor Collot d'Herbois had accused him of sowing dissension in the country. In fact, by the time Danton rose to defend the Minister, the warrant for his arrest had already been signed. But Danton's speech was so vigorous and effective that the Assembly disavowed Collot, and Garat was reinstated; however, sensing fresh trouble ahead, he finally resigned on August 20.

Two rival candidates entered the lists as his successor: Jules

his own apartment, where he would find her giving the children their supper when he got home.

A day came when he began to miss the morning sessions, too. Marat, denouncing this absenteeism, printed a somewhat daring allusion to the "Committee of Public Ruination." This sort of thing could not go on. Danton had two alternatives before him: he must either resign or rewed; either abandon his public career or else rediscover, in the emotional security of a second marriage, that peace of mind and sensuous satisfaction which would enable him to guide his country's destiny once more.

Less than four months after Gabrielle's death, he asked M. and Mme. Gély for Louise's hand. Though they had been expecting this proposal, the girl's parents nevertheless made difficulties. They disliked the idea of surrendering a fifteen-year-old child to this giant of thirty-four; especially they disliked the idea of doing so without a church ceremony. Marc-Antoine and his wife made great play with their own, and Louise's, piety and tried to fob Danton off by declaring that they could not possibly let their daughter marry a man who refused to go to Confession before his wedding. Furthermore, such Confession must not be made to a conformist priest. To their great surprise, Danton accepted these conditions. He agreed to everything— Confession, church wedding, and all—so long as it meant his getting this adorable ingénue.

The marriage contract was signed on June 12. Danton's previous contract, with Gabrielle, drawn up in 1787, provided for joint possession of property. This new one, on the contrary, established separate endowments for husband and wife. Danton made over to Louise a capital sum of 40,000 *livres*. Since Gély could not match this, Danton provided the *dot* himself; first, a sum of 10,000 *livres*, made over as a loan to his future father-in-law, interest-free and for life; and a second capital endowment of 30,000 *livres*, supposedly offered by an old aunt of Danton's, Mme. Lenoir, to her future niece-by-marriage. In this way Louise's fiancé avoided wounding her self-respect. He did not want anyone to be able to say that he had *bought* her.

This contract sheds a good deal of light on Danton's concern for his family. By marrying under the "separate property" dispensation (a very rare choice in his day) he was protecting the

possible, to conclude a separate peace. At this precise moment Lebrun was caught up in the general purge of the Girondists. Though he was not thrown into a prison cell—Danton managed to secure this concession for him—he was placed under house arrest, guarded by gendarmes, and forced to conduct his negotiations henceforth under the added handicap of this unconstitutional detention.

On several occasions English spies saw him escorted like a malefactor from his home to the Pavillon de l'Égalité, where he and his masters worked together. All Europe soon heard of his alarming predicament. France was made a laughingstock, and the discussions collapsed. Poor Lebrun was the first victim. Hauled out of his room by the gendarmes, he somehow managed to escape and thus avoided joining the Girondists in prison. But he was recaptured; and so this skilled diplomat paid for his moderation, foresight, and love of peace under the knife of the guillotine.

A few days after the arrest of the Girondists, Danton was chatting with Robespierre and Marat in the private bar of a café on the rue du Paon. "It was here," as Victor Hugo later wrote in *Quatre-Vingt-Treize* ("Ninety-three"), "that there used to meet, secretly and intermittently, men who were so powerful, and so constantly under observation, that they shrank from talking together in public." From the whole discussion among the three men—a classic display of skeleton-rattling in the family cupboard—one need recall only one remark, supposedly spoken by Marat toward the end of the exchange, and that because it contains a suggestion which Danton in the end followed. *"Let me give you one piece of advice, Danton. You're in love, you're thinking of getting married again. Be a sensible fellow and stop meddling in politics."*

Danton's matrimonial plans, it is true, were by now known to everyone. Moreover, his energy and zest for battle had undergone a marked decline. Even in the Pavillon de l'Égalité his colleagues saw him less often. They sat every morning, from nine till midday, and again in the evening from seven o'clock onward. But however urgent the problems to be dealt with, Danton never turned up for the evening session. He preferred to spend the time in Louise's company, either upstairs with her parents or in

benches for the Deputies and galleries for the public. These galleries rested on a single enormous beam which withstood everything—the crowds, the shouted abuse, the fury, and the chaos.
It bent but it never cracked, even in those famous days of June
of 1793 when the Montagnards crushed the Gironde.

Both sides had supposed that this change of venue would enable them to legislate in peace. But party rivalry had already
passed the point of no return. The Girondists were accused of
"Federalism," a fearful crime against the "Republic one and in-
divisible." While Marat, Robespierre, and other Montagnards
attacked them from the rostrum, Hébert's troops, together with
20,000 National Guardsmen under the leadership of their new
commander, Hanriot, proceeded to besiege the Tuileries. Sweating with fright, the Deputies of the Plain joined the Montagnards
in voting for the arrest of twenty-nine Deputies and two Ministers, accused of trying to "break up the country's unity and
replace it with a federation of autonomous regions." All the
leading Girondists found themselves in prison: Vergniaud, Brissot, Gensonné, Carra, Valazé, Lasource, Ducos, Sillery, and
others. One or two managed to get away, however: Barbaroux,
Pétion, and Guadet to Normandy, Lanjuinais to Brittany. Condorcet stayed in Paris but went into hiding in his mistress's
apartment. Roland and Buzot joined each other at Rouen, but
Manon—the former's wife, the latter's lover—was arrested in her
house and thrown into the Abbaye Prison.

Even if Danton did not himself plan the downfall of these
men—and of that one woman—he certainly gave Marat and
Robespierre a free hand to do so. Doubtless Danton regretted the
arrest of Lebrun, the Foreign Secretary, that valiant pacifist who
had kept England neutral for nearly a year by posting Chauvelin, Talleyrand, Noël, and Maret to London. When it came
to negotiating with the crowned heads of Europe and attempting to best them by diplomatic means, the Committee of Public
Safety bowed to traditional usage and made the Foreign Secretary responsible for all this secret bargaining. Now at the time
Danton was putting out some very delicate feelers: to England,
a country he wanted to see pull out of the coalition; to Turkey,
Sweden, Denmark, and Switzerland, in the hopes that they
would not join it; and to Prussia, with whom he intended, if

[11] Camille Desmoulins.
Portrait by Boze. (*Photo by Bulloz*)

[12] Hérault de Séchelles.
(*Photo by Bulloz-Viollet*)

[10] Robespierre. Portrait by Boilly. (*Photo by Giraudon*)

[9] Louise Gély and Antoine Danton ("L'Optique), by Boilly. (*Photo by Josse-Lalance*)

CHAPTER XIV

The Revolutionary Tribunal

WHEN DANTON REACHED BELGIUM on March 5 he was confronted with a disastrous situation. The inhabitants, exasperated by the excesses of the National Commissioners, were in revolt against the French army. That very morning the bodies of some murdered soldiers had been found in a lonely part of the countryside. The Austrians, taking advantage of this reaction, had crossed the Roer and defeated Valence, one of Dumouriez's divisional commanders, at Aldenhoven. The Duke of Württemberg had recaptured Aix-la-Chapelle, while Miranda—another of Dumouriez's divisional commanders—found himself obliged to raise the siege of Maestricht, fall back on Liège, and then abandon Liège and retreat as far as Louvain. Dumouriez began to panic. From his headquarters in Brussels he sent out a constant stream of orders to his field commanders, but he could not inspire them with the will to win. Their hearts were no longer in the job.

Faced with a catastrophe of such magnitude, Danton had no option but to turn about and make straight for Paris. On March 8, only five days after his departure from the capital, he caused a sensation by reappearing in the Riding School. For the first time in six weeks he mounted the speakers' rostrum. Members gasped at his appearance. The double burden of grief he bore, as a widower and an anguished patriot, accentuated his ugliness. One had only to look at him to measure the extent both of his private distress and of the disaster that had befallen the nation.

Paris. Thuillier, a notary called Bévière, and a sheriff's officer drew up a descriptive inventory of all movables, chattels, and items of clothing. Their owner did not stay to oversee the cataloging of his library. The bookseller appointed by Thuillier would take several days to carry out a complete valuation, and Danton had to return to Belgium. He therefore left his brother-in-law to act in his name, and boarded a carriage for Brussels. This time he was accompanied by Robert, whom the Assembly had appointed a delegate to the Commission. Though a Deputy in the French National Convention, Robert was a Belgian, born at Liège, and delighted by the prospect of receiving "that parental embrace of which tyranny had for three long years deprived him."

The two friends crossed the border at Belleville on the morning of March 3. Danton found difficulty in restraining his emotions. For the first time he was leaving Paris with the absolute and ghastly certainty that he would never see Gabrielle again. What he did not know, as yet, was that the luck she brought her husband had been buried with her; that when Gabrielle died, it was as though his good angel had abandoned him.

us pay her the tribute of our tears; she is worthy of them. Yes, it
is Citizen Danton's wife of whom I speak! Her husband was
absent, and she lay confined to her bed, having just given birth
to a new citizen. It was at this moment that Roland and his
followers dealt her a mortal blow. . . . Danton was away in
Belgium: these cowardly creatures took advantage of his absence
to charge him with the responsibility for selecting the victims
to be murdered during September 2 and 3! When his poor wife
read this monstrous libel in the papers, she died of shock!"

The fact that she had died in childbirth was conveniently
ignored. The whole speech was an abominable travesty of the
facts, and Danton publicly dissociated himself from it. This did
not stop him thanking Collot when the latter, accompanied by
Robespierre, came to offer his condolences. After them all Danton's friends appeared: Desmoulins and his wife, the Roberts,
the Legendres, and many others.

That same day, February 17, Danton had to make arrangements for the future of his children. There were now three of
them. History has preserved no trace of the newly born infant,
and everything suggests that it lived only a short while. But it
was still alive when its father authorized Antoine Charpentier,
brother of the deceased, to "summon a meeting of relatives and
friends to appoint him [i.e. Danton] guardian of his *three*
children." This family council was held on the 22nd, presided
over by M. Thuillier, justice of the peace. It duly recognized
the widower as official guardian of his three children, with M.
Charpentier, his father-in-law, as deputy guardian. This latter
appointment was all the more necessary in that Danton had to
return to Belgium. It was also why he had granted Antoine a
power-of-attorney.

By the terms of this authorization Antoine was required to
"demand the removal, without inventory, of the seals set in place
after Mme. Danton's decease"; or, "if such removal without
inventory should be contested," to "call for any summary court
order that might be necessary, and proceed thereafter to make
an inventory of all goods and chattels," and then "to effect the
sale of the furniture."

The seals were lifted on the 25th, in the presence of the
person principally concerned, Danton himself, who was still in

the political organization of the country between them. Danton and Lacroix took the provinces of Namur and Liège, as far as Aix-la-Chapelle. They attempted to impose "fraternization" in the towns and villages, with varying degrees of success. Sometimes they had to call in the troops to help them. Nevertheless, Danton himself was never responsible for any atrocities—which is more than can be said for the National Commissioners. Still, he upheld the latter with his authority. "What did the Belgians think we'd send them?" he remarked one day. "Young ladies?"

Personally, he was anxious to please all those under his administration, especially representatives of the fair sex. Though he loved his wife, he was not averse to a little variety. While he was at Liège, Merlin, the Deputy for Douai, saw him "occupied with his pleasures." A man named Foliot described him, in a letter to Carra, as "always sitting down at table, surrounded by girls." He was so constituted that he could not help being unfaithful to Gabrielle. A great drinker and trencherman, this massive, oak-like figure generated an overabundance of sap. Besides, many women were offering themselves to the victors, if only to save a father, a brother, even a husband who had been arrested by the occupation authorities for some offense against their troops. Could the bull from Arcis resist such temptations?

Meanwhile in Paris the King's trial had got under way. Since December 11 the Convention, transformed for the occasion into a court of justice, had been subjecting his actions to a close and relentless scrutiny. Louis XVI made a very bad defendant. It was not a role with which he was familiar, and he floundered badly under interrogation. Sometimes he told such open, unblushing lies that he seemed doomed in advance.

Dumouriez at the time was very anxious to return to Paris. He had two ends in view: to prevent the King being condemned, and to get the decree of December 15 annulled. By pleading overwork and exhaustion he obtained thirty days' leave. Before he set out from Liège he had a discussion with Danton and the latter's London agent, the former Abbé Noël. Among themselves they worked out a scheme for saving the King. Noël had just arrived from France, where he had met Miles, the Englishman Mrs. Elliott had introduced to Danton some time previ-

Lastly, France "would regard as her enemies" all those who, "rejecting freedom and equality," attempted to "restore or treat with the monarch and members of the privileged classes."

When Dumouriez received notification of this charter his anger knew no bounds. In his proclamations to the Belgian people he had promised them liberty; and now he found himself compelled to act like a conqueror. His chagrin and fury were such that he had the decree printed and posted up without appending his signature to it in token of approval; and so hard did he chafe on the bit that from now on he scarcely ever left the Palace of the Prince-Bishops. (In his *Memoirs* he declared that this ukase was partly occasioned by Danton's determination to have his revenge on the little town of Ath, which had refused him a lodging for the night during his journey. No doubt this statement is exaggerated; but it has a certain air of plausibility.)

When Danton left Paris on the evening of December 15, it does not look as though he found time for a quick detour to Sèvres to see his wife. He wrote her from Liège on the 17th—an indication of the speed with which he habitually moved around the country. "Don't forget to take care of sending my saplings to Arcis," he told Gabrielle. "And remind your father to go ahead with the arrangements for his house in Sèvres. Give Antoine lots of kisses from me, and tell him that Daddy will try not to be away too long." In another letter he wrote: "I hope to be with you on January 1, after spending a day or two in Arcis." But Brune, who was still Commandant of the Horse Requisitioning Center, told Gabrielle that her husband's mission would keep him in Belgium for a good two months. Disappointed, she wrote to Danton, who replied: "Our friend Brune really does exaggerate."

Brune was, in fact, pretty near the mark. Danton saw a lengthy task ahead of him, and one that would monopolize all his energies. The Belgians refused to accept the decree of December 15; they disliked bullying tactics. Arguments flared up between them and the thirty National Commissioners of the Convention, who had been sent out to help Danton, Lacroix, Camus, and Gossuin enforce the law. The four of them parceled out

Camus having made the trip depends on the merest hearsay; but there is one really striking piece of evidence which points to Danton as the messenger. It was on December 8 that he and Camus discussed the political situation with Dumouriez. On the 9th they decided that one of them must return to Paris. On the 13th Danton was in Maître Finot's office at Arcis-sur-Aube, where he signed the deed of purchase for "the coppice known as Les Quittainies," at a price of 600 *livres*. And on the 15th the Convention ratified the decree requested by whichever of the two Deputies had returned to Paris for this purpose. But the one who left Liège must have been Danton: his signature on the notary's deed at Arcis proves it. The distance between Arcis and Paris is less than a hundred miles, and a glance at the map shows that such a detour on Danton's part would have been quite feasible.

The decree which the Convention approved on December 15 had been worked out by Danton in Liège and was put before the Deputies by Cambon. Its text made no specific reference to the annexation of Belgium, but laid down a series of principles governing the occupation of Belgian territory—and, in general, of any foreign territory which the French army might subsequently invade. The decree contained a dozen clauses. It commanded the victorious generals to proclaim, there and then, the "sovereignty of the people," together with the abolition of feudalism, the nobility, and entrenched privilege of any sort. The people were to be convened in primary assemblies for the purpose of electing a provisional government. All property confiscated "from the Treasury, the monarch, his abettors, and from all bodies and communities, whether lay or clerical" was to be placed in the keeping and under the protection of the French Republic. Proclamations were to be made to the effect that the Convention would nominate National Commissioners, chosen from its own members, to go and "fraternize with this provisional Assembly, and take counsel jointly with it and with the French generals as to what defense measures were desirable and what methods should be employed in order to procure such clothing and rations as were necessary for the armed forces." The provisional administration would end as soon as the inhabitants "organized a free and popular form of government."

Dumouriez's misleading lecture as loudly as anyone. That evening Mme. Roland invited the General to dinner. She thought it a clever move to confront her pet demagogic aversion with the victorious warrior, across the same table. But she also had a surprise in store. The party was not held at the Ministry of the Interior, but in the Tuileries Palace. For five days now Danton had ceased to be a member of the Council. Manon had taken advantage of his absence to install *her* Ministry in the King's Palace. She and her husband were now occupying the apartment that had belonged to Mme. de Tourzel, the former royal governess. (Danton remarked that, despite everything, "Queen Coco" hadn't had the nerve to occupy Marie-Antoinette's chamber.) He accepted her invitation; but the food, which was no better than that in the rue des Petits-Champs, soon triumphed over his false bonhomie. Two hours later he turned up at the Opéra, accompanied by Dumouriez. The audience recognized them both—Danton such a huge figure, the General so diminutive—and a tremendous ovation greeted them when they appeared in their box.

Danton was no longer living like a Parisian, but rather in the style of some provincial in town without his wife—so much so that friends and relatives had given up inviting her, in the certain knowledge that the invitation will always be turned down.

Gabrielle had her consolations—though these did not include the company of Lucile or Louise Robert, from both of whom she was drifting steadily further apart. Lucile's reputation was being blackened by so much gossip nowadays that Gabrielle could hardly help regarding her as a rival. In Louise's case, it was she who had fallen out with the Danton *ménage* rather than *vice versa.* Besides, Gabrielle's fourth pregnancy, unlike the others, was proving a difficult one. She scarcely went out at all, except to take her children for a walk in the Luxembourg Gardens. Often her little neighbor from the floor above would accompany her on these expeditions. As she grew older—if one can apply such a phrase to passing the age of fourteen—Louise Gély was acquiring an air of self-assurance unusual in a girl of her age. Intelligent, understanding, and reasonably pretty, she very soon became Gabrielle's dearest and most intimate friend. The two little boys, Antoine and François-Georges, looked on

to the monarchy. Not the Ancien Régime, that's gone forever
. . . A democratic monarchy will be established. And while
France will never again tolerate the senior branch of your family, in your own case it's another matter. You have fought under
the tricolor flag, and you stand a very good chance of ascending
the throne. Your duty, therefore, is to hold yourself in reserve."
Louis-Philippe did hold himself in reserve—until 1830.

On October 14 Dumouriez reached Paris and was given a
tumultuous ovation by the crowds. When invited to speak at
the Jacobin Club on the Battle of Valmy and the Prussian retreat, the little general's first action was to embrace Robespierre.
Danton, welcomed with equally enthusiastic applause, accepted
the presidency of the Club. "We are not exhausted by any
means," Dumouriez told them at the end of his lecture. "Very
soon I hope to have a force of sixty thousand men with which
to pull down kings and save the common people from tyranny."

Ah-ha, his listeners thought, so freedom was to become an
article of export, was it? Camille Desmoulins took the same line
in the Convention on September 28, when he came out in favor
of a "war of conquest"; Danton dared not point out how fal-
lacious this argument was, since the majority of those present
shared the same attitude. He therefore fell back on the well-
tried gambit of siding with the strongest party, and expanded
on the theme that Desmoulins had sketched. "Let the Convention," he thundered, "become a General Committee of Insurrection against all monarchs throughout the world!" (And why
not? Hadn't the Regent, the Sancy, and Anne of Brittany's
Ruby all been recovered? Plenty of good fresh troops there . . .)
But when his rhetorical temperature fell to normal again, Danton felt he had once more overstepped the mark. Though he
avoided repudiating his actual statement, he nevertheless turned
his coat. ("The really absurd man," as Barthélemy was to say
later, "is the one who never changes.") As far as this war of
conquest was concerned, Danton's speech on April 13, 1793,
went back on the opinion he had expressed during October of
1792. He even got the Convention to pass a motion declaring
that "the Republic would not interfere in any way with the governments of other powers."

Meanwhile—still on October 14, 1792—Danton applauded

Cordeliers. It was with some relief that she found herself in the
same home, and occupied by the same daily round, that she
had abandoned fifty-nine days before. That she no longer slept
in the canopied four-poster once occupied by Chancellors of
France did not distress her at all. She had got back her old
room, complete with its twin beds. She had even begun to regain
her husband's affections—somewhat in abeyance after the re-
proaches she had leveled at him on September 4. Though she
had not forgotten her grievances, at least she was now prepared
to forgive her husband his Pilate's role in the September massacres. Poor Gabrielle, it was lucky she remained ignorant of
Danton's terrible confession to Louis-Philippe. Besides, she was
once more suffering from the early symptoms of pregnancy—
her fourth. The child, she calculated, was due about the beginning of February: four more months of patience and precautions.
The doctor insisted on her going to bed early.

Danton took advantage of this regimen to go out in the eve-
nings without his wife. He, Fabre, and Desmoulins were often
seen together in the Palais-Royal restaurants, accompanied by
women of dubious reputation. Was he ever seen crossing the
threshold of "the lady from the rue Bleue?" There is no clinch-
ing evidence on this point one way or the other. Agnes, who
was still passionately devoted to Philippe d'Orléans, had no
further motive for keeping in with Danton after his resignation
—or at least, so she thought. Deputy Danton and Citizen
Égalité were now equals in the eyes of the law; they sat side by
side on the benches of the Assembly, among lawyers, merchants,
carriers, and horny-handed sons of toil. For a descendant of St.
Louis this seat on the Mountain represented a terrible comedown.
Drawn on by his inevitable destiny, the unhappy Duke did not
realize how fatal the course upon which he had embarked would
prove. He no longer desired the throne, which in any case had
slipped beyond his grasp. Doubtless, too, his son did not return
to the army, after that interview with Danton on September 22,
without telling his father the gist of the following remarks that
the Minister made: "This Republic we have just proclaimed
won't last long. There'll be a great more blood spilled yet; but
France's vices, and maybe her virtues too, will bring her back

Chauvelin, for his part, took advantage of the suspicion with which he was regarded to make approaches to the opposition and urge them too toward a position of neutrality. But he went about the job without finesse, and Lebrun was obliged to repair his diplomatic gaffes by sending him a second mentor, the ex-Abbé Noël, who was accompanied by two of Danton's nominees: his mother's stepson, Georges Recordain, and his cousin Mergez. Recordain was a daring young man who, with the impulsive enthusiasm of his twenty years, had volunteered to act as a courier between London and Paris, carrying mail too dangerous to entrust to the post. It was absolutely vital that England should remain neutral—an object which Talleyrand, Chauvelin, Noël, and Georges Recordain, obscure advocates of a great cause, successfully achieved.

It was in the full flush of this diplomatic victory that Danton appeared before the Convention on September 21, the day of its opening. His eyes shone with self-assurance, his step was brisk and confident. Knowing the strength of his position, he received with a cheerful smile the ovation which greeted him as he entered the Riding School. Wearing a blue coat and a white cravat, he strode into the Chamber, shaking hands as he went. There was a fresh burst of applause as the galleries caught sight of him. Yet news of the victory at Valmy, eighteen hours earlier, had not yet reached Paris.

Less through any false modesty than to make his own position quite clear, Danton ignored the ministerial bench and took his place on the Left of the Assembly, with the "Mountain," where his various friends—Jacobins, Cordeliers, Orleanists—were gathered. From here he could observe the Right, which comprised the Gironde, Brissot's group, and the various hangers-on of Roland and his wife. These two major parties were separated by the "Plain," or "Marsh." Deputies who occupied the Plain, and showed, by their cautious attitude, that they would rather pursue a policy of opportunism than express frank and possibly dangerous opinions, were known as *crapauds,* or "Toads."

Now Danton mounted the rostrum and, for the first time, spoke there not as a Minister but as a Deputy. Better still, and a great surprise to his audience, was the following declaration: "The incompatibility of the executive and legislative powers force

CHAPTER XII

Deputy or Minister: The Hour of Decision

SINCE MARCH 30 the Marquis de Chauvelin had been the King of France's ambassador in London. But it was M. de Talleyrand, the former Bishop of Autun, who really represented the government. As unofficial ambassador, Talleyrand proved a useful mentor to the twenty-five-year-old official diplomat. Both were well known for their liberal views, and the government of August 10 therefore confirmed them in their posts.

On the other hand, the British government no longer recognized the Marquis. Alarmed by the overthrow of Louis XVI, Pitt and his Ministers preferred not to maintain official diplomatic relations with France. However, they allowed both Chauvelin and Talleyrand to remain in England—a neat enough way of keeping up contact while severing public communications. The link was all the more useful to the two countries in that Danton, with his habitual cunning, was dangling the offer of a French colony in front of Pitt's nose, in return for England's guarantee of neutrality during the war.

Lebrun, the Foreign Minister, was in correspondence with both Chauvelin and Talleyrand. The latter pleaded France's case at the Court of St. James along the lines Lebrun laid down; he was at great pains to emphasize Louis XVI's bad faith and double-dealing during the events which led to his downfall. With discreet allusions to the death of Charles I, the Bishop argued that by deposing the King and confining him to the Temple the victors of August 10 had saved his life and were now holding him in reserve.

Danton would automatically compel the latter to refuse his offer—unless he wanted to have La Rouairie, the King of Prussia, the Emperor, and the *émigrés* all accusing him of treachery. The whole elaborate plot, the prime object of which was to compensate for French military weakness, would then have collapsed like a house of cards.

This is why, though we cannot be certain that the precious stones found among Brunswick's heirlooms were brought him by Carra two days before Valmy, it is equally impossible to assert as a fact that the Commander-in-Chief *must* have bought them from some receiver, for cash.

In one of his novels Hugo devotes seven lines, no more, to this murky affair. He pictures Robespierre, Marat, and Danton arguing fiercely with one another in a bar down the rue de Paon. The date is 1793. Hugo makes the People's Friend ask Danton, angrily: "What about the robbery from the National Archives? What about the Crown Jewels?" Eventually, after trying a dozen times to dodge the issue with some irrelevant answer, Danton replies:

> "I halted the enemy's advance. I barred the way to the Austro-Prussian alliance."
> "Prostitute!" said Marat.
> Danton rose to his full, terrifying height.
> "Yes," he cried, "I am a whore. I admit it. I sold my body—but I saved the world!"

In fact, what he had saved was the Declaration of the Rights of Man—which amounted to much the same thing.

Force in several successive groups. The first lot, comprising ten men, was let out by a jailer. (The authorities, we may note, never made any serious attempt to discover this accomplice.) The ten escapees made their way across Paris from the rue du Roi-de-Sicile, where the prison stood, to the former Place Louis XV. No one raised the alarm in La Force, and no one attempted to apprehend the group elsewhere. Yet they took their time, and did not conceal themselves. They made various visits and collected enough accomplices to keep watch for them while they were breaking into the Archives. A quick climb up a ladder and the thing was done. They crammed their pockets with fabulous loot but were unable to take everything at one go— to begin with because there was too much of it, and also because they had promised to leave some for their fellow crooks.

The following evening a new group went into action, led by a man called Meyrand. Again, it comprised about a dozen thieves; and again, all of them had got out of La Force— "escaped" is hardly the word, since they had no more trouble in leaving that most curious prison than Miette had had the day before. After these, the third team had its turn. Under the direction of one Deslanges, it followed the now well-beaten trail blazed by its predecessors, but had even better luck, picking up both the "Regent" and the "Sancy." The first, a diamond by which Marie-Antoinette set great store, weighed 137 carats and was a stone of the very highest quality. It was an heirloom from Louis XIV's nephew, the Regent: hence it's name. This ancestor of Égalité's had bought the famous brilliant from a Hindu, in 1717. The Sancy was an equally fine stone, though it weighed only fifty-three carats.

When Deslanges and his fellow robbers met Miette, Meyrand, and *their* gangs (on the premises of a café-proprietor named Retour) to divide the loot—some hundreds of stones—they quarreled so violently that they failed to reach any kind of agreement. Just as the argument was on the point of degenerating into a brawl, a man called Douligny pulled them all up short by remarking: "There's enough jewelry still left in that strong room to give everyone a fair share."

So it came about that a fourth raid was carried out. It took place two nights later, thus allowing the thieves a day's rest be-

discovery of the theft. How did Roland happen to be so well informed? If Danton was in fact involved in the affair, it does not look as though Roland could be entirely innocent. According to the version he produced later, a version contradicted by the note referred to above, it was only *three or four days after the robbery* that he received a visit from two police informers. "Citizen Minister," they told him, "we have some extraordinary revelations to make to you." The two men were called Lamy-Evette (sometimes known as Brière) and Cottet. According to Roland, the following represents their stage-by-stage account of the conspiracy.

On August 10, various looters mingled with the Federates who were fighting their way into the Tuileries Palace. These profiteers laid hands on so much valuable plunder that they were arrested and locked up in La Force Prison. There they made the acquaintance of a character called Miette, who was serving a sentence of several years for fraud. Miette dumbfounded them by suggesting that they should do a job on the National Archives. He knew the interior of the building well. The treasure was kept inside five locked cases, in a chamber the doors of which were under seal. But no seals had been placed on the windows that looked out on the open-air colonnade. To get up there the only equipment needed was a good long ladder. The danger of being spotted was negligible. Nobody ever came near the square at night. Once up in the gallery, all one had to do was to break a window and put one hand through to slip the catch.

"That's all very well," said one of the prisoners. "But we've got to get out of here first!"

Miette roared with laughter. Get out of La Force? An easy task. A warder would open the gate for him whenever he liked.

History does not relate how Roland, at this point in the two informers' story, chose to accept a version which cast grave suspicion on the integrity of a service directly responsible to his colleague M. Danton, as the Minister of Justice. One cannot help thinking of Fabre d'Églantine, now Danton's Principal Private Secretary, and of his visit to Mme. Roland.

However, let us stick to the official thesis for the moment. Miette admitted about forty prisoners to the plot. They left La

if no one had the slightest knowledge as to who might have done the deed, and expressed amazement that nothing had leaked out about it in advance. . . . I let him rattle on, said very little myself, and revealed nothing of my inner thoughts. Eventually he took his leave, and I never saw him again.

"When my husband and I next met, I told him: 'One of the men who robbed the National Archives was here this morning, to find out if he was under suspicion.' My husband asked who it was. 'Fabre d'Églantine,' I said. 'How do you know?' 'How do I know? So bold a move can only have originated with our master of boldness—I mean Danton himself. Whether this will ever be proved, in the formal sense, I don't know; but I'm absolutely sure it's true.'"

Though Manon Roland was an intelligent woman, with excellent sources of information, her evidence must be treated with caution. She composed her *Memoirs* in the Abbaye Prison: her alliance with the Girondists—as we shall see later—had cost her liberty and, ultimately, her life. By now she had come to regard Danton, who was at least partly responsible for her incarceration, as the devil incarnate. Nevertheless, the behavior of the Minister of Justice, as revealed in the course of this analysis, does leave room for suspicion.

Government Commissioners, appointed by Roland, now took over from the police officials whom Restoul had called in; and a group of jewelers, under the direction of Lemoine-Crécy, the previous curator, made an expert appraisal of those diamonds which the thieves—owing to Camus's sudden appearance—had not had time to remove.

In the box of documents pertaining to this affair (now housed among the archives of the Public Record Office) there is one very curious letter. Written by Roland and dated September 18, it advised one M. Gerbu, a goldsmith in the rue du Harlay, that two individuals would be calling on him that same day (i.e. the day following Camus's discovery) to offer him some pieces of jewelry "stolen from the National Archives." Roland urged this goldsmith "to take all available steps to recognize these men, and to secure their arrest."

Now September 18 was less than twenty-four hours after the

sponse was: "I don't give a f—— for the prisoners, they'll have to take their chances." When the tocsin—as foreseen in his speech the previous day—began to ring out all over Paris, Prudhomme, the librarian, similarly hastened to the Place des Piques. "Don't be alarmed, it's the tocsin of victory!" Danton told him.

"But there's talk of a massacre—"

"Yes," Danton said, "we might *all* be massacred tonight—the most loyal patriot as soon as the next man. But the people are aroused. They're determined to take the law into their own hands."

Desmoulins, who was present during this exchange, modified the statement a little: "The innocent will not be confused with the guilty. All those vouched for by their local authorities will be handed over to them."

Partially reassured, Prudhomme took his leave.

Dr. Saiffert came to request the release of his patient, the Princess de Lamballe, who was interned at La Force. Danton told him: "I cannot do it. Anyone who tried to oppose the justice of the people would be regarded as their enemy."

In the general atmosphere of panic, Ministers even began to fear for their own safety. There was a remark of Mme. Roland's which went the rounds at this time: "Robespierre and Danton hold the big knife over us all. Danton is the man responsible for this mob, behind the scenes." (At one point she really thought her last hour had come. An unruly crowd, stinking of alcohol, forced its way into the Ministry in the rue des Petits-Champs and called on Manon—by now half dead with fright—for arms to deal with the traitors and to march on Verdun.) In the City Hall the Administrators signed warrants condemning Roland, Brissot, and a score of other Deputies. Danton spotted these documents on the Public Prosecutor's desk, slipped them into his pocket, and showed them to Pétion, the Mayor, who nearly fell through the floor. Without Danton's intervention Roland and Brissot would have joined Mme. de Lamballe in La Force.

In order to canalize this "justice of the people" somewhat better, the Minister of Justice had decided that the Council should conduct its deliberations in the City Hall. When he left Pétion's office, he found his colleagues awaiting him in a nearby room, where he had summoned them for a meeting. Together

permanence of "at all times" by tacking on that "yet more," which crowns and amplifies it, as though, in his patriotic fervor, he wished to prolong what was already eternal. This hints at the major artistry of Danton's eloquence; it explains why Choudieu, the Deputy for Maine-et-Loire, rushed up to Gabrielle, exclaiming: "My God, how splendid he was! There's never been anything so moving. . . ."

But Mme. Danton would have felt happier had he been a splendid family man or lawyer, rather than aspiring to the perilous splendors of a politician's career. She said as much to her husband when she congratulated him. "Be on your guard against all these men," she warned him. "They may be acclaiming you now, but tomorrow—who knows?—they could turn and tear you to pieces." Then he promised her, in his cups, that when the enemy had been driven back across the border, he would go back to live at Arcis, in the peace of the countryside. For him, as for all true patriots, to believe in victory was to be victorious already.

Meanwhile the Prussian advance continued. Now their armies were no more than sixty leagues from Paris. The dictator's call for boldness removed any lingering scruples that still existed in the City Hall. Since the Chief had commanded it, they would indeed use boldness—in the prisons. Sergent and Panis, the Administrators of the Committee of Public Safety, dictated the following translation of the concept to Méhée de la Touche, the Clerk to the Committee: "Before hastening to the border, we must be sure we have left no traitor or conspirator behind us."

The Committee appointed a number of "judges," who were to go around the prisons and personally to recruit the men to carry out their sentences. How many such amateur executioners did they find? The answer is about five hundred—not, as legend later asserted, the entire population of Paris. But if these good folk were not actively responsible for the September massacres, neither—being thoroughly terrorized themselves—did they make any effort to stop them.

On learning of the measures being taken by the Committee, Roland's Private Secretary hurried around to the Chancellery and informed Danton. According to tradition, Danton's re-

A gigantic ovation rose from the benches and poured down from the galleries. Danton had galvanized everyone's energies: even his fiercest enemies applauded him. As one of them afterward wrote: "When he uttered those final words, this hideous man was beautiful." Yet how—since shorthand as we understand it did not yet exist—could history preserve a record of this famous tirade? Beneath the speakers' rostrum there stood a circular table, around which there worked fifteen secretaries, sitting side by side. Each of them would memorize a sentence, or part of a sentence, as the speaker delivered it, or perhaps an interruption from the body of the Chamber. Then, jogging his neighbor with his elbow, he would hastily jot down this sentence, or intervention, on a numbered sheet of paper. The next secretary, following the same procedure, would also listen to a short bit of the speech, or some fresh interruption; then, as he was about to note it down, he would jog the third copyist, who would go through the same procedure with the fourth, and so on till the flow of speech had been picked up all around the table and came back to number one again. Then all that was necessary in order to obtain a transcript of the proceedings was to arrange the notes in numerical order. This work of synthesis took place in the shorthand writers' box—that same little room through the window of which Louis XVI had, on August 10, observed the debate which led to his dethronement.

Inevitably, errors crept into the shorthand writer's transcript. For this reason it is not certain that Danton, when he improvised his famous aphorism, actually delivered it in the traditional order ("boldness, and yet more boldness, boldness at all times, and France will be saved"). But did he say every word of this? Merlin de Thionville afterward wrote that "Danton saved the country with these words: *Boldness, and yet more boldness, and yet more boldness still!*" There is a third version: according to several papers, he said: "Boldness, boldness at all times, and yet more boldness, and France will be saved!" Here the natural crescendo from "yet more" to "at all times" is reversed; yet however illogical it may seem at first sight, this arrangement of the phrase strikes me as more in keeping with Danton's personal style. Having proclaimed that what was needed was "boldness, boldness at all times," he reinforced the

the Sovereign People." France had to be informed of the changes that had taken place in the capital, and Desmoulins, the group's literary figure, was skilled in the art of misrepresenting facts. To the various *départements* he explained that "a vast plot in the Tuileries Palace recently came to a head when the Swiss, by an infamous strategem, lured the Federates of the eighty-three *départements* into their lair and proceeded to massacre them. . . ." This was why the Parisians, hurrying to rescue these imperiled provincials within their walls, had toppled the King from his throne, and, in the process, had killed a certain number of his hired assassins. But it was not to be thought that France as a whole should follow the example Paris had set. The government was responsible for maintaining order, and intended to do so. "The sword that we must turn against all traitors and enemies of our country is the sword of the law. Let the courts begin to render justice, and the people will cease to take the law into their own hands."

Danton's signature is appended to this circular, but had he in fact read it? Did he, we may well wonder, so much as pick up a pen and scribble his name at the foot of the text? Probably not. Even during his spell with the Commune, in the Public Prosecutor's department, Danton already possessed a signature stamp. This stamp he entrusted, when he became a Minister, to Camille Desmoulins, who lent it on occasion to Fabre d'Églantine, Robert, and Paré. Many notes signed "Danton" Danton himself never saw at all. Fabre d'Églantine took advantage of this state of affairs to feather his nest very extensively. To begin with he submitted his financial requisitions for approval; but it was not long before he dispensed with this preliminary. If a government department was to run efficiently, it had to have money. One day it would be a draft for 3000 *livres* on some Minister's funds, the next for 20,000. The various treasurers always paid up for the warrants bore Danton's signature. But there seemed to be no end to such demands.

The new Minister was not unaware of this racket, but he had to rely very heavily on his subordinates. Already overwhelmed by the pressure of top-priority work, he had no time left to deal with lesser matters. National defense, purging the country's unreliable elements, relations with foreign powers, speeches before

Hitherto one official had combined the functions of Private Secretary to the Keeper of the Seals and Permanent Private Secretary to the Ministry of Justice. The new Minister soon abolished this economy. Camille Desmoulins was appointed to the first post, and Fabre d'Églantine to the second, at a salary in each case of 12,000 *livres*. Robert, whose ambitions were more modest, was well content to be made *chef des secrétaires particuliers,* an office roughly equivalent to head of the Civil Service. We do not know what salary it carried—only that, his duties obliging him to sleep at the Ministry, Robert drew 2400 francs from the Secret Fund in order to purchase the necessary furniture but never did so, since it was provided from existing supplies.

Danton's departmental staff appointments included Jules Paré, his former chief clerk, Collot d'Herbois, Barère de Vieuzac, and a former King's Bench Counsel named Dupont. Robespierre was offered a position, but refused; he did not wish, he said, to become a financial burden on the State. Danton also found places for several old friends outside the Ministry of Justice. Brune, the Cordeliers' regular printer, was put in charge of the Horse Requisitioning Center, which supplied mounts for the cavalry. Armed with an Adjutant General's commission, he set off for the provinces in full-dress uniform, and this appointment of his was the springboard, as it were, which afterward made him a Marshal of France. Marc-Antoine Gély, Danton's fellow tenant, had suffered by the abolition of the Paris Parliament, in which he held a post as court usher. When his neighbor on the floor below became a Minister, he found Gély an identical appointment in the Ministry of Marine. Danton, in fact, took the whole Gély family under his wing—especially little Louise, who was now fourteen and a constant companion of Gabrielle's. A very mature girl for her age, Louise also used to have political discussions with Danton himself. Finally, the Minister freed Lucile from the embarrassing attentions of that overromantic soul Fréron, whom he sent off to the Moselle region as Commissioner of the Executive Council in Metz. The salary was a mere pittance of 1500 francs.

Installed in the Place Vendôme, which had been renamed the Place des Piques, Desmoulins drafted the inevitable "Report to

A song was composed which translated this tribute into somewhat more popular language:

> Condorcet said of an evening
> To more than one confrere:
> I have a scheme in my noodle
> Which you may like to share:
> What we must establish, you see,
> Dear friends, in this countree
> Is a *ré ré ré*
> A *pu pu pu*
> A *ré*, a *pu*,
> A *république*
> Of form unique.
>
> Danton he wanted Louis
> To sit upon the throne—
> But Danton quickly changed his views
> To mine, and mine alone;
> For he thinks, just like me,
> Nothing better can be
> Than a *ré ré ré*
> Than a *pu pu pu*, etc.

There were two more stanzas in the song; one wonders whether Danton ever got a premonitory shiver when he heard the following lines:

> A hero is honored no longer
> Than it pays to have him about:
> We reap the fruit of his labors
> And then we boot him out.
> This may not be fair play
> But it's still the usual way
> With a *ré ré ré*
> With a *pu pu pu*, etc.

Whoever wrote this verse was a true prophet. More than one French Republic was to adopt the technique it describes.

There was another practice, even less seemly and still very much in vogue, which can be summed up by the perennial slogan "Jobs for the boys." Danton could hardly be expected to break with so very human a custom.

though," he said. "I'm afraid I may not be able to carry the people with me."

"Oh yes," Lucile insisted, "the plan will go through all right, never fear."

What made her so certain? Perhaps something she had heard from her Marseillais dinner guests. She was a little tipsy, chattering away brightly and laughing without restraint.

"How can you *laugh* at a time like this?" Gabrielle demanded.

Her spirits suddenly evaporating, Lucile lowered her voice: "It'll bring me tears enough later. Perhaps tonight."

Mme. Charpentier rose; it was time for her to be going—not back to Fontenay-sous-Bois, but to her son's establishment in the rue de la Vieille-Monnaie, where she sometimes stayed when she was in Paris. Anxious to have a moment alone with Desmoulins, Danton suggested that Gabrielle and Lucile walk a little of the way with Mme. Charpentier.

The three women went out together. It was a fine, clear evening, and, though France was on the edge of a volcano, the neighborhood seemed very peaceful. After strolling a little way, they sat down outside a café. Suddenly a detachment of cavalry trotted past, followed by a group of "patriots" singing obscene songs. Lucile and Gabrielle took fright again, but Mme. Charpentier remained unperturbed. She said good-by and proceeded on her way alone. The two scared girls ran all the way back to the Cour du Commerce.

Danton and Desmoulins were no longer alone in the apartment. There were about a dozen men there, stacking guns in one corner by the light of oil lamps. Beside them stood pretty Louise Robert, watching these preparations for battle with some emotion. The sight of Desmoulins holding a musket made Lucile burst into tears. She asked Louise if they would sound the tocsin. "They're sure to," Louise replied. Lucile hated the noise of the tocsin; she found it peculiarly depressing.

Among those present was Stanislas Fréron, who took advantage of the occasion to make Lucile one of his usual disguised declarations of undying love. As he picked up a gun (while she looked on) the would-be lover proclaimed, in a melodramatic voice, that he was tired of life and would welcome

on the King's deposition, the Assembly was cooperating with
the anti-Royalists—which meant, in effect, with Danton. It was
a strange kind of plot, since, contrary to what one might
logically expect, everything went on in the open—in the streets,
the clubs, even in the palace itself. Here Louis, who received
hourly reports on the development of events, seemed sunk in
a mood of apathetic resignation and indifference to his fate.
In this he made a striking contrast with the Queen, who displayed great courage and a stubborn determination to resist at
all costs. To her still-faithful Swiss Guards and the few aristo-
crats around her who had not fled with the rest, Marie-
Antoinette transmitted a mood of astonishing coolness and self-
confidence.

Danton, too, was making the rounds of his *quartier,* though
more with the intention of attempting to calm the people than
with the aim of arousing them further. This did not stop him
from announcing: "Tomorrow the people will be victorious, or
I shall be dead!" Meanwhile Madame Elisabeth was telling a
group of intimate friends in the Tuileries: "There's no danger:
Danton will take care of us." In her innocence she believed
that the demagogue had been *bought* by her brother; whereas
in fact he had merely been *paid.* There is a subtle distinction
between the two.

Lucile Desmoulins was to leave a vivid sketch of the night
of August 9 in her *Journal.* Since her baby (together with
François-Georges Danton) was away in l'Îsle-Adam, the young
mother was able to help her husband entertain several Marseillais at dinner. It was a cheerful meal, spiced with the broad
accents of the Midi and all the more lighthearted because the
guests were convinced that the monarchy's last hours had come.
They took their leave after the dessert, and Desmoulins and
Lucile walked down the rue de l'Odéon to spend the rest of
the evening with Danton.

But when they arrived they found Gabrielle in tears and
Mme. Charpentier vainly trying to reassure her daughter. The
moment he saw Desmoulins, Danton announced his determination to finish off the Throne that very night. "I'm worried,

8th, a letter arrived from Fabre d'Églantine. Speaking on behalf of the Cordeliers, the poet begged him to return. Robespierre and Desmoulins felt his presence to be indispensable. How could a plot be carried through without the master plotter? This finally decided Danton. He hired a post-chaise and returned to Paris as fast as he could.

He arrived in the rue des Cordeliers, unannounced, on the morning of the 9th. Here he found Gabrielle and his elder son, who had returned from Fontenay the night before, and a few close friends from whom he learned what had been going on in his absence. It was impossible to control the slum districts or the Marseilles contingent much longer. A recent decision of the Legislative Assembly had added fresh fuel to their wrath. By 406 votes to 224, the Assembly had rejected the motion to bring La Fayette to trial for his unauthorized trip to Paris. When the Deputies emerged after the session was over, the crowd booed them. Some members were seized by the scruff of the neck and forced to defend themselves against physical assault.

That same day, August 9, the Assembly at last discussed the matter of the King's deposition—though the debate was so brief that it is hard not to regard this, too, as an element in the plot. "The real signal for the insurrection," wrote Eymery, the bookseller, "was the adjournment of the 'Deposition Debate.' And here one might vindicate the Legislative Assembly of the charge that it was unduly influenced by the 'patriotic' societies—in other words, by the Jacobin faction." In fact, nothing could have been more apt to arouse the mob against the King than a delay in his deposition. This truth appeared so self-evident that Roederer took the floor to denounce a motion approved by Santerre's Quinze-Vingt constituency, which declared that "if by Thursday, August 9, the National Assembly had not approved the King's deposition, tocsin and drum will sound at midnight and summon the people to revolt."

"This motion," Roederer told the Deputies (who knew very well what was afoot), "was circulated to the other forty-seven constituencies. Only one division, that of Le Roi-de-Sicile, has repudiated it." It is all plain enough; by adjourning the debate

an influence over them that rivaled his own, and—above all—
since a newcomer called Santerre had arrived, bringing with
him his reputation as "the Father of the Back Streets." This
was what the humble folk in the *quartier* called him: Santerre
was always ready to lend a sympathetic ear to their troubles. A
brewer by trade, he had been present at every major affray of
the Revolution. He had fought beneath the walls of the Bastille
and had, besides, saved the lives of several wounded defenders
whom he took into his own house and had nursed by his family.
As a battalion commander in the National Guard, he had
followed La Fayette to Versailles on October 5, 1789, and
attempted, though unsuccessfully, to protect the palace. A partisan of the Revolution (though opposed to pointless atrocities)
Santerre was experienced enough to sense, the evening before
June 20, 1792, the first warning symptoms of the storm that
was to culminate in the famous invasion of the Tuileries.
Whipped into a frenzy by mob orators, the whole of Saint-
Antoine swore to take revenge for the dismissal of the Ministers
by slaughtering the royal family. La Fayette's letter was the
last straw, the ultimate excuse for an outburst of mob violence.
Agitators from the Jacobins and the Cordeliers, eager to fish in
these troubled waters, hurried down to the Faubourg Saint-
Marcel and urged its inhabitants to join their comrades from
the Quartier Saint-Antoine.

Since he could not arrest this torrent, Santerre resolved to
place himself at its head and canalize its flow, so as to avoid
the worst. Accordingly he preached revolt throughout his constituency. He was joined by Pétion; and so it came about that
the Father of the Back Streets and the Mayor of Paris found
themselves leading a memorable demonstration, in which Danton
played no part. The brewer maintained discipline of a sort
among those who profaned the sanctity of the Throne; and
though he could not stop the crowd manhandling Marie-Antoinette and forcibly adorning Louis XVI with the red cap
of liberty, at least he saved their lives.

For about four hours the people filed past that little group—
the King, wearing a galley slave's bonnet; Marie-Antoinette,
worn to breaking point yet still maintaining an outward air of
impassivity; Louis's sister, Madame Elisabeth; and the royal

thinkable." Was he relying on these "brave troops" of his to restore order in Paris—and, if need be, to carry him, La Fayette, to power?

In the Legislative Assembly, for all that the Girondist Guadet described him as "a second Cromwell," most of the Deputies approved of the General's attitude. For some time now the unwarranted interference practiced by the clubs in political matters had been irritating them considerably. After all, Deputies were elected by the people; they regarded themselves as quite experienced enough to conduct the business of legislation without any advice from the Jacobins and the Cordeliers, whose membership did not depend on public suffrage. They were getting thoroughly fed up with these irksome nuisances. However, they did not dare make an open attack on men such as Danton, Robespierre, or Marat. After a heated discussion, therefore, they decided to take no immediate or dramatic action on the letter from Maubeuge, and passed to the order of the day.

But at the Jacobin Club it was a very different matter. Danton had found a sublime, magnificent, and quite unexpected chance to attack his old adversary, with all the invective at his command. After Collot d'Herbois, Robespierre, and Desmoulins had worked off their indignation, Danton took the floor. He began, ironically: "Doubtless we should regard the day on which La Fayette reveals himself in his true colors to all France as something of an auspicious occasion. Now all the masks are stripped away, he can never again be quite so dangerous." Then, in more serious tones, he demanded the dispatch of two petitions: the first to the National Assembly, asking that it should request the General to appear before the Bar of the House; and the second to all the constituencies, begging them to send similar petitions to the Legislative Assembly themselves.

Danton also flattered himself that he could foresee La Fayette's reaction: even if the Deputies did not refuse such an appeal, the General was sure to. "He will not obey, I am convinced of it," Danton declared. "He'll go over to the enemy, without a doubt."

At the same moment, a similar debate was going on in the Club des Cordeliers. Danton had attended the Club's meetings less often since he had found Legendre and Marat acquiring

to which she is entitled." Thus "the House of Austria, which has always brought troubles upon France," would no longer have any private or dynastic motives for interfering in her domestic politics.

This was to neglect the fact that it was France, not Austria, who had declared war; but Danton cared nothing for such logical quibbles. It also left out of consideration the personal will of a sovereign who, appearances to the contrary, did not lack for stubbornness.

If this scheme of a royal divorce caused amusement among the plebs, it thoroughly alarmed Dumouriez, and left La Fayette speechless with rage. Dumouriez resigned on June 16. While the King was forming a new Cabinet of obscure conservatives, the Legislative Assembly received a letter from La Fayette, in "the entrenched fortress of Maubeuge." This communication begged them to safeguard the fate of France by taking some thought for the French army, which was desperately short of all essentials—men, munitions, food, and clothing.

"Do not reject this plea," La Fayette wrote. "It comes from those who are the true friends of your authority." To this request he appended certain others, concerning the immunity of the executive and the independence of the sovereign, as laid down by the Constitution. Finally—and here was the bomb that was to explode in Danton's hands—the General demanded that "the régime of the clubs be extirpated at your hands, and replaced by the rule of law; that their usurpations of power give way to the firm and independent exercise of properly constituted authority, and their anarchic slogans to the two principles of freedom; that their frenzied fury yield before the calm and unwavering courage of a nation that knows its rights, and is determined to defend them; that their sectarian conflicts be subordinated to the true interests of the country as a whole, which, in a moment of crisis, should unite all those *who do not regard its enslavement and ruin as a subject for vile rejoicing and infamous speculation.*"

This red-hot verbal broadside of La Fayette's was obviously aimed at Danton and his supporters. Since he felt no fear of them, he was able to write, in justification of his outspokenness: "Here, among my brave troops, timid sentiments would be un-

only mocha coffee but every other kind of drink was available. Zoppi was a native of Florence, and a fellow countryman of Danton's mother-in-law, Mme. Charpentier. With the one, as with the other, Danton enjoyed chatting in Italian. *"Mi da un cappuccino bollente,"* he would say, heavily stressing the tonic accent, and Zoppi would reply: *"Subito, Signor sostituto!"*

Another customer *chez Procope* was Legendre, who did not envy Danton his linguistic skill: all a butcher needs to know is how to cut up meat, and his friend remembered the 50,000 *écus* that were offered Legendre as an inducement to perform that service on Danton himself. Without Legendre's declaration, Danton would never have known a thing about this murderous project. The two of them spent many hours together at Zoppi's, talking politics with d'Églantine, Marat, Hébert, Saint-Huruge, or Momoro, whose support for Danton was mingled with a certain jealousy; of all his companions there was only one who felt nothing but admiration for him, and that was Camille Desmoulins.

While their wives were embroidering bibs or discussing their coming *accouchements,* the two friends were doing the rounds of the theaters. They were often to be seen at the Théâtre du Palais-Royal, then known as the Théâtre Montansier, from the pseudonym of its director, Marguerite Brunet. The First Deputy Public Prosecutor, according to gossip which he did his best to suppress, was one of the Montansier's sleeping partners. From the auditorium of this celebrated theater he would applaud famous actors and plays with revolutionary themes. Backstage, in Mme. Brunet's apartment, he met the admiring circle who paid court to this great performer. Conversation would go on far into the night, to the accompaniment of champagne and *petits fours.* It was here that Danton met the beautiful and coquettish Agnes de Buffon, still determined to lure him, by the promise of her favors, into joining her beloved Philippe's party. When the Duke of Orléans approached the pair, did he observe the dangerous game his mistress was playing? With a man like Danton, any woman was best advised to be on her guard. Or did the Duke intend to draw the demagogue over to his side at last by deliberately shutting his eyes until the crucial moment was reached? Incapable of arresting the movement he

Gabrielle's pregnancy was nearing its term: the doctor gave her another ten days or a fortnight. Lucile Desmoulins was also expecting a child, but she still had over five months to wait. The two women visited each other regularly and went out for walks together, the one displaying her condition, the other her beginner's fears concerning that unknown quantity, motherhood.

Since he did not want to tire his wife unduly, Danton no longer invited friends home to dinner. He was proposing numerous reforms in the Commune and in order to win support would entertain the waverers at meals in the Palais-Royal chophouses. This cost him a good deal of money, and his detractors made such burdensome "love feasts" a ground of complaint against him, claiming that he spent anything up to 300 *livres* a head on them.

What came a good deal cheaper, on the other hand, were the long sessions Danton spent in Zoppi's, a café on the rue des Fossés-Saint-Germain (today the rue de l'Ancienne-Comédie). Zoppi himself was an Italian, who, like his illustrious forerunner Procopio, made the best mocha coffee in Paris. On the chairs where Danton rested his vast hams, men such as Boileau, Racine, or La Fontaine, and, later, Voltaire, d'Alembert, and Diderot, had sat before him. Everyone knew the history of this famous establishment. Procopio had come to Paris from Palermo in 1684, with the idea of spreading the coffee-drinking habit among Frenchmen. He opened a little shop in the rue des Fossés-Saint-Germain, opposite the Comédie, the most fashionable theater of the day. He served his customers with nothing but this blackish brew of his, to the exclusion of any other beverage. Mme. de Sévigné, whose literary and gastronomical predictions were equally shaky, declared that "Racine is a passing fad, like coffee." She did not like this new drink herself, and was irked by the spectacle of carriages stopping outside the "café" (a neologism coined for the occasion) while the occupants had a cup of the stuff brought to them without leaving their seat. Inside, in a large room with walls painted to resemble marble, a subdued gathering did homage to the new fashion and sat sipping the strange nectar from tiny ritual cups.

When Zoppi took over, this exclusiveness ended: in 1792 not

from that religion of the people which they formerly defended. This is what my life has meant."

Having sketched this impression of his past, Danton now blocked in, with large, bold strokes, the general lines of his future. The defunct Assembly had drawn up a Constitution; the King had gone to the Riding School and sworn to uphold it. Time now for Danton to proclaim his allegiance to this charter. He said: "Whatever my individual opinions concerning men and affairs may have been at the time of the Constitution's overhaul, *now that it is sworn* I would demand the death penalty for any man—were he my brother, my friend, or my own son—who raised a sacrilegious hand to attack it. Such are my feelings in this matter. The general will of the French people, made no less solemnly manifest than their adherence to the Constitution, will always be my supreme law. I have consecrated my entire life to the people. No longer will their enemies attack or betray them with impunity. Very soon they will rise and purge the earth of all its tyrants, unless tyranny abandons the league it has formed against them. If need be, I will die in the defense of their cause—"

"We will die with you!" a voice called out, and a chorus of assent rose from the benches: "Yes, yes, we will die, too!"

Danton's peroration was a fine piece of soapbox rhetoric: "The people will have my dying prayers; only the people deserve them. Their courage and enlightenment have raised them from abject nothingness; their courage and enlightenment will render them immortal!"

"Bravo!" cried his audience, and even the moderates could not but help acclaim him. Then the Mayor took the tricolor sash of office and bound it around the First Deputy Public Prosecutor's waist. In one of the front seats, Gabrielle dabbed at her eyes, and her husband blew her a kiss. Proud and happy, he had just outlined, in this ringing yet calculated manifesto, the pattern of his militant destiny. As Aristide Briand was to declare, "a political speech is not a work of literature, it is *an act*." One hundred and thirty years earlier, Danton had come to the same conclusion. This "act" of his on January 20, 1792, this resounding personal testament, was to make him one of the pillars of the Revolution.

his visit. The Prime Minister was a man who kept himself aloof.
This task was doubtless carried out by his secret agents, who
were unlikely to make the fact public. Their department contained numerous filing cabinets, each with its label—"Spanish
Affairs," "Polish Affairs," "Prussian Affairs," and so on. Only
one had a French title, and that because there was no exact
equivalent in English for the thing it described: *Agents Pro-
vocateurs*. If a file with Danton's name on it existed in this
cabinet, no proof of the fact has survived.

On the other hand, we are less likely to be wrong if we
assume that the traveler met Thomas Paine, author of *The
Rights of Man*, and Thomas Christie, another admirer of the
Jacobins' ideals. But it is not true that it was Talleyrand who
introduced Danton to the two Londoners. In August and
September of 1791 that revolutionary prelate had not yet crossed
the Channel. His official mission to London only began the
following year, on January 24, 1792. But despite this, Danton
may well have made the acquaintance of both Paine and
Christie; and they in turn may have put him in contact with the
leaders of the Whig Party: Sheridan, Fox, and Lord Stanhope.
The last-named was in fact the Prime Minister's brother-in-law;
though he attacked Pitt's policies in public, he privately supported them.

Thanks to this lucky coincidence, Danton could play a double
game. He could satisfy his patriotic conscience by attaching
himself to the Whigs, who were dreaming of an alliance with
the country that had formulated the Rights of Man. But through
the good offices of their leader, he could also establish himself
on a better footing with the agents of the Prime Minister, who,
after all, was the man who held the purse strings. It did no harm,
either, that Pitt's secretary and *éminence grise* was none other
than his niece, Hester—Lord Stanhope's daughter.

Danton's precise relationship to both these political groups is
yet another of the mysteries which crowd his double life, com-
pounded in equal degree of a genuine, and ardent, passion for
universal liberty, equality, and fraternity—and a no less powerful love of money.

During his London exile he learned that Leopold of Austria was at long last beginning to take some interest in the

CHAPTER VIII

Deputy Public Prosecutor to the Commune

AT THIS PERIOD the Austrian Emperor and the King of Prussia were more concerned over Catherine the Great's ambitions in Poland than over Louis XVI's internal difficulties. The Empress of Russia herself, anxious to be left a free hand on the Vistula, was pressing the Courts of Vienna and Berlin to intervene in France. As for England, a revolution which damaged her rival's maritime power could not but be welcome across the Channel. William Pitt, the Prime Minister, was establishing numerous agents in Paris, some English, some French, and some Swiss. Was Danton one of them? Various reports and letters which only came to light long afterward (and which we shall refer to later in the chronological order of their discovery) confirm the probability in a manner tantamount to proof.

Unfortunately for history, little is known about Danton's visit to England. There is no evidence as to where he stayed in London and Birmingham. He wrote few, if any, letters during his time there—not through fear of compromising himself, since he often displayed a quite childish lack of caution (as his property deals make clear); but rather because of his natural bent for off-the-cuff oratory, which left its mark on his way of life in general. Even if he kept up a correspondence with Gabrielle, which might have enlightened us about this period, his family either destroyed or concealed his letters after his death. We know only that he did not dally in England, since he remained there a mere six weeks.

There is very little likelihood that Pitt received him during

should go over to Birmingham. But he could not meet the expenses involved, and spoke no word of English.

Danton, whose English was fluent and who had money and to spare, offered to go with him. A young relative, a cousin named Georges Mergez, accompanied them. All three carried daggers and pistols. Later, Fouquier-Tinville was to call this trip an "emigration." To which Danton replied from the dock: "Despotism still flourished unchecked in Paris. I therefore chose exile. I banished myself and swore not to return to France until liberty had been established there."

Of his intention to return we have one corroborative piece of evidence: he did not take his wife and child with him. But that intention is also implicitly contradicted—again, by Danton himself—in that clause of the power-of-attorney Antoine Charpentier received which required him to terminate Danton's lease and sell his furniture. Besides, the exile could very easily summon his wife by letter to join him.

So on that hot August morning in 1791 Danton was parted from Gabrielle for the first time. The three travelers must have left by post-chaise or hired carriage. We can imagine Danton's sad expression at that leave-taking, and Gabrielle's tears as she held out their son to him. They embraced, and then the driver whipped up his horses and was gone. As he rattled along, Danton may well have felt that Bailly and La Fayette had won the final round.

influence over the masses), Danton was still hesitating between
the two possible options. Republic or regency? No matter; that
could be settled later. He threw in his lot with Laclos—though
reserving the right, if all went well, to take whichever side he
liked, to proclaim a republic, and, if need be, to throw Laclos
himself into prison.

Meanwhile, however, he accepted, from the hands of his
fellow conspirator, a petition that had been drawn up by a
third rogue. This was Brissot, the founder and editor of *Le
Patriote Français,* and another friend of Philippe d'Orléans's—
though an unreliable friend who affected a wavering brand of
Republicanism and whom Laclos likewise hoped to use for his
own ends. The object of this petition was to arouse the people
against Louis XVI. On July 16 Danton took it down for
approval by the members of the Club des Cordeliers.

A huge crowd filled the Club to hear him. It was a hot
summer day and passions were running high, so that the sweat
stood out on his listeners' foreheads. From the rough scaffolding which served as a rostrum, Danton read out the text of the
petition. Its central demand was for the King's removal from
power. The audience did more than applaud: they screamed
insults at "the Austrian woman" and "Fat Capet."

Legendre, who was in the chair, delegated forty-eight "patriots" to carry a message to each of the forty-eight electoral
divisions. A fortnight previously, the City Council had invited
all Parisians to congregate on the Champ-de-Mars on Sunday,
July 17. The idea was that they should celebrate—very simply,
by the mere gesture of assembly—the anniversary of the events
that took place on July 14. (The three days' delay was to avoid
the loss of work which this would otherwise entail.) Laclos and
Danton intended to use this public gathering for their own
purposes. The emissaries of Legendre were instructed to tell
each division: "Tomorrow, when the citizens of Paris assemble
on the Champ-de-Mars, the petition of the Club des Cordeliers
will be offered to them for their signature."

Desmoulins went to the Jacobin Club in person to ask if its
members would associate themselves with the venture. But the
Jacobins rejected such a plebiscite, on the grounds of illegality.

dashing Colonel of the Reserve and corpulent Counsel, the one fifty and the other thirty-two—though to look at them one might well have reversed their ages. Laclos seemed far younger than he actually was: he devoted a great deal of care to his appearance. His wig was scrupulously brushed and powdered; his complexion was miraculously free from wrinkles; he dressed with dandified and foppish elegance. Danton, on the other hand, seemed a good deal older; excessive weight put years on him. Yet Laclos's *Poésies Fugitives* and *Les Liaisons Dangereuses* had been in all the booksellers' shops at a time when young Danton was still playing truant from school. Later, when General Marmont was in command of the First Consul's artillery in Italy, Choderlos de Laclos was his adjutant. In his *Memoirs,* the aged Marshal devoted one word only to his former subordinate, whom he described as the "celebrated Laclos." Marmont's hand was shaky enough by the time he came to pen this phrase, but the hint was enough, both for him and his readers. It is easy to see how much, back in 1791, a person like Danton could be flattered by the friendship of this elegant officer. Laclos's eyes were aglint with shrewdness and subtlety; his high forehead—another sign of intelligence—rose above them like some gleaming miter. The gigantic Danton, overshadowing his visitor with his corpulent presence, nevertheless gave the impression of being his foil. Their interview makes one think of the fight between David and Goliath. But here the object was not so much to defeat one's opponent by force of arms as to bamboozle him with clever arguments.

Whether there should be a republic or a regency did not matter for the moment. The most urgent and essential thing was to prevent Louis getting the reins of power back into his hands. Laclos brought Danton around to the idea of a *coup d'état.* He had no idea whether, once the King was overthrown, Danton would opt for one form of government or the other. But he calculated that once victory was assured, he could force the demagogue's hand in favor of Philippe d'Orléans. As for the Duke himself, if he found himself with his back to the wall he would no longer try to shuffle out of his responsibilities.

Though won over to the idea of a popular pronunciamento (which he had undertaken to bring about by virtue of his

right which the Constitution gives me to exercise that office; I might go so far as to say that, after making so many sacrifices in the interests of the people, and for the sake of freedom, I can no longer leave the class in which I have placed myself, that of the ordinary citizen. . . ."

This was a bombshell for Laclos and his ambitions. But though initially taken aback, the wily intriguer soon recovered himself and lost no time in coming to a private agreement with Danton. Then, sure of the support he needed (there is no formal proof of Danton's part in this affair but subsequent events make it a near-certainty) the novelist asked leave of the President of the Assembly to appear before the Bar of the House. On July 11 his request was granted. In an adroit speech he attacked the notion of a republic, while at the same time acknowledging Philippe's withdrawal; to everyone's surprise, he gave the impression that he was pleading for the present King. But what Laclos in fact was doing, from a practical viewpoint, was giving the Duke's supporters enough time to mount a *coup d'état.*

The conservative majority did not fall into the snare Laclos had laid for them; indeed, they went so far as to use some of this apprentice Machiavelli's arguments to succor the King. Two days after Laclos made his speech, the Standing Committees of the Constituent Assembly presented their report on the flight to Varennes. This document recommended neither the King's removal from power nor the setting up of a regency under anyone whatsoever. Two days after its publication Barnave asked leave to speak in the Assembly. Together with his colleagues Pétion and Latour-Maubourg, he had brought the royal family back to Paris. Moved by the distress of the Queen, he proposed a motion confirming the inviolability of the King's person. The Deputies, who were alarmed equally by the prospect of republic or regency—the first suggested by mob agitators, the second by an ambitious junta—voted in favor of this motion. By declaring the King inviolable, they *ipso facto* restored his powers as a constitutional monarch.

The news of this decree made Choderlos de Laclos almost inarticulate with fury. If an Orleanist *coup d'état* did not take place at once, it would be too late. The Duke's private secretary hurried to Danton. The two men made an interesting contrast:

one battalion to another, no longer capable of making them obey
his orders. For two hours he cajoled and argued, but without
success. When, at last, Marie-Antoinette retreated up the steps
into the Tuileries, she could not help turning to the troops of the
National Guard and saying: "You must at least admit that we
no longer have our freedom."

The next day Louis XVI went to lodge a complaint before the
Constituent Assembly. The session was being presided over by an
obscure Deputy named Chabroud. Without addressing Louis as
"Your Majesty," much less using the third person, Chabroud
replied to his protests: "You must be quite well aware that noisy
demonstrations are an inconvenience which always accompanies
the progress of liberty!"

When he got back to the Tuileries, the hapless monarch found
a somewhat unusual letter awaiting him. It was, officially, from
the Directory of the *département,* but in fact had been composed
by the inevitable Danton, together with Count Armand de
Kersaint. In reprimanding tones it counseled the King to remove
from his company all refractory priests, "who shed hypocritical
tears over religion." It concluded by enjoining him to send a
declaration to the other Courts of Europe that he was living as
free as the fish in the ocean. Louis XVI, however, could not
write this lie to the monarchs of neighboring countries. He merely
drank the bitter cup of his defeat to the dregs, vaguely conscious that once again Monsieur Danton—one of his own Advocates—had triumphed over him.

First at the Jacobins, and then in the Club des Cordeliers, the
hero of the day was welcomed with a great ovation. In both places
he made a speech, which was largely an attack on La Fayette.
"He has resigned!" Danton roared. "Why is he still with the
National Guard?" Fréron went further still. Recalling that the
Constituent Assembly, when it abolished hereditary titles, had
decreed that no citizen might henceforth bear any name "but
the true name of his family," printed the following piece of advice
in Desmoulins's journal: "Citizens, know who are your friends,
and who your declared enemies! Bailly and *Mottié* are un-
worthy of your trust. It is Danton the patriot you should elect
Mayor—and *ça ira!"*

ensuring that it went off without a hitch—in other words, to disobey La Fayette's orders.

The announcement of this restrictive move provoked a debate in the Municipal Council. La Fayette, supported by Bailly, asked members to proclaim a state of martial law and the compulsory mobilization of reservists. With his sharp, hard-hitting oratory Danton managed to whip up a majority against the motion—whereupon La Fayette, in a state of furious annoyance, offered Bailly his resignation. "Only a coward," Danton growled, "could desert his post in the hour of peril! And besides, your commission is not from the municipal authorities. If you want to resign, you will have to take your resignation round all the forty-eight electoral divisions that made you a general."

What "peril," in fact, did Danton have in mind when he spoke? That a refractory priest should celebrate Mass in fact bothered him not at all. What really made him apprehensive was the suspicion that Saint-Cloud might be the first stage in a longer journey—which, if accomplished, would bring Louis XVI to the heart of La Vendée, where the inhabitants had been in revolt against Paris ever since the Civil Constitution of the Clergy.

La Fayette, naturally, did not go around the forty-eight constituencies offering them his resignation. The following morning, Monday April 18, he arrived at the Tuileries bright and early, leading the battalions that he had detailed for duty the day before, and counting on his own personal authority and popularity to get the royal procession safely through.

The carriages were waiting by the front steps of the palace. The King, his family, and their suite got into them. Alerted by the posters that had been put up all over the Théâtre-Français electoral division (which was, of course, Danton's), a vast crowd had gathered behind the railings. It was making a clear demonstration of its hostility toward the King's departure. The battalions that followed one another in at the palace gates—that of Les Cordeliers in particular—did not appear much disposed to let him go, either.

The mob cheered the troops, yelled insults at Marie-Antoinette, and were sarcastic at the King's expense. The royal children were in tears. Saber in hand, La Fayette galloped from

innocent project of the King's that finally drew him out of his neutrality and hurled him into the heart of the religious struggle.

The oath taken by conformist priests caused the King great heart searching. As a monarch of calm and conventional piety, he could not bring himself to see the nation meddling in the affairs of the Church. Furthermore—by a *concordat* which dated back to the reign of Francis I—French sovereigns "by the grace of God" had the right to appoint bishops. Now, it seemed, the Constituent Assembly was stripping Louis of his spiritual privilege. Caught between his Catholic conscience and his duties as a constitutional monarch, he felt that his private moral dilemma would very soon cross the dividing line and become public property. Now, about three months before Mirabeau's death, La Marck had passed on to the King a remark the "plebeian Count" had made, to the effect that "the royal family was lost if it did not leave Paris." With Mirabeau gone, Louis XVI had only one idea left in his head: to follow the dead man's advice.

In order to see which way the wind was blowing, he decided to go away on April 18, 1791, to spend the Easter holiday at Saint-Cloud. He warned La Fayette of his intention, and the Commander-in-Chief of the National Guard took adequate measures to ensure the royal family's safety. He detailed several battalions to cordon off the approaches to the Tuileries, so that the royal carriages could drive through without any trouble. By an unfortunate oversight, the Marquis included the Bataillon des Cordeliers in this detail. It was at this point that Danton, informed of what was in the air by the battalion commander, Villette, emerged from his period of self-effacement and intervened with all his old fiery impulsiveness.

That evening, Palm Sunday, the day before the royal family's projected departure, Danton buttonholed La Fayette in the City Hall. Since the morning a rumor had been going about that a refractory priest, a Jesuit named Lenfant, had celebrated Mass in the Tuileries Palace. At Danton's instigation, the Cordeliers battalion had unanimously agreed to draft a public notice denouncing the "culpability" of Louis XVI, "first public servant, whose duty is to uphold the law, but who prefers to flout it." This poster also called upon other battalions of the National Guard to prevent the departure for Saint-Cloud, instead of

FRATERNITÉ ("Freedom, Equality, Brotherhood"). This slogan was born in the Club, invented by Danton, and destined to become the motto of the various French Republics of the future.

In this assembly the tribune from Arcis possessed a weapon that matched his ambition. He could stand on equal terms with them all now—Robespierre, making his academic speeches to the Jacobins: Bailly, the life and soul of the conservative Club des Feuillants; the Deputies busy with their legislation in the Riding School. The "poor man's Mirabeau" now possessed a megaphone which was to project his brazen voice, his coarse chuckle, and those startling metaphors of his to the four winds of public opinion.

How did he intend to employ this "cannon," as he himself once described the public platform? To begin with, by forcing Bailly to become one of its servants. The anecdote has some unexpected twists to it.

There was, at this period, a certain obscure Deputy in the Constituent Assembly whom Providence and Allah were later to make famous. His name was Menou; he was a baron and the son of a marquis from Touraine. Elected by the nobility of his bailiwick to represent them at the States-General, Menou had gone across to the benches of the Third Estate, where he made loud proclamation of his liberal opinions. (We find him, in later years, a general in Egypt under Bonaparte, Commander-in-Chief after Kléber's death, converted to Islam, given the Moslem name of Abdullah, marrying a Moslem girl, and affecting Turkish costume. Defeated by the English, repatriated to France after the Peace of Amiens, and restored to the bosom of the Church, he was to end his adventurous life as Governor of Venice in 1810, a Grand Officer of the Legion of Honor, and a Knight of the Iron Crown. But at present Deputy Menou's unpredictable and dilettante career still lay ahead of him, and he was devoting himself to attacking Louis XVI's government.) On October 19, 1790, Menou mounted the speakers' rostrum and proceeded to take several members of the Cabinet apart. M. de Montmorin and M. de Fleurieu, who were respectively Minister of Foreign Affairs and Minister of

to Paris in 1792, as a Deputy to the Convention. The former had lodgings in the Palais-Royal, where he occupied the post of secretary to the Duke of Orléans. The latter was on reasonably good terms with Bailly—who had just been re-elected Mayor with a big majority. In these circumstances, there is nothing to prevent us assuming that it was the Duke's secretary who briefly held the presidency of the Club—and was nominated to this position with a view to having the Commune remove the seals that barred all entrance to the monastery. This near-certain hypothesis is yet another indication of collusion between Danton and the Duke.

The Commune, then, now permitted the Club of the Rights of Man to establish its premises in the former monastery: hence its new name, the Club des Cordeliers. However, the City Hall would allow it to hold meetings only in the "theological lecture room." But a few days later the Club occupied the chapel by main force, and Bailly dared not object, much less take a stern line over its action.

Chateaubriand, who visited the Club in 1792, left the following sketch of it in his *Mémoires d'outre-tombe:* "The monastery had been stripped of all its veils, curtains, sculptures, and paintings: the basilica was scraped bare, and offered nothing to the eye save its naked bones and vaulting. At the east end of the church, where wind and rain came in through the glassless rose windows, there stood some joiners' benches, which did duty as a desk for the President when the session took place inside the church. The speakers' rostrum consisted of four small propped-up beams, each pair resembling a vertical X, with a plank running between them like a piece of scaffolding."

The Jacobin Club was a quasi-parliamentary association, where one had to show one's credentials to gain admission, and the most marked characteristics in debate were caution and casuistry. At the Cordeliers, on the other hand, entrance was free to all, and anyone who chose could get up and harangue a highly mixed audience, which might well be equally amused or furious. There was only one rule imposed on all speakers: they had to put on the "red cap" before climbing the ladder that served as a staircase. There was a long strip of calico nailed to the wall, which bore the legend *LIBERTÉ, ÉGALITÉ,*

The main object of the *Club of the Rights of Man* is to denounce, before the tribunal of public opinion, all abuses of authority, in whatever sphere, and any infringement of the rights of man; the Club therefore, after due deliberation, invites any citizen to acquaint it with any instance of oppression or injustice which they may have suffered, or concerning which they possess information, and to furnish therewith the evidence on which such complaints are founded.

The *Club of the Rights of Man,* having satisfied itself as to the legitimacy of such a complaint, will lose no time in giving it the greatest possible publicity, and in exposing the author of the crime to public obloquy. . . .

It hardly seems necessary to add that dozens and, later, hundreds of such denunciations poured in to the Secretary. The new Club would certainly not lack for business.

The original premises were in the rue des Boucheries-Saint-Germain, close to the Abbaye. A person called Cirier, who owned a ballroom, was willing to make it available to "Dufourny de Villiers"—or, in other words, to Danton. The first meeting, announced by means of handbills which Brune ran off, drew only a small audience. There were young girls under the gallery handing out copies of the Declaration of the Rights of Man. The assembled company, led by the President as though by a priest, read this prayer of the new religion aloud, in unison. Then the speeches began. There were attacks on the municipal authorities, the Constituent Assembly, the Throne, and the Church.

As the weeks went by, the audience grew till M. Cirier's ballroom could no longer hold them all. Every evening people had to be turned away. Momoro suggested reoccupying the church of Les Cordeliers, though both it and the monastery were still under seal. To get the seal removed required authorization from the City Hall, where Danton was by no means *persona grata.* Such a request was bound to meet with refusal. The conspirators therefore played a more subtle game. Dufourny de Villiers resigned the presidency in favor of a certain Peyre, or Pieyre, whose name is variously spelled on the Club's official records. When we consider the success of the intervention, it seems likely that the man in question was actually Pieyre rather than Peyre. The latter, a native of the Basses-Alpes, only made his first visit

As far as Marat was concerned, the incident seemed to be closed. He had gone into hiding, and that was that. But the sheriff's officers returned to his lodgings the following day. No one made any effort to stop them when they placed seals on the door of his room, nor when they proceeded to immobilize the printing press he employed. For the time being *L'Ami du Peuple* was dead: four months were to elapse before its next appearance.

In Danton's case, the consequences were different. The Châtelet continued to place an unfavorable interpretation on his speech of the 22nd. The judges of this tribunal remembered only his violence, and neglected the spirit of reconciliation which had succeeded it. They therefore instructed the examining magistrate of the Garde des Marets to lay charges against him. This official signed a warrant for Danton's arrest, on the grounds that he had "made speeches prejudicial to public law and order."

Coming so soon after the Marat incident, would an *affaire* Danton finally cut this infernal district down to size? Not yet: the examining magistrate proceeded to go cool on the job. He held the warrant in abeyance, deciding to wait until passions had cooled before executing it. Not surprisingly, every Paris newssheet took cognizance of these events. One pamphlet, sold on the streets and in the public gardens, treated the whole affair in humorous vein. Its title gave the prospective reader a fair idea of its contents:

> GREAT motion on the
> GREAT crime of the
> GREAT M. Danton, perpetrated in the
> GREAT district of the
> GREAT CORDELIERS and upon the
> GREAT retinue thereof.

At last, the ambitious District President was renowned throughout the capital. So at least he declared in the presence of his wife and friends. But this was a mere façade. Underneath he was highly apprehensive at the prospect of his arrest, with officers of the watch arriving and beating on his door. One or two hints that he slipped into speeches before the District Assembly persuaded that body to address a protest to the Constituent Assembly. Danton's electors, declaring that the pro-

patriotism to permit the execution of the Assembly's decrees rather than obstruct them."

Here was a real setback for Danton. He had to admit defeat, and went back across Paris in a very crestfallen mood. But what was this? Everybody had disappeared: the crowds thronging his route, General Plainville's troops, the battalion protecting the Hôtel de Fautrière, all those serried ranks of uniforms and riders, that vast mob of local inhabitants and screaming women—all gone, vanished as though they had never been. What had happened in Danton's absence?

The truth was that La Fayette, being no more anxious than Danton to provoke a civil war, had capitulated and ordered his subordinate commander to pull out. Marat himself had disappeared. Sacrificing his usual attire—the headscarf, the shirt gaping open at the neck to expose his hairy chest, the old and filthy jacket—he had walked out of his house in a smart frock coat and hat, smiling, clean-shaven, and quite unrecognizable. Thus disguised, he had passed unchallenged through the crowds and the military cordon. Danton, on learning what had happened from the neighbors, went back home to Gabrielle, who had been sick with anxiety during his absence and was only too glad to hear his cheerful laughter once more.

Next day, January 23, the lucky victor went to take his seat in the City Hall. Elected a member of the Commune together with his friend Legendre, he appeared in the old *Parloir aux Bourgeois* and was greeted by much loud whispering. The Chamber was less enamored than ever of this person and of the way he invariably attempted to block municipal decisions. New members took the oath in alphabetical order; when it was Danton's turn, loud protests were voiced. The man was a disturber of the peace who had always hampered the Commune in its lawful duties—had, indeed, fought its decisions tooth and nail within the last twenty-four hours. How could such a pestilential agitator be allowed a place among its members? Faced with such an attack, Danton found himself constrained to plead in his own defense, emphasizing his love of the people, his respect for the law, and his devotion to reason. The eloquence he displayed won him some votes; but without the threat of a new plebiscite in his favor at district level, he would not, it was clear, obtain his validation.

[sic], who are barricading the main thoroughfares and blocking all access to or from the district, we would spring to arms instantly! If the tocsin were to be rung now, if we sounded the general alarm, twenty thousand men would rally at our call and these troops would blanch at the sight of them. But God forbid that we should do such a thing: our cause is too fine a one to risk spoiling. The only arms we must employ are those of reason!"

The orator, then, it would appear, was renouncing any possibility of fraticidal strife—and with good reason. The citizen militia of Les Cordeliers would never bring themselves to cross bayonets with the citizen militia from other districts. Fearing desertions, Danton decided to negotiate with the executive. In any case, there was no need to sound the tocsin or beat the drum to bring the crowds into the streets. From her window Gabrielle could see her neighbors all flocking out to engulf La Fayette's nine hundred men.

At the headquarters of his District Assembly, Danton proposed that a deputation should be sent to the Riding School, requesting the Constituent Assembly to arbitrate in this matter. There was general applause, and Danton himself was chosen to head the delegation. He set off at once, together with three of his constituents and his friend and chief clerk, Paré. A vast crowd cheered them on their way. Outside Marat's house—now cordoned by Villette's battalion—Legendre shouted: "While I am here the People's Friend is safe! No one shall touch so much as a hair of his head!"

When they reached the Tuileries, Danton and his group requested a hearing at the bar of the Assembly. The request was refused. Danton then sent in a note to the Deputy presiding over that session, a lawyer named Target. The latter—convinced that Danton, far from seeking a reconciliation, was deliberately encouraging violence—replied that he was going to lay the matter before the Constituent Assembly there and then. The Deputies—after a stern talking-to from Target—passed a motion calling upon the Cordeliers District to show proper respect for the law. A secretary was sent out to inform the petitioner, who had been pacing around the colonnade, that the National Assembly "disapproved of his conduct" and that it "relied on his sense of

[3] Citizens from the suburbs of Saint-Antoine and Saint-Marceau on the march, June 20, 1792. (*Photo by Giraudon*)

[2] The first Madame Danton (Gabrielle Charpentier). Portrait attributed to David. (*Photo by Josse-Lalance*)

[1] Georges-Jacques Danton, King's Counsel, from a contemporary
cameo. (*Photo by Josse-Lalance*)

plain sense of justice, they refused to comply with the demands of sixty Paris districts—the entire city, in fact—what a splendid addition it would be to the case he was building against them!

But the General and the Mayor did not fall into the trap. With some regrets, no doubt, they ordered the transfer of Besenval to the Châtelet prison. Now all they had to do was to find various excuses for continually postponing his trial. This they did with some success. The mercenary was not tried for another five months, and then he was acquitted. Danton did not press to have the hearing speeded up, for during those five months he was already enjoying the fruits of his victory and he saw his influence over the masses increasing daily.

This incident reveals something fundamental about Danton's character. He demanded the return of Besenval simply to boost his own popularity, which he felt was not advancing fast enough. But once he had got what he wanted, he was quite content to leave the Colonel to slumber undisturbed in his cell, because he knew very well that the poor man was innocent. Can we, perhaps, infer from this that he was by nature a kindly person?

At Versailles, Marie-Antoinette was becoming panic-stricken. She, too, had no love for La Fayette and Bailly and Mirabeau; nor, indeed, for any of those who had labored to bring about the great social revolution. She regarded them all as enemies. Yet the Queen was not a bad woman. Overspoiled by the life she had led, too far isolated from the miseries of the people, she was wholly circumscribed by her own soft, luxurious universe. When she saw these lightning flashes playing across the sky, she suggested to the King that he should flee, with her and their children, to Metz. From here the army of General Bouillé, Governor of Lorraine, would be able to escort them back to Paris and re-establish the absolute power of the monarchy. Louis allowed himself to be talked into this scheme. In order to facilitate their departure, he summoned the Flanders Regiment to Versailles. When this unit arrived, the King's Bodyguard entertained its officers at dinner. The banquet took place on the stage of the royal theater. A lady-in-waiting in the palace, feeling that such a spectacle might reassure the Queen, advised her to go

map in front of him and trace the route to Switzerland with his finger. This gesture aroused the suspicions of his fellow guests. In his *Memoirs* he afterward wrote: "I was on the point of leaving when I heard the tocsin being rung with furious urgency; and within seconds the inn was surrounded by two or three hundred peasants armed with guns, sticks, and spits. Their leader informed me that I was 'very probably an aristocrat on the run,' and asked my permission (!) to imprison me. My cell turned out to be one of the rooms in the inn."

The next day his captors took Besenval to Brie-Comte-Robert, and shut him up in a ruined castle. An attorney named Bourdon, together with a squad of lawyers' clerks, was assigned to guard him. La Fayette, informed of the arrest, sent down an aide-de-camp to Brie-Comte-Robert. "After some polite chitchat," Besenval writes, "this officer told me that M. de La Fayette required my word of honor that I would not attempt to escape if the occasion presented itself. 'Monsieur,' I replied, 'the best possible guarantee I can give M. de La Fayette of my remaining here is the risk to which I would expose *him* were I to escape.' My days were by no means disagreeable: I read, and amused myself observing the pranks that the clerks got up; sometimes I had a game of tric-trac with the local priest. . . ."

It is interesting that Bourdon also notified Danton of the arrest: why him, and not the President of any other district? Doubtless because the attorney knew the Counsel, either personally or by reputation. Danton at once convened his electors and told them of this "plot against the nation, with Besenval playing cards instead of submitting to the lightning stroke of justice." On his request the Assembly passed a motion inviting the other districts to copy that of Les Cordeliers. Fifty-nine similar resolutions were delivered with Danton's to the City Hall, which was thus faced with sixty demands that the Colonel should be transferred to a Paris prison, for "immediate judgment."

In reality, Danton did not care at all about Besenval. This hired officer, this Swiss mercenary, had done no more than carry out the duties he was paid for. He certainly was not guilty of "insulting the nation." What Danton hoped to do by attacking him was to annoy La Fayette and Bailly. If, from a

been responsible for it and the sobriquet "Madame Veto" now began to be applied to her.

It was at this point that M. de Saint-Huruge dispatched his dangerous letter to Bailly, as President of the Constituent Assembly, and to his Secretary. If circumstances arose, he informed them, which would lead the "aristocratic coalition" to "tip the scales in the direction of the veto," then the ebullient marquis-turned-radical would require "exemplary reprisals" for such behavior. The essential thing about this letter was the thinly disguised threat of murder it contained. At all times, and under any régime, such an act has been liable to severe penalties, and three officers of the watch were accordingly sent to arrest Saint-Huruge at his home.

That same evening, Danton was presiding over his District Assembly. He announced the fact of Saint-Huruge's imprisonment and spoke up in his defense. The marquis, he said, was a hothead but he was also a patriot. Besides, it was no bad thing that patriotism should be seasoned with a dash of hotheadedness. Without the second, the first was liable to go soft. "We are not eunuchs!" Danton bellowed. Saint-Huruge, he went on, was a fine man, a decent fellow who—even with a gun in his hand—wouldn't so much as hurt a fly. He must be released from the Châtelet at once. The President demanded a resolution from the District Assembly. The Assembly so voted and insisted on Saint-Huruge's release. A letter was drafted and dispatched to the City Hall. Whether out of fear or generosity, Bailly gave in. Saint-Huruge would lie in his dungeon no longer.

Sometimes, however, instead of demanding a man's release, Danton was likely to press for his incarceration. Such was the case with the Baron de Besenval, for instance. This Swiss officer was in command of the mercenaries stationed on the Champ-de-Mars during the events of July. Indeed, for a few days, while Marshal de Broglie was detained at Saint-Denis, he was acting Commander-in-Chief. But being afraid that he might suffer the same fate as the defenders of the Bastille, M. de Besenval deserted on the morning following July 14. On the 19th he reached Villegruis, a village two leagues from Provins. When he was sitting at table in an inn, he was unwise enough to spread out a

rumors that traveled back from Versailles. Since June, Mirabeau had been publishing the *Journal des États Généraux;* Gorsas, the *Courrier de Versailles à Paris;* Barère, *Le Point du Jour;* and Brissot, *Le Patriote Français.* Reading these kept Parisians abreast of fresh events. It was through them that they learned of the Tennis Court Oath, Mirabeau's famous apostrophe to the Marquis of Dreux-Brézé, and the transformation of the States-General into a National Constituent Assembly.

The whole population took an impassioned interest in these happenings. In the gardens of the Palais-Royal people discussed them with frenzied excitement. Built by the Duke of Orléans some years previously, the buildings that surrounded (and still surround) the vast and verdant enclosure ringed it with a circle of shops and restaurants. It served, at one and the same time, as a meeting place for persons of fashion, the main public square of Paris, a central stage for every kind of tub-thumper, and an open-air cloister where thinkers could stroll about and exchange ideas.

The crowds surged to and fro beneath the trees. Respectable women and ladies of easy virtue jostled each other outside the shopwindows, admiring the dresses and jewelry and finely bound books on display. There was much pushing in the crowded entrance of the Caveau—a café still in existence today, the one survivor from this period; there were arguments over tables on the sidewalk outside La Grotte Flamande, renowned for its beer; there was the Café des Italiens, with its vast and globular Dutch stove that attracted customers in chilly weather; and the Café de Chartres, where the young Duke of that name, Philippe d'Orléans's elder brother, had his portrait on view; and lastly the Café de Foy, where they sold the *eau-de-vie d'Andaye* that connoisseurs went into ecstasies over.

But what a bear garden the Café de Foy was! This was where the Patriotic Society of the Palais-Royal held its meetings—outside in the open air, with orators standing on chairs, sometimes on tables, unless they were put off stride by a rainstorm. The fieriest speakers were men like Saint-Giniès, Loustalot, Harivel, and Collard. But the real organizers of the group were Danton, the Marquis de Saint-Huruge, and Camille

vate residence. Driven off by a strong police detachment, they
turned their wrath on the owner of a saltpeter refinery, M.
Henriot—though he, in fact, had sacrificed part of his fortune
to keep his personnel fed. Troops were brought in, but it took a
couple of days to get the rioting under control. More than a
hundred corpses were found lying in the streets afterward.

The feverish atmosphere in the capital had not yet subsided
when the States-General opened at Versailles. The first session,
on May 5, took place without the Third Estate Deputies from
Paris. The slowness of the voting procedure, the moral pressure
exerted around the polling booths (which reduced the 40,000
primary electors to a mere 11,706)—all these obstacles combined
to prevent the twenty Parisians elected from appearing in the
Assembly before May 23.

Among them there were very few people destined to achieve
fame. All the same, they included M. Bailly, member both of the
Academy of Sciences and the French Academy; Dr. Guillotin,
whose name needs no introduction; and the Abbé Sieyès, author
of the famous pamphlet on the Third Estate referred to before.
("What is the Third Estate? Nothing. What should it be?
Everything . . .") Danton knew these three men well: he used
to meet them at the Lodge of the Nine Sisters.

Two more of his friends were included among the Deputies:
Maître Camus, the lawyer who bore Mme. Recordain's maiden
name, and Maître Dosfant, who had drawn up Danton's marriage contract and employed Gabrielle's brother Antoine as his
clerk.

Danton might have put forward his own candidature. Did he
consider doing so? It would seem improbable. If he wanted to
make a living and pay off his debts, it was better, surely, to stick
to his legal practice rather than go off and live in a rented room
at Versailles. The eighteen *livres* that a Deputy received as an
allowance for each session would hardly have begun to fill the
financial gulf which his love match had opened up under his
feet. In order to act as the people's representative, he would
have had to leave Paris and let his cases gather dust there. Such
an ambition called for the kind of resources he did not possess.

Nevertheless, he was able to follow all the deliberations of the
Assembly, thanks to a rash of new broadsheets and the various

them, would then participate (if elected) in the task of designating the twenty Paris Deputies.

Naturally, such a novel procedure provoked discussion. When their electoral duties were concluded, the voters did not go home. They stayed in the church, moving from one group to another to press home their various points of view. Sometimes they would get up on a chair and express them to the entire gathering. Their function was not restricted to choosing the electors of the twenty Paris Deputies. They still had the task of formulating various demands and complaints and submitting them in tabulated form—the so-called *Cahiers de Doléances*—to the States-General.

Denied the right to vote because they did not pay sufficient taxes, the common people were seething with well-justified indignation. But it was a completely false rumor that drove them over the edge. Word went around that a certain M. Réveillon, a papermaker from the Faubourg Saint-Antoine, had declared on his way to the polling station: "The workers can manage perfectly well on fifteen sous a day! I have some under me who make twenty, and they go around with watches in their fobs—very soon they'll be better off than I am!"

Apocryphal or not, this story went around Paris like wildfire. It reached the Dantons, who—despite their lively interest in public affairs—paid scant attention to it: they had other things to worry about. Their son, who was now just over a year old, had succumbed to an illness which the family doctor could do nothing to cure. The poor child went into a swift decline and died on April 24. The funeral took place two days later. Gabrielle was heartbroken. Being an extremely devout woman, she went to seek consolation in a religious atmosphere. Her husband, on the contrary, inveighed noisily against Providence. He accompanied Gabrielle as far as the church door but would not cross the threshold with her. His ugliness intensified by anger, he strode away, staring straight in front of him, pacing the streets and mingling with the various groups that were all excitedly discussing the supposed remarks of the factory owner from the Faubourg Saint-Antoine.

On the 27th, three days after the death of Danton's child, some hotheaded demonstrators besieged the manufacturer's pri-

tonished that so large a man could have produced so tiny a baby. The child squalled, and Danton rocked it in an unsuccessful effort to quiet it. But he was also delighted: the new arrival was obviously going to have his father's powerful voice.

M. de Barentin, the President of the Board of Excise, had been—as we observed above—the new Counsel's first client. On that occasion there had been a conflict between two different tribunals. Certain forges situated at Conches, in Normandy, and forming part of a family inheritance, had been sold by the heirs of one René de Capelles. The creditors, who objected to this sale, demanded that the Châtelet—the court which had criminal jurisdiction over the Paris region—should take cognizance of the matter. The opposing party wanted the case to be tried by the bailiff's court in Conches. Danton was briefed by M. de Barentin, pleaded the case before the Court of Dispatch, and succeeded in having the case referred to the Châtelet.

As a result of this victory the President of the Board of Excise developed a high opinion of Danton's professional abilities, so much so that he retained the young man to take care of all his interests. Admitted to Barentin's confidence, Danton became something very like his intimate friend. During their discussions Gabrielle's husband would talk politics with his client. The latter, struck by Danton's original ideas, one day introduced him to Archbishop Loménie de Brienne, the Minister of Finance. Barentin thought that since both men were from Champagne, they ought to get on fairly easily. The prelate was born in Brienne (his château is still standing there), a small town just over sixteen miles from Arcis, with a military school that was afterward to acquire fame from Napoleon's having studied there.

Danton drew up a scheme of social and economic renovation for his illustrious compatriot's benefit. He incorporated in this project much of the introductory discourse he had delivered before the College of Advocates. It was vital that the King should stop this running battle with Parliament. Let him convince its members—with rather more subtle arguments than a ukase of provincial exile—of the pressing need for his reforms. Finally, let both the nobility and the clergy, who had a share in the payment of taxes that hit the Third Estate hardest, forego some

ment placed Paris under martial law. Troops began to patrol the streets.

In September another incident took place which drew large crowds—this time on the Seine—and produced a fresh case for Danton to handle. Demolition workers set about removing the Pont-au-Change. The shanties which ever since the Middle Ages had crowded this bridge from side to side now vanished in clouds of dust. To demolish the bridge meant the expropriation of its inhabitants. One of them, a tailor named Sansac, received from the municipal authorities an indemnity of 33,500 *livres*. Since he himself estimated his loss at 42,000, he briefed Maître d'Anton to take charge of his interests. The case was heard on December 7, and—for the first time—Danton lost.

Meanwhile Parliament had come back from Troyes. Louis XVI lifted his interdict in the belief that the members of that ancient assembly, having been made contrite by their exile, would prove more amenable in the future. The King was mistaken, however; next year Parliament refused to ratify two further edicts, one extending civil rights to Protestants, the other authorizing a loan of 420 millions.

On October 24, M. Charpentier sold his café business: this was four months after his daughter's wedding. No doubt the Inspector of Tax Concessions felt that the wife of a Counsel to the King's Bench should not have a father who was a café proprietor. He sold Le Parnasse for 41,200 *livres*, to a man named Pascal Maulu. With this money he purchased a house and garden at Fontenay-sous-Bois, and settled down there with his wife.

Their daughter visited them there frequently: Fontenay was an easily accessible suburb. Mme. d'Anton had become very elegant—*noblesse oblige* in more senses than one—and made a great impression on the local residents. In the end they came to call her "la belle Gabrielle," and their mayor gave her name to a new thoroughfare in Fontenay. (This Avenue de la Belle-Gabrielle is still in existence, though popular tradition attributes its title to a memory of Henri IV's mistress.) At the same time, Mme. d'Anton began to develop a certain telltale plumpness. The child was born at the rue des Mauvaises-Paroles in April of 1788. The young father picked up his son in clumsy hands, as-

Republican Danton, who not two years ago was calling himself
M. d'Anton."

It would, indeed, have been impossible for M. d'Anton to
prove his nobility by adducing—as he did for the Vicomte mentioned above—twenty-three relevant documents in evidence. Nor
could he have written on his own behalf remarks such as the
following, taken from the draft statement composed for the sons
of this aristocrat (whose rank some opponent had challenged):
"The hand of the Vicomte du Chayla, member of the Order of
Chivalry, impressed on several of the documents in evidence ad-
duced by the supplicants, will not have pointed out in vain that
they owe their being to the same source from which he is sprung,
since *His Majesty* will find no flaw in the attestation of this
noble warrior, whose name already stands hallowed by history,
which has passed down to posterity the valor with which a du
Chayla helped to rout that redoubtable enemy force at whose
hands the fortunes of *His Majesty's august forebear* long hung in
the balance on the field of Fontenoy."

For a man who was to denounce all "tyrants and their lack-
eys" from the platforms of various revolutionary clubs, this "august forebear" of "His Majesty" smells too much of the cour-
tier. But the advocate of those days had only one aim in view:
to win his case. And as for Danton's style . . . ! We shall have
further occasion to observe that this brilliant orator was a very
mediocre writer.

In a case somewhat similar to that of the du Chayla brothers,
that of the Marquis de la Devèze, Danton was to declare that
"nobility is the most precious of possessions." He was to change
his tune a few years later, when political developments had
rendered hereditary titles the worst sort of stigma.

During 1787, meanwhile, the situation continued to deterio-
rate. In August the King signed a general decree, over his own
seal, against Parliament as a whole. Since this body still refused
to ratify the new tax measures, the King ordained its banishment
to Troyes. This removal of the highest officers of the realm was
not carried through without incident. Seditious broadsheets appeared, pasted up on walls. Faced with the hostility of the people, who threatened to oppose this forced exodus, the govern-

meeting of the States-General; Dom Gerle, who made his mark on the occasion of the Tennis Court Oath, and the Abbé Sieyès, who was to compose that incendiary pamphlet beginning: "What is the Third Estate? Nothing. What should it be? Everything . . ."

The Grand Master, the supreme Head of the Order, was none other than His Royal Highness the Duke of Orléans, cousin to Louis XVI, First Prince of the Blood, and—paradoxically—one of the régime's most severe critics.

In fact the entire Revolution was contained, in embryo, in the Lodge of the Nine Sisters. Danton, "The Republican," could not have failed to acquire, from such company, the stamp that afterward made him "The Man of August 10."

It is very unlikely that he would have described his initiation to the proprietor of the Café de l'École, or given any details of the investiture ceremony either to Gabrielle or her mother—such as the swords of the Brethren pricking the thighs and calves of the neophyte as he lay on the ground, prostrate and blindfolded, while the Venerable Master pronounced the ritual formula of initiation over him; or the white apron, with set square and compasses embroidered on it in gold, which was tied around his waist; or, finally, the "steel arch" of swords under which he must pass, humble and happy, after his affiliation. The mysteries of a secret society are not to be divulged, even to the woman one loves. Danton had "seen the light," but the pleasures of that illumination he had perforce to keep to himself.

But there were other pleasures involved—not least the new acquaintances which the Lodge brought him. Among these was a Brother who did not, on the face of it, seem likely to play much part in Danton's career as a lawyer. This was an obscure general named Dumouriez, a funny little man who turned up in the rue du Pot-de-Fer wearing the civilian dress of an ordinary bourgeois. Little known, despite the twenty-two wounds that had earned him a pension, he had more of a reputation for espionage than for strategical skill. Louis XV had employed him as a secret agent, sending him on missions to Corsica, Prussia, and Poland. While passing through Hanover, Dumouriez had made the acquaintance of a German Freemason, the Duke of Bruns-

at present possess. According to Mme. Roland, he was getting
nowhere in his career, and the modest meals he ate would seem
to confirm her statement. Anxious to get on in the world and
widen the circle of his acquaintances, he began knocking at
various doors which opened without any trouble—that of Free-
masonry, for instance.

This mysterious organization, exclusively philanthropic in its
aims, was based on, and inspired by, the tenets of Christian
morality. Imported from England, it did not rank as heretical,
and a man still imbued with Catholicism—as Danton was at the
time of his affiliation—could find some satisfaction for his hu-
manitarian urges in belonging to it. This was why, about 1786,
he "saw the light" in the Reverend Lodge of the Nine Sisters.
He was regarded as possessing the "talent and qualifications"
needed to do so.

The mysteries of the Lodge were celebrated in a house on the
rue du Pot-de-Fer. A famous astronomer, Joseph de Lalande,
held the grade of Venerable in this Lodge, and various other
savants figured among the Masters and Companions: Lacépède,
Condorcet, Bailly, Guillotin, and others. There were well-known
artists, such as Hubert Robert, Joseph Vernet, and Greuze
(the "Adonis portrait" of Danton dates from this period).
There was a famous sculptor, Houdon, and several successful
writers: Choderlos de Laclos (the author of *Les Liaisons
Dangereuses*), Florian the fabulist, Chamfort the moral essayist,
and the poet Parny. There was a lawyer later called upon,
by a quirk of Providence, to defend the King: this was Raymond
de Sèze. There was a parliamentary Judge of Appeal, Duval
d'Éprémesnil; a prince, Msgr. de Rohan; a duke, M. de la
Rochefoucauld; and a marquis, M. de Beaumont.

Among the Apprentices, the lowest grade of the Order,
Danton found three of his colleagues from the Law Courts:
Maître Camille Desmoulins, whose inflammatory speeches were
to lead the mob on to storm the Bastille; Maître Pétion de
Villeneuve, who later brought back the King from Varennes;
and Maître Brissot, also known as de Warville, who became one
of the leading Girondists. Besides these he made the acquaintance
of Mirabeau, already a well-known figure in Paris; Rabaud-
Saint-Étienne, who was to press for freedom of worship at the

belief that Greuze's sitter was Danton is mistaken or else Greuze was determined to flatter his client. There is no trace in his treatment of the face which Manon Roland found so "repulsive and hideous."

When his evening meal was over, the young lawyer would talk for hours with the Charpentier family and his fellow customers. Sometimes he would leave them early for a visit to the theater—but more often to go home, where he would be joined by his former classmates who had now followed him to Paris.

Françoise Duhauttoir was the only woman present at these meetings. But then was she not—like Louis Béon, Courtois, Saint-Albin, and Jules Paré—a native of Troyes? Béon had by now been ordained as a priest. Another, rather older priest used to join them from time to time—none other than that Father Béranger who had wanted to punish Paré in college, and who was now a close friend of the group. These, together with a few new acquaintances picked up in the capital, formed Danton's permanent audience. By now he felt the zest for battle surging up in him. They would discuss such topics as philosophy, law, or public finance, and often the discussion went on till well after midnight.

When the guests had departed, did Danton join Françoise in her apartment? It does not appear so. On the contrary: though Mlle. Duhauttoir may well have solaced his leisure hours when he was working for Maître Vinot, it looks as though the relationship was now strictly platonic. Better still, either deliberately or by accident Danton was to play a part in bringing about his friend's marriage. One day he introduced her to Maître Huet de Paisy, a lawyer and Counsel to the King's Bench and the two fell in love with each other. First as lover and mistress, and later as husband and wife, Maître Huet de Paisy and Mlle. Duhauttoir—partly through the fact of their marriage, partly by a most odd combination of circumstances—helped to bring about Danton's own marriage to Gabrielle Charpentier.

Danton had no great hopes—for the immediate future, at any rate—that such a match was within his reach. To maintain a domestic establishment required the kind of situation he did not